SACRIFICE

Other books by Denise Grover Swank:

Rose Gardner Mysteries

(Humorous southern mysteries)
TWENTY-EIGHT AND A HALF WISHES
TWENTY-NINE AND A HALF REASONS (June 2012)

The Chosen Series

(Paranormal thriller/romance/urban fantasy)
CHOSEN
HUNTED
SACRIFICE
Untitled (The Chosen #4) Winter 2013

On the Otherside Series

(Young adult science fiction/romance)
HERE
THERE (November 2012)

SACRIFICE

DENISE GROVER SWANK

Kelly
What would you
Sacrifice for love?

Denise Grover Swank

This book is a work of fiction. References to real people, events, establishments, organizations, or locations are intended only to provide a sense of authenticity, and are used factiously. All other characters, and all incidents and dialogue, are drawn from the author's imagination and are not to be construed as real.

TO my readers,
you make all the hard work worth it

CHAPTER ONE

SHE was dead.

No. She only wished she was. Her body lived, though she felt as if her heart had been ripped from her chest. The organ mocked her with each beat, spreading her grief to every cell of her body.

"Emma, we need to go," Raphael's voice called through her haze.

She lifted her face from the damp forest ground and stared into his impatient face. Her anguish turned to rage. Will, the only man she had ever loved, the only person who had loved her in spite of herself, was gone. His memories of her—the love he felt for her, his urge to protect her at all costs, *everything*—had been stolen from him before he was beaten, thrown into a van, and carted away.

All while Raphael had used his hypnotic charm to keep Emma from saving him.

She stood, the tears drying on her face as the cold wind whipped her bloody nightgown around her legs. "You did this."

Raphael's dark eyes widened. "*I* did this? How is this my fault? I just saved your life by hiding you."

The power inside her began to build, scorching her chest as though she were burning from the inside out.

His voice softened. "Emma. You need me."

"Need you? *Need you?*" Her hands shook at her sides. Sparks flew from her fingers, illuminating the dark forest around them. "Because of you, I've lost Will. I've lost Jake. I lost my baby. I've lost everyone I *love*." She choked on the last word, tears burning her eyes. She pushed her pain into the energy, feeling it swell. A golden light surrounded her.

He released a throaty laugh, reaching for her. "Don't do anything hasty, Emmanuella."

She gritted her teeth. "Don't touch me."

His hand dropped to his side. "Emma, I didn't have anything to do with Jake or the baby. That was Alex. And Aiden, your father. They're to blame." He lowered his face, his eyes level with hers. "Together we can get even."

She sucked in a breath, and pain shot through her side. Earlier in the evening, she'd been kicked by one of the men sent by a political group intent on harnessing her power and using her baby. A baby prophesied to have great power and to rule the world. Will's baby. Only she'd miscarried the child just minutes ago, a result of the beating she'd incurred during her fight to escape.

A small smile lifted the corners of his mouth. "You need to focus your revenge on Aiden. You can save Jake, but you need me to do it."

Her five-year-old son was a pawn, held by her father as incentive for Emma to fight in the contest of elemental immortals to gain control of the world. But something else needed her immediate attention. She lifted her chin. "What about Will?"

Raphael's shoulders relaxed. "Emma, I'm sorry, but Will is dead. We both saw them throw his body in the back of that van."

"You let them kill him!" Rage overtook her and she thrust her hands forward, shooting her energy toward him. The golden light flashed in an arc, creating an eerie glow as it lit the dark forest. A green light met hers, shooting flashes in all directions.

She jumped in surprise, her energy fading as the green light edged closer.

Raphael beamed and he lifted an eyebrow, an evil glint in his eye. "You're going to get yourself killed, Emmanuella. You've just proven how much you need me."

Her light shortened as his filled the space, stopping inches from her outstretched hands.

She flung her hands to her sides, sending energy flying into the trees, leaves igniting from the sparks. "Do it then! Kill me!" Grief overwhelmed her and sobs rose in her throat. The sudden exertion of power sapped what little energy she had left and her knees buckled as her vision faded.

The green light disappeared and Raphael moved to her, pressing his chest to hers. He held her up before she fell. "I don't want to kill you, Emma. On the contrary, I want to rule with you." His hand snaked around her back, pulling her closer.

Her strength returned with Raphael's touch.

The trees smoldered, and gray smoke wisped into the sky. Vaguely aware of an acrid odor filling her nose, she stared into his dark eyes, lured by the hypnotic pull he aroused, drowning in her body's physical need for him. "Will," she whispered.

His mouth hovered over hers and he whispered, "Will is gone."

The words penetrated the fog in her head. *Will.* She shoved his chest, breaking contact. The mist burned off as she shook her head. "Don't you touch me or I'll—"

He laughed. "Or you'll what? Kill me? Empty threats, Emma. Look how well your last attempt went." Raphael took a step backward, a cocky smile covering his face.

She shook with rage and frustration. "We both know there are plenty of other ways to kill you."

He lifted his chin, studying her. "You're much more impetuous than I expected. Watching you with Jake made me think you were more clearheaded. Still, it's a trait we can use to our advantage."

"Who the hell do you think you are?" But she knew. Raphael and Alex were the elements earth and air. Her father, Aiden, the fire element, had tricked them into handing over most of their power in a millenniums-long game. The prize was Aiden's daughter, and whomever she chose regained his power along with his realm. The other would be cast into the shadow world. They lived mortal lives, reincarnated time and time again, locked in an eternal fight for Aiden's previous daughter Emmanuella. While Emma shared her name and image, nothing else about her was the same.

"You know who I am. Even if you've changed, we have centuries of history. You are meant to be mine. Not Will's. We can defeat Aiden's new game together."

Aiden. The chilly wind cooled her temper, defeat following in its wake. If she couldn't kill Raphael, how could she beat the more powerful Aiden?

She wanted to wake up from this nightmare. The winner would rule the shadow world alongside Aiden. She didn't want to rule anything. She wanted Jake and she wanted Will, but he was gone.

No. Will couldn't be dead. How could she go on without him? Closing her eyes, she lifted her head toward the sky. "I need him."

"You only needed Will to grow your powers, and now they're fully developed. You no longer need the pendant to use them. Now you just need to learn how to channel your energy. You no longer need Will."

That wasn't what she meant. Not that she expected Raphael to understand. She reached out with her mind. *"Will! Are you hurt? Tell me where you are!"*

Silence hovered in her consciousness, but also something more foreboding. Before, she could at least sense him, even if they couldn't talk. Now there was absolutely nothing. "I can't feel him."

"Who?"

"Will! I can't feel Will. I could sense him before, but now it's gone. Why can't I feel him?" Her hysteria rose at the implication.

Raphael sighed, his voice softening. "Because he's dead, Emma. You have to let him go. Unless you develop the power of resurrection, there's nothing you can do."

She gasped. "Can I do that? Develop the power of resurrection?"

Raphael shook his head, pity drawing his mouth into a thin line. "No. If any of us could, it would be me. I possess power of the earth. From ashes to ashes, dust to dust..." His eyes softened. "But even I have no control over death, Emma. Especially in this weakened state. Death is final."

"Just because I can't feel Will doesn't mean he's dead. But without his mark, the Vinco Potentia have no reason to keep him alive. I have to go save him." *The mark.* The mark Jake had branded on Will's arm to mark him as Emma's protector. Hope bobbed to the surface and she clung tight. "I can't feel him because his mark is gone! And I think mine are gone too. I felt a burning on my back when Will's mark went away."

Raphael spun her around, pulling down her nightgown to reveal her shoulder blade. "I can't make out the trident." He angled her back toward the moon. "All that's left is fire."

"So Will's mark and the water mark are gone."

"What water mark?" He grabbed her shoulders and turned her to face him.

"Why would I still have fire but lose the other two?"

"*What* water mark?" His fingers pinched her shoulder and she faded again, the longing for him returning. He dropped his hands, cursing. "I know about the mark of fire and Will's mark, but you've never had water before. When did it appear?"

"I don't know. Sometime after I met Will, his mark and water appeared."

Raphael's jaw dropped before he twisted his lips. Fury replaced the shock in his eyes.

"That's not important." She brushed past Raphael and started toward the road.

"Where do you think you're going?" he called after her, irritation bleeding through his words.

Moonlight lit her path as she picked her way through the undergrowth. "Will drove here and I have his keys. I'm going to find his car and go get him."

"Even if Will was alive, you don't know where they took him."

"I have a pretty good idea." *South Dakota.* It was so obvious, but then Will had never been Kramer's true prize. Emma was, and Kramer knew Emma would come looking for Will.

Raphael moved beside her, matching her strides. "Emma, this is suicide. For all you know he'll be dead by the time you find him."

She stopped and spun to face him. "He'll be dead for sure if I don't."

"I won't let you do this."

Clenching her fists at her sides, she glared. "Here's a surprise for you—you can't stop me."

His fingers dug into her bicep, and liquid warmth flowed through her arm and heated her chest. Raphael smiled at her reaction. "See, Emma? That's where you're wrong." His fingers swept the hair off her cheek and tucked it behind her ear. "I can stop you if I need to, for your own safety." His mouth lowered to her exposed ear. "You're not thinking sensibly, my love."

She relaxed into him, needing to be closer.

His hand caressed her cheek, lightly tracing the swelling where she had been hit. "That's my Em. Let me help you see reason. Will is no longer necessary and the sooner you accept this, the easier it will be."

The mention of Will's name wiggled in her mind, pushing against Raphael's magnetic pull as his mouth found hers. Sanity scrambled for a foothold. "No," she mumbled against his lips.

His kiss deepened and her consciousness struggled for control. Her fingers splayed against his chest and she pushed him away. "No!"

His grip around her back tightened.

Will. The image of his prostrate body in the woods filled her mind, and her connection to reality strengthened.

"Emma, look into my eyes." Raphael held her chin and lowered his penetrating gaze to hers.

His dark pupils pulled at her consciousness until there was nothing but him.

His hand slid to her cheek. "Will is dead. I know how upsetting that is for you. He meant everything to you, but he's gone."

A wave of grief stole her breath and her legs collapsed.

Raphael held her against him. "It's okay, my love. I'll help you through this." His face lowered and his lips hovered over hers. "Will is dead. Say it."

Her psyche fought his command.

"Emma," he cooed. "I know how difficult this is for you, but you need to accept the truth, and the first step is to say the words aloud. Say it: Will is dead." His eyes narrowed.

Agony ripped away her resistance. "Will is dead." Her voice cracked, the surety of it seeping into her marrow as she said the words.

He smiled and stroked her cheek. "Good girl. Yes, he's dead and you must let him go."

A voice called out behind Raphael. "There you two are."

Raphael's body stiffened before he spun around.

His gaze broke contact, releasing her tunnel vision, and she fought to focus.

"Alex, you're interrupting a private moment. I was consoling Emma over Will's death."

Alex stood less than six feet away. His mouth lifted into a mocking grin. "My condolences for your loss, Emma."

Raphael pushed Emma behind him. "Are we really going to do this now, Alex? Hasn't the poor woman been through enough tonight?"

"Raphael, as always, you have the unfair advantage. I'm only here to even the playing field. Emma's almost always chosen you before, but things are different this time."

Without Raphael's touch, Emma's sense of reality returned, grief hitting her like a tsunami.

Alex took a step closer. "Emma, Raphael's motives are—"

The ground shook and Emma struggled to stay upright. A crack split the ground, separating Alex from Raphael and Emma.

Clouds churned overhead and a strong wind swept through the leaves. Alex heaved an exaggerated sigh. "Raphael, I'd hoped it wouldn't come to this so soon."

Raphael grabbed Emma's hand and his warmth flowed through the contact into her body. "I need you to run with me, Emma. *Now.*"

His command sank in as he took off, pulling her behind him. She struggled to keep up with his longer legs.

The gusting wind pushed against them and her legs burned from the exertion. Raphael dragged her behind him, his hand squeezing hers.

Aiden's voice floated in the air around them. "Eager to start fighting so soon." He laughed, the sound echoing off the trees. "Save your energy, children. Your big battle is in six weeks."

Raphael ignored him, pulling her deeper into the darkness.

"A little earthquake isn't going to stop me, Raphael." Alex's voice echoed through the air.

Raphael looked down at her. "Emma, set the trees on fire."

"What?" She shook her head, her mind fuddled from his touch and her agony.

He jerked to a halt. "Listen to me. You need to concentrate. Set the forest on fire."

The events of the evening were too overwhelming. "I can't."

"Yes you can," he hissed. "Now do it."

"No."

His fingers dug into her arms as he gave her a shake. "We need each other to win, so consider this our first battle. Make a fire!"

"You do it!" she shouted, jerking out of his grasp. "You two think I'm some fantastic prize? Well, guess what? I don't know what the fuck I'm doing!"

He leaned closer, anger darkening his eyes. "If you want to save your son, you will set the woods on fire. If you don't, Alex will make damn sure you never see him again."

The thought of Alex kindled a spark of anger. A low level of power filled her chest. She shot it forward. Flames leapt from a few tree branches. *Pathetic.* She fell to the ground, sobbing.

Raphael growled and cursed under his breath. "You have to do better than that."

Rain pounded the leaves over her head.

She'd failed Will. Now Jake would die because she was powerless to stop the newest monster in the darkness. "I can't do this."

Raphael jerked her off the ground, his eyes burning into hers. "That rain is Alex trying to stop you from creating a fire. He's trying to keep you from Jake," he spat through gritted teeth. "You need to do this now or it won't work. *Make a fire!*"

Rage burned her chest. She aimed for the trees, pushing every bit of energy with it. A deafening explosion filled the air as flames ripped through the forest. Thick smoke enveloped her, filling her lungs. Blackness hung in her peripheral vision before swallowing her whole.

She welcomed the nothingness.

CHAPTER TWO

WILL woke to a dull roar filling his aching head. His hands were cuffed behind his back, his cheek pressed to a cold metal floor. Peeking through a cracked eyelid, he took in his surroundings.

From the curved walls, the cargo netting, and the hum he now recognized as engines, he realized he was in the back of a cargo plane. A man in camouflage sat in a jump seat, a semi-automatic weapon at the ready.

How the hell had he gotten here?

Will reached back into his fuzzy memory. He'd been in a forest with a woman he'd never seen before, but she seemed to know him and warned him that they were in danger. Then the gunmen showed up. The last thing he remembered was the stinging in his neck and then blackness.

Goddamned tranquilizer dart.

But the thought of the woman flooded his head, accompanied by worry and anxiety.

What the hell?

Forcing his rapid breath to slow, he pushed aside his fear for her and focused on what he knew, which was nothing. The entire night, other than his snippet of memory, was a complete blank. Had he been on a job? He had to have been. It wasn't as if gunfire followed him around. In spite of his mercenary job, gunfire was rarely part of his life anymore. Not since he left it behind in Iraq.

He silently cursed, pissed that he'd thought about Iraq. That shit was better left in the past.

But why couldn't he remember the job? Tranquilizers knocked you out. They didn't steal your memory. Had someone slipped him a roofie? Will couldn't even remember the last time he ate or drank.

What the hell happened before he found himself in the woods, and why was he with that woman?

What little he saw of her in the moonlight, she didn't seem his type. She was short and brunette, not to mention she was wearing an old-fashioned white nightgown splattered in blood.

Panic stole his breath at the thought of her being hurt.

What the fuck? Why would he care about some random woman? He stopped caring about women years ago. Or anyone else, for that matter.

A nagging unease chewed at the edges of his brain, and there was no denying it had nothing to with him being captured and bound.

He was losing it.

Think, Will. What do you remember before the woman?

An empty crevice stretched in his mind, but he continued pushing back until he stumbled upon a foggy scene. He was accepting a job that offered a lot of money.

Why couldn't he remember what it was?

Someone stepped over him toward the jump seats. "Has he moved at all?"

"Nope. Out like a light," a voice shouted. "That dart was loaded and would keep an elephant down for a week. He ain't going nowhere."

"He's gonna wish he could sleep forever when Kramer gets done with him."

Kramer? Who was Kramer? He couldn't remember any Kramers from any past jobs, but honestly, there'd been too many men to keep track of them all. Not to mention his clients often went by fake names. It crossed his mind that he'd pissed off the husband of one of the many women he'd screwed, but he just as quickly dismissed it. How many husbands had military cargo planes at their disposal?

Military cargo plane.

Shit, did this have something to do with his history in the Marines?

The plane sloped forward.

"You better take a seat," one of the men warned. "We're gonna land soon and they said it's a pretty short runway."

"What about him?"

"So what if he slides around a bit? He'll be out for hours. He can add the bumps and bruises to all the others he's going to wake up to."

Will started a mental tally of who to get even with once he broke loose. Opening his eyelids a slit, he decided that the stockier guy was the first dipshit on the list.

The plane descended and Will slid across the floor, banging into a metal box that jabbed his shoulder blade, but he kept up the unconscious ruse. The guards would be less cautious and he could use it to his advantage. Once they landed, he needed to be ready to bolt. Too bad his hands were bound with handcuffs instead of rope or zip ties.

The plane touched down and bounced as Will's body slid the opposite direction. One of the men stomped on his back and Will bit the inside of his cheek to keep from flinching. "Where do you think you're going, buddy?"

The men laughed.

Now both assholes were on his shit list.

Once the plane came to a halt, they grabbed his shirt at the top of his shoulders and slid him across the floor toward the cargo opening. As the back door lowered, Will cracked his eyes open enough to see it was still dark. And that he faced an empty tarmac.

He could use that to his advantage too.

The two men dragged him to the sloping edge. Before they started down the ramp, Will tucked his legs and bolted upright, jerking out of the two stunned men's holds. He gave a hard kick in the knee to the man on his right who had stomped on his shoulder. The other man regained his senses and lifted his gun, but Will kicked it out of his hands and planted his heel in the man's abdomen. The guard doubled over in pain.

Will made it down the cargo ramp and onto the pavement before light flooded the airstrip. He stumbled and came face to face with over a dozen men pointing semi-automatic weapons toward him.

Shit.

A dark-haired man in a suit walked through the gunmen, his gaze on Will. He clapped, a slow, methodical applaud, while a mocking smile spread across his face.

"Bravo, Mr. Davenport. You entertain me every time we meet."

Will lifted an eyebrow, trying to place him. "Have we met?"

The man laughed, but it sounded hard and cold. "You're on a roll, Will. But enough of this nonsense. Where's Emmanuella?"

This guy had to be Kramer. "Who?"

The man's eyes narrowed. "You've always been cocky, which has its time and place. But now is the time to cooperate. I've grown weary of your games."

"Then that makes two of us," Will spat. "Because I don't know what the fuck you're talking about."

Kramer pursed his lips and furrowed his brow. "I'd really hoped you'd learned by now, Will. I have to admit that after our last encounter I'll take pleasure in having you at my mercy."

A chill ran down Will's spine. Why did this man think he knew him? And if Will did, why couldn't he remember?

Kramer turned and walked through the armed men. "Take him to the holding cells and keep eight armed guards on him at all times. He's not to be underestimated."

Shit. What had he gotten into now?

****

Emma roused, sitting in a chair with something strapped against her lap, holding her in place. Her eyes flew open in alarm as she flinched, her hands gripping chair arms.

"It's okay. You're safe." Raphael patted her hand.

Her breath came in short pants as she surveyed her surroundings. They were in a small luxury jet with only two rows of seats and a bench seat along a side wall. She was strapped into a seat, with Raphael in the seat across the aisle. The other seats were empty.

She turned her face to him, her heart thumping wildly against her ribcage. "What happened? How did we get here?"

"You created a raging forest fire, much like the one in Minnesota. Unfortunately, it didn't kill Alex, only deterred him long enough for us to get away." Raphael's finger lightly stroked the back of her hand. "You used too much energy and passed out. One of the first things you need to learn is how to control your energy flow. It's amazing you haven't killed yourself by now."

Her head ached and her mouth was dry, as though she had a really bad hangover. She needed Will's touch. He always helped her through this part, after she'd done too much.

Will.

The pain hit her full force, sucking her breath as she gasped. "Will..." The tears gushed without permission and she lowered her face into her hands, wailing.

Raphael unbuckled her seatbelt and pulled her from her seat. She collapsed into him, her legs giving out.

Will. Her pain hemorrhaged with her violent sobs.

"I know, love. I know." He held her to his chest, stroking the back of her head. His languid warmth seeped into her, soothing the pain.

"No!" She jerked back, tripping on the frame of the seat behind her. She refused to betray Will, especially now.

Raphael reached out to steady her, but she swung out of his reach.

"Don't touch me!"

"Emma—"

"NO!" she screamed, taking another step back, her loose nightgown twisting around her legs. Frantic, she swung her head, searching for a way to escape. She spotted a door in front of the first row.

Alarm filled Raphael's eyes. "Emma, I know you're upset and you see me as your enemy right now, but we're thirty-five thousand feet in the air."

She didn't care. She'd rather plummet to her death than succumb to Raphael's pull again. Her muscles tensed, prepared to leap for the door.

"Emma, don't do anything—"

She bolted, barely getting past him before his fingers dug into her arm. He pulled her against his chest, a fire in his eyes. "I know you'll hate me for this when you wake up, but hopefully you'll thank me for it later."

His lips lowered to hers and he kissed her with his pent-up frustration. To her agony, she answered his call, giving herself to him. The familiar fuzziness filled her head and she sagged before his arm tightened around her back, holding her to his chest.

He continued to kiss her until she was aware of nothing but him. Then he laid her down on a seat, tucking a blanket around her and smoothing her hair. "Don't worry, Emma. Everything will be all right."

His words were faint and far away, but she wondered how could anything be all right without Will.

****

The guards escorted Will into a cargo van. Looking through the back window, he could see that they drove past a small compound surrounded by a chain-link fence, then through a guard station with wooden gates. One gate was unpainted and looked as if it had recently been replaced. He almost laughed. What the hell kind of security was that?

A heaviness filled his chest, nearly suffocating him with grief. He held his breath in an attempt to slow his racing heart. What the hell was going on with him? Will shoved his fear into the recesses of his mind. If he was going to get out of this, he needed a clear head.

No streetlights lit the road so he wasn't sure where they were until the vehicle stopped and the back doors opened. Six guards fell in around the back of the van as the four armed guards inside escorted him out. As flattered as he was, Will wished they'd underestimated him instead.

They paraded down a sidewalk and stopped at one of the middle buildings, taking Will through the front doors and to an elevator bank in an office lobby. A security guard at the front desk eyed Will with distrust.

An uneasy sense of déjà vu swept through him, making him hesitate. "I don't really care much for elevators. I'm a bit claustrophobic."

The guard on his right curled his lip but remained silent.

Will couldn't let them see his apprehension. Everyone had a part to play and his was the cocksure asshole. He checked their uniforms for stripes and found none. "You boys Army? Marines?"

"Freelance," the man on his left said.

One of the other guards elbowed him.

He winked. "Freelance, huh? Whaddaya know? So am I. Maybe we can work out some kind of arrangement."

The men remained silent.

"So that guy out on the airstrip—was he Kramer?"

The man on his right shifted his eyes as though Will were crazy.

The elevator door opened and someone dug a gun tip into Will's back and pushed. "Enough chitchat. Playing stupid isn't going to get you anywhere."

Six men packed the small space with Will, pressing him against the back wall. "So where are we? Some secret government facility?"

The guard who had been on his left shook his head. "Like you don't know. You've busted out of here twice. Last night you stole a plane and crash-landed it in Wyoming."

"Mitchell, shut up," one of the men grunted.

Will turned to face the talkative guard. "Mitchell, is it? I think you've got the wrong man. Seems to me I'd remember stealing a plane." Will grinned. "Although it does sound like something I'd do. Always go for the dramatic exit." Which was a lie. Covert was always better. "What was I here for anyway?" The question released the anxiety he'd held at bay, catching him by surprise. Someone was in danger and he needed to save him. Or her.

Mitchell pressed his lips together in a scowl.

The elevator doors opened and the group filed out. Fluorescent lights flickered overhead.

Will angled his head to the ceiling. "Nice touch, fellows. A-plus for creepy effects."

Four armed men flanked a door in the hallway. Will was deeper in the building, surrounded by ten men total, and his hands were still cuffed behind his back.

One of the guards opened a steel-plated door, the hinges creaking.

"Can I at least know what I'm being held for?" Will asked over his shoulder as they pushed him through the opening.

The slammed door was his answer.

"Hey! At least take these fucking handcuffs off."

The door remained closed and Will turned to inventory the room. A flimsy metal frame and a bare mattress. A metal toilet. Four rectangular small vents close to the ceiling on two opposite walls. No chairs. No sink. No window. That made things trickier.

Surrendering to underlying panic that had nothing to do with his own safety, he sat on the bed, the frame sagging beneath his weight. He closed his eyes and tried to sort out his mess of emotions. Fear. Worry. Love.

Love?

And all those feelings spiked whenever he pictured the woman in the woods. Was she Emmanuella? Just the thought of her name tightened his chest with dread. Who the hell was she?

He sucked in a deep breath, his body twitching with distress. A new fear slid in to join the existing one. Will was a man used to being in control. He'd not only slipped down the ladder of control, he was on the bottom rung about to fall off. He had to get a grip and he had to figure out where all these emotions came from.

There was little doubt he'd been on a job and he must have failed, which was why he was here now. The woman in the woods must have been the job. Concentrating on the phone call, he remembered that he was supposed to bring a woman to South Dakota for a ridiculous amount of money. The memory spiked his anxiety and his breath caught in his throat, sending his heart racing. He fought to stifle the panic and his mind instinctively retreated to a familiar behavior that had been his mind's coping mechanism during extreme situations in Iraq.

He thought of his mother.

Given the sting of her rejection three years ago, concentrating on happy times as a child with his mom only made his terror worse. His mind scrambled to find another buoy. It wasn't an image, only a feeling, yet much more powerful.

Belonging.

Choking back a sob of surprise, he clung tight, overwhelmed with the power of the feeling, the one thing he'd craved his entire life. He didn't question where it came from, only that he knew it was real and it was his. It lapped through him, filling him with a sense of calm.

Belonging to what? Or who?

The image of the woman appeared along with a fresh wave of emotions. On the brink of tears, an overwhelming urge to save her filled every part of his head and his panic returned. She was in danger and he couldn't do anything to help her. He'd never felt like this about anyone in his entire life and his hysteria was tied to a woman he didn't even know.

Calm down. They've fucked with your head.

He took a few quick breaths as he twisted the idea like a puzzle piece, trying to make it fit with what little he knew. That had to be it. If his feelings were real, he'd remember her. Remember her fucking name, for God's sake. Maybe he'd been the guinea pig of some new mind-control project he didn't know about. Will liked the idea, as farfetched as it seemed. If only because the other alternative was one he couldn't face: he was losing his mind.

She was a figment of his imagination, or at least his feelings were. The only person who needed saving was himself.

Working his hands under the edge of the mattress, he groped for loose metal pieces to unlock the cuffs. It took him ten minutes before he found a section that had any give. Concentrating on a task returned some clarity to his head. He needed to focus on the situation he was in *now*. The frame was entirely too new, as was the mattress, which told him that the holding cells were rarely used. If at all.

Why had he been escorted to a compound in the middle of nowhere and placed in a cell that rarely saw prisoners?

He bent the thin metal stick of the frame back and forth, spinning it around.

Kramer knew whom he was, calling him by name, which in itself was disconcerting. Will rarely gave his real last name. Aliases worked best, considering the company he tended to keep in his business. The fact that Kramer knew his real name let him know that this wasn't a case of mistaken identity. But Will had never been here before and he'd sure as hell remember stealing a plane the night before.

The terror and panic returned. *Focus on the task at hand. One step at a time.* His anxiety retreated, hovering in the background.

The piece snapped and Will looked over his shoulder to angle it to the keyhole. It took several attempts to insert the shard into the locking mechanism, but after a few quick jerks and twists, the cuff popped open on his left hand. He rotated his arms to the front and freed himself from the other restraint.

He got up and moved around the room. Pressing his ear to the door, he heard muffled voices filter through the metal, but he couldn't make out any words.

Will realized he wasn't going anywhere. The space offered no chance of escape. Even the door hinges were on the outside.

With a grunt of frustration, he lay down on the bed and closed his eyes. He had no idea how long it would be until someone came back, but he figured he should get all the sleep he could beforehand.

He had the feeling he was going to need it.

CHAPTER THREE

JAKE stirred. Something in his memory tickled his consciousness. A shadow almost, it hovered at the edge, teasing him with the feeling of something forgotten. Something important.

His eyes opened as the haze burned away and he found himself in a room, laying on the edge of a bed clutching Rusty, his stuffed dog.

"Señor Jake, you're awake." An older woman sat in the corner, knitting a scarf.

Mommy had tried to knit once, a long time ago. The thought of her sent a pain through his stomach. Where was she?

The woman set her yarn and needles in a basket on the floor. "My name is Maria and I'm here to take care of you. Are you hungry?"

He sat up, his anger building. *He* said that he was taking Jake to see his mother. "Where's my mommy?"

Confusion clouded the woman's face. "I don't know. Señor Aiden only said you were coming."

"Who's Aiden?"

Her eyes filled with fear as she leapt out of the chair, wringing her hands. "*Tu abuelo.* Your grandfather."

A man stood in the doorway. "Not to worry. Jake has had a difficult night and is confused."

Jake recognized the voice. It was *him*. "Where's my mom?"

Maria stood in the center of the large room, swinging her gaze between Aiden and Jake.

"That is all, Maria," the man said.

She hesitated, watching Jake with terrified eyes.

Aiden took several steps into the room, his cold eyes watching her while his face remained expressionless. "I said that is all, Maria."

Her hands shook as she hurried past him.

His gaze followed her with a look of boredom. He turned his attention to Jake.

Jake jumped off the bed, his hands clenched at his sides. "You told me that you were taking me to see my mommy!"

Aiden cocked his head to the side. "No, that's not what I said at all. I said we were going to get your mother."

Jake's breath came in short bursts. "Then where is she?"

Sitting on the side of the bed, Aiden leaned forward, clasping his hands. "Lesson number one, Jacob: Always make sure the person states in very clear and concise words what they mean. Is their language ambiguous? Make them clarify. Take Raphael, for example. He thought he pinned me down and made the situation fit his desires. Yet he forgot that there are always loopholes to squeeze through."

Aiden laughed like he'd said something funny. But Jake was mad. He wanted answers and Aiden was talking about someone he didn't know. "I don't care. I want my mommy!" His chest filled with fire.

Aiden raised an eyebrow, yet looked bored. "You *should* care, Jacob. If you had asked me to clarify last night, I would have told you that we were getting your mother but letting her go. For now."

"I never saw my mother." But he didn't remember anything that happened last night after Aiden took him from the house, either.

Aiden placed his hand on Jake's head. "You were there. You just don't remember."

Jake wanted to ask why, but with Aiden, anything was possible. "I want to see my mom," he said in slow, even words.

Aiden laughed. "You're a stubborn child, aren't you? You're a lot like your mother, you know. She was stubborn too."

"How do you know my mom?"

Dropping his hand, Aiden's smile fell. "I'm her father."

Maria had said that Aiden was his grandfather, but Jake didn't believe it. First, Aiden looked closer to Will's age instead of the grandfathers he'd seen on television. And second, Mommy said she didn't have a dad.

"Everyone has a father."

He'd read his mind.

Aiden laughed. "After all our conversations, it shouldn't surprise you."

He was right, but somehow it didn't seem right with him right next to Jake.

"Now you know how your mother felt when you first tried it with her."

Guilt coursed through him. She'd hated it. Just like he did now. "I want my mom. I want her *now*." His fingers tingled with energy.

Aiden sighed. "We all want things. It doesn't mean we get them. Take me, for instance. I want your mother to do what I ask, to fight for you, yet I have no guarantee that she will."

Fear mingled with Jake's anger. Was Mommy in danger? She loved him and would do anything to save him. "Fight what?"

Aiden stood and walked to the window. "You have a lovely view from this room. One of the best views of the estate."

Jake didn't care about views or estates. He wanted his mother.

Twisting his upper body to look at Jake, Aiden's mouth lifted into a smile that didn't reach his eyes. "All in good time, Jacob. All in good time." He moved to the doorway. "You will begin training after breakfast."

The door closed behind him and Jake looked around the room in dismay. The room was nicer than the ones Alex had kept him in, but he knew it was a jail, despite the huge, fancy furniture lining the walls.

He tried to swallow the lump of disappointment in his throat. This was supposed to be over. Aiden had tricked him and told him he'd get to be with Mommy. But Aiden didn't say when. A loophole, he'd called it.

Jake didn't know what to call it. The only hole he knew about was the one in his heart that grew bigger every day. One day he'd fall into it and never come out.

Flopping on the bed, he buried his face into the pillow and sobbed out his frustration and loneliness. He broke his rule, calling out to her, begging her to come save him, but the one time he needed her, she didn't answer.

He was alone.

****

Will jerked awake when the metal door swung open and four armed men entered the room. Within a second, he shoved down his disorientation, clasping his hands behind his head and crossing his feet at the ankles. "Good morning. You boys bring me breakfast in bed?"

Two men reached down and grabbed his arms, pulling him to his feet.

"Got your handcuffs off, I see," the shorter guard said.

Will shrugged. "I needed my beauty sleep and I like to sleep on my back. A little lumpy with the cuffs on."

"Funny guy, huh? We'll see how funny you are once Kramer is done with you."

They pulled him into the hall, where eight more guards waited. They marched down the hall and turned the corner. Two more guards stood by a door and snapped to attention when they saw the group approach.

One of the men opened the heavy metal door. "Kramer said to bring him in and he'll be here shortly."

"Tell Kramer it's rude to keep his guest waiting," Will said as he walked through the opening. Worried about what he'd find on the other side, he was relieved to see a table and two chairs and a mirror covering one wall. A simple interrogation room.

The door closed behind him.

They were watching him through the glass. As heavily as they guarded him, he knew they didn't expect him to show signs of weakness. Nevertheless, they hoped to glean something by observing him in isolation. What they wanted from him, he had no idea, but this was all part of the game. Make him wait and worry.

He pulled out the metal chair, the feet screeching across the bare concrete floor. Once he sat, he kicked back with his elbow on the table. Lesson number one when going undercover: you can make people believe anything if you play the part right.

But Will wasn't undercover, and he had a feeling it wasn't going to work this time.

Fifteen minutes later the door opened. Will raised an eyebrow in greeting but remained silent as Kramer walked into the room. The sight of the man sent ripples of apprehension through Will that had nothing to with the exchange they were about to have. Acknowledging his fear ignited the worry he'd felt for the woman last night, a worry that burned Will with an intensity he wasn't prepared for. He stifled his gasp.

Kramer took a seat in the chair on the other side of the table. "How did you sleep, Will?"

Will took a moment to recover from his dismay. He hadn't felt anything for her since he went to sleep last night. He'd hoped it was a bad acid trip. Will smirked. "Those peas under the mattress really disturbed my rest. If you plan to let me stay here longer, I hope you have someone look into that."

Kramer folded his hands on the table and stared into Will's face with cold, hard eyes. "Keep it up while you can, Davenport. Pretty soon your cocky attitude will be beaten out of you."

Dread filled him, but Will *tsked*. "What kind of hospitality is that?"

Kramer lifted his mouth into a grim smile. "Where is she?"

"You can't tell them," a voice said in his head. A voice that wasn't his own. Will's heart skipped a beat. He'd imagined it, yet he felt an urge to obey. "Who?"

Kramer shook his head. "Seriously? We're playing this game?" His brow furrowed. "Trust me, with the press catching wind of Alex's disappearance from the public eye and some bimbo coming out of nowhere claiming to have had an affair with Senator Warren, I have enough trouble to deal with without adding you and this infuriating woman into the mix. And considering what a pain in the ass you've been, I'd love nothing more than to take my frustration out on you."

Will's mind kicked into gear, trying to sort out why they were holding him. Kramer must have hired him to find the woman in the woods. If he played along, he might get more information. "Senator Warren? You mean the guy running for president? What does he have to do with this? Is the woman you're asking about the one claiming to have slept with him?" He forced himself to sound cocky, every word at odds with his rising fear.

Kramer sighed. "You're full of idiotic questions, when what I really need is answers." He placed his palms on the table and leaned forward. "Where's Emma?"

Emma. The name sent waves of love crashing through him. Fear, dread, worry, belonging—all pinned themselves on the single word. His whole reason for living was tied to a woman he didn't even know.

That was impossible. And crazy.

"Tell them nothing. You have to buy her more time," the voice said.

A new hysteria raged, a fear for himself. He was losing his fucking mind.

Lowering his eyes to hide his traitorous emotions, Will growled, "How the hell should I know?"

The man sighed and looked up at the ceiling. "I have several options at this point."

Will raised his head and glared.

"We could do nothing with you and wait." Kramer lowered his chin as his eyes pierced Will with cold disinterest. "I have no doubt she'll come for you. It's just a matter of how soon and what she's capable of doing." He grinned. "But why not extract information from you while we wait? Maybe after some coercion you can be persuaded to tell us more about her powers, and we'll be more prepared."

The hair on the back of Will's neck prickled. "No need to get hasty, Kramer. I'm sure we can reach some kind of understanding."

"You'll actually mean that in a few more hours, Will. I'll check in on you later and see if you're more forthcoming then."

Kramer left the room as six armed men entered.

Damn, this didn't look good.

****

Lush green scenery flew past her car window in a blur. There was no denying the beauty of the rolling hills and fertile pastures, but the images were like a reflection on moving water, blurry and out of focus. Her mind tunneled inward, barely acknowledging her surroundings.

Her chest was so heavy she fought for every breath, desperation and despair filling her blood with their toxicity.

Was it possible to die from grief?

She'd come to her senses by the time the plane had landed at the small airport, but she didn't fight Raphael when he led her down the steps of the plane onto the tarmac. Everything around her moved in slow motion, her reactions a second behind. A tiny part of her told her to run as she walked to the waiting car, but she ignored it. Will was dead and Raphael was her only chance to save Jake.

She had to save Jake.

The thought of him should have given her strength, fueled her need for vengeance. But she felt too desolate to find the energy to do anything but put one foot in front of the other and slide into the front seat.

Will was dead. What did it matter who she was with?

Raphael made a few attempts to talk to her, but his words were muffled. Emma leaned her head against the window and closed her eyes, trying to block out her new reality.

She was completely alone.

Raphael pulled through a remote-controlled iron gate and drove up the circular drive, stopping in front of massive wooden doors.

"Welcome home, Emma."

A flicker of anger sparked and just as quickly died. Let him think what he wanted. She didn't care.

They walked into a two-story entry with a monstrosity of a chandelier hanging over their heads, and for a brief moment she wished it would fall, crushing her to the floor.

Surely a quick death was a better alternative to slow suffocation.

He showed her the house, which was a joke. Her mother's house could fit in the living room. But she said nothing, following him like a zombie. A zombie in a bloody nightgown. She didn't give a fuck about his house, but it would take too much effort to tell him. Instead, she put one foot in front of the other, which she realized she'd been doing her entire life anyway.

Just one more day. Just one more minute, hanging on for dear life. For what? Before Jake, it was for the elusive hope that her life could be better. After Jake, it was because he was her entire world. The sun rose and set on loving and protecting that little boy. Her life could be broken down into four words: before and after Jake.

Until Will.

The burning in her throat threatened to ignite and burst into flames. Could she do that? Could she use her power to spontaneously combust?

Raphael stopped in front of a partially open door. "This will be your room. For now." He pushed it open to reveal a room with a bed covered in fluffy white linens. Two floor-to-ceiling windows featured a second-story view of an endless green lawn.

When had they climbed a staircase?

"You've had a trying night and it's now midmorning. Perhaps you'd like to rest?" he asked gently. Under different circumstances, Emma might have believed he cared. "You can shower and change into clean clothes first."

Ignoring him, she pushed past him and laid down on the bed, her gaze focused on a tree in the yard.

He moved beside her and hesitated before reaching down to caress her cheek. "It will get easier, Emma. I promise. Just take it one day at a time." When she didn't answer, he turned and left the room, shutting the door behind him.

She closed her eyes, thinking that he sounded like someone who spoke from firsthand experience.

CHAPTER FOUR

JAKE sat at a massive dining room table, dragging his fork through the runny eggs on his fancy plate. A wall of windowed doors looked out onto the gardens, a fountain in the middle. Shrubs shaped like dolphins and bears flanked the patio. A month or two ago he would have been curious enough to investigate. Now he just wanted to go home. Whatever or wherever that might be.

Maria stood to the side, watching while he ate.

"You must eat, Señor Jake." Her thick black hair was pulled back in a bun. Her mouth turned down into a disapproving frown.

"These eggs are gross," he sighed.

Maria reached for the plate, muttering in Spanish, as she took it to the kitchen doorway. She returned several minutes later with a plate full of fruit, scrambled eggs, and bacon.

"This is better, no?" she asked with a kind smile.

"Yes, it's better. Thank you," he said, picking up his fork. He wasn't hungry, and while he didn't understand all the thoughts in her head, he knew she'd watch him until he ate something.

"You have such good manners, Señor Jake."

"Of course he does," Aiden said, walking into the room.

Maria jumped and crossed herself as she scurried backward, away from the table.

Jake lifted his gaze from his plate. His grandfather walked toward him, a smile spread across his face.

"Do you like your room?" Aiden sat next to him.

Jake shrugged, tilting his head to study Aiden. He reminded him of Alex somehow. He just couldn't figure out how.

"It's because we are both elementals."

"What's that?"

"It's a bit complicated for you to understand, but we can control the elements. What you recognize is our power, the energy we emit. You're a natural at it, which is why you came into your powers so much sooner than your mother. That and the fact that you have two parents who are elemental."

Jake twisted his mouth. "What about Will?"

Aiden's smile fell. A ripple of irritation rolled off of him, filling the room. "You don't need to worry about Will right now. You have too much work to do." Aiden looked up at Maria, his eyes darting with anger. "Why is he still eating? I told you to have him ready by now."

Maria's eyes widened and she backed into the wall. "I'm sorry, Señor Walker. I—"

"It's my fault." Jake dropped his fork on his plate with a clang. "I didn't like the eggs and she got me a new plate."

Aiden watched Jake with a puzzled look, suspicion in his eyes. Jake felt him scanning his mind to see if he was lying. Waiting for him to finish, Jake tried to push into Aiden's mind, hitting a solid wall.

Aiden laughed. "You are kind to stand up for Maria." His smile fell and his eyes hardened. "But benevolence is a weakness. Benevolence will get you trampled."

Maria made a gurgling noise and Jake turned to her. She grabbed her throat and her face turned blue before she fell to the floor.

Jake's mouth dropped open in shock.

Aiden continued, ignoring the dead woman on the floor. "You need to be ruthless to defeat your enemies."

"Enemies?" Jake's breath caught in his throat, forcing his words out in a wheeze.

"Yes, and you must prepare to fight them." Aiden stood. "There's no time to waste. We start now."

****

Will stood naked with a hood over his head, his hands cuffed behind his back. A metal collar around his neck tethered him to a wall. He knew about CIA interrogation procedures. Enough to feel the slow trickle of fear seep into his head.

Kramer wanted information about the woman in the woods.

Will knew nothing about the woman in the woods other than his psycho obsession with her. And he couldn't admit that.

Goddamn it to fucking hell.

The door creaked open and footsteps echoed in the room.

The hood was jerked off his head and his eyes adjusted to the blinding light.

Will tensed and gritted his teeth. His cheek stung when an open hand slapped him. He knew it was coming, but it didn't make it any easier. Standard CIA terrorist interrogation procedure. For Iraqis.

Which begged the question: Was he being held by the CIA, or someone familiar enough to know their techniques?

A beefy guy stood in front of him, wearing a grim smile. "Okay, Davenport. You can tell me what I want to know and we can spend the rest of the day eating bonbons, or you can do things the hard way."

Will cocked his head. "I don't really care for bonbons, but I could sure as hell use a beer."

He was prepared for the next slap.

"Do you know the current location of Emma Thompson?"

He'd warned himself that this would be hard, not just physically but because of the madness that persisted no matter how many times he told himself what he felt wasn't real. Nevertheless, the sound of her name tightened his gut. "No."

"When was the last time you saw Emma Thompson?"

Why couldn't he remember her when the mere mention of her name opened the floodgate of emotions? His tightly strung nerves were close to breaking and the interrogation had only begun. He was a dead man. How ironic that he had survived all those hellish years in Iraq, only to meet his end in some senator's basement all because of a woman. A woman he couldn't even remember.

"I asked you a question. When was the last time you saw Emma Thompson?"

A hard slap to his cheek rattled his head, returning him to sanity, if only for a temporary reprieve. He refused to believe this was the end. He'd been through worse than this, even if he couldn't come up with anything at the moment. "I guess in the woods, just before your boys showed up."

His interrogator raised his eyebrows. "You're being awfully cooperative."

"You can't show any weakness or you are dead." He latched on to the voice in his head, ignoring that it wasn't his own. "I'm not a real fan of getting the shit beat out of me. I'll tell you anything I know."

"*Really?*" the man titled his head.

What the hell was there to tell? It wasn't like he had information they didn't. They knew she'd been in the woods. But the need to protect her overrode all reason. "What's she to me, anyway?"

He wasn't prepared for the next slap or his head slamming into the plywood screwed into the wall. The man's forearm jammed the metal collar into Will's neck, pressing him against the board.

"I think you skipped step two and moved on to step three," Will choked out. "You're not following proper interrogation procedure."

"Smartass, huh? That last answer told me everything I need to know. Everything you've said is a fucking lie." He jerked Will away from the wall. "Let's start again, shall we? I want truthful answers this time. We know she wasn't in the woods. Our men searched for her and came up with nothing."

"Then maybe she ran off. She was there when your men showed up. She was the one who warned me to run."

The man grabbed Will around the throat. "Let's say that she was there and warned you. Where is she now?"

"How the hell would I know? I can't fucking read her mind."

"We think you can."

Like the voice he heard in his head seconds ago? A chill washed over him. The voice in his head was Will losing grasp with reality, not something real or supernatural. He dug deep to find his bravado. "I bet you believe in the tooth fairy and Santa Claus too."

Another slap to the face as well as his stomach.

"What the fuck do you want from me?" Will growled.

"Answers that you shouldn't be so willing to give up. What are her powers? Where is her son? Have you seen Alex Warren?"

Will shook his head. *Powers? What the hell?*

"Is she still pregnant?"

That one sunk into his core, catching him off guard, though he had no idea why.

"Aw, hit a nerve, did I? Then let's talk about the baby, shall we?"

"What baby? What the hell do I care about a baby?"

His interrogator paused and crossed his arms. "Because it's yours."

Will snorted. "Mine? You're mistaken there. I take great care to make sure something like that doesn't happen."

"Nice try, asshole. You've already admitted to Kramer it's yours."

After several more rounds of abuse, the man cleared his throat. "Let's try again, shall we? Is Emma Thompson still pregnant?"

The image of her came to mind: her nightgown bloodied between her legs, catching his breath in his chest. His knees buckled and he struggled not to hang himself on the collar around his neck.

Another slap. "Is she still pregnant?"

"You have to tell him yes. Her life depends on it."

Who knew what the blood was from? But he knew, the anguish gripping his heart told him everything he needed to know, even if he couldn't remember it. "Yes."

The interrogator grasped Will's cheeks, his fingers digging deep. "See? That wasn't so hard, was it?" He released his grip and slapped Will's face again.

Will's cheek burned. Son of a bitch. This had just begun.

"Let's talk about her powers. What is she capable of?"

Will shook his head to clear his lingering grief. "What the hell are you talking about? What powers? Like special skills?" Maybe she was some rogue CIA agent or a terrorist they thought he was associated with.

His answer earned him a head slam into the plywood wall. "Wrong answer, pretty boy. We already know she can create explosions and use mind control. What else can she do?"

An operative could handle explosions, but the mind control? That wasn't possible.

The man slammed his head into the wall several more times. "What else can she do?"

"I think she can fly."

The interrogator stopped, his hand clenched in Will's hair. "Fly? How?"

What the fuck? This shithead believed him. "You know, fly."

His head slammed again. "Wrong answer."

"No fucking shit," Will said through gritted teeth as his head hit the wall. "I don't know anything about this woman. Why do you keep asking me?"

The man released his hold on Will and stepped back. He looked over his shoulder at the man in the corner. "Time to move on to the next phase."

"Already?" the guard asked.

"Kramer needs answers fast and this obviously isn't working." Will's interrogator released a heavy sigh. "I'd start talking if I were you."

"And here I thought we were having a nice chat."

The man turned and left the room.

Will closed his eyes and prepared himself. He had a pretty good idea what the next phase involved.

He was right. Hours later, Will shivered uncontrollably, water dripping from strands of hair onto his face. The room had been cooled, probably into the fifties if they followed standard procedure, and two men took turns dousing him with buckets of icy water.

His interrogator would return and ask more questions then leave unsatisfied with Will's answers. Then the men would come back and start again. The voice in his head offered sporadic encouragement.

His legs were rubber, but when he sagged the collar on his neck choked him. For the first time in his life, he wondered if he'd get out of this.

"You can survive this. Hang on."

The door opened again and he darted a glance toward the man who entered the room.

Kramer. He wore a satisfied smirk and leaned against the wall. "How's it going, Will?"

"Oh, you know." Will's voice shook from his chattering teeth. "Just hanging out with my new friends."

"With friends like these, I'd hate to meet your enemies." Kramer took several steps closer. "Help me out, Will. There's something I don't understand. You seem so adamant that you don't know her. Why the pretense?"

"You can tell him. She's safe now." Will nearly cried with relief. "Maybe because I don't."

"Will, you and I were in her hospital room when I saw your mark. Is this one of your attempts to protect her? Because it's really not working."

Will closed his eyes. How was he going to get off this fucking merry-go-round? "I'm not protecting anyone. What mark?"

Kramer laughed. "You're going to play stupid with that too?" He looked over his shoulder at one of the guards behind him. "Uncuff him."

"But sir—"

"Do it."

The guard stepped behind Will and unlocked his restraint.

"This mark." Kramer grabbed Will's left arm and pulled it forward, revealing his forearm. Kramer looked up, his mouth gaping. "Where's your mark?"

"*What mark?*"

"The mark on your arm. The mark of the Chosen One!"

"*What the hell are you talking about?*"

Kramer dropped Will's arm, the color draining from his face. "You really don't remember, do you?"

"I never met this woman until last night. I have no idea what you're talking about."

Kramer took a step back. "You have no recollection of Emma Thompson?"

Overwhelming emotions for her? Yes. Memories of her? "No."

"Or her son, Jake?"

"Is that the baby my new friend keeps asking about?" His answer was flippant but pain shot through his chest over the loss.

Kramer tapped his hands behind his back. "This changes everything."

"Finally," Will exhaled. "Now you know this was a huge misunderstanding."

Kramer looked at him. "But you remember last night?"

Will hesitated.

"Tell him."

He knew it was possible to go insane from extreme interrogation methods, but he'd hope it would take him days to lose his mind, not half a day or so.

"Your life now depends on it and you need to live. Tell him."

Tears burned his eyes. Damn, he couldn't lose what limited control he had. "I remember standing in the woods with her and another man. She told me we had to run, then your boys showed up. They shot me with a dart and the rest is history."

"And what's the last thing you remember before that?"

Tell him.

"Getting a phone call about a job." Will's head jerked up. "I think it was you."

"Do you have any powers?"

"Again with the powers?"

Kramer laughed dryly. "I guess that's a no." He watched Will through hooded eyes. "Do you know anything about Alex Warren, Senator Warren's son?"

"Nothing I haven't heard on TV."

Kramer watched him again before releasing a heavy sigh. "I guess we're done with you then."

"Finally."

Kramer turned to the interrogator. "Take him out and shoot him."

Will's eyes widened. "Wait a minute. There's no need for that. I told you what I know."

"Which, unfortunately, is no help at all. I have no idea why you've forgotten the last month and a half, but you're of no further use to us."

Month and a half? He'd lost a month and a half? "What about Emma?"

Kramer narrowed his eyes. "What about her?"

"You said she was coming back to get me. Don't you think you should keep me alive as bait?"

Grumbling under his breath, Kramer headed for the door. "Take him back to his room while I make a call, but do not underestimate him. He only looks weak and pathetic."

Will wanted to take exception with that, but if his body looked anything like his tattered psyche, he had to agree.

Several men pointed guns at him while one guard unlocked the collar on his neck. When freed, he fell to his knees.

"Hold it together."

He was too weak to get up on his own. Two guards hoisted him up and dragged him to the door, still naked.

Some strength had returned to his legs by the time they threw him in his cell. Will stumbled as he fell to the floor. He considered putting up a fight, but he'd never be able to overpower them in his weakened state. He'd only get himself killed.

"Good news, pretty boy."

Will looked up to see a guard's face in the partially open door.

"You've just got yourself a temporary stay of execution. Let's hope your girlfriend shows up soon."

The lights turned off, plunging the room into total darkness. Will crawled onto the bare mattress and curled into a fetal position in an attempt to get warm. Would she come for him?

Will wasn't counting on it.

CHAPTER FIVE

"EMMA, you have to get up. You're still wearing the clothes you wore when you got here, and the room reeks of smoke and wet dog." Raphael threw open the drapes, flooding the room with light. "You have to eat and get your energy back. It's time to get to work."

Flinching, she squeezed her eyes shut. She'd lain in bed for two days, refusing to get up other than to go to the bathroom.

He grabbed her arm and pulled her into a sitting position then squatted in front of her. "I know you're still upset, but this isn't you. You're a fighter. You don't give up."

After lying in the dark so long, she had to squint to look at him. "You don't know jack shit about me."

He grinned, his eyes lighting up. "Ah, she speaks."

"Shut the fuck up."

"Gladly, if you'll talk instead."

She tried to lie back down but he held her up.

"Sorry, Sleeping Beauty. I've listened to you cry and call out for him long enough. You're done."

His hypnotic effect washed through her and she jerked out of his hold. "Get your hands off of me."

He put his hands in the air in an exaggerated gesture. "Deal. As long as you get up. You've wasted two precious days of our six weeks to prepare that we couldn't afford to lose. It's time for you to start working."

Her anger flared. "This is pointless. You saw the other night what I'm capable of. We also saw that I didn't even come close to touching Aiden. Do you really think we have a chance against *that*?"

Raphael stood, turning his back as he moved to the window. "Honestly?"

"Yes."

"I don't know."

Biting her lower lip, she swallowed the lump of fear in her throat. She never expected him to admit it, even if he wasn't sure of it.

He twisted around to face her. "But I know that we don't stand a chance if you don't at least try to save us. And I know if you're dead that you'll never get Jake back. If you're defeated, what's to stop Aiden from doing away with Jake too?"

Her breath caught and she had to force herself to exhale. "Aiden wouldn't kill him."

Raphael walked toward her, grim determination in his eyes. "We don't know that. To Aiden, people are expendable. You included." He sat on the bed next to her. "While you're unique this time, your predecessor was reincarnated time and time again. Just like Alex and me." He paused, tears glistening in his eyes. "Emmanuella was Aiden's daughter and he did away with her to create you." His fingers clenched into fists in his lap.

"Why? Why would he do that?"

"Who knows why Aiden does what he does? I grew weary of trying to figure out his games centuries ago."

To what lengths would her father go to be entertained by this stupid game? Maybe the more accurate question was what wouldn't he do? "No, no, no," she mumbled frantically, shaking her head. "This is crazy! Things like this don't happen!"

He stood. "You can live in denial all you want, but it doesn't make it any less real."

A fresh wave of grief washed over her. If denial could change reality, Jake would be with her and Will wouldn't be dead. But she'd dreamed of Will in her twilight state the past days. He felt so real, answering when she cried for him, telling her that he was there. It only upset her even more. He wasn't there. He was gone. Wasn't he? "Raphael?"

He paused in the doorway.

"How do you know Will is dead?"

He hesitated before pity filled his eyes. "Emma, you and I both saw his body. Do you really think they would capture him and keep him alive?"

The question sent a shaft of pain through her heart.

"No. The answer is no. He's of no use to them without his mark. And you know yourself that while Kramer's men were ordered to capture you alive, they were none too gentle about it. You suffered a beating, bruises, and worse."

Worse. She still wore the proof of worse. The stiff fabric scratching her thighs. She couldn't think about her baby. She could barely think of Will.

"They killed him in the woods that night," Raphael said. "And you know it deep inside."

Did she? She was certain of it that night when Raphael made her say it out loud, but could she really give up on him so easily? "I dreamed of him."

His expression fell away and he seemed to choose his words carefully. "Everyone has dreams, Emma."

"Not like this. It felt real. Like he was *there*."

He paused again before his eyes bore into hers. "Did you experience this when Will had the mark? Did you have dreams of him?"

Disappointment swept away her hope. "No."

His mouth lifted into a smug grin. "No. You didn't, but you did dream of someone, didn't you?"

She heaved an angry breath and stood. "I'm not doing this with you right now."

He took a step into the room. "Why not? Let's get it out here in the open, Emma. Who did you dream of?"

"You know damn good and well who I dreamed of."

"Say it."

"Is this some fucking ego trip for you?"

"No, this is pointing out the facts. I told you that you were meant to be mine and the dreams prove it. You didn't dream of Will. The only thing you had with Will was a shared mark and a baby. Now they're both gone."

"How dare you!" She released a sob of despair. "Don't you dismiss him like that. He meant much more than that and you know it."

"You loved him. Yes, I am fully aware of that. Don't you think it was hard for me to see you with him when I thought you were my Emmanuella? Don't you think I wanted to rip the man's head off? But he had his part to play and I had to stand back and watch until it was done. And the fact remains that he's human, Emma. He's not like you and me."

Her eyes flew open. "You said he *is* human. Present tense. You think he's alive."

He rubbed his forehead in frustration. "Look, I understand your need to grasp for straws." His hand dropped. "But the sooner you accept this, the sooner you can move on and prepare. It was a slip of the tongue."

"But the dreams—"

"Do you feel him now?"

Her eyes widened in surprise. "What?"

"Do you feel him now? Reach out to him. You said you felt him in your dreams. Before last night, you could feel him and talk to him when you were awake. That seems like a more certain link than vague dreams that in reality are your subconscious's way of dealing with your grief. At least your dreams of me pointed to your future. Did your dreams of him do that?"

Her eyes welled with tears.

"The surest way to know if he's still there is to reach out to him. So do it. Prove that he's alive."

Flustered, she squeezed her eyes shut, focusing on Will. *"Will? Are you there?"*

Silence was her answer.

"Will. Please. I'm begging you. Don't leave me. I need you." Tears streamed down her face as she choked back a sob.

Raphael cleared his throat and she expected to find him gloating. Instead, he stared at the floor.

"You're not alone in losing someone you love, Emma." He looked up, his eyes burning with pain and anger. "We both lost someone two nights ago, but we can grieve later. Now we have to concentrate on defeating Aiden."

She knew this, but she couldn't let Will go yet.

Raphael shook his head and turned to leave. "Get showered and dressed. There're clothes you can wear in the closet. You're thinner than she usually was, but they should work. Then come down and eat and we'll get started."

The door closed and she considered lying back down, but he was right, as much as she hated to admit. She needed to save Jake.

Avenging Will's death was pure bonus.

She stripped off her gown and held it in her hand, a fresh wave of tears falling. The gown stunk of bonfire, mildew, and metal. She threw it into the trash can, telling herself that what was done was done. Crying wouldn't solve anything, but the tears fell anyway as she showered, washing away the grime but reopening the pain. When she turned off the water, she stood at the stall threshold, a towel wrapped around her body. The air-conditioned breeze cooled the water droplets on her skin, sending chills through her body, but she hesitated.

I can cry in here and I can cry when I go to bed. But when I walk out of this shower, no more tears.

When her foot hit the tile floor, a change swept through her. Her heart hardened and her back straightened, determination replacing her despair. Aiden would pay for what he'd done.

She found clothes in the closet as Raphael said she would, grabbing a pair of jeans and a T-shirt. Pulling them on, she tried to ignore that these were meant for someone else. That Raphael might be in pain too. Because to admit that he had suffered a loss made him more like her than she could afford.

He stood in front of the stove when she went downstairs. The smell of onions and butter, reminded her stomach that she hadn't eaten in days. He smiled and gestured to a small round table in front of windows with a view of the backyard. "Have a seat at the table. I hope you like omelets."

She turned her gaze to the table set for two and her back stiffened. "Look, we need to set some ground rules before we start this. Dining socially is not acceptable."

He set down the plate and her traitorous stomach growled loud enough to hear.

"I have to make sure you eat."

"No. You don't. When and what I eat are none of your business. What we have is strictly a *working* relationship. I will work with you to save my son and then we are done."

His gaze narrowed as his smile fell away. "Whether you've eaten or not *is* my business. You're entirely too thin and you need your strength to do this. It's going to be hard work, and frankly, I'm not sure you can do it."

She clenched her teeth. "Then what the hell am I doing here?"

"Because I'd rather take a chance with you than team up with Alex. I loathe the man and honestly, he's not much stronger than you at this point."

"Are you serious? Did you see the storm he created?"

His eyebrow raised. "Did you see the fires you've created?"

She hadn't seen the final results of the last fire, but she had seen the first one in Minnesota. She didn't want to think about how many people she'd killed. "This is pointless. Sure, I've created two massive explosions and nearly died as a result. If Will hadn't saved me the first time..." Mentioning Will brought a sharp stab of grief, but she swallowed it down.

"And I saved you the second. But you can learn how to do it without killing yourself in the process. You just don't know how yet."

"And you're going to teach me? Fine, then we need rules. The first is you are not to touch me under any circumstances."

"I'm not sure I can agree to that." His hard stare told her he was serious.

She took a step back. "Then we're already done."

"What do you think saved you after you created that fire? What kept you from leaping out of a jet flying over the Midwest? I *gave* you energy. I won't agree to not touch you, but I will agree to only touch you when I deem it absolutely necessary."

She shook her head. "No way. You could claim anything you want to be 'absolutely necessary.' Why would I agree to that?"

A derisive laugh rumbled in his throat. "You think you're the one holding all the cards here. You think you can set these terms and that I have no choice but to kowtow to your wishes." His voice lowered. "But you forget that you need me just as much. Without me you have no chance of saving Jake."

Her grief boiled into rage, her chest burning with power. "I don't need you. I can always side with Alex."

"Alex." He laughed again, looking at the ceiling. "That's rich. You think I'm going to believe that you'll side with the man who raped you and kidnapped your son? You claim I don't know jack shit about you, but I know you'd sooner die than team up with him."

Anger filled her, her energy begging for release.

Raphael's glare softened to disappointment. "You're still so young and impetuous. You don't even know how to prevent what you've just done."

"Fuck you, Raphael."

"Close your eyes."

She narrowed them instead, her anger and hatred increasing the pressure.

"For God's sake, Emma, if you can't trust me in this one thing then we're doomed."

Taking a deep breath, she closed her eyes.

"As impossible as this sounds, try to relax."

She bit back a retort before a jolt shot through her body, then the pressure was gone. Her eyes flew open in alarm. "What happened?"

He turned around and poured a cup of coffee. "Sit down and eat."

"What happened?"

"I pulled your energy away."

"How?"

"All in good time. Now you eat." He picked up a crystal juice glass off the counter and sat in the chair next to her place setting.

"But—"

He looked up at her with a hard stare. "You have your conditions and I have mine. The first of mine is you let me do this my way. I teach what you need to know when I think you need to know it."

She glared. "I'm not allowed to ask questions?"

"You can ask all the questions you like. But don't expect me to answer all of them."

She sat in the chair and picked up her fork. "I have a lot of questions, so don't expect me to just sit here and let you spoon-feed me."

He nodded, his lips pursed. "I'd be surprised if you didn't have questions. In the past, at this point in the game you'd know all the answers. They would have just come to you. Of course, we never made it to this point before, so it's all a moot point. But in past experiences, you had memories of your previous lives and your purpose in it all."

She gave him a hard stare. "I never would have chosen you, you know."

His gaze held hers, his face expressionless. "I know."

"I never would have chosen Alex, either."

"I know this too."

"Has that ever happened before?"

"No."

"Did she always love you?"

"No."

"So sometimes she loved Alex?"

"In the beginning." He watched her eat with a serious expression, lifting his glass of amber liquid to his lips.

She frowned. "That doesn't look like orange juice."

Smirking, he raised the glass to her. "How perceptive of you."

"A little early in the day to be drinking, isn't it?"

"You have your vice—loving a human—and I have mine." He took another drink then grinned.

"You're creeping me out. This is the second time you've watched me eat. Why aren't you eating too?"

"I already ate hours ago. It's nearly lunchtime."

"How long have you done this?"

His mouth lifted into a crooked grin. "Watch you eat or have breakfast before lunchtime?"

They'd spent centuries fucking with her life and he joked about it. "This might go faster if you actually volunteered some information."

With an exaggerated sigh, he shifted in his seat. "In the very beginning, it was a more level playing field. Our life experiences were fresh each time and it was easier to find one another. Travel was an ordeal and people often didn't stray more than twenty miles from their homes their entire lives. Consequently, at least in the very beginning, we all often lived in the same village or town. By the time we knew who we really were, we already had a history."

"How far back does this go? Middle Ages?"

"Further."

"Prehistoric man?"

He snorted. "It was B.C., but not that distant."

"But when exactly?"

"What does it matter? Ancient Greece. That specific enough for you?"

She took a sip of her coffee, watching him over the rim. "That's a helluva long time."

"You have no idea."

Centuries sounded so vague until she put it into perspective. For two thousand years this had gone on and on. How could Raphael do this time and time again? To be so close and lose it all again. To lose the person he loved time and time again. But at least he knew he'd see her again at some point in the future. She'd never see Will again. She tried to ignore that Raphael had lost his Emmanuella forever too.

"So go ahead. Ask more questions."

Taking a bite of her eggs, she looked out the window. "Where are we? It wasn't this green in Montana and Wyoming."

He watched her for a moment. "Tennessee."

"Is this your house?"

He twisted the coffee cup in his hand. "Yes."

"If I wanted to walk out the front door and turn my back on you, could I?"

He paused. "Everyone has free will."

She snorted. "Apparently not."

He leaned forward on the table. "Okay, my turn. Do you want your son back?"

Her fork dropped with a clang. "You really have to ask that question?"

"Apparently you need to be reminded of it." He looked at her plate and raised his eyebrows. "You haven't eaten even half of that. We can't start until you eat more. You need the energy."

"Again with the energy." But she knew he was right. Will had figured out that when she used too much, one way to re-energize her was give her food. And his touch. She pushed away the memory of Will's touch. She couldn't afford to let her mind go there. Not right now.

Raphael sat back. "I suspect you've only used energy from your own body to make fire. But there are other sources. In fact, you should only use your own energy for small things and if there's no other source. Any other time, you need to pull it from elsewhere. Still, it will be hard on you at first. This is all new to you. Emmanuella..." He paused and took a breath before continuing. "Emmanuella had lifetimes of memories stored. Once she began to remember, she could use those to help her. You have nothing."

"That's encouraging."

He shrugged. "It is what it is. That's why I got so frustrated with you and Will. Will was supposed to protect you while you regained your memories and learned to channel your power, until you no longer needed the pendant to help you. In the past, once your protector was marked, your human enemies were always hot on your trail. And once you no longer needed the pendant, your protector's job was done and you released him."

"So that's why you got so angry when I said I wasn't practicing."

"Practicing always helped the memories return faster. When you told me that Will thought it was too dangerous to use your power, I wanted to kill him. Literally. But you couldn't come into your full power without him. Aiden set that little trick up just to add complications."

"You had said you couldn't be around me or it would inhibit my powers."

"Yes, but that part's not important." He looked away. "Just more of Aiden's rules."

She lowered her gaze. "What would have happened if Aiden didn't steal Will's memories and I didn't release him?"

"It was unprecedented. You never loved your protector before."

"From what you said, me not picking either of you was unprecedented. The whole thing is unprecedented."

"Very true. Also unprecedented was the length of time for you to prepare. You were usually given months to remember. This time was a month and a half. Then again, there was nothing for you to remember. Honestly, it's a wonder you didn't get yourself killed."

"You already said that."

"It doesn't make it any less true."

"What does it mean?"

"It means the world has tilted off its axis."

She grimaced. "Very funny."

"The world may not have literally tilted but the rules of everything have changed. It's anyone's guess what happens now."

Maybe so, but she'd do her best to make sure it wasn't left up to chance.

CHAPTER SIX

"AGAIN."

Emma stood in the field, hanging over her bent knees. "In a minute."

Raphael watched her, his arms crossed. "No. Now. Again."

"You think it's so goddamned easy, then you do it."

The log she'd been trying to move shot ten feet away from her without warning. Raphael put his hands on his hips. "There."

"Go to hell."

"Thanks. I'd rather stick around here on earth. Which means you need to try it again."

She was so tired. She'd never been so exhausted in all of her life, but she'd never admit it to him. It didn't help that she got little sleep at night. It was the one time she allowed herself to grieve, and she spent most of her time in bed crying for Jake, crying for Will, which left only a few hours for sleeping.

The first two days she was sure Will was there, answering her when she called out for him. But last night, there was nothing but silence. She'd held out hope that her dreams of him meant something, but she forced herself to accept the truth.

Will was dead.

Jake was more difficult. During the day, he kept himself shielded from her, but at night when he slept, he let his guard down. He cried for her in his sleep, smothering her with his fear and loneliness. She tried to answer him, to use their connection to give him comfort, but their connection had become one-way since the night her father changed the rules. All of his feelings flowed out, without her love and reassurance going back.

He thought she'd forgotten him.

In his sleep, he begged for her to come to him and save him. Even if she knew where he was, she couldn't save him. If she couldn't move a log ten feet, how would she defeat her father?

Then there were the new dreams, a scene from the vision she'd received in Kansas City after her encounter with the crazy homeless man. It was only one part of the vision, but enough to frighten her. A valley lay below her with multiple fires spread across the landscape, and a voice tickled her ear. *"You are the destruction of the world."*

If she weren't so irritated, she would have laughed at the idea. There was little chance of her being the destruction of anything. In two days of practicing, she'd made little progress and Raphael had become more and more frustrated.

"You need to focus. Point your energy to the log and push it with your mind."

"I thought you were going to teach me how to use other power sources."

He scowled, anger filling his eyes. "You have to learn how to use your own energy to do simple tasks without killing yourself. Once you've accomplished that, you can move on to bigger things. You can't run until you learn to walk."

"I'd settle for learning to crawl," she muttered.

Raphael released a guttural growl. "If you refuse to take this seriously, then we might as well quit now."

She put her hand on her hip, her anger building. "I'm taking this seriously. I'm the one out here for hours on end trying to do stupid-ass shit like move a log two feet."

"Then quit talking about it and move it."

She took her brewing anger and focused the energy on the wood. "Move!"

The log shot sideways a couple of feet, jerking and hopping before coming to a stop.

"No. No. No." Raphael groaned.

"I'm trying!"

He rubbed his face with his hands. "We're not getting anywhere, so let's call it a day. Besides," he moved in front of her, looking into her face. "You look exhausted, and crying all night isn't helping matters."

"What I do in the privacy of my own room isn't any of your business."

"Wrong." He took a step forward, his chest almost touching hers. "Sleeping falls under the same category as eating. It's obvious that your lack of sleep is interfering with your progress, so you have two choices tonight. You either take medication to help you sleep or you let me help you sleep."

Fury instantly ignited. She could only imagine how he planned to *help* her go to sleep. "Don't you even think about touching me."

"Then you'll take medication."

"And if I refuse?"

"I believe this falls under the 'deemed necessary' category."

She'd heard enough and spun around to march back to the house, when he grabbed her arm. His energy flowed through her, filling her with a need for more. She recognized it for what it was now, but she was clueless how to stop the flow. She doubted Raphael would ever teach her how to block it. It was his weapon against her.

"I hate you," she spit through her gritted teeth, forcing herself to stay in control.

He pulled her against him and stared into her face. "You only think you do. One day you'll thank me."

She closed her eyes to weaken her connection to him.

"I can help you forget him."

Her eyes flew open and she tried to jerk out of his grasp. "No!"

"Think about it, Emma. No more pain. No more loneliness."

She shook her head, frantic. He was capable of it and she knew he would do it. A sob escaped as she felt her body giving in to his. She had to fight this. "No, please, Raphael. *Please.* I've lost everything else. Don't take that from me too."

Caressing her cheek, gentleness softened the anger in his eyes. "I only want to help you, Emma. I'm not your enemy."

"Then please don't do this." She hated begging, especially to him, but she couldn't lose her memories of Will.

"Then tonight you'll take something to help you sleep and tomorrow we'll start fresh." He leaned forward, his lips brushing her cheek before he dropped his hold on her.

She stumbled backward, hate filling her every cell. She hated him for taking advantage of her that way, but she hated her own body and its traitorous reaction even more. One day she'd figure out how to stop it. Then she'd turn it around and use it against him.

****

Will had lost all track of time. His room had been dark since they'd thrown him in and he hadn't seen anyone since. Which meant he hadn't eaten or had anything to drink either. Gauging from his hunger and thirst, he suspected he'd been in the room at least a day, perhaps two. He'd finally resorted to crawling to the toilet and drinking from the bowl to stave off dehydration.

He toggled between consciousness and sleep, spending hours caught in the in-between. Images of Emma filled his head from the few moments of memories he had of her. He had a bizarre need to know that his love for her was reciprocated. The horror on her face, after he first became aware of his surroundings, reassured his ego. The way she grabbed his hand and tried to pull him to safety. The panic in her voice as he ran off after the gunmen.

If he'd stayed with her would she have been captured too? Or would they be somewhere safe and together now? Would holding her in his arms fill the ache in his soul?

He replayed the scene over and over, his need to remember her so strong. He picked apart every detail. He spent the most time on the first few hazy moments when he tried to figure out where he was. Her arms wrapped around his neck as her tears wet his face. Her lips pressed to his unresponsive ones. And if he pushed back to the very edge of the haze, where his memories hit a wall, the very first thing he remembered was her voice. "Will! *Please*. Don't leave me. I love you."

He clung to her words as they parted his delirium and proved he was still sane. He didn't love a stranger or a ghost. She was real and she loved him too.

But when the chaos in his memories erupted, another man stayed with Emma through it all, trying to lead her to safety. For the most part she'd ignored him, focusing on getting Will out of the woods, but there was no denying the hungry look in the other man's eyes.

He wanted her.

And there wasn't a damn thing Will could do about it.

When Will slept, he dreamed of her. There were no images, yet he knew it was her. She cried for hours, her sobs taunting his need to protect her. She often called his name along with Jake. The interrogator said Jake was her son. Did Kramer have him too?

Her despair mixed with his, pulling him deeper into his madness, the weight so heavy he thought he might sink through the rickety mattress and down into the earth until it sucked the life out of him.

In moments of lunacy, he tried to reach her, her presence hovering just out of reach. When he first heard her, he called to her, telling her that he was there. He eventually stopped because it seemed to upset her even more.

And that's how he knew he'd really gone mental. People couldn't talk to each other in dreams.

That and the other voice in his head.

The voice he'd heard during the interrogation was still there, offering encouragement.

"Don't give up, Will. He's coming."

At first Will tried to figure out who was coming, then gave up. There was no voice. No one was coming. His subconscious had kicked into self-preservation mode.

In his rare saner moments, he tried to make sense of where he was and why he was here. He knew it involved Senator Warren and Kramer, and somehow Emma fit into it all. Kramer and his interrogator claimed that Emma had powers, whatever that meant. What he most wanted to know at the moment was how he lost a month and a half of memories. And why.

When the door to his cell opened, he was sure he was hallucinating. He turned to the light, but before his hand shielded his eyes, he was sure he'd seen James. His eyes burned, tears streaming down his face.

"Will?"

Will shook his head slowly. Now he heard James's voice too.

Maybe he was dead.

Will tried to open his eyes, but the room had flooded with light.

"Son of a bitch, what the fuck have they done to you?" Someone squatted next to his cot and set something on the floor.

"*James?*" Will's tongue was heavy and slow to move. Squinting, he caught a glimpse of James's horror-stricken face. Will sank into the mattress. "What...I don't know...How did you get here?" His voice was raspy. He had to be hallucinating.

James's head leaned forward, examining Will's face. "They captured me and threw me into this cell. What did they do to you?"

"Interrogation."

"Interrogation? *Naked?*" James sat back on his heels. "That's why they gave me this bundle of clothes. Come on, let's get you dressed."

Will had been curled up so long that his arms and legs protested when he stretched them out.

"Shit." James grasped Will's arms to help him up.

"I know I look like hell, but if you try to take advantage of me right now, I can still kick your ass."

James swung Will's legs over the side of the bed and pulled him upright. "You fuckhead." He pulled the shirt over Will's head and helped him put his arms through the holes. "I'm too good for you."

Will's mouth lifted into a smirk. "You wish." Will stood on shaky legs while James helped him put his pants on.

James helped Will sit on the cot, grim determination on his face. "We have to get out of here."

Exhausted, Will leaned over his legs. "I don't understand. How did you get here?"

James stood and paced. "They found us while you were in White Horse."

Will's stomach cramped. What was James talking about?

"We need to figure a way out of here."

"Yeah, good luck with that. I'd settle for a drink of water." Will's mouth felt like it was coated in sandpaper.

James stopped in midpace. "How long has it been since they gave you something to eat or drink?"

He closed his eyes. "They haven't."

"They haven't given you *anything*? How long have you been here?"

"I don't know. I've lost track of time. Since they captured me the night in the woods."

"The night they tried to take Emma?"

Will looked up, his mouth gaping. "You know about Emma."

James narrowed his eyes, his brow furrowing. "Of course I know about Emma. What that fuck are you talking about? Now answer my question: Did they take you the night they tried to take Emma?"

"I think so." James not only knew about Emma but also about the woods. Relief washed through Will like a summer shower, warm and full of hope. It was real. All of it was real.

"That's four days, Will!"

"They threw me in here, waiting for Emma to show up. Guess they forgot to send her an invitation." Will looked up. "You've been here all this time?"

"Yeah, and it looks like they've treated me a hell of a lot better."

"Lucky you." Too lightheaded to stay upright, Will eased himself down. The mattress creaked in protest. "So why are you in here now?"

"I think they think I can get information out of you." He lowered himself to the floor next to the bed, resting his head in his hands. "What a fucked-up mess."

They sat in silence before James grunted and shifted his weight. "So why didn't she come?"

Will hesitated. James just admitted that he was sent here to get information. But this was James. His oldest and most trustworthy friend. "I don't think she can."

James cocked his head. "Why do you say that?"

"Because she cries for me in her sleep."

James stared at the wall by the door. "So you think someone has her?"

Will's heart sputtered. First, James wasn't surprised when Will said she cried for him. Like he thought it was entirely possible that Will would know this. But the second reason caused Will's muscles to tense. James was nervous. "I don't know."

"She'd come get you if she could, right? Did you guys have a fight? Was she the one who turned you over to Kramer?"

Memories of the night in the woods flashed in his mind. "No, she definitely didn't turn me over. She tried to protect me."

"How did you find her? After Kramer's men showed up..." He shot Will a nervous glance.

"I don't know. I don't remember any of it."

James's eyebrows rose. "What do you mean?"

"It means my memories of her are all gone. Kramer said I'd been with her a month and a half. But I remember standing next to a fire with her and she was terrified that I'd get caught when Kramer's men showed up. My only memory before that is getting the call to take a job to bring a woman to South Dakota."

James's shoulders relaxed as he released a long exhale. "You don't remember any of it?"

Why did James look so relieved?

"James is not to be trusted."

"Did you hear that?" Will asked, struggling to sit up.

James reached over and grabbed Will's arm. "Hear what?"

"That voice?"

James shook his head with a wary look in his eyes. "I think you've gone too long without eating, dude. You're hallucinating."

Maybe so, but he wondered if he should listen to the voice in his head anyway. "Yeah, good luck with that, although if I have any hope of breaking out of here, I need to get some strength back."

James got up and pounded on the door. "Hey, can I get something to eat and drink in here?"

Within minutes, the door opened and the guard put a tray on the floor, the door closing behind him. James picked up the tray and set it on the cot. "Eat it slow."

"I know, James." Irritation bled through his words and he hoped James thought it was crabbiness from hunger. James was up to something.

Although Will knew he should eat slowly, once he saw the rice and chopped meat on the plate, his stomach growled in protest. Will sipped from the bottled water first, coating his dry mouth and soothing his throat. He had to resist the urge to guzzle it.

James settled on the floor next to the bed. "So you don't remember anything? You have no idea who took Emma?"

Will capped the bottle with shaky fingers. "Why do you think someone took her?"

"Because in spite of all of her other flaws, she'd never leave you here if she knew you were in danger."

Rice spilled on the mattress as Will tried to scoop it into his mouth with a spoon. "What flaws?"

James hesitated and started to raise his hand to his mouth before he caught himself and put his hand back down. "Look, I'm not here to bash your girlfriend."

"Why *are* you here?" Will didn't hide the hard edge in his voice.

James's eyes flew open. "I told you already."

"You told me the first part—that they thought you could get information. But you forgot the second part, James. What kind of deal did they give you?"

James jumped to his feet and paced again. "Goddamnit, Will. I got us both a deal. *Both of us.* They just want Emma. They told me your mark was gone and they don't need you anymore. Just help them find her and they'll let you go."

"Are you really that fucking naive, James?"

James's eyes blazed with anger. "No, Will. I'm not. That's why I have insurance. If we're not released, I have information on them they don't want made public."

Will's hand fisted around his spoon. "So why not use that information now, James?"

"Will, you don't even remember her. Why are you protecting her?"

He didn't answer, taking several bites of food. "Why do they want her? What's so special about her?"

James paused. "They want her baby."

"And you're just handing her over?"

James's eyes hardened. "It's an easy choice, Will. Her or you. I'll pick you over her any damn time."

"You forgot a minor detail. You're handing over my baby, James. *My baby.*"

The color drained from James's face. "You don't know that. I always suspected she lied to you about that."

"You have to protect her."

Will swallowed the lump in his throat. "I do know, James. The baby is mine." It was a pointless conversation. There was no baby now, but he'd be damned if he was the one to tell them.

"I'm sorry, Will. I didn't know."

But he did.

Will thought he'd hit bottom, yet it kept going deeper. James. But he needed James to get out of here. He took a deep breath. "So now what? I don't know anything. I can't give them any information. What does that mean for you?"

"You obviously have some limited knowledge if you know the baby is yours."

"Kramer told me it's mine. He said I admitted it sometime in my not-so-distant-yet-elusive past."

"You said you were with her before you were captured. What do you remember?"

"Tell him about Raphael."

Raphael. Was that the man with her? Did he have her now?

"Tell him about Raphael." The voice was more insistent.

Tears burned Will's eyes, his control dangerously close to the edge. He was losing his mind. "There was a man." His voice shook and he cleared his throat.

James glanced up with an anxious look.

Will refused to betray her and James's eagerness to do so made the few bites of food in Will's stomach churn.

"They can't touch Raphael."

Will took a deep breath to steady his fear. "He was in the woods and he insisted that Emma escape." He reached for the bottle of water so he didn't have to look James in the eye. "He might have Emma."

"Raphael? Dark-haired guy? Dark eyes? Sexy as hell?"

Will looked up. "You met him?"

"No, but you told me all about him."

"I called him *sexy as hell?*"

"No, but any man who made you feel that threatened had to be."

He felt threatened by this guy before he lost his memory. Now he was really worried about her. "So you go tell them that I think Raphael has her, and then what?"

"Do you have any idea where Raphael is? Where he might have taken her?"

"Not a fucking clue." If he did, Will wouldn't tell those assholes.

James rubbed his forehead. "That's probably okay. They know you've lost your memory so they can't expect much."

Why had James acted surprised when Will said he'd lost all memory of her? Lucky for Will, James had gotten sloppy.

"You need James."

"Shut the hell up!" Will shouted.

James jumped. "What the hell?"

Will shook his head. He wasn't losing it. He was already gone. "Nothing. Sorry. I think I'm hallucinating."

"Maybe you should lie down." James picked up the tray and sniffed it before setting it on the floor. "You need to rest, Will. I'm going to take care of everything."

Reclining, Will looked at him. "Are you, James?" Recklessness kept him from hiding the distrust in his voice.

Hurt flickered over James's face. "Don't I always?"

Will closed his eyes, too weary to keep them open. He welcomed the darkness that called to him.

CHAPTER SEVEN

JAKE lay in bed, the nightlight in the corner casting scary shadows against the walls. Shadows that crept toward him.

He thought he'd imagined them at first. Shadows didn't move, but these did. Edging along the wall slowly, like they tried to trick him by sneaking up on him. He'd mark the progress with his memory. The top of the dresser's shadow came to the middle of the window, but when he looked again it had moved to the edge of the sill. Every time he opened his eyes, the shadows weren't where they were the last time he saw them.

But far more scary things lurked in the house than shadows, even shadows that moved. Aiden was somewhere, watching everyone. When people didn't do what Aiden asked, they had to pay.

Aiden appeared in his doorway, an evil gleam in his eye.

Aiden was upset with Jake. He wasn't making the progress Aiden wanted.

Jake had to be punished.

Rusty, his stuffed dog, rose into the air and hovered next to the bed.

"Do you know what happens to disobedient little boys?"

Shaking his head slowly, Jake's heart raced.

"They lose things they love."

Rusty burst into flames and fell to the rug in ashes.

"Tomorrow, I expect you to do better." Aiden turned and left the room.

Jake buried his face in his pillow, sobbing until the linens were soaked. Rusty was the only thing he had left and Aiden had taken him away. "Mommy! Mommy!" he cried over and over.

Why wouldn't she answer?

She didn't have to talk, just be there with him, close enough to feel even if she wasn't really there. Mommy had done it before, when Alex held Jake in Montana. Why didn't she come to him now?

Maybe she forgot him. She had the new baby now. And Will. She didn't need Jake any more.

Mommy had given up on him.

****

Emma had turned off the shower and wrapped in a towel when she heard banging on the bathroom door.

"Emma! Open the goddamn door," Raphael said, slurring his words.

He must have been listening for the water to turn off.

She hurried into the closet and threw on a nightgown.

"Open the door, Emma!"

Flinging it open, she found Raphael holding a pill bottle. "Time to make a choice, Emmanuella. Sleeping pill or me?"

Fear washed over her. He was drunk and belligerent.

She tried to keep her fear out of her eyes. "I already told you that I wanted the sleeping pill."

With unsteady hands, he opened the bottle and grabbed her wrist, his thumb stroking the soft inner skin. He looked up, his mouth parted. "Are you sure you prefer drugs?"

Biting her lip, she nodded, scared of provoking him. Her body had already begun to react to his touch.

He poured several pills into her hand. "There you go. You've made your choice. You'd rather be drugged than touch me."

Her heart thudded in her ears as she counted the pills in her hand. Five. "That's too many."

Leaning forward, he whispered in a loud voice, "We want to make sure you go to sleep." He gave her a slight push toward the sink. She filled a glass of water, keeping her gaze down.

Raphael leaned into the doorframe as he watched her. He was going to make her take them all.

"I'm capable of taking pills on my own, Raphael." She glared at his reflection. He studied her body and she wished she wasn't standing in front of him in a clingy nightgown.

"You're capable of many things, my love. You just don't always choose to do them."

He referred to her disappointing results over using her power. During dinner, he'd been short and had more alcohol than food. He accused her of purposely trying to sabotage their union by holding back, even when she assured him over and over that she was trying her best. Holding back didn't help her save Jake.

She put a pill in her mouth and swallowed it with the water. "There. Happy now?"

He moved behind her, watching her reflection in the mirror with an unfocused gaze. His breath reeked of alcohol. "Now the others. This was your choice. Unless you've changed your mind."

Her stomach twisted in knots. He'd promised not to touch her if she took *a* sleeping pill, not five. She didn't trust him. Especially drunk.

"I said, take the pills," he growled.

Putting her hand to her mouth, she dumped them in and took the glass of water he held out to her. She swallowed, fear churning her stomach.

His hand reached out to her hair and he lifted it, leaning over to smell it. "You look like her, did you know that? Exactly like her."

She froze, choking on her fear. "I took them, Raphael."

"Sometimes I look at you and I forget." Threading her hair in his fingers, he closed his eyes. "I always loved your hair, Emmanuella."

Her body tensed as she waited. Should she move away? Should she let him exorcise his demons?

"It's agony to have you so close but so far. I've waited so long, so very long." His voice broke and his other hand skimmed her waist. "I want you."

If he used his power over her, she wouldn't be able to stop him. In fact, she'd probably welcome him. *Oh, God.* "I'm not her, Raphael."

"Emmanuella..." He buried his face in her hair, tightening his grip.

"Raphael! Stop! I'm not Emmanuella."

His hand slid up, stopping underneath her breast. "Do you remember the joining words?"

Her body was fading, his energy overpowering hers. "No! Remember? I don't know them. I'm not her."

His mouth lowered to her neck, trailing to her shoulder blade.

"Raphael...stop."

Moving to her side, he lifted her chin. "I can make you love me."

Her heart beating wildly, she shook her head. "No, not this way."

His mouth lowered to hers, hungry and demanding. Her body answered with demands of its own, the pain of her body's betrayal cutting deep.

His hands roamed her body, pulling her gown up.

An ember of anger blazed within her and she latched on to it, feeding it with her indignation. She had to stop him. Stop herself. With a sharp burst of power, she pushed against him and he flew several feet away, tripping as he tried to regain his balance. He landed on the bed, a bewildered look in his eyes.

"Get. Out," she seethed. "Get the hell out of here or I'll *kill* you."

He got to his feet and took a step toward her. "You want me too. I can feel it."

"*No*. That's not real. Maybe it was with her, but it's not with me." Tears burned her eyes, but she refused to let him see her cry again. She was sick of crying. "Get out of my room."

Staggering to the door, he stopped and pointed at her. "I was right. You have been holding back your power."

"Get out. NOW!" she screamed, barely holding on to her control.

He slammed the door shut and she locked it with shaky fingers. A lock wouldn't keep Raphael out, but at least it would slow him down.

She ran to the bathroom and knelt in front of the toilet, making herself gag. Splashing water on her face, she refused to look into the mirror. The event was too close to her encounter with Alex years ago. She crawled into bed, pulling the covers over her head and giving in to her tears. She had to figure out how to stop his control over her. Was it rape if she didn't fight him at the end?

Fuzziness filled her head and she realized that she'd thrown up too late. Some of the sleeping pills made it to her bloodstream. If Raphael came back, she'd be too drugged to stop him.

****

Will dreamed of her again, but this time was different. She walked toward him through the darkness, surrounded by a golden glow. She wore a white gown, more fitted than the one in the woods and not bloody. Her dark hair fell around her face and rested on her chest.

She stopped in front of him, reaching a hand to his cheek. Tears glistened in her eyes. "Is it really you?"

He nodded, the burning in his throat too strong to speak through.

"But you're dead. How are you here?"

"I'm not dead, Emma." He cupped her cheek, thankful he could touch her. God, she was more beautiful than he remembered.

"How do you know me?" A tear slid down her cheek. "Aiden stole your memories."

"He didn't take everything." He couldn't believe she was here with him.

Her chin trembled as his thumb brushed her lips. She rested her head on his chest, wrapping her arms around his waist. "This isn't real."

Maybe not, but he'd take what he could get. He soaked in her flowery scent, surprised by how perfectly she fit against him. "Where are you, Emma?" He lifted her chin so he could stare into her dark brown eyes. "Tell me where you are."

A smile lifted the corners of her mouth. As she started to speak, her face faded into the darkness.

No. He couldn't lose her yet.

"Will! Wake up. Something's going on."

Will jerked upright, surprised that the sirens now piercing his ears hadn't woke him. The loss of her sucked his breath away. He'd touched her. Held her in his arms. If he'd only had a few more seconds, he'd know where she was.

No, it wasn't real.

"Are you okay?" James asked.

Will shook his head. He had to focus. If he could get out of here, he'd find a way to find her. "Yeah, fine."

Relief filled James's eyes. "Thank God. I thought you had to be dead if this noise didn't rouse you."

"What's going on?"

"I don't know. The sirens have been going off for a minute or so. I can hear guards running down the hall, but nobody's saying anything."

Will stood, wobbling with dizziness. "Does this have anything to do with your collaboration? Or the information you slipped them while I slept after you drugged me?"

James's jaw tightened. "No."

So he didn't deny it. "Do you have a plan?"

"No."

"What? They didn't slip you a key?"

"Goddamnit, Will. I only—"

The sirens stopped.

Both men moved next to the door, pressing their ears to the metal panel.

Will stepped away first. "Nothing. Absolute silence."

"I hear footsteps," James hissed.

Will leaned his head against the metal. James was right. A set of footsteps clicked on the concrete floor, approaching at a leisurely rate. Taking several paces back, Will surveyed the room for a potential weapon. Nothing. Even the tray with his food was gone. He glared at James. "Did it occur to you we could have used the spoon before you sent it back with room service?"

"They specifically looked for the spoon, you asswipe."

The lock on the door clicked, the mechanism turning.

James took a step back.

The door opened and a face peered in. "Good evening, gentlemen. Or maybe I should say morning since the sun's about to rise. I hope I haven't disturbed you."

"Alex Warren," James muttered under his breath.

Alex eyed Will up and down with an amused grin. "I have to say, this isn't your best look, Will."

"Fuck you."

Alex laughed. "That's more like the arrogant asshole I remember. It's your lucky day, boys. Consider this your get-out-of-jail-free card." Alex's eyes filled with a mischievous glint. "Tell Emma that she owes me. I gave her something, now I want her to give me something in exchange."

Will's shoulders tensed. "What?"

Alex smiled. "Now if I wanted you to know, I would have told you. Trust me, she'll know what I'm talking about."

Will didn't like the sound of that, but he wasn't in a position to negotiate. "What makes you think I'll see her again? I've lost all my memories of her. Why would I find her?"

Alex raised his eyebrows as a mischievous glint filled his eyes. "Who said I thought you would be the one looking?" He stepped into the hallway. "You better get out of here before someone shows up to investigate this mess."

Will was about to ask what mess, but stopped when he saw the hall littered with bodies.

"I never heard any shots," James whispered.

"No, you wouldn't. I don't need guns." Alex smiled then waved his hands forward. "Shoo! You're supposed to be escaping, not taking a leisurely stroll."

James moved down the hall, Will following behind in disbelief. Bodies lay on the floor, no sign of struggle or injury of any kind.

Will spun around, his chest constricting with fear. Alex stood in front of Will's cell, his smile gone. Expressionless, he stared into Will's face.

A chill shot down Will's spine. What had Alex done and what was he capable of?

CHAPTER EIGHT

"WILL, come on." James grabbed his arm and pulled him down the hall.

His feet moved like they were stuck in molasses. He knew he was mixed up in some crazy shit, but this proved it even more.

"Will!" James gave him a jerk.

He stumbled and recovered, glancing back at Alex, but he was gone.

James stopped next to a guard and pulled a gun out of his holster.

Swiping his hand over his mouth, Will surveyed the hall. "What the hell happened here?"

"This was your world, Will. Not mine." James leaned over another guard and grabbed another gun, then put it in Will's hand. He rummaged around the bodies, pulling out ammunition and stuffing it in his pockets. "You're white as a sheet. You need to get your shit together. We may have to fight our way out of here."

The question was, who would they have to fight? He could fight just about anything with guns. But this? Will shook his head, taking several deep breaths. It was one thing to hear a voice in his head and fantasize about a woman he'd seen for ten minutes. But this...

James searched several more bodies, finding a high-powered rifle on one. He looped it over his shoulder.

"Okay, I say we take the staircase and try to find a car to get away."

Will nodded, still struggling to get up to speed. "Yeah." He nodded, sucking in a deep breath. "Sounds like a plan."

They entered the stairwell and moved up the stairs in silence, Will having to rest a couple of times to catch his breath. When they reached the first floor, they stopped at the door. Will peered out the small window into the lobby.

"There're bodies here too."

"I suspect there're bodies everywhere," James whispered.

Will suspected James was right but refused to admit it, swallowing his rising anxiety. The fact that he was so unnerved only fueled the undercurrent of panic.

"There's a parking lot in the back," James said, sliding back the rack on his gun. "I say we steal the keys off a guard out there and borrow his car."

"How do you know there's a parking lot in back?" Will narrowed his eyes.

James straightened his shoulders. "What exactly are you accusing me of? I'm in this ass-deep shit because of you and your girlfriend, and you're now pinning some kind of blame on me? What the fuck, Will?"

Will heaved a breath. "I'm sorry." Rubbing his forehead, he tried to pull himself together. He was paranoid. James's life was in danger too, and he was helping Will escape. Given Will's current mental state, he wasn't so sure how well he would have fared on his own.

James relaxed. "I happen to know about the parking lot from when we broke in here a week ago."

"So that really happened? I hear I stole a plane."

James snorted. "You were always such a drama queen."

"I'm gonna need a bigger tiara." Joking soothed his apprehension.

Glancing out the window again, James grabbed for the doorknob. "We'll enter the lobby and if the coast is clear, we'll turn left and head out the back door. The compound has a circular drive. The buildings are all at one end of an oval. The guard house at the exit is at the other end."

Will nodded and focused on James's words. "I remember the security checkpoint. It seemed pretty inadequate."

"I suspect they hadn't seen much action until you hit 'em." James smirked. "Over and over again. You ready?"

Will nodded.

James studied him, the worry in his eyes telling Will that he didn't believe him. James pressed his lips together. "Okay, let's do it."

Will opened the door and James slipped out first, his gun raised as he looked out the front doors and down the hallway. He turned to Will and motioned him out.

Exiting the stairwell, Will's instincts kicked in. James reached into the pocket of a dead guard. Five bodies added to the twelve downstairs, no marks or sign of trauma. They all looked like they had fainted and fallen to the ground.

James had said this was Will's world, yet James seemed more unaffected than Will. James had to have been part of it to accept everything going on around them. With a glance, James motioned down the hall before he took off.

Will followed behind, covering the front door. They burst outside.

The sun had begun to rise, casting a red glow on the horizon that threw an eerie pall over the half-full parking lot.

A car chirped and James ran for the driver's door. Will twisted around, surveying the area for guards before he climbed into the car. The compound was quiet, with no signs of life.

Because everyone was dead.

A chill crept up his spine and he shook it off. He'd seen plenty of dead men before. It wasn't something he wanted a Boy Scout badge for, but it was a fact of life for a Marine in the middle of action. The bodies in war were often bloodied and ripped to shreds. At least these bodies were clean. In theory, the neater crime scene should be easier to stomach, but it only reinforced to Will the reality that he was out of his element.

James started the car and drove around the back of the buildings.

"You have a plan for once we get out of here?" Will asked.

"Nope."

They drove up the circular drive to the guardhouse, finding two bodies lying on the sidewalk next to the small building. The gate was up.

"What the hell did Alex do to them?"

James shrugged and pulled onto the highway. "Who knows? Although if Emma had done it, they'd be piles of ash."

Will sucked in his breath as a fresh wave of anxiety hit him. "So she does have powers?"

James hesitated. "Yeah."

"What is she?"

Gripping the steering wheel with both hands, James tensed. "That's an interesting question, and even more interesting is that I never once heard you ask that question before you lost your memory. Before, it was all about protecting and defending her and...yeah." He cast a glance at Will. "You were trying to get answers, which was the whole reason you broke into the compound in the first place, but I never heard you put it that way."

Will latched on to every word, trying to piece his life together. "You still didn't answer my question. What is she?"

"I don't know. You were trying to find out, part of the reason you stole the book. But as far as I know, you never found the answer."

"She wouldn't tell me?"

"She didn't know herself. She'd never shown any type of powers until she met you."

Will took another breath. "How did I meet her?"

James gave him a hard stare. "You were never totally forthcoming with all the details, but I know that she was your big job. The Vinco Potentia hired you to bring her to them."

"Wait. Who?"

"Kramer works for the Vinco Potentia, a secret political group that Senator Philip Warren is the head of."

"Why would they want her?"

"She was part of a prophecy. She was supposed to have a baby that had powers they planned to exploit."

"But you said she had powers. Wouldn't they want her for those?"

"They did after they found out she had them. Of course, they were scared shitless of her after they realized what she could do. But your purpose was to deliver her to them so they could make one of their members the Chosen One. They figured one of their guys would get the mark and have the power. Double the power, double the fun."

"So did one of them become this Chosen One?"

"No, you did."

Will's heart skipped a beat.

"The Chosen One got a mark, like a tattoo or a brand."

"On my arm. It was on my arm."

"Yeah. How'd you know?"

"Kramer." Will sighed, rubbing his eyes. "So did I have powers too?"

"No. You said you could talk to her in your head when she was really scared, but other than that it was just an obsessive desire to protect her. That was the Chosen One's purpose—to protect the queen."

"She's a queen?"

"That's what the prophecy calls her, although you were never sure if that was literal or not."

A queen. This was insane. But if she had supernatural powers and he really could hear her in his dreams, that meant that the voice in his head could have been real. But who was it? "Who's Jake?"

"Her son."

"So where is he now?"

"Last I knew, Alex Warren had him. Right before Kramer showed up to capture Emma, we'd tracked Alex to Montana. Not only were you trying to get more information about what Emma might be, you were also trying to recover her five-year-old son."

"Why would Alex want him?"

"Because he has powers of his own. He can see the future."

"Shit." If he hadn't already been exposed to everything else, he wasn't sure he could believe all of this. "Wait,"—he braced his hand on the dashboard—"we have to go back. If Alex has Jake, we need to get him back."

James shook his head. "No fucking way. We are *not* going back there. Besides, I'm fairly certain that Alex doesn't have him anymore. They kept asking me if I knew where Jake was. Before this, Kramer knew that Alex had him."

"Then Alex lost him or gave him to someone else."

"So it appears."

"Then who has him now?"

"Your guess is as good as mine. Maybe Emma has him back."

Will knew that wasn't true, judging from her cries for Jake in his dreams. "So now what?"

"Now?" James raised his eyebrows. "Now, we try to put our lives back together."

"What the hell are you talking about? We have to find Emma."

James snorted. "We most certainly do *not* have to find Emma. We need to stay the fuck away from Emma. You claimed you loved her, but she was a manipulative bitch who tricked you into becoming part of all of this mess. She almost got you killed several times and she definitely gifted you with some powerful enemies. The best thing that happened to you was losing your memories of her. I have no idea how that happened—more supernatural mumbo-jumbo shit, I'm sure—but we'll take it as a sign that your job is done and you're free of her."

Giving Emma up was the last thing he could do. "Why do you say she manipulated me?"

"Think about it. When have you ever fallen in love with a woman? Messed around? Sure. You even had some steady girlfriends in the past. But head-over-heels in love? Never. So what are the chances you're going to fall hopelessly in love in less than a few weeks with someone you're hired to transport?"

Will wasn't sure he wanted to know where this was headed.

"You're branded with a fucking magical mark by a woman with magical powers and you just happen to fall in love with her? She's cast a spell on you, Will."

Will shook his head. "There's no such thing as magical spells. That's insane."

"No. It's not. She possesses power you can't even dream of. She can use mind control. She can create massive explosions. She's killed countless people, Will. Countless."

"That doesn't mean that she made me fall in love with her."

"She freely admitted that the mark made you feel compelled to protect her. If she branded you with that, what's to stop her from making you love her? Wouldn't that be in her best interest? Wouldn't you want to protect her even more if you thought you loved her?"

Will's stomach twisted. What he felt wasn't real. Or was it? "I dreamed of her."

"What?"

"Not only did I hear her crying when I slept, calling out for me and Jake, but when you woke me up because of the alarms, I was dreaming of her. It was real, like she was really there." He turned his head to James. "She was surprised to see me alive. She was happy to see me."

"What did she want?"

He gave his head a shake. "Nothing. She just wanted to be with me."

James remained silent for several seconds. "That might have been real."

Will nearly collapsed with relief.

"But you said she cried for you in the other dreams? You think she's being held captive?"

His defenses went up. "Yeah."

"What if she needs you to save her? What if she visited you so you would search for her?"

"She didn't ask me to save her, James. She said she thought I was dead and was happy to see me."

"Yeah, of course she was. Because she needs you to save her."

Will shook his head. "No. I don't think—"

James tapped the steering wheel with his thumb then pulled the car to the side of the road. "We need the book."

"What book?"

"The book you stole from the compound. The book you thought had answers. We need to find the book and figure out how to free you."

Will wasn't so sure he wanted to be freed. But he wanted answers and he also wanted to find her, James be damned. "So where's the book?"

"Last time I saw it was in Montana."

Leaning back into the seat, Will's eyes sunk closed. "And where are we now?"

"South Dakota."

"Do you have any money on you, Daddy Warbucks? How are we going to pay for this little field trip?"

James shoved Will's shoulder and laughed. "Oh, ye of little faith." His hand slipped into his pocket and pulled out a wallet. "Those guards back at that compound don't need these anymore."

****

When Emma opened her eyes, she found Raphael sitting in a chair next to the window. Her heart skipped a beat as she sat up.

His elbows rested on the chair arms, his fingers laced and under his chin. Dark circles underscored his eyes. He sighed when he saw her move and lowered his hands to grip the chair arms.

Emma's first reaction was to jump out of bed and make him leave. But his glazed expression made it obvious he was hung over. After last night, provoking him seemed a bad idea. Instead, she froze, waiting to see what he wanted.

His eyes bore into hers. "I'm sorry for my behavior last night. I was drunk and obviously out of control."

While his apology was surprising, it also angered her. "It couldn't wait until breakfast? I sit down to eat a bagel and you sip your coffee murmuring 'sorry about terrorizing you last night.' Why are you in my room watching me sleep?"

He rubbed his face with his hands. "After I calmed down, I realized I'd made you take several sleeping pills. I wanted to make sure you didn't stop breathing."

"Wow. Am I supposed to thank you for that?"

He shook his head and he stood. His eyes glistened. "Again, my behavior was inexcusable and I've damaged what little progress we've made. I'm sorry."

She pointed to the door. "Get out."

His gaze focused on the floor as he walked to the door and paused at the threshold. "You cried for him again."

Her breath caught as her pulse sped up.

"We're days behind and I need you to be focused. The sleeping pills were supposed to help you get enough rest so you could concentrate."

Her anger swelled, overtaking her caution. "Maybe I didn't sleep well last night because some maniac threatened me."

He hesitated for several seconds. "You need to get ready. We have a full day of work ahead of us. After your demonstration of power last night, it's time you showed me what you're really capable of. What you've been holding back."

Hours later, Emma had been unable to repeat her use of power the night before, not that she didn't like the idea of blasting Raphael across the lawn. She just couldn't make it happen.

Desperation made Raphael short-tempered and dangerous. "Center yourself," he said, making her focus on the same log from the day before. "Find your energy within yourself and concentrate on making the wood burst into flames."

She narrowed her gaze, searching for the burn in her chest, then pushing it out.

Tiny flames licked at the tree trunk before sputtering out.

A vein throbbed in Raphael's temple. "What is your game, Emma? What do you hope to achieve?"

Her hair clung to the side of her sweaty face. The afternoon was hot and humid and she was short-tempered herself. "What could I possibly gain from holding back my power from you, Raphael? You've said you won't teach me the next step, getting power from other sources, until I master this one. And seeing how I really need to move to the next step so that I have even the slightest chance of saving my son, *why would I hold back*?"

He moved closer to her, his skin blanching around his mouth. "I don't know, Emma. Perhaps manipulation of some kind."

"Oh, isn't that calling the kettle black. Seems to me you own the market in manipulation, Raphael."

His pupils dilated and turned a faint red. "Do not push me."

"Or what? You'll get drunk and come to my room again?"

She wasn't prepared when he backhanded her cheek.

Pure rage filled her and she lashed out, forcing her energy to him.

He stumbled backward, wisps of smoke wafting off his shirt. Squaring his shoulders, a murderous look filled his eyes. "Is that what it takes, Emma? Extreme emotional distress? Maybe you need to fight for your life to make your power work."

The ground shook under her feet and she struggled to maintain her balance. A loud crack filled the air on her right and a tree fell toward her. She jumped out of the way, the tree branches scratching her arm as the massive oak crashed to the ground.

"Use your power, Emma!"

The tree skidded across the yard to her, knocking her face forward on the ground. The air flew out of her chest and she fought to suck in a breath.

"Get up," he snarled.

He'd lost his mind.

He strode toward her and jerked her off the ground, then gave her a shove as he stepped away. "Defend yourself, Emma."

She found a small burst of energy to shoot, which he easily blocked with the wave of a hand. The ground shook again and a small crack split the earth, zigzagging from Raphael and stopping at her feet.

Hands clenched at her sides, her chest heaved. "Do it! Finish it, Raphael!"

His eyes locked with hers, a green glow surrounding him. He looked wild and dangerous before he broke contact and turned away. "We're taking a half-hour break, then resuming." He stomped into the house.

Once he'd gone inside she allowed herself to pat her swollen cheek and wipe the blood from her lip. Tears burned her eyes before it occurred to her that he'd left her outside. Alone.

Her pulse quickened. He said he'd be gone a half an hour. How far could she get before he realized she was gone?

Did she dare leave?

The fact remained that while Raphael's mental stability deteriorated by the hour, he was the only one who could help her at this point.

Unless she found Alex.

The thought made her skin crawl, but Raphael had quickly ascended the list of most hated people in her life, a hard list to climb. Still, there were so many problems with her plan, or lack thereof. She had no idea where Alex was, and Raphael was sure to find her before she got far. He tracked her somehow, and she was sure it had to do with her energy. All the more reason to learn to control it.

She walked down to the creek that ran in the trees along the back of the property. While she couldn't run from him yet, she could get away from him for a short while. Kicking off her shoes, she sat on the bank and put her feet in the stream, the water cooling her down. She closed her eyes.

Raphael freely admitted he withheld information from her. The question was why? He must be spoon-feeding her, only giving her information absolutely necessary to finish this level then move on to the next. But what if she could figure out some of it herself? What if she really did do the very thing he accused her of—progress and hide her true powers from him?

The idea teased her need to retaliate.

Raphael controlled the earth. She'd seen him create earthquakes and make trees fall. He could move simple objects. He could control her. The last filled her with anxiety, but if she could figure out how it all worked, she was certain she could stop him and regain her free will.

Alex was air. Storms and rain and wind. He could probably do other things she hadn't considered. He could control weather associated with clouds, but could he change climates? Could he control things in the air, such as planes?

She and Aiden were fire. She already knew she could create massive fires and make small items explode. She could turn men into piles of ash. She could control minds. Surely there was more. The fact that she needed extreme anger to use her power was crippling. During her skirmish with Raphael, her fear overpowered all fury, squashing her energy. She'd learned weeks ago that fear didn't work for her energy source. Her power was fueled by pure anger. Lord knew she had plenty of anger to go around, but even she had her limits. She had to figure out other sources. And she'd be damned if she told Raphael what she was doing.

Dipping her foot deeper in the water, Emma let her guard down and thought of Will. If he were alive, he would rip Raphael apart for the way he'd treated her the last two days. But Will wasn't here and the fact remained that Will was no match for Raphael's powers. Even if he were alive.

Raphael had been right. She cried for Will again, but she'd dreamed of him too. A more concrete dream than the previous ones. He appeared to her in the darkness of her grief and not only knew who she was, but held her in his arms and looked down at her with love. But four words in her dream ate at her resolve.

I'm not dead, Emma.

She scooped up her hope and held it tight in her fists. Could it be true? Raphael insisted that Will had died.

Raphael insisted.

It made sense that he would encourage her to leave Will behind. Raphael saw Will as a threat, even in death. But would he lie to her and tell her that he was dead for his own benefit? Hell, yeah, he'd do it.

Yet she couldn't ignore that Will's presence wasn't out there anymore. The mark had to be the reason, but if their marks were gone, how could they have a connection in their dreams?

Jake didn't have a mark and she could communicate with him telepathically. Until Aiden's interference. But Jake was half-deity, or whatever they were. That had to account for something.

Could Will be alive? Raphael was right about one thing—when she searched deep in her heart for the answer, the cold truth ached in her bones. Will was dead. They had tossed his dead body into the van. The surety permeated every part of her. But her subconscious just couldn't let him go yet.

When she allowed her head to consider the bigger picture of who she was, she found herself on the verge of a panic attack. Most people would jump at the opportunity to be part of something bigger, something immortal, but Emma had always craved normalcy. The chance to live a safe and ordinary life. And as sucky as her existence had been the last twenty-seven years, an eternity of it was more than she could stomach.

A week ago she would have settled for life with Will, Jake, and their baby, driving a minivan, and complaining about Will forgetting to take out the trash.

Now she didn't know what to hope for.

CHAPTER NINE

"JAMES, how can you be sure that the bag is still at the cabin? First of all, wouldn't Kramer and his men have taken it? And if it had been left behind, wouldn't the management have taken it?"

"I told you I had insurance. This was just one of many pieces. I knew you had the book and I figured Kramer would want it. So I hid it in the crawl space under the cabin after you left to go look for Jake. How many campers are climbing into dirty, cobwebby crawl spaces? Trust me. It's there."

"So what are the other pieces?"

James's chin jutted then he turned to Will, his eyes full of worry. "We can talk about this later. You need to eat more of that grease feast in a bag and get some sleep."

Will shook his head and tossed the fast food bag into the backseat. "I think a couple of hamburgers will hold me for a few hours."

"You need sleep. You look like shit."

"You're no beauty queen yourself." James was evading him. *No.* Will was paranoid and crazy. James was concerned about him and wanted him to rest. It was no secret that James was the mother hen of the two. James had always gone to great lengths to protect him, acting like the brother Will never had. Will had almost died in the compound and it didn't take a rocket scientist to figure out that the realization had kicked James's protective instinct into high gear.

Still, the voice had warned him.

Will nearly laughed at his thought. The voice. He was listening to the advice of a mysterious stranger over his best friend of twenty-plus years? That was fucked up. There was no voice. The voice had been his mind's way of trying to cope with the situation.

Will leaned back into the seat and closed his eyes. "I need to know what happened. What I've been doing the last month." He needed to know more about Emma.

He felt James tense. "You're supposed to be sleeping."

"Consider it a bedtime story."

He hesitated then shifted his weight. "I'm not sure you want my version. It's not pretty."

James's answer was no surprise, but Will wasn't sure he was ready to let go of the fantasy in his head.

"You showed up on my doorstep after getting the shit beat out of you. Emma was with you and had brought you to me."

"So she knew about you? That's totally unlike me."

"I know. I guess you told her because you were desperate. In any case, you were in bad shape, with broken ribs and, I suspected, a punctured lung. I told you that you had to go to the hospital and you refused. You said they'd find you there and get Emma. Emma, to her credit, wanted you to go as well. But then again, you weren't any good to her if you were dead."

Will tried to associate the cold, calculating woman James painted with the woman in the woods and in his dreams. The two didn't correlate. "Wait. How long ago was this? If I had broken ribs and a punctured lung—"

"No jumping ahead in the story. Like an idiot, I agreed to let you stay at my house, and that night I woke up to Emma screaming. You couldn't breathe and had turned blue, so I told you I was in charge and ran out to pull my car up to the door to take you to the hospital. When I came back I nearly shit my pants."

Will opened his eyes. "What happened?"

"Emma was leaning over you in the bed, surrounded in this bright yellow light, and a spark of, like, electricity shot through you. Then Emma passed out."

"What was she doing?"

James released a heavy sigh. "She healed you. All of your broken bones were gone, you could breath, even your bruises were gone."

"How could she do that?"

"Her pendant. She had a pendant of fire that gave her power. But it's gone now. Kramer took it."

"So she's powerless?"

"Yeah, I guess so."

But that didn't ring true. Will remembered Emma using her power in the woods. The grease in his stomach tumbled like a washing machine.

"The next day you left her with me to run off to South Dakota so you could figure out how to steal the book. She got pissed and ran off to Raphael."

"The guy in the woods? The guy who might have her now?"

"One and the same. See? If he has her now, she's there of her own free will. She left you to die in that compound."

Will wasn't so sure about that, but kept his opinion to himself.

"That night, Kramer's men found her in town and tried to capture her. She got away but caused a massive forest fire in the process. You arrived back in town in time to help her get out of the woods alive."

"The town several miles from your lake cabin?"

"Yeah."

That made no sense. If she left James's place to run off with Raphael, why was she only miles from James's cabin? There was nothing in that podunk town to keep her there. "How long had I planned to be gone?"

"A few days."

"Why did she leave?"

"Let's just say that Emma and I didn't make good roommates."

Will knew how confrontational and snide James could be. What if Emma left James but waited in town for Will? It still didn't explain why she would run off with Raphael.

"After the fire, I insisted on going with you to help you steal the book out of the compound and gather information about the Vinco Potentia and the Cavallo."

"Who?"

"The group that kidnapped Jake. They kidnapped him when you were taking Emma to South Dakota."

"How the hell did I let something like that happen?" God, had he gotten sloppy? Maybe he'd botched everything so badly that his mind shut out the last month so he could forget it. He quickly dismissed the idea. It sounded preposterous, even in light of everything else.

"I'm not entirely sure. I think you said Emma had fallen down a cliff and you'd left her son in the truck to go down and save her."

"Where *is* my truck?"

"A molten mass of metal on a Colorado roadside." James shot him a quick glance of sympathy. "The Cavallo blew it up when they kidnapped Jake. You and Emma thought they had killed him."

How could he forget all of this? It was totally crazy. Just like his feelings for a woman he couldn't remember and a voice in his head. "You said I loved her."

"I said you *thought* you loved her."

"But you saw us together..." How did he ask this without sounding like a needy teenage girl? "Did it look like I cared about her?"

"If you're asking if you couldn't keep your hands off her, the answer is yes. You even insisted on her sleeping with you when you had your broken ribs." James scowled. "But you and I both know that lust and love are two completely different things. I think Emma took those feelings and made you think they were something else. We also know you're not the kind of man to think with his dick. She manipulated you."

"So we went to South Dakota and stole the book, then we stole a plane to get away—"

"You and Emma stole the plane, after she blew up a lot things in the process, and you crash-landed in Wyoming, where I picked you two up the next morning."

"We crashed?"

"Your fuel tank and oil line got hit by bullets during your takeoff."

His frustration with his memory loss grew. People didn't forget things like this.

"Then we went to Montana. You and Emma had found out that Alex had Jake there—"

Will shook his head in confusion. "I thought the Cavallo had Jake."

"Alex stole Jake from the Cavallo—keep up." James snorted. "We stayed in a cabin a couple of towns away from White Horse, where Alex had him. I'd made a list of rental houses that I thought they might be keeping him in, and you left to go check it out."

The part where his present consciousness took over was coming up soon. "And I left Emma with you?"

"Yeah, I suggested she stay and rest," James said defensively. "She was pregnant, exhausted, and she'd just suffered a concussion. She didn't have any business traipsing around in the middle of the night."

Why would James care about Emma if he thought she was a controlling bitch? This story was disturbing him more than he expected it to. And not only because of what happened to Emma. "And Kramer showed up."

James shot Will a glance. "Yeah, about forty-five minutes after you left."

"Did he hurt her?" He didn't even remember her, but the thought of what she went through set his nerves on edge.

James hesitated for several seconds. "No, I don't think so."

That didn't fit either. In the woods, her face was bruised and the nightgown she wore was bloodied. "What was she wearing?"

"*What?*"

"Was she wearing a white nightgown, way too big on her?"

James shook his head slowly. "No..."

Either James was lying or she'd changed somewhere before he lost his memory. "Okay, so Kramer showed up. How'd he get her?"

James's hands twisted on the steering wheel. "Emma was exhausted so I sent her to bed. I was at the kitchen table working on research on the Vinco Potentia when the door busted open. I didn't even have a chance to reach for my gun." His eyes darted sideways then back to the road. "They held me at gunpoint and Kramer sent his men into the bedroom to get Emma."

"Did she put up a fight?"

"No, she was drugged." Pursing his lips into a thin white line, James took a deep breath. "Kramer's men drugged her."

"How do you know that if you weren't in the room with her?"

"Because they said they were drugging her, you dickhead. What the fuck are you accusing me of?"

Leaning his elbow on the car door, Will rubbed his eyes. "Nothing. I'm sorry. Go on."

"They carted her out to a van, put me in another van, and left."

"And you don't know how she got away?"

"Not a clue."

"But most prisoners are kept together. If she had broken loose or someone broke her out, your van would have stopped. In fact, the person breaking her out probably wouldn't know which van was hers."

"Again with the accusations?"

"It wasn't an accusation, James." Will lowered his voice. "Why are you so fucking defensive?"

"Because I expected you to beat the shit out of me for letting them take her."

"I don't even remember her. Why would I beat the shit out of you?" But he did want to beat the shit out of him. Just not for the reason James expected. He took a breath to settle his temper. "Then what happened?"

"I don't know. The next time I saw you was at the compound."

"And you have no clue how she got away?"

"How many times do I have to say it?"

James's story sounded unlikely. Part of the story, anyway. There was a huge gap of time between when Kramer's men put Emma in their van and Will was with her in the woods. And Raphael.

What if James was lying to him?

But why would he do that? What motive would he have? James wouldn't lie to him. Would he?

"You're supposed to be sleeping."

"Yeah," Will grumbled, sure he'd never sleep with all the doubt dancing in his head.

****

Jake and Aiden stood on a hill at the edge of Aiden's property. Aiden rested his hand on Jake's shoulder, his fingers pressing into Jake's flesh just enough to let Jake know who was in charge, but not enough to hurt. Being so close to Aiden usually made Jake nervous, but his hand kept him from wiggling. Aiden didn't tolerate fidgeting.

The air was hot, but not sticky like it had been in Texas and Arkansas. The cloudless blue sky stretched until it ended at the tops of the mountains on all sides. Sprawling vineyards dotted the landscape.

"It's beautiful here, don't you think, Jake?" Aiden asked.

Answers were always tricky with Aiden. Jake often thought he wanted one answer when Aiden actually wanted another. The wrong answer brought punishment of some kind, even if it was a stare. Aiden's stares weren't normal. His eyes would capture Jake's and a fire would burn through Jake's body.

Jake clenched his fist, his nails digging into his palms as he gazed into the valley below. Mommy would think it was pretty here. "Yes, sir."

Aiden swept his hand in a dramatic arc. "This can all be yours."

Jake glanced up to see if he was joking.

As always, Aiden read his mind. "No, Jacob. All of this can be yours. And I'll tell you how: You are very special. My most special creation yet. Do you know why?"

He shook his head.

"You are the child of two very special parents. Your father is air and your mother is fire."

Tears filled Jake's eyes at the thought of her, but he blinked them away and lifted his chin. The way Aiden liked.

"You have the ability to control two elements. We've been working on fire, which admittedly isn't going as I had hoped. I've decided to try your other element. Whether you realize it or not, you've already controlled air as well."

"I have?"

"Yes, but those times were accidental. You were very upset and created a storm. When you learn to control it, you can do so much more."

Jake was scared to try it. Aiden was already upset over his failure at fire. What if he couldn't control air? He peeked up at Aiden through his eyelashes. Aiden seemed absorbed in his speech and his promise of the valley and hadn't noticed his thoughts.

"Raphael is earth and he has your mother in his possession, but things aren't going well." Aiden scowled. "I may have to intervene."

Fear clutched Jake's stomach. Was Mommy in danger?

Aiden's mouth lifted into a smile, which looked all wrong. Like a Mr. Potato Head earpiece jammed into the mouth hole. "Jacob, you will be stronger than all of the rest of them combined. We just need to teach you how."

That was the part that frightened Jake the most.

CHAPTER TEN

DINNER was almost as uncomfortable as the previous night. Emma had tried to excuse herself, but Raphael insisted they dine together under the pretense that they needed to become more unified. After the disastrous afternoon, Emma wasn't sure that was possible. The last thing she wanted was to be with him, but he'd threatened to coerce her into staying, which meant touching her. She avoided that at all costs.

She had to figure out how to break his hold over her. What she didn't understand was why Alex's touch didn't affect her the same way. Raphael and Alex were supposed to be equals. Granted, her exposure to physical contact with Alex was more limited, just the night Jake was conceived and the night he came to her bedside at the compound, but she'd never felt anything with him. Other than revulsion.

Perhaps it did mean that she was meant to be Raphael's. The thought shot an arrow of anger into her fear. She refused to accept that possibility. She'd rather be dead.

Raphael looked at Emma's plate, his brow lowering. "Emma, don't you like your dinner?"

Although she wanted to tell him to go to hell, she forced a smile. "It's great. I'm just not very hungry." In spite of her efforts, her hatred slipped into her words.

Raphael set his fork down and rubbed his temples. "I had hoped that we could eat together and get past our earlier unpleasantness." He looked up and lowered his hands. "I'm sorry for my behavior this afternoon. It was inexcusable and I sincerely apologize."

The regret in his eyes almost made her believe him. And she might have, if it wasn't the second time Raphael apologized for predatory behavior within twelve hours. Still, she had to play along, as grating as it was. She lowered her head and stared at her plate, trying to look subservient. "You've been under a lot of stress."

He gasped and placed his hand over hers. "Yes! You do understand. I knew you would if given enough time."

The pull to him was automatic and her heart fluttered in fear. Could she remove her hand without arousing his suspicion? She raised her eyes as she pulled her hand loose, reaching to pat his upper arm. "Of course, how could I not?"

He poured himself a glass of wine and took a sip, his shoulders relaxing. "Time is short and your lack of progress is quite disturbing. I hadn't anticipated this. You're capable of powerful acts. You've done them before. Why are you holding back now?"

Gripping her fork, she bit her lip and considered her response. "I'm still upset, Raphael. I'm sure that has something to do with it."

Raphael slammed his hand on the table, rattling the dinnerware and making her jump. "I should have made you forget him already."

She made herself answer slowly. "No. I just need more time."

He balled his fist. "Time is one luxury we don't have. I'm grieving as well, Emma. But we need to put our past behind us and move forward with the future. A new future." Raising the wine glass to his lips, his face softened before he turned to face her. "Perhaps that's exactly what we need. A new future."

She froze. "What do you mean?"

"You are meant to be mine and the only thing holding you back from accepting our union is Will. Will is dead. I didn't want to rush you too soon, but the fact remains that we need to join together before we face Aiden and Alex. If we join sooner, then you'll receive the benefit of my powers as well."

"I'm not joining with you." The words slid over her lips before she could restrain them. While she meant every word, telling Raphael was suicide. "Yet," she added.

He glared.

"I'm sure I'll make more progress tomorrow. Besides, you said I needed to have my full powers for us to join."

"You do have them. You no longer need the pendant."

"But my powers don't work yet. I can't use them on command. What if joining stops my progress?"

"That's not supposed to happen," he said, but doubt filled his words.

Her tension dropped a notch. He was listening. "But how do you know? You said everything is different this time."

"True..."

"I say we give it more time. We need for us both to be at our best to win this."

He sipped his wine, his eyes focused on her. "You will agree to join with me?"

Oh, God. She couldn't do that, but she couldn't tell him no, either. She smiled the sweetest smile she could muster. "We'll both know when the time is right, Raphael. I don't want to join with you with Will still fresh in my heart."

"I can make you forget him." His words were husky as he exhaled.

"And who will make you forget Emmanuella?"

His exuberance faded. "She's the past. You are my future."

She lowered her gaze. "You can't love a woman for centuries, then simply forget her when the next one comes along, Raphael." Looking up with a small smile, she added, "At least, I hope you don't forget me so quickly."

"There will only be you, Emma."

They ate in silence, Emma choking down her food so she had an excuse to leave the table.

"Perhaps you'd like to take a walk around the property," Raphael said, pouring more wine. "The sun will be setting and the view from the top of the hill in the southwest corner is breathtaking."

The food in her stomach twisted. "Thank you." She smiled again, trying to sound sincere. "But I'm really tired after our busy afternoon." *After you tried to kill me, you maniac.* "I think the best thing for me is a good night's sleep so I can be ready to try again." She stood and placed her napkin on the table. "I want us to have a fresh start tomorrow."

Raphael rose from his chair and moved next to her, kissing her lightly on the cheek. "Of course, love. That's a wonderful idea. Until tomorrow."

She gave him one last smile before picking up her plate and silverware and carrying them to the kitchen sink, grabbing the small pair of scissors lying on the counter.

Emma wasn't going to be defenseless if he came back to visit her tonight.

****

By the time James and Will pulled into the campground, the sun had set hours earlier. Most campers had turned in for the night. Only a few stragglers sat around campfires, their voices carrying in the evening air.

"That's good," James said. "We can sneak around to the crawl space without being noticed."

Will had a raging headache. He wanted to get the book and go. What he did after that was a giant question mark. While James hoped the book would help exorcise the demon of Emma from Will's head, Will wasn't sure he wanted to let her go.

James parked the car in a lot by the beach bordering a small mountain lake. He'd found a flashlight in the glove compartment and turned it on when he climbed out of the car. Will followed him to the gravel road that ran through the campsite, amazed that he'd been here less than a week ago and didn't remember any of it.

How did something like that happen? The more he thought about it, the more he realized it had to be mumbo-jumbo shit, as James called it. But who wiped out his memory? From his limited memories, he knew it wasn't Emma. Could it have been Raphael? Or Alex?

"Hurry your ass up," James whispered over his shoulder.

Will had fallen behind, lost in his thoughts. He shook his head and reached for the handle of his gun in his waistband out of reflex. "Get your shit together," he muttered to himself. Carelessness would get him killed. He'd come too far to get killed walking on a campground road talking to himself like a deranged person.

"How far is it?" Will asked once he fell in step with James.

"The cabins are on the back row, close to the woods. Ours was at the end. I figured we'd go past it, head up in the woods, and circle back. The opening to the crawl space faces the trees."

Campers looked up from their fires, watching the two men pass with open curiosity. James tried to carry a conversation about fly-fishing and the best lure to use, but Will grunted and volunteered only one- or two-word answers.

Will was off his game. He knew it, and as much as he tried to focus, he couldn't. A slow dread rolled through him, fear oozing from his pores. Never, not even in his early days in Iraq, had he been this incompetent. He was in deep shit.

James turned off the road between two campers. "We need to get to bed," James said loud enough for a couple across the road to hear. "Five a.m. will be here before you know it."

"I know."

James glanced back with his eyebrows raised in exasperation. At the edge of the campers, he flicked off the flashlight and leaned into Will's ear. "Now we head straight up into the trees."

Will nodded and focused on the tree line. Once they were several feet into the woods, James doubled back. When they reached the cabins, James squatted down and surveyed the structures. Will knelt next to him.

"It looks like the occupants are in for the night," James said "All the lights are off. We're going to run up to the back left corner—the door to the crawl space is there. I'll grab the bag, we'll head back to the woods and keep going until we get to the store, then cut across the parking lot to the car. Okay?"

Will nodded. "Yeah."

"Your job will be to look out for trouble. You think you can handle that?"

"I'm not a goddamned baby."

"I never said you were, but you've had a rough couple of days."

"I said I can handle it. You wimping out?"

James didn't answer, just stood up and took off toward the cabin, leaving Will to follow.

Crouching down at the corner of the house, James felt for the edge of the crawl space opening, sliding out the panel without a sound. He crawled halfway in, flicking on the flashlight for a second. He pulled out two duffel bags, then crawled back under the house.

After peeking around the corner toward the road, Will lifted one bag and put the strap over his shoulder.

James emerged then slid the panel in place before grabbing the other bag and motioning to the woods. The trek through the woods and back to the car was uneventful. As they threw the bags in the backseat of the car, Will couldn't help wondering if it was too easy. He wasn't suspicious. He was paranoid.

They headed back to the highway, Will's mind a tattered mess. How could he doubt James? James helped him escape, helped him steal the book from the compound, helped protect Emma.

But why? Why would he protect Emma if he thought she had manipulated Will? The James he knew wouldn't have stood for it.

"I say we head several hours away, find a motel room for the night, and figure out where to go tomorrow."

Will nodded, unable to answer. He'd never felt so unsettled in his entire life. He dozed, waking up hours later when James pulled into a motel parking lot. After James checked in, they carried the bags into the room and tossed them on the dresser.

"You stink," James said, heading to the bathroom. "But I'm showering first, then going to bed. You can wait since you've been sleeping all day."

"Yeah." He was fully awake, aware that the bags in front of him possibly held answers to the past month. The shower turned on as Will unzipped the first bag, finding several T-shirts and a pair of jeans. Digging deeper, he found a brown leather-bound book in the middle: *The Complete Essays of Lorenzo de Luca* emblazoned in gold letters on the cover. This had to be it.

Sitting on the edge of the bed, he opened the book, the leather binding creaking. The beginning held a bunch of philosophical sayings, but the last quarter of the book was different. Most was written in a language he didn't recognize, with English translations written underneath some passages. He wondered if James would be able to figure out what language it was, with his communications background. Maybe he already had.

Will found a translated prophecy.

The Chosen One will serve
The mother of the two
Elevated and Supplanter
Will battle for control
Their influence will be felt
Across the lands

The elevated one will
Conceive in the full moon
After the summer solstice
Born of great sorrow
The mother shall accept
Her Chosen One
And he will bear her mark
Protecting her until the end

Was this the prophecy the Vinco Potentia had used to decide Emma was the queen? He had no idea how they could tie her to this godawful poem. They had to have some other information because this shit was too vague. He flipped through the book trying to find something that tied Emma to the mess. When he didn't find her name, he flipped back to the prophecy and read it again, trying to wrap his head around the words.

James said that Will had been the Chosen One, and he'd had a mark. According to the prophecy, his job had been to serve her. Two were supposed to battle for control. Was Emma the mother of the elevated and the supplanter? She had a son and had been pregnant. Were they the prophesied ones?

He turned the page and found a drawing of an elaborate trident. Glancing down at his forearm, he wondered if it was the same mark James claimed he'd bore. His eyes closed. He couldn't believe he was open to believing any of this, but then after everything else, an appearing then disappearing tattoo seemed minor. It was the fact that he was involved in all of this and then forgot every bit of it that made his chest tighten in anxiety. Rubbing his hands over his face, he took a deep breath. Get it together, Will.

He flipped back to the prophecy. The mother shall accept Her Chosen One, And he will bear her mark, Protecting her until the end.

Should he be protecting her now? Was that why he still felt this love for her even when his memories had fled? He may not have a mark on his arm, but a nagging ache in the pit of his stomach suggested she wasn't safe. Unfortunately, there wasn't anything he could do about it. He didn't even know where she was.

Setting the book on the bed, he got up and continued digging in the bag, finding several pieces of women's clothing. His breath stuck in his chest, although he told himself he shouldn't be surprised to find her personal items. They'd been traveling together. It made sense her things would be with his. He pulled out several shirts and a couple of skirts. Without thinking, he lifted one to his face, breathing in a floral scent like he'd smelled in his dream.

That couldn't be a coincidence.

He clutched them for several moments, hoping to absorb some remembrance of her. Scent was supposed to be the strongest prompter of memories, but when Will concentrated on her smell, his mind hit a huge blank wall. Disappointment coursed through him, now even more desperate to make a connection to her.

He found more items. A few toiletries, but no cosmetics other than some mascara and blush. That alone told Will that she wasn't his usual type, even if he hadn't figured it out by now. He couldn't believe he'd dismissed her so quickly in the woods.

Carefully replacing her clothing, he found several guns and ammunition in the bottom of the bag, thankful he was armed. He zipped it closed, then opened the other bag and found a laptop computer and papers on top. Most of the papers had a "VP" handwritten in the upper corner of dossiers on businessmen, attorneys, and politicians. Some were names he recognized, others he'd never heard of. All had photographs attached, except for one. Aiden Walker. Reading the name sent an unexplained chill down his spine. The dossier gave a birth date and place, and his profession was listed as entrepreneur. What about this man made him apprehensive? Underneath the dossiers were papers with rental properties listed. Will plugged in the laptop and powered it up, finding James's name on the logon page.

James said he was doing research when Kramer showed up. If James was doing research, how did his laptop and papers get under the house?

Things didn't add up. But then again, if he were honest, things hadn't added up since James got tossed into Will's cell.

James lied to him.

The shower turned off and Will unplugged the computer, stuffing it and the papers back in the bag. He sat down on the bed and opened the leather book, pretending to be absorbed in the text when James opened the door.

"Found the book, I see."

"Yeah, interesting stuff."

"Getting answers to your questions?"

"Some." Not enough to suit Will. So far there were more questions than answers.

James opened his bag and pulled out a fresh set of clothes and took them to the bathroom. "We'll get a good night's sleep and figure out what to do in the morning."

Will had a lot of things he needed to figure out.

CHAPTER ELEVEN

SNEAKING outside had gone easier than Emma expected. She'd waited in her room for several hours until the house became quiet, hoping Raphael had gone to bed and wouldn't come to her room, especially after the sliver of hope she'd given him.

She'd never join with him. If it came down to saving Jake, she'd figure out another way. Maybe Aiden would be willing to negotiate saving Jake's life for her agreeing to not join with Raphael. That had to be in Aiden's best interest too.

What she hadn't expected was the soft voice that called out her name for over an hour. Raphael's schizophrenia had rubbed off on her.

The voice stopped when she stepped out the door, replaced by the sounds of crickets and cicadas that filled the still night air. Even though the sun had set hours earlier, humidity hung in the air and a fine layer of sweat lined Emma's forehead and neck within moments. She made her way to the edge of the property and took off her shoes, rolling up her jeans to wade through the creek into the neighboring pasture. The tree line surrounding the creek would hide her from Raphael if he happened to look outside.

The creek water was cool as she stepped in, but a thin layer of clouds covered the moon, making it difficult to make her way through the murky water. Her foot slipped on a rock and she nearly fell before righting herself.

"Careful, we can't have you getting hurt now, can we?"

Emma's heart sputtered and she stumbled backward, splashing water all over her jeans.

The clouds parted and moonlight spilled out to illuminate Alex as he stepped from behind a tree on the creek bank across from her. She wasn't sure whether to be relieved or frightened it was him instead of Raphael.

"Out for a midnight stroll?"

"Why do supernatural creatures like to stalk me in the middle of the night?"

Alex laughed. "You have *others*?"

She shook her head in irritation. She refused to tell him about Raphael's visit at a motel pool in South Dakota. "What are you doing here, Alex? Are you here to see if I'll join with you?"

He leaned his back against a tree, his knee bent while he braced his foot on the trunk. With his arrogant grin, he reminded her of the first time she met him nearly six years ago. Not a pleasant memory. "What are you doing out here in the middle of the night?"

She had no plans to move until she figured out which direction was safest. "You answer my question first."

"Waiting for you. I've been calling you for over an hour."

"That was you? Why didn't Raphael hear you?"

"Really, Emma. You ask the most mundane questions."

Her temper flared and a golden glow reflected off the water. "Then why were you calling me? Why are you here?"

"Checking on your progress. How's it going with Raph?"

"You really think I'll answer that?"

He cocked his head and winked. "Let me take a guess. It's not going well."

"What makes you say that?"

His smile fell. "The bruise on the side of your face, for one."

She resisted the urge to touch her swollen lip.

"You don't have to stay with him. The fact that you're sneaking out in the middle of the night tells me that you're not happy here."

She narrowed her eyes. "That and the bruise on my face."

"Exactly."

"Funny, I don't remember anyone caring about my *happiness*. I thought it was more a matter of survival."

He shrugged. "Fair enough." Eyeing her up and down, his grin returned. "You plan on staying in that creek all night?"

"I haven't decided yet." She lifted her chin. "Are you here to try to convince me to go with you?"

"No."

Her mouth gaped in surprise.

He laughed. "You weren't expecting that, were you?"

"Then why are you here?"

"I told you already—to check on you and see how your progress is going."

"If you don't want me to join with you, then why do you care?"

He raised an eyebrow with a mischievous look in his eyes. "I never said I didn't want to join with you. I just don't want to *now*."

"Why not?"

He laughed again. "Don't look so hurt. Five seconds ago you would rather die than join with me. Now that I don't want to, you're suddenly jealous."

Anger fueled her power, and the glow grew denser. "I am not—"

"You're not ready." Alex stepped away from the tree, moving closer to the creek edge. "I want to join with you, but your power's not strong enough yet."

She lifted her face to look up at him. "That's what I told Raphael tonight when he insisted on joining."

"Then obviously you're the more rational of the two of you at the moment."

She couldn't trust Alex, but he seemed the most rational of the three of them. While he said he didn't want to join with her now, she had to wonder if his information was trustworthy. "Why are you telling me all of this?"

"Because you're not going to progress with Raphael and he's too stupid to see it. That or he's jumped even further into madness."

She thought Raphael had already boarded the train to crazy town.

"In fact, I would guess your powers are weaker when you are with him."

Her eyes widened. "Yes."

"That's not surprising. But if you want to have a shot at survival, you're going to have to figure out how to grow your powers and learn what you're doing on your own."

"But if I leave, won't he find me again?"

"Yes."

"Then how can—"

"You need to learn to mask your power. How do you think I found you in the creek? You glow like a freaking nuclear power plant. Raphael has you hidden with his own power, but once you left his property, his protection stopped."

"So how'd you know he brought me here?"

He twisted his lips into a grimace. "Raphael is a creature of habit. He's predictable."

"So how do I learn to hide from him? Will you tell me?"

Shaking his head, he laughed. "Not yet. If I teach you how to hide from Raphael, you'll be able to hide from me as well."

"Then how can I make progress if I'm stuck here with that lunatic?"

"By what you're doing right now. Try to sneak away and practice on your own."

Emma took several steps toward the creek bank. Alex stood less than six feet from her and here was her chance to see if Alex had an effect on her or not. Both times Alex touched her had been before he knew his true identity. "I don't know what I'm doing. Have you got any pointers?"

It was either incredibly stupid or incredibly brave. What if he could control her too? The fact that he didn't want to join with her now boosted her confidence. Nevertheless, she was about to touch the man who raped her six years ago and possibly hand over her free will on a silver platter. She stepped onto the bank and wrapped her fingers around his wrist before he realized what she was doing.

His eyes flew open at the spark between them, followed by a flow of energy. Only she didn't lose control, she felt more powerful. Alex jerked his arm away and backed up several paces.

The power disappeared and she found herself craving more. No wonder Raphael wanted to touch her. What the hell had just happened?

Alex took small, shallow breaths. "You're stronger than I thought."

"What happened?"

He paced, covering his mouth with his hand.

"Alex!"

He stopped, spinning at the waist to stare at her. "Raphael exerts an influence over you."

"Yes! How does he do that?"

"Everything is cyclical. The circle of life and all that bullshit. The world must have checks and balances. Everything has a counterbalance. Raphael is yours."

"So he's stronger than me?"

"No, not necessarily stronger. Think rock, paper, scissors. Each possesses equal traits, but has power over another. All are kept in balance." His eyes were wide. Not only was he surprised, he looked frightened.

"I'm your balance," she whispered.

He lifted his chin and his eyes held hers. "Yes."

"I can control you."

His mouth contorted before his face became expressionless. "In theory."

"Which is why Emmanuella always picked Raphael in the later years. He controlled her."

"Yes."

"But Raphael said she picked you in the beginning."

"She had an advantage with me. But we loved each other as well and I would have willingly given myself to her."

"You make yourself sound like a martyr. You would have benefited."

"A martyr? On the contrary. I know you find this difficult to believe, but I'm capable of loving someone. I loved her. In the beginning, anyway. But I grew to resent her and the power she held over me. Then over time Raphael developed an obsession with her that went far beyond survival and the game. He stole her time and time again, convincing her that she was destined to be his until she not only believed it, but remembered it with each new reincarnation."

"'You're meant to be mine,' that's what he keeps saying," she whispered.

"Exactly."

"So why did you kill her all those times?"

"Because I knew I never had a chance and I refused to be exiled to the shadow world." His mouth lifted into an evil grin. "The fact that it pushed Raphael further and further into madness every time was an added incentive."

"So I have you to thank for that?"

He lifted his hands from his sides and lifted his shoulders into an unapologetic shrug.

"So if Raphael is my balance and I'm yours, who is Raphael's? Who do you have influence over?"

He hesitated then looked away. "Water."

"Water?" Why hadn't she thought about it before? Fire. Air. Earth. Water. There were *four* elements.

"He was one of us many years ago."

"So water is a he? Where is he now?"

Alex scowled. "Water was outcast long ago."

"Why was he outcast?"

"Water never participated in our game. And with most of Raphael's and my power, Aiden was strong enough to send him away."

"So he became a shadow?"

"No, but he hasn't been seen for about a century. Every so often he turns up and tries to stir up a bit of trouble, and slinks away."

"So why not team up with him and beat Aiden in this grudge match?"

"For one thing, like I said, he hasn't been seen for at least one hundred years, so I wouldn't know where to even look. He shields himself perfectly. If he's still around, he's either very far away or turned off his power. And second, he'd never side with either of us. There was never any love lost between any of us and there's the fact that I have power over him. Let's just say he's no fan of mine. And while Water would enjoy nothing more than defeating Aiden, he'd never side with either of us to do it. When I said 'stir up a bit of trouble,' I meant that he showed up every so often and tried to kill Raphael or me. But I guarantee if he showed up for the battle, all chaos would break loose."

"He never tried to kill Emmanuella?"

"No."

"But he could control Raphael?"

Alex hesitated. "Yes."

"Then I have to find Water."

He shook his head with a derisive laugh. "You think you can find him after all this time, when we haven't seen him in ages?"

"Have you looked?"

"Well, no..."

"You say he hates Aiden?"

Alex's mouth lifted into a smug grin. "*Hate* isn't a strong enough word, which is why he'd never talk to you. He'd kill you first. You're Aiden's daughter."

"Then I'll just have to convince him that I hate Aiden even more. Besides, he never tried to kill Aiden's daughter before."

"Emma, that's crazy."

"Any crazier than anything else going on? Is it any crazier than the wacko nut job in the house who tried to kill me with a sleeping pill overdose? I refuse to let that man have power over me. Is there any other way to stop him?"

"Well, you could stay away from him."

"I'd love nothing more than to stay away from him, but you won't teach me how to hide myself, and if I leave, he'll just find me."

"Did he really try to kill you?"

"Which time? The sleeping pills or this afternoon?"

"Gods be damned. He's crazier than I thought." Alex covered his face with both hands and rubbed his eyes. "You can't leave him yet. You need to grow stronger so you can defend yourself if he finds you, not to mention you'll need to defend yourself against Water if you go through with that crazy scheme and find him. Just keep practicing and I'll be back in two nights to check on you."

She narrowed her eyes. "Why would you help me?"

"I haven't hid my motives. I hope you'll agree to join with me later. If I help you, you might help me."

"I won't promise anything."

"I know, but at this point, I'm willing to take my chances. Besides, between you and me, you're the one with all the power until we join. Literally."

She nodded. "Okay, so tell me what I'm doing wrong. Raphael said I need to be able to do small things with my own energy, then I can use other energy sources for bigger things."

"He's right. What's your own source of power?"

Hesitating, she considered her options. She worried revealing too much could give him an advantage against her. Alex claimed she had control over him, but what if he lied? Or what if he hoped to glean information to use against her as leverage? At this point, she didn't have a choice.

"Anger. I use anger."

He raised an eyebrow. "Interesting. Extreme emotions work, but be careful with that—you can also lose control just as quickly as you gain it."

She knew that to be true from firsthand experience. "So what else can I use?"

"Honestly, it may be too late to change it. In the past, Emmanuella always used her core energy, which, while fairly even-keeled and reliable, isn't as strong as an emotion. That must be why you're stronger than she was."

"So can I find my core energy?"

"You can try, but I suspect you're already hardwired to use anger. Is it difficult to generate?"

"Anger? Generally, no." She snorted. "So why isn't my power as strong around Raphael? Because he has control over me?"

"Partly. I suspect with his erratic, irrational behavior that he's also made you afraid of him and your fear inhibits your power."

She bit her lip, refusing to answer.

"The only way you'll be able to use your power to its fullest around him is if you are fighting him."

"He tried that this afternoon. It didn't work. Not effectively anyway."

Alex sighed. "The problem is we've never reached this point before, and even if we had, you would have already reached your full powers. The old rules stated that the one's presence could stunt the growth of the other. What Raphael probably didn't tell you was that the stronger of the two stunted the growth of the subordinate. Raphael's presence could literally be stunting your development."

"Which is why you don't want to be with me right now."

"If I have the chance to grow stronger, I don't want to risk it. But be careful to keep him from touching you as much as possible. There's a rush of power, as you just discovered, and it can be quite addictive. Mixed with Raphael's insanity..."

Just what she needed. A crazy addict. "But what about you and Raphael? Do you two affect each other?"

"No, because we're on opposite sides. Think of all four elements as points on a square, and our energy flows counterclockwise. Fire is at the top and water is at the bottom, polar opposites. Raphael and I are polar opposites. We exert no control over one another."

"You know all of this and I know nothing. It's so goddamned frustrating."

He moved closer, his face softening. "I carry my memories from one life to the next. Once I realize who I am, I can remember all of the things I did in past lives, which helps me figure out what I can do now. But you have only this lifetime. You're figuring it all out like Raphael and I did centuries ago."

"And Emmanuella."

"Yes, and Emmanuella. Although she was never around very long after all her memories returned."

"A few times, thanks to you." She needed to remember that.

He gave a noncommittal shrug. "That's enough lessons tonight." He moved toward her, his hand outstretched. "Take this, but only use it if absolutely necessary."

She cautiously reached her hand out and he placed a folded piece of paper in her palm.

He turned and walked across the pasture without a backward glance. "See you in a couple of nights."

Watching him walk into the darkness, she was even more confused. Alex might be helping her now, but at his core he was a monster, and she needed to remember that.

CHAPTER TWELVE

WILL woke up exhausted and with a dull headache, the sound of the shower gurgling through the bathroom wall. His sleep had been plagued with dreams of James and Emma. In the light of day, they were vague and foggy, and he was sure they were ordinary dreams. His subconscious was telling him that he feared James betrayed them both.

His subconscious had wasted its time. He already knew that.

Will reluctantly admitted that he'd hoped to dream of Emma, but there'd been nothing this time, not even her tears. Maybe she'd forgotten him already. Or maybe they were never real to begin with. He wasn't ready to accept that, further evidence of his disconnect to reality.

Sitting up, he tried to orient himself in the crappy motel room. James sang an off-key rendition of Aretha Franklin's *R-E-S-P-E-C-T* behind the bathroom door. Will stepped into his jeans and grabbed the ice bucket off the dresser. His throat still felt like it was on fire.

The sun blinded him when he opened the door, and he raised his hand to shield his eyes. Two men rushed him and shoved his face into the exterior wall.

"Thought you could get away, huh?" one grunted into his ear as he lifted Will's free arm at an awkward angle behind his back.

Stupid. He'd forgotten his gun inside. "Haven't you heard, if you love something set it free?"

"Too bad there's no love for you as far as Warren's concerned."

"The feeling's mutual." Will thrust his head back into the man's nose. His would-be captor's hold loosened and Will swung around, punching him in the throat. The man doubled over and gagged.

The man next to him reached for his gun. Will swung the ice bucket into his temple then shoved his head into the wall. His attacker's body slumped as it slid down the wall, the gun clanging to the concrete.

Will picked up the firearm and held it to the gagging man's head.

"Why are you here?"

"Warren," he choked.

"What about him?"

"He wants you back."

"Why?"

"The woman."

Emma.

Will's finger tightened on the trigger.

"Having fun without me?" James asked from the doorway.

The captor reached for Will's arm. Will brought the handle of the gun down on the man's head. He fell face down on the pavement.

"I can't leave you alone for a minute." Will glanced at James, who stood in the doorway, a white towel wrapped around his waist and water dripping down his chest. He leaned over and grabbed the man closest to the door, dragging him through the opening. "Time to clean up the trash."

Will tugged the other man inside and dropped him next to the guy on the floor. "Looks like we're still wanted."

James pulled a shirt out of his bag and pulled it over his head. "We need to focus on getting some dirt on these members, something to hold as leverage to get them off our asses."

Will rubbed his temples. "It shouldn't be hard to dig up shit on Warren. He's a politician, for God's sake. Isn't a closet full of skeletons a requirement to run for a political office? In fact, Kramer said something about a current scandal involving a woman claiming to have an affair."

Frowning, James shook his head. "Old news and dismissed by the press already. Besides, nothing sticks to Warren." He opened a folder and flipped through several pages. "We could focus on Simmons from Simmons Industries. It looks like he's got some shady deals involving some overseas accounts. And he's got Warren in his back pocket. We could nail them both and take out two key guys in the organization."

"What about his son?"

James continued reading. "Simmons doesn't have a son."

"Not Simmons. Warren."

He froze, raising his head. "Alex? What about him?"

"There has to be shit on him."

"You're fucking insane. You do *not* want to go there. You saw what he did."

"Exactly. Can you imagine if the media got a hold of that?"

Shaking his head, James set down the paper and placed his palms on the dresser. "I know what you're doing, Will."

"You don't know shit about what I'm doing."

"You're trying to find *her*."

James had started to refer to Emma as *her*, refusing to say her name, as though not mentioning her name would make Will forget about her quicker.

"I know I'm not going to find her, jackass. I'm trying to save our necks. We're not just dealing with the Vinco Potentia, and we can't ignore there's supernatural shit going on. It would be a huge mistake to dismiss it."

"So, what? You tell the media that Alex magically killed a compound full of men?"

"No—"

"Because how are you going to prove that? Not to mention the crime scene has almost certainly been cleaned up by now. Warren's been tied to so much shady bullshit that always gets swept into the corner while the circus clowns waltz in and distract the crowd. Warren's the master at it. So even if the media got wind of it, and actual bodies were produced, guess who was in the compound at the same time? A couple of ex-Marines from the special forces who happen to know a lot of creative ways to kill a man and who just so happened to be locked up at the same time and escaped."

Will ran a hand through his hair. "Okay, you're right, but I still say we can't dismiss it."

"Oh, trust me, I have no plans to. I intend to keep him in plain sight. From a distance. I know a cobra's dangerous, but that doesn't mean I have to cage it. I can let it slink off into the forest and terrorize other creatures."

This was all backward. Will was the leader of the two and James usually followed, further evidence of Will's decline.

James looked up, determination in his eyes. "I've figured out what we need to do. You're right. We need to think of the bigger picture. We need to focus on our end goal."

Will cast a glance at the unconscious men on the floor. "I'm listening."

"Our end goal is to extricate ourselves from the Vinco Potentia without repercussions. We need to make them trust us."

"What do you propose?"

"We go back to one of your original goals before you lost your memory. We find Emma's son, Jake."

That was the last thing Will expected. "Holy shit."

"Now hear me out. We find him and prove to Alex that we're on his side. Alex gets his son back. The Vinco Potentia gets the boy and we prove ourselves useful."

"You don't know that. You said they never wanted the boy. You said they wanted Emma."

James shrugged. "When plan A doesn't work out, you go to plan B. The boy can be their plan B."

"I'm not so sure we should hand him over to Alex. Shouldn't he be with his mother?"

"Alex is his father. If they want to have a custody dispute, they can take it to court. But this way we prove ourselves friendly to the Vinco Potentia and Alex. It's a win-win."

After listening to Emma cry for Jake for hours in his dreams, Will wasn't certain he could give Jake to Alex. But they could concentrate on getting Jake first, then figure out who to give him to.

"Small problem," Will said with a grimace. "We don't have a clue where Jake is."

"So we focus on what we do know. We know the Cavallo took him. Then Alex took Jake from them and went to Montana. The next time we saw Alex was days later in South Dakota and we learned from Kramer that Jake was no longer with Alex."

"So either Alex gave him to someone or they stole him from Alex."

"And you don't think Emma has him?"

Her cries still echoed in his head. "No."

"We need to figure out who else has a motive, and our best source is Emma."

Will's breath hitched in his throat. "You're saying we should find her? You think she's going to agree to getting her son back and then turn him over to Alex?"

"No, I have no intention of finding her. Even if I did, I don't have a fucking clue where she is. But she might have left clues when she was with you. We backtrack and retrace your steps with her."

"How can we do that when I can't remember any of it?"

"We focus on what we know. I know you were at the compound with her. And while you were there you saw the book, which we went back and stole."

Will nodded. "Yeah, that's good."

"I know you were in Arizona at some point looking for the boy, but you said he'd been moved, which he had. To Montana. I don't know what you did after you left Arizona, but you went to your apartment right before you came to see me. We should go to your apartment and see if either of you left any clues there."

Home. He released an exhale of relief. Finally, something solid from his past to latch on to.

****

"It's a little thing, Emma. Why do you refuse me?" Raphael stood in the backyard with his feet shoulder width apart, hands on his hips.

She blew a strand of hair out of her face. "I'm not refusing, Raphael. I'm trying."

Raphael's eyes narrowed as he scanned her up and down. "You look exhausted, my love. I thought you planned to get a good night's sleep."

"I did, Raphael." She lied, which killed her, even if it was a lie to Raphael. She'd stayed out in the pasture half the night learning to focus and control her power. By the time she'd gone to bed, she'd made real progress. Unfortunately, none of her improvements showed today in Raphael's presence. Which wasn't surprising after Alex's revelations.

"Then why can't you move a stupid log, Emma?"

He'd been ordering her around all morning and afternoon, becoming more and more irritated with her lack of development. Her temper snapped. "Maybe I'm not supposed to move a stupid log, Raphael. Maybe that's in your job description, not mine."

He moved next to her before she had a chance to react and threaded his hands through her hair, jerking her toward him. She rose on her tiptoes, crying out before she could stop herself.

Raphael smiled, his eyes filling with perverse pleasure. "We must learn to work together," he said in a soothing tone, then jerked harder. "Your lack of cooperation is disconcerting, my love."

She gritted her teeth, refusing to give him the satisfaction of hearing her cry out.

"I want you to move the log, Emma. It's such a little thing to ask."

"I...can't..." she panted, her scalp screaming in pain.

"You can."

"You're earth...I'm...fire..."

He paused, then loosened his hold. "Perhaps you're right."

"Let me try..."

His hand dropped, releasing her.

Stumbling backward, she seethed in anger. Her chest burned and a golden glow surrounded her. While biting back her tears, she reached out her hand and shot a mass of energy toward him.

His reaction was delayed half a second and he jumped sideways as he reached for her, making the ground shake.

She struggled to stay upright. "That good enough for you, Raphael?"

He laughed, taking a step toward her. "Looks like someone found herself."

"You stay the fuck away from me!"

He took another step. "I think you're ready for the second step."

Sucking in several short breaths, she watched him, her nerve endings screaming in anticipation. "Stay back."

"You've asked for this, Emma. Don't you want to learn how to get power from another source?"

She did, but not from him.

He took another step, less than an arm's reach away. He was too close.

Stretching out her arm, she released her power. He lunged and pushed her arm sideways as a burst of energy shot into the trees, the foliage igniting.

Raphael wrapped an arm around her waist and pulled her to his chest, leaning into her ear. "Good show, my love. I think you've earned a reward."

Her resolve faded, his presence turning her head fuzzy. She tried to concentrate, to stay out of his control, but his energy overpowered hers, demanding subservience.

"Don't fight me, Emma." Keeping her in his arms, he dragged her closer to the house. "Let me show you what we can become."

Panic flooded her mind as she fought for control, desperate to find a lifeline. Will. His image popped into her head. Thinking of him always helped her keep her grasp on reality. She latched on to her memories of him. *Think about Will.*

"You can get energy from so many sources, Emma. It's best to start small and work your way up." He stopped beneath a power line and smiled. "But time is short so I'll give you a larger demonstration of what can be yours. Be *ours.*"

She was losing herself, falling down the rabbit hole.

His arm dropped and she stepped back in surprise as her senses returned. Her anger, which bobbed below the surface of her control, ignited.

Raphael leaned closer. "Good, Emma. Very good. Let it build, let it boil."

Her anger grew, her insides a raging mass of energy. She would kill him.

"What do you use to make your power? What's your source? Tell me."

The pressure crushed her internal organs. She wasn't sure how much longer she could last.

"Do you know what would happen if I touched you right now when you're full of power?"

She shook her head, her eyes wide with fear. Would she join with him? "No!"

"If I let my power build to match yours..." His eyes glowed and a green light encased him. "If we joined together, we could be indestructible."

Panic clawed at the surface of her consciousness. "Will!" But Will was gone. The only one who could save her was herself. "No."

Raphael's eyes danced. "It would be magic."

She pushed her power toward him, but the flow stopped when his hand touched her arm.

Raphael pulled her to his chest, wrapping an arm around her back. A rush of emotion and sensations assaulted her. Hot and cold. Pain and ecstasy. Belonging and loneliness. Terror and anger.

Satisfaction filled his eyes and he grinned. "Do you feel it, Emma?"

She couldn't answer, paralyzed by the overstimulation.

"And do you know what would happen if we add more power with the two of us united together?"

She couldn't move, couldn't think.

"This is what happens if we add more power."

The sparks flew from the power line overhead, surging through her. Her every nerve ending begged for release.

"And just a little bit more." He grinned as light bulbs on the outside of the house exploded, a shower of glass raining down around them but avoiding them directly. Their glows filled the space around them, sending strands of sparks and electricity in all directions.

The pain was unbearable. She made a desperate attempt to release the energy, but Raphael's connection stopped her flow out while adding more from his source. He was going to kill her.

Her body arched back and she began to fall before he pulled her to his chest. "That is only the beginning. If we say the joining words, we would be unstoppable."

Was this what he planned to do? Kill her if she didn't join with him?

"Do you remember the words, darling?"

"No," she choked out. The burning tears streaming down her cheeks offered a miniscule relief. "I don't know them."

The pressure increased, power pinpricking every inch of her skin. *"Will!"* It was pointless to call for him but she was past rational thought, running on instinct. Her vision fading, Raphael's face was the last thing she saw as she screamed then passed out from pain.

CHAPTER THIRTEEN

"GODDAMN son of a bitch piece of shit car." Will kicked the tire and spun around on the highway shoulder in frustration.

"Yeah, that's gonna make it start." James laughed. "Calm your ass down. It's just overheated. It'll cool down and then we'll add water and move on."

"For the second time today."

"It's a motherfucking heat wave and beggars can't be choosers. It wasn't like we went car shopping. I don't know about you, but I didn't feel like sticking around and testing out all the keys from those creepy dead guys."

James was right, but Will had been on edge since he'd heard Emma scream his name in his head several hours before. He thought he'd left crazy-ass shit back in South Dakota.

"The forecast is for cooler weather tomorrow with some rain. It might be best to find a motel for the night and start again tomorrow. I'd rather be sitting around on my ass in an air-conditioned motel than sitting in the godforsaken heat on the side of the road."

Will grunted his approval, not that he had much choice in the matter. James was right again, but Will had a sudden urge to be home, to make contact with something familiar. His apartment could wait until tomorrow night.

Once they added the water to the radiator, they headed to the nearest town and checked into a motel. After an early dinner, James researched on his laptop while Will sprawled on the bed and watched a baseball game.

His eyelids grew heavy and he fought to keep awake before everything faded to black. He plunged into total darkness before a voice called out to him.

"Will."

It wasn't Emma and it wasn't the voice in his head at the compound. This was a child's voice.

A soft light filled the darkness and the scene became an outdoor garden overlooking a vineyard. A child with curly blond hair sat on an ornate concrete bench, staring at the view. "Sit with me, Will."

Nerves tingling, Will took the few steps to the bench and hesitated.

A little boy looked up, his big blue eyes too serious for a child his age. "We have to hurry before he finds out."

Will sat. The concrete beneath his ass felt more real than any dream he'd ever had.

The boy's mouth pursed. "This isn't a dream. You have to listen to me."

"Okay." Will's voice shook. *Get it together.*

The boy turned back to the view, his small hands twisting in his lap. Tears filled his eyes. "He's killing her."

"Killing who?"

"Mommy."

Will's mind scrambled to piece this all together. Who was this boy and who was his mother? Even as he asked, he knew. His stomach plummeted.

Emma. This had to be Jake.

"He's doing it wrong. He's killing her."

Will's breath froze. "Who's killing her?"

Tears slid down Jake's cheeks. "I heard her in my head when she screamed for you."

Holy shit. That was real.

No it wasn't. This was just a dream.

With a scowl wrinkling his forehead, Jake's chin quivered. "I think she's still dying." He looked up, his huge blue eyes holding Will's. "Will you make sure she's okay?"

Will choked on his fear. "I...how..."

"Through your dreams. You can find her and then tell me. But we can only do this once. Aiden will find it out and I won't be able to try it again."

She was dying. But if this was a dream or even if it wasn't, how could he save her? "Tell me what to do."

"Close your eyes and think about her. Do you feel her?"

Will's eyes sank closed as he thought about how crazy this was, but it wasn't any crazier than what he experienced in captivity. Besides, he had nothing to lose by trying. He focused on her and the dream that had felt so real two nights ago.

Her warmth washed over him, then her faint floral scent. His pulse picked up. "I think I've found her."

"Call to her." Jake said.

"Emma. Emma, it's Will." Nothing. "She won't answer."

"I don't think she can." Jake's voice broke and he sniffed.

A small hand slid onto Will's outstretched palm. His fingers curled around the smaller ones.

"Now push through the darkness toward her."

The black surroundings were a thick fog. Will shoved through, concentrating on her while maintaining his grip on Jake's hand. A soft light appeared and then a room. It was a bedroom, and a woman lay on the bed. She appeared to be sleeping, but a heavy pall hung in the air.

"Do you see her?"

Her long dark hair was a sharp contrast to her overly pale face. Will watched the shallow rise and fall of her chest. "Yes, but something's wrong."

Jake squeezed Will's hand. "You can help her."

"How?"

"Just touch her."

Will sat on the edge of the bed and took her hand in his free one.

She lay still and unresponsive.

Anger burned through Will like a wildfire. "What did he do?"

"He wants her power."

Emma's fingers wiggled in Will's hand and she released a sigh. Her eyelashes fluttered open. "*Will?*" Her voice broke.

"She's awake," Will whispered, and Jake squeezed his other hand, his nails digging into Will's palm.

Emma's eyes glistened. "I miss you."

And then she was gone.

****

She woke with a start. "Will!"

Disappointment sucked her breath away when she realized she was alone in the dark. Her dream had felt so real, that Will had really held her hand.

"You're still dreaming of him."

Her head whipped around to the voice. Raphael sat in the chair in the corner, his face hidden in the shadows.

Her disappointment increased and fear rolled down her back. She forced her words to sound firm. "What are you doing here?"

He uncrossed his legs and leaned forward. The moonlight streaming through the windows cast long shadows across his face. "I was worried about you. I wanted to make sure you were okay."

Okay? She was far from okay. Terrorized and traumatized, she wanted to bury her head into her pillow and sob, but she refused to give him the satisfaction. "You almost killed me, Raphael."

He stood and inhaled a deep breath. "I know... I don't know what I was thinking." He grabbed his head in his hands. "Your progress has been so slow and I've been so frustrated." Pivoting, he looked down at her, his eyes wild. "I'm pinning everything on you. My entire existence. I was sure you were hindering your progress to get back at me."

"That's crazy. Why would I want to get back at you?"

His mouth opened and closed before he pinched his lips. "You blamed me for everything. Losing Will. Losing your baby. I figured this was retaliation."

She hated him for those things, but that wasn't what kept her from progressing. "No, Raphael. You've pushed too hard and made me too nervous. You scare me."

He moved to the bed and sat next to her, reaching for her hand then stopping himself.

She held her breath. She couldn't do this again so soon.

Silhouetted in the moonlight, his face was unreadable, but she smelled the alcohol on his breath. "I know. I'm sorry."

"I think I just need a good night's sleep. Tomorrow I'll be better."

"But you keep saying that, Emma, and it just doesn't happen." The sharp edge was back in his voice.

She released a tiny exhale of fear before she could contain it. "I'm trying my best, Raphael."

"Your best hasn't been good enough, Emma."

"Raphael, please." Her voice broke. She was so fucking tired of being at his mercy, but she couldn't fight him. Only one person could.

His hand reached for her hair and stroked lightly. "I'm sorry, Emmanuella. I'm sorry." He leaned forward and buried his face in her neck.

"No."

"Shh, Emmanuella. I'm so sorry, I've hurt you again." He pulled her head to his shoulder, stroking the back of her hair. "I love you, Emmanuella. I don't want to hurt you."

His touch made her lightheaded, but she was prepared. She pushed against his chest. "No!"

He pulled her mouth to his, his lips bruising hers in his desperation. Wrapping an arm around her back, he held her to him.

She was drowning, spiraling down into her pit of abandon. If he took complete control of her, she might as well be dead.

Fight.

The word floated in the void and she latched on to it. *Fight.* She couldn't give up.

One hand held her hair while the other held her against him. *Fight him.* She searched for her power, finding a small spark. The hand on her back reached under her shirt, fueling her anger. She sent her power through her hands into his chest, only slightly stronger than a strong spark of static electricity.

He sat back in surprise, his hands falling to his sides. His head turned so the moonlight lit one side of his face, revealing his eyes wide in confusion.

"Raphael, please go. Don't do this. Don't make me hate you." If she appealed to his need for her to love him, he might leave her alone.

His mouth twisted. "Do you hate me, Emma?"

It was a trick question. She couldn't tell him yes, yet she refused to encourage him. "I'm tired, Raphael. I almost died and I'm just so tired." Her voice betrayed her again, revealing her fear.

He reached for her and she shrunk back.

"You're really frightened of me."

She bit her tongue.

"I can make you love me."

"No. Just go."

He started to rise, then abruptly leaned forward and pushed her back on the bed, kissing her.

She sobbed her frustration as she faded again, her body craving his.

The scissors.

They were under her pillow. Her hand reached behind and slid under, searching.

"I love you, Emmanuella. I've waited for you for so long."

Her hand stilled as his power overcame hers. He was right. She was his. *No*, a small voice in her head protested. She made one last half-hearted swipe under the pillow, her hand brushing cold metal.

Her fingers curled around the handles before she toppled into the need he generated. His power lapped at her in waves, sending licks of craving throughout her. *Don't fight him. I'm his.*

No.

Concentrate. Make this count. Fighting the fog of desire was like pushing into strong wind. She focused every bit of concentration on swinging the scissors as she pushed him with her other hand.

He rolled to the side and she held the scissors at his neck, the points poking into his flesh.

His eyes flew wide in alarm.

"Get the fuck away from me, Raphael."

He scooted away from her on the bed, closer to the door, his mouth twisted in shock as blood trickled down his neck.

She leaned forward to keep the scissors against his pulse point, careful to keep from physically touching him.

"Emma..." His Adam's apple bobbed as he swallowed.

"I'll kill you if I have to. Get out."

He reached the edge of the bed and slid his feet to the floor.

Emma retracted her hand but held out the scissor points toward him.

"I'm sorry. I shouldn't have…" He left the room without looking back.

The scissors shook in her hand as the adrenaline rush peaked. She stumbled to the door and locked it even though she knew it wouldn't keep him out. Collapsing in a heap, she crawled to the bed, still weak from what Raphael had done to her that afternoon. She needed food but was scared to leave the room. Perhaps the next best thing was sleep, but she was terrified to lose consciousness. He could come back, and by the time she realized what he was doing it would be too late. She glanced at the clock on the nightstand. It was two a.m. She'd been out for hours.

He really had almost killed her.

She had to figure out a way to escape. To do that, she needed to be stronger. Which meant she had to practice, but she couldn't even walk out of the room, let alone walk out to the pasture. To fall asleep meant she'd be at Raphael's mercy. She was sick to death of being at anyone's mercy.

When Alex came back the next day, she had to get him to teach her how to mask herself. Raphael was getting crazier and crazier. The next time he might go too far.

She lay on the bed, sliding the scissors under her pillow but keeping her fingers curled around the handle.

****

The shadows danced around the room, no longer hiding their movement, spinning faster and faster until Jake hid under his covers.

Aiden was coming.

He sensed his movement through the house, felt the sickening warm wave as Aiden made his way to Jake's bedroom.

Jake would pay.

But Mommy was alive and safe for the moment. Will had saved her this time. Raphael was dangerous, even Aiden knew it from comments that slipped out. But now Aiden knew he could talk to Will.

Yet he wasn't sorry, even if Will was in danger. He felt his mommy through his connection with Will, even if it was only for a few seconds.

The door slammed against the wall as Aiden threw it open and Jake lowered his sheet. There was no hiding from Aiden.

The shadows had stopped, lurking on the walls with curves that looked like hooks. Jake preferred the shadows to Aiden.

Aiden stood in the doorway, his eyes glowing in a golden light. "What have you done?"

Jake sat up, his chin trembling.

"He's alive." Aiden's voice boomed through the room, making the furniture shake.

Had Aiden thought Will was dead? He wished he knew what happened between the time he left the house in Montana with Aiden and he woke up in this room. Dread mixed with fear spiraled around Jake's chest and squeezed.

"Not only is he alive, but he knows about Emmanuella. How does he know about her?"

Of course he knew about Mommy. What was Aiden talking about? "Raphael was killing Mommy."

"How did you know this?"

"I heard her. Raphael was killing her and she screamed for Will."

Aiden's eyebrows rose and his voice lowered to a whisper. "You heard her? And so did Will?"

Jake nodded, Aiden's face blurry through his tears.

"This changes everything."

****

Emma felt better the next morning But at breakfast she convinced Raphael that she was still too weak to practice. Guilt swept over his face and he wouldn't look her in the eye.

"Emma, I'm sorry."

If he said that he was sorry one more time, she really would stab him.

He took a drink then lowered the glass as he studied the amber liquid. "I have an errand I need to run. If you feel well enough, I'll leave you here alone, but I'll be gone all day and won't be home until late tonight. Will you be all right by yourself?"

She hoped her relief wasn't too obvious. She wanted to tell him she'd be safer without him here, but worried if she was too antagonistic he wouldn't leave. "Yes."

"I'll leave my cell phone number in case you need me for anything, but it might take some time to get back to you." He paused, worry filling his eyes. "Are you certain you'll be okay? Maybe I should wait until you get better."

"No," she said too quickly, then gave him a quick pat on his arm. "No, I've already been enough of a burden. You go and I'll be fine." But curiosity got the better of her and she glanced at him through her eyelashes. "Where are you going?"

He hesitated. "You don't need to concern yourself with the matter. Just rest assured that I'm seeking outside help to smooth out your difficulties."

"Difficulties?" Her breath stuck in her throat, making her words sound squeaky.

His eyes softened. "I know you're trying. I see your fear and I've been too hard on you. I think I might know a source that will tell me what the problem is. I'd take you with me, but I'm worried it might be dangerous, especially in your weakened condition." He rose, taking his plate to the sink. "But I need to leave soon. I've left my cell phone number by the phone here in the kitchen."

Emma had been excited about the phone when she first saw it days ago, until she realized she didn't have anyone she could call. Even if she called the police, Raphael would find her and potentially kill people to get her back. She couldn't risk it.

Now she wondered if there was someone she could call after all.

CHAPTER FOURTEEN

THE sun had begun to set, a thick haze hanging over the yard. Emma found a small bag and packed several changes of clothes and some food. She went into Raphael's bedroom and discovered a small stash of cash tucked in a dresser drawer. His room hadn't been the dark, oppressive décor she'd expected. Instead it was light and airy, with a small portrait on an easel in a corner by the window.

A portrait of her.

No, not her. Raphael's Emmanuella.

The girl in the portrait was much younger and her eyes sparkled with innocence and youth. Emma doubted her eyes had ever looked like that. Her life had never afforded innocence.

The girl's hair was pulled up into an elaborately curled hairstyle. She wore a red ruffled dress that was cut low, the skirt full. Emma guessed the painting to be several hundred years old from the clothing and the cracks in the oil paint. How had Raphael gotten it?

If he had a portrait of Emmanuella, he obviously loved her in his own way, which made Emma almost feel guilty about what she was about to do.

Almost.

At eight twenty, she walked down the long circular driveway to the road. She hadn't seen the front of the house since Raphael had brought her here almost a week ago.

A car with darkened windows parked perpendicular to the driveway as she approached. As it idled, she hesitated. Was this really her only option?

Yes.

She opened the door and slid in the front, tossing her bag over her shoulder into the backseat.

"You're early. Eager to see me?"

Her eyebrows rose with a smirk. "I could ask you the same."

Alex grinned as he pulled away from the curb. "Raphael's going to be very upset with you, Emma."

"Like I give a flipping rat's ass."

He chuckled. "You *have* changed."

"Why does everyone presume to know me? You don't know shit about me."

"You might want to consider at least pretending to be nice. Otherwise I could dump you on the road right here and let you take your chances with Raph."

She crossed her arms. "You won't."

"Be careful making that call, Emma. While it might be true now, the day is coming that you'll be fair game to the both of us."

The truth of his words deflated her momentary relief over her escape. Alex was right. At some point, one or both of them would cut their losses and probably try to cut out their competition. Emma hoped that day of reckoning didn't come until the very end. But she worried about Raphael's reaction when he discovered she was missing. He was borderline psychotic at best. Would he find her and drag her back or would he kill her now and be done with it? "You have to teach me how to hide myself."

Alex snorted. "I don't *have* to teach you how to do anything."

"If you don't, Raphael will just track me down and your rescue trip will have been for nothing."

"I'm masking you, so Raphael can't find you right now. And when the time is right, I'll teach you, but only after conditions are met."

"What conditions?"

He held up a finger and waved it back and forth. "Uh, uh, uh. You'll find out in due time. First things first, we need to make some ground rules."

Emma rolled her eyes. "I thought that was my line."

"Ha, very funny. The first rule is you don't touch me. Also, we will be in close proximity as little as possible and you will refrain from using your power around me unless it's absolutely necessary."

"You're making me feel unloved."

He shot her a *go to hell* look.

However, his requests made sense. If she was capable of doing to him half of what Raphael did to her, he had made a calculated risk helping her leave Raphael. "So why did you help me?"

"Honestly?" He cast her a sideways glance. "I'm not sure."

"That doesn't sound like you at all."

"To quote someone I know: You don't know shit about me."

"I know you raped me six years ago." That reminder made her question her own sanity for sitting here next to him. At least Raphael had acted in his love-crazed delirium. Alex had been cruel and sadistic.

"Maybe that's why I'm helping you now."

Doubtful. Most likely Alex figured that if he helped her, then she'd feel a need to repay him for his kindness later. By joining with him. But the truth was that Alex had a lot riding on her survival and he couldn't stand by and let Raphael kill her.

"Do you have any idea where Raphael went today?" Alex asked as he pulled onto the highway.

"He said he had to run an errand. Something to smooth out *my difficulties.*"

Alex laughed. "So that's what he's calling it. Figures." He shook his head. "I happen to know where he went, although it was a wasted trip."

"So where'd he go?"

"To the Vinco Potentia compound in South Dakota to get the book of De Luca's writings."

Emma's head swam. She swallowed her nervousness and concentrated on appearing curious. Did Alex know that she knew about the book or the prophecy? "What?"

"Lorenzo De Luca was the guy who wrote the prophecy that's sent humans all atwitter for several hundred years."

"Don't go getting all judgmental. Only a month ago you were one of those humans destroying other people's lives because of that prophecy." Hers included. Gut instinct told her not to let Alex know she had taken the book.

Could she pull off the next part with what she knew? "Why was it a wasted trip?"

"Because the book is gone. I was there a few days ago and it was missing."

"If it just has the prophecy, what's the big deal?" That's all Will claimed to find, other than some dates with incidents that had happened or that the Vinco Potentia had averted. But then, she'd been too distraught about Jake when he looked at the book to give him her full attention.

"Because it's the official record of the rules of the game."

"What?" Will hadn't found anything about the rules. Unless it was in the section written in another language.

"The rules appear in the book, mystically. The book has changed over the years. In the beginning, it was just papyrus paper, but over time, it evolved into a bound journal. But in addition to the physical properties of the book, every time there was a tweak to the rules, they changed inside the book. I was hoping to find the book and read the official rules. I don't trust Aiden to give us all the information, and apparently neither does Raphael."

"So where is the book now?"

"I have no idea."

Emma guessed that the book was with James, and if it contained half of what Alex said, she needed to get her hands on it. Alex may have helped her escape Raphael, but that hadn't bought her trust. "Can you find it?"

He shrugged with a heavy sigh. "I'm not sure where to look. I'll have to backtrack and see who saw it last, which is going to be hard to do since Scott Kramer is dead."

Her eyes flew open in surprise. "What? How?"

Alex swallowed and gave her a crooked smile that didn't reach his eyes. "Why, Emma, I didn't know you cared about Kramer. Especially since he was the one who hired Will Davenport to bring you to them."

When he put it that way, she wondered if she should thank him after all. But the mention of Will sobered her, dropping a heavy veil of grief around her heart. Kramer's death was a very odd coincidence considering the current events. "Yeah, Kramer and I were buddies. How did he die?"

"Let's just say Kramer had a little industrial accident."

Resisting the urge to press for more, she made herself accept that he wasn't going to share what he knew. In the grand scheme of things, what did she care how one of a shitload of assholes died?

"So what's our plan?"

His eyebrows rose with a sarcastic smirk. "*Our* plan?"

"Fine, your plan."

"You're awfully self-assured for someone being held prisoner."

She laughed. "Prisoner? Really? I realize that you're the one in control right now, but we both know how quickly that can turn on you."

A scowl furrowed his brow and she almost felt like an ass. She was no better than Raphael. But she needed to remember that Alex would sell his grandmother to the devil himself if he would aid him in any way. She should have no guilt in getting what she needed from him.

"Where are we going?"

"First the airport. Then a private plane to Missouri."

Her heart flip-flopped. Her mother was in Missouri, but so was Will's apartment. Why would Alex want to go to Missouri? Maybe he knew Will had taken the book after all, and this was some big con job on his part to use her to get it.

Anticipating her question, he grinned. "Nope, it's a surprise. But I will tell you that you and I will part ways tomorrow."

Her mouth dropped in surprise. "But…"

"I'm not going to tell you, so you might as well save your breath."

She had a million questions, but they would all have to wait. She was safe from Raphael, at least for a little while.

****

The drive to Kansas City was unsettling, the gray overcast sky matching Will's mood. He found it difficult pretending he didn't know about James's duplicity. He continued to remind himself that he needed James. But he couldn't get past the question that drove him closer to the edge of insanity.

Why?

Why would James toss away over twenty years of friendship to betray him? And if he didn't betray him, why would he lie? Had Will done something to lose James's trust? Was it that James hated Emma so much? Would he really risk their friendship?

James knew Will wasn't himself, but Will excused it as still recovering from his incarceration, which wasn't a lie. Between his dreams, the torture, and the question of

James's loyalty, Will's mind wandered and struggled to focus. He needed a plan to find out what James knew and wasn't telling him, then where to go and what to do from there. James was right. They needed to extricate themselves from the Vinco Potentia, but he didn't agree that turning Jake over to Alex was the solution—if nothing else because it would hurt Emma even more. If they had spent a month trying to recapture Jake from Alex, then it seemed crazy to give him back. They didn't even know if Alex wanted Jake back.

If Jake was still alive.

His stomach churned at the thought, but he reminded himself that Jake had visited him in a dream last night. *Listen to yourself. You're turning dreams into facts.* But the dream felt so real, and there was no denying the tiny half-moon nail cuts on his palm, cuts that were far too small to have come from his own nails.

They arrived in Kansas City after dark and James parked several blocks away from Will's apartment, in case the building was under surveillance. Another wave of déjà vu swept through Will as they walked down a dark street and passed a parking lot, but he shook it off. Even if it was a buried memory of his time with Emma, he doubted it would surface.

Instead, he focused on getting into his apartment, The goal was Will's sole purpose for existence at that moment. He convinced himself that if he could just get inside and surround himself with something familiar, he would become himself again—confident and decisive. He wasn't sure how much longer he could continue living in this haze.

He entered the building without incident, his anticipation growing with every step. When they exited the stairwell onto his floor, he stopped halfway down the hall and lifted the edge of the carpet to retrieve his emergency apartment key. "It's gone."

James's hand moved to his gun, hidden under his shirt. "Do you remember taking it out?"

Still squatting, Will ran both hands through his hair. "No, but I probably took it out when I was here with Emma. If my truck blew up, my keys probably blew up with it. The question is, why didn't I replace it?"

"Maybe you thought you wouldn't be back."

Will rose slowly, letting the finality of James's statement soak in. The idea made sense.

"You haven't been here for a month," James said, glancing up and down the hall. "Which means you haven't been around to pay your bills for over a month. Is the apartment still yours?"

Will forced himself to concentrate when his touchstone to reality was less than twenty feet away yet agonizingly out of reach. "Um, yeah. I never knew when I'd be here or on a job, so all of my bills were set up on automatic electronic payments."

"Until the Vinco Potentia seized your bank account a month ago." James rubbed his chin. "But they give you a grace period, so you're probably okay. Now we just need to get in."

Will hadn't come this close just to be thwarted. He pulled out his lock-picking kit and set to work unlocking his deadbolt.

A minute later, James scowled, leaning over Will's shoulder. "What the hell is taking you so long?"

Will grunted in frustration. "I put these locks in to keep unwanted visitors out."

"Oh, the irony," James laughed, slapping Will's back. "And here you're supposed to be the master at this."

"Shut the fuck up."

James pulled out his gun. "Here's another way to do it."

"You can't shoot my door, you asshole. Have you lost your mind?"

"Well, your way's obviously not working."

Will stuck a pick between his teeth and mumbled, "Just give me a minute."

"I've given you two."

The lock clicked and the door sprang free.

His stomach twisting, Will walked over the threshold. The apartment looked the same as always. Neat and clean. And impersonal. In his desperate search for normalcy, he'd ignored the fact that his apartment had never felt like home. His sister had decorated it for him, but he rarely spent time there. Home had always been his mom's. Not that his mother's house was an option.

"There's an empty ice cream container in the sink," James said, looking over the counter into the kitchen.

"My emergency cash stash was hidden in there. We had probably run out of money. My guess is that all my weapons are gone too." He knew some were in his duffle bag.

"You showed up at my place with a small arsenal."

"It wouldn't hurt to check it out." Will moved into the single bedroom. A thick layer of dust covered the furniture and the closet door stood open. A quick glance in the back confirmed he'd taken all of his guns and ammunition as well as all of his fake IDs. James was probably right. He hadn't planned on coming back.

"You have three messages on your answering machine."

"Megan." Only two people had his land-line number. James and his sister. He went through so many cell phones that the land-line was the only certain way to contact him other than e-mail. But Megan rarely called and she wouldn't have left that many messages unless something was wrong.

Will walked to the kitchen and pressed the play button.

"Will." Megan's voice spoke through the scratched answering machine tone. "I need you to call me back as soon as you get this message." The machine time-stamped the message as having been a week ago.

James caught Will's eye. "I wonder if the Vinco Potentia paid a visit to your sister. That was right before they captured you."

Will's breath caught. He had so little contact with his family that he'd given it little thought.

The next message played, his sister again. "Will, I've sent you an e-mail and I still haven't heard from you. I need you to call me. It's important."

If Kramer had messed with his sister or her family...

The next message started. "Will, now I'm really worried about you. Listen, I didn't want to leave this in a message but I have to tell you. Um..." She paused. "Mom's in the hospital. She's got advanced breast cancer and she's dying." Her voice broke and Will heard her take a breath to compose herself. "She's asking for you, Will. She wants to see you before she dies, but she's failing fast and I'm not sure how much longer she's going to last. Please, Will. I need you to come home."

The machine beeped and said the call had been made that afternoon.

His mother was dying.

Will sat down on the sofa, looking up at James with wide eyes. How much more could he take?

James's face paled. "Do you think this is a set-up?"

Will shook his head. "What? No. I don't think so."

His mother was dying and she wanted to see him. The real question was, did he want to see her?

James pulled his laptop out of his bag. "I'll do some digging and see if it's true."

Lowering his face into his hands, Will growled, "If the Vinco Potentia set it up, they'd have to use my sister and I don't even want to go there. But if they are responsible, they'll be thorough enough to plant fake medical records and show her as a patient at the hospital. You're wasting your time."

"So what are you saying? That you don't want to see your mother? What if she's really dying?"

"So I'm supposed to give a fuck about her now because she decides it's convenient for her to see me? What about the last three years?"

James groaned and set down his computer before going into the kitchen. He returned with a bottle of whiskey and two glasses, which he set on the coffee table with a clunk. "If anyone ever needed a drink, you do, my friend." He unscrewed the cap and poured two generous glasses.

"I don't drink. Not anymore."

"Yeah, I can see that. The bottle I gave you two years ago was still unopened." James picked up the glass and set it in Will's hand. "But tonight you do. I know you swore off anything stronger than beer after your weeks-long drunken spree when you came home after your discharge, but tonight you need to make an exception. Consider this medicinal."

Will held the glass in his hand, swirling the amber liquid. "And what really drove me to my weeks-long drunken spree, James? It sure as fuck wasn't my court-martial."

James pushed the glass up. "Stop thinking and just drink."

Will brought the glass to his lips and swallowed a generous gulp, the whiskey burning as it went down.

"Lucky for you, getting the alcohol in your system is more important than savoring a sixty-dollar bottle of eighteen-year-old Jameson, or I'd wring your neck for that."

"I'll tell you what drove me to my drunkfest. My mother."

James sighed and rested his hand on Will's knee. "I know."

Will leaned back into the sofa and put his feet on the coffee table. "She deserted me when I needed her the most. For him. She didn't even love him. Why?" He gulped another mouthful, suddenly eager to deaden his pain. It bombarded him from too many directions.

"All the more reason to see her. Ask her that very question. She owes you."

"Yeah." He sucked the last of the whiskey from his glass. "She owes me."

James poured more into Will's glass. "I'll do some digging and if it all checks out, we'll go see her tomorrow."

He was going to see his mother.

CHAPTER FIFTEEN

"RISE and shine, sleepyhead!" Alex called out in a cheerful voice.

Emma pulled the covers over her head. She'd had the best sleep she'd had in weeks. It was amazing how easy it was to rest when you weren't terrified for your life.

"It's Freedom Day and we've got a drive ahead of us. Let's go."

She lowered the blanket and sat up. "You're serious. You're going to let me go?"

Alex rolled his eyes. "I made it perfectly clear that I want to be around you as little as possible." He shrugged. "No offense."

She climbed out of bed. "None taken." She grabbed a change of clothes out of her bag and headed for the bathroom. "I need a shower."

"Make it quick. Turns out we're pressed for time."

Pausing in the doorway, she glanced over her shoulder. "We have an appointment?"

"Something like that." Alex walked into his adjoining room, his words muffled. "Bang on my door when you're done."

Freedom was a foreign concept after her week with Raphael. But she and Alex had flown on a private jet into Kansas City, and checked into two adjoining rooms in a hotel downtown. She could have left any time she wanted, which in reality was a lie. Raphael would have found her. But Alex chose to let her make her own decision, no pressure either way, which surprised her. She'd considered him more manipulative.

Showering quickly, she dressed in jeans and a T-shirt, almost regretting her decision to not bring skirts. While cooler in the Midwest heat, they were difficult to run in if necessary. She'd deal with the discomfort.

Alex said it was Freedom Day, but they had to drive somewhere. Where were they going? And would he give her money to live on for the next few weeks? All she had was the little cash she'd stolen from Raphael. She'd never asked for a handout in her entire life, but she didn't have time to work for minimum wage or wait tables for crappy tips. Besides, these assholes owed her.

After a quick blow dry of her hair, she knocked on Alex's door.

He opened it and eyed her up and down, his eyebrows raised in appraisal.

For the first time since she'd seen Alex a couple of days ago, she felt intimidated by him. Why was he looking her over like she was about to be put up for auction?

He shook his head and smiled, eerily close to his father's political mask. "Well, okay. Let's get going!" He grabbed her bag off the dresser and led her into the hall.

Following behind, she was suddenly unsure she'd made the right decision, but there wasn't much she could do about it now.

****

James drove to Morgantown, Missouri while Will slumped in the passenger seat, nursing a hangover. He rubbed his temples, shutting his eyes to the blinding sunlight.

"You ready to see your mom?"

Grunting, Will sunk lower into the leather. In the history of asinine questions, this had to top the list, yet Will knew that James grasped for something to ease the tension.

"Well, you better get ready. We're about five minutes away."

Will didn't even answer with a grunt. He wished he hadn't drowned his sorrows quite so much last night. Instead of facing his mother with a clear head and carefully thought-out questions, a piercing pain stabbed his skull. One thing in his favor was that he didn't dream of Emma. Maybe she was gone, exorcised from his brain like James wanted. Did Will want that too? He couldn't deny his life, not to mention his sanity, would be better off. Yet, something inside him still clung to her.

James pulled into a parking garage and found a spot on the second level. "We're entering through an auxiliary building. That way if the Vinco Potentia is watching, we might be able to elude them."

Two men sat in a car close to the entrance as Will and James approached. "What do you think?" James asked.

Will rubbed his aching forehead. "Looks suspicious. We need a diversion."

James pulled Will between two parked cars and squatted. "Yeah, I'm on it."

A woman pushing a stroller and tugging a school-aged boy approached from behind. James tugged a baseball cap over Will's head. "Meet you inside, Daddy."

Will fell into step with the family, grateful that the mom was distracted by the whiny toddler in the stroller. He passed through the doors, touching the boy lightly on the shoulder. The men cast a quick glance in his direction, then looked way.

Hiding around the corner, Will waited for several minutes before James walked in, pushing an elderly gentleman in a wheelchair and wearing a safari hat on his head.

"That was easy," Will mumbled as he moved down the hall.

"Speak for yourself. I had to break into a car to get this hat, then I had to convince Mr. Turnball I wasn't going to assault him."

"Well, we're in now." With Will's every step, a rebellion festered. Once again, he'd let James call the shots. For days he'd followed James like a fucking lost puppy. Yeah, his life was shit. But it had been shit before and he could guarantee it would be shit again. This wasn't him. Hiding and cowering behind James's skirts wasn't Will Davenport. It was time to take charge.

They rode the elevator to the third floor and James followed Will into the hallway.

"Stay in the waiting room, James."

Wide eyed, James looked around, spotting the nearby waiting area. "Why?"

"I need to do this on my own.

James's shoulders relaxed. "I know, but after everything you've been through, you need me watching your back."

"No," Will enunciated slowly, "what I need to do is to go see my mother by myself. When I'm done, I'll come find you."

"Will—"

"Why don't you want me to go on my own?"

James grabbed Will's elbow and dragged him toward the chairs, away from a nurse passing by who narrowed her eyes at their exchange. "Will, be reasonable. You're still recovering and we have no idea if this is a trap or not."

"We both know my mother is lying in a bed down the hall, dying. They may be waiting to ambush us, but I'm doing this on my own."

"Will."

"You've treated me like a two-year-old since you walked into my cell days ago, and for some bizarre reason, I've let you. But it stops now."

James leaned his forehead closer to Will's and lowered his voice. "Will, you've been through a major trauma that would have flattened most men. You just don't bounce back from something like that."

"You treating me like a child is making it worse. Let me work through this my own way. And going to see my mother by myself is the first step."

James rubbed his chin, looking around at the dilapidated vinyl chairs. "All right. I'll wait here. But if you're not back in thirty minutes, I'm coming looking for you."

"Fair enough." Will's arm brushed James's as he pushed past.

James grabbed his elbow, his gaze locking with Will's. "Good luck."

Will nodded and pulled loose. God, that felt good. He even felt like a sliver of himself.

****

The sun had only been up a few hours but a wet fog hung in the air. A fog Jake had created.

Aiden beamed. "Very good, Jacob. How do you feel?"

It was a trick question. Aiden was full of them. "Great," Jake answered with as much enthusiasm as he could muster.

"This is a very good start. Next you will make clouds."

Easy for Aiden to say. Jake wanted to tell him to make clouds himself.

"Disobedience will not be tolerated." Aiden's anger rolled off of him, washing over Jake in waves.

Catching his breath, Jake struggled against the toxicity that choked him. Once it eased, he shifted his feet apart and closed his eyes.

Fog had been kind of easy. Fog was tiny drops of water that clumped together and hovered over the ground. He had to control the air around it, but the water readily obeyed. Clouds were harder. The water droplets had to cling differently so that they were lighter and fluffier, almost like steam. He centered himself, drawing his power from deep inside, his body almost singing to the molecules in the air, forcing them to push the water.

"Very good."

Jake peeked through his slitted eyelids. The fog had folded in on itself, becoming thicker and denser, a three-foot fluffy mass that looked like white cotton candy.

"Now you need to make it bigger."

Jake closed his eyes to hide his tears. He was so tired and doing things like making clouds made him more tired. After Aiden's nighttime visit to his room, he'd gotten little sleep. Jake was worried about Mommy, worried about Will. The shadows had begun moving the moment Aiden left, creeping across the floor and lapping at Jake's bed, yet he still preferred them to Aiden.

What would Aiden do to Will now that he knew Will was alive?

"You don't need to worry about Will." Aiden's voice sounded like thick honey, slow and sweet. He used that voice when he meant the opposite of what he was saying.

Jake opened his eyes, pulling his lower lip between his teeth.

Aiden smiled, his eyes glowing. "I'll take care of everything in due time."

****

While Will acknowledged James had legitimate concerns about the Vinco Potentia showing up, he was glad he was alone as he walked down the hall. He took a moment to steady his nerves before searching for his mother's room. He took in the view of the town through a wall of windows he passed, appreciating the fact that his mother had chosen to raise Will and his sister in Morgantown, close to his grandparents. The alternative was to traipse all over the world and be raised as military brats.

It had also spared them a lot of years with their controlling father.

Squaring his shoulders, he turned down the hall and found her room number. It was time to get some answers. He pushed through the door, stopping short as it swung closed behind him.

He hadn't seen his mother in over three years, and at first glance he thought he was in the wrong room. The frail woman lying in the hospital bed looked decades older. Her eyes were closed, but the door hinge squeaked and she turned her head, her mouth dropping in disbelief. "Will?"

"Mom," Will whispered, his heart sinking as he moved to her side. How did this happen?

Her chin trembled. "You came. You really came."

Will sat in a chair next to the bed and took her hand. "Yeah, I came."

They stared at one another for several moments. Will wasn't sure what his mother saw. Longer hair than his old military cut. A few wrinkles and a harder expression in his eyes.

What he saw stole his breath. His mother, always a small woman, was now tiny and frail. Her arms were like shriveled toothpicks covered in saggy skin. She reached a bony hand to his face. Will was astounded that she looked more like eighty than fifty-five.

"Megan...she said she couldn't reach you." She patted his cheek. "After everything... I wasn't sure you'd come."

Will swallowed the lump in his throat. "I had to come, Mom. Once I knew you actually wanted me to. I didn't want to come all this way for you to kick me out."

She closed her eyes. "Oh, Will..."

He was an ass to bring it up, but the pain of her rejection still stung. More than stung. Ate at his soul. His father's he could understand, but his mother's...it had been the final blow, shoving him headfirst into his pit of self-destruction.

"Despite what you think, I never stopped loving you."

He shook his head, turning to face the wall. "Wow. You had a funny way of showing it. Dad, I understood. But you..."

"I wasn't strong enough."

He tried to swallow the burning in his throat, but it hung there, bringing tears to his eyes. That was a lie. She'd been one of the strongest people he knew. Maybe he shouldn't have come. What did he hope to gain? "Does Megan come to see you a lot?"

"Every day. Sometimes she brings her boys with her. They're growing like weeds. She's got a baby girl now too. Just turned a year old." She dropped her hand to cover Will's. "Megan misses you."

He nodded, trying to control his emotions. "I miss her too. But after Dad found out that she helped me with my apartment... It just seemed easier for her to not see me anymore."

"Your father has quite an influence."

Will's brow furrowed. Talk about an understatement.

"How are you doing, Will?"

With tears in his eyes he gave her a cocky smile. "Just great, Mom. I work in a big high-rise and wear a three-piece suit to work."

She frowned. "Don't you take that tone with me, William." Three years ago, she could have pulled off the statement. Three years ago she did. But her voice shook, losing the edge it needed to be a true threat.

"What do you want to hear, Mom? That I'm married with two kids and a dog? Because I'm not. My life is royally screwed up. And you know what? I take full responsibility for my mistakes. But I counted on you, Mom." His voice broke as he held back tears. "I counted on you to help me put the pieces of my life back together and tell me everything was going to be okay. Instead, you sent me away."

She released a sob. "I'm so sorry."

"Why? Why did you turn your back on me?" There it was. The real reason he came. He had to make sense of her betrayal.

Her chin quivered as her grip on his hand tightened. "You will never know how much I regret what I did, Will. But we both know how difficult it is to go against your father's wishes."

"After everything he's done over the years. Missing all those family activities. And the mistresses."

Her eyes widened.

"Of course I knew about the women. Everyone knew. All those years it was just you and Megan and me while he was on his missions. When he was gone, our lives were good, but when he was home...no one could live up to his expectations. God knows I tried. I tried so hard to be just like him, I no longer knew what part of me was really me and what part was him."

"Will..."

"No, Mom. Let's just get it all out there. I was the one there for you, all those years being the man of the house. I would have done anything for you, Mom. I loved you and I was so lucky that your love was enough to make up for that bastard's expectations."

"William. Please." Her voice broke with tears.

What had he expected? But now that he'd started this, he had to see it to the end. "When I needed you the most, you took his side." Will's shoulders shook. "How could you take his side, Mom?"

"Because I was scared, Will. I'd just found out I had cancer and I worried that your father would leave me if I stood up for you. I needed someone to take care of me."

Her face was blurry through his tears. "I would have taken care of you, Mom."

"I couldn't ask you to do that, Will. You had your own life."

He laughed bitterly. "My own life. Yeah, that's rich. My own life has been one lowlife job after another, dealing with the scum of the earth. I have to take responsibility for that too, but your betrayal didn't help."

Her voice quivered. "Will, I'm so sorry. If I could do it over again, I would. I'd change it all. I wouldn't have thrown you away."

He shook his head, choking back years of grief.

"There's not a day that goes by that I don't think about you. From the moment I wake up to when my head hits the pillow at night, you're in my thoughts. You're in my heart. I thought I was protecting myself by siding with your father, but what I didn't realize was that I threw away the greatest gift I'd ever been given. You."

He pinched his lips tight, breathing through his nose as he looked up at the ceiling. He refused to break down in front of her.

"I've hated myself for three years for letting you leave with your father's ugly words filling your head. There's a reason he treated you like he did, and that's my fault too." Her voice shook and she took a deep breath, a coughing spell in its wake. When her breathing came under control, her grip on his hand tightened. "You are not a monster, Will. You are a good man and I'm so proud to call you my son."

His tears broke. He'd waited years to hear her say this again. Why didn't it make everything better?

"There's another reason I wanted you to come."

Gritting his teeth to still his trembling chin, he waited.

"I wanted to give you something." She pointed a hand to the nightstand. "It's there in that drawer."

Pulling it open, he saw a handful of objects.

"That blue pouch. Hand it to me."

Will retrieved the small silk bag, drawn closed with a corded drawstring, and placed it in his mother's outstretched palm.

With shaky fingers, she pulled it open and poured a small object into her hand. Silver glittered in the overhead light.

She looked up at him with a faltering smile, tears in her eyes. "I wanted you to have this, but I couldn't be sure your father would give it to you." She grabbed his right hand and slid a silver band on his ring finger. "It fits perfectly. It's like it belongs on you."

Will examined the thick band with a central blue stone.

"It belonged to someone very special to me. I want you to have it."

"Who?" He studied her face.

The smile fell from her eyes, replaced with a longing that caught him off guard. "Never you mind that part. The important thing is that you have it now. I should have given it to you years ago, but life got in the way..." She lay back against her pillow, looking even more tired than she did before.

Life got in the way of lots of things. Will lay his head on the bed next to her.

She placed a hand in his hair, stroking in a halting movement. "So your life...is it still unsettled?"

The loving gesture, one she'd done countless times years ago, broke the dam to his heart. "Yes," he choked out through his tears.

"I'm so sorry. I'm so very sorry." She continued to run her hand over his head as he cried into the blanket. "I'd change it if I could." Her voice turned wistful. "I'd change so many things..."

Will knew better than anyone that what was done was done. He sat up and wiped his face with the back of his arm. "We can't change the past, Mom. We can only go forward."

She pinched her trembling lips and nodded. "So tell me. Is there anyone special in your life?"

"Have you been talking to James?"

Her eyes lit up. "So there is someone."

Hesitating, he considered his answer. Where did Emma fit into his life? He didn't even know her, yet the fact that he worried about her right now, wondering if she was safe...that had to mean something. "Yes."

She cocked her head with a raised eyebrow, the same expression she'd used when he was a boy withholding information.

I love a woman but I don't know anything about her other than she has magic powers. God, he was crazy. "Her name is Emma. She has a little boy, Jake. He's five."

"So no children of your own?" she asked with a hopeful tone.

He looked down at their clasped hands. He'd had a baby but not any more, the grief still fresh. "No."

She patted his hand. "So what do you do for a living now?"

Releasing a derisive laugh, he looked over her shoulder. "I'm currently between jobs."

"I see..."

His eyes pierced hers. "Have you been happy, Mom? Did Dad try to make you happy these last years?" He hoped she would say yes, so that his pain would have been for something.

She shook her head. "No. I regretted forcing you to leave the moment you drove away. Your father blamed me for what happened."

"Why?"

"He said if I'd been firmer with you years ago..."

"I'm sorry."

Tears filled her eyes. "No, none of it was true, but I deserved every bit of it for the choices I made. All of them." She paused. "If you love this woman, then whatever you do, no matter what, don't let her go." Her eyes burned with an intensity that frightened him. "Don't let things or circumstances separate you two. If you love her and she loves you, fight for her."

The ferocity of her words made her sound like she spoke from firsthand experience. Was she referring to losing Will or someone else? He glanced down at the blue stone on his hand.

Placing her fingertips on the band, she twisted gently. "This ring is very special to me. Promise me that you'll take care of it."

He nodded. "Who did it belong to?"

Tears filled her eyes and she gave him a tight smile. "Some things are better left in the past."

They sat in silence for several moments before Will looked at the clock. James would come find him soon. "I'm going to have to go soon."

"I won't see you again, will I?"

Will choked back his tears. "No."

"Well, then I guess this is goodbye."

"Yeah." He laid his head down on the bed and she stroked it as the blanket under his cheek grew damp with tears.

"When you were a little boy you used to be afraid of the dark, until I let you keep that old mutt that turned up on our back doorstep. Rusty."

"I loved that dog."

"I know." He heard the smile in her voice. "But before he showed up you were plagued for months with nightmares. Do you remember?"

"Yeah, it was about water and fire and terrible storms and losing someone I loved. I was sure it was you. I was terrified you were going to die and leave me all alone."

"Yes, that's what you'd always say when you woke up so frightened you'd refuse to go back to sleep. So I'd have you lay down and I'd run my hand over the top of your head, until you drifted off. You'd hang on to consciousness, afraid to fall asleep and lose me." Her voice broke. "For three years, I've been scared to go to sleep, terrified I'd drift off forever and lose you. Now that I've found you again, I'm no longer afraid."

"Mom." Will raised his head, choking back his tears.

She cupped his face. "My baby, no matter where you are, no matter what you do, I will always love you. There's nothing you could ever do to make me not love you anymore."

Will covered her hand with his.

"If you love this woman, don't let her go, Will. Love her with everything you've got. Love is a precious gift. Don't squander it like I did."

The door pushed open and an orderly in scrubs walked in with a chart. "Mrs. Davenport, we're ready to take you down to radiology now."

His mother looked stricken.

Will leaned his forehead into hers. "It's okay. I have to go anyway."

She nodded, closing her eyes as she swallowed. "I love you, Will."

"I love you too, Mom."

The orderly wheeled her bed away and Will studied the moving cars in the parking lot, refusing to watch one more person leave him.

CHAPTER SIXTEEN

ALEX and Emma climbed into Alex's rental car and drove north of Kansas City.

"Are you going to tell me where we're going?" Emma's apprehension had soared after driving two hours. The fact that they were in spottily populated farmland didn't help her fears. After his momentary switch to smarmy Alex in her room, she didn't trust him.

With a wink, he laughed. "Not one for being patient, are you, Emma?"

"You said it was Freedom Day. What does that mean?" Her imagination ran wild with the possibilities.

"Exactly what it sounds like, Emma. God, you're paranoid."

"With good reason."

"Maybe so, but I've told you multiple times, even though I need you on my side to win this fight with Aiden, I don't want you around me now. What is so evil about either of those things? Seeing how I'm one of your least favorite people, you think you'd be glad to be rid of me."

Did he plan to hide her in the boonies? Keep her trapped with some magical force field to hide her from Raphael?

He pulled off the highway into a midsized town. Continuing through town, he pulled into a hospital parking lot and turned off the engine.

"Why are we at a hospital in Morgantown?"

He laughed. "Do you know how much fun it is watching you squirm?"

"Go to hell, Alex."

"I suspect I will someday, or our own special version of it, but hopefully not today." He opened the car door and pulled out her bag. "Let's go."

"Why do you have my bag?"

"Because you and I are parting ways here."

She had little choice but to follow him inside. Her stomach twisted. God only knew what Alex had planned.

****

Will sat in a faded vinyl-covered chair, staring out the window. He couldn't believe he actually saw his mother. Or that she apologized and said if she had to do it over, she would have chosen differently.

Or that she'd soon be gone.

He was losing everything and everyone. His mother. Emma. The baby. He sat up, grim determination squaring his shoulders. He didn't have to lose Emma. He'd figure out a way to find her and find out if this was all real.

The decision slid into place and for the first time since he lost his memory, he felt a renewed sense of purpose. He needed a plan. He didn't even know the first place to look for her, but with all of James's secrets, he might know where she was or at least have some clues. Eager to corner James, Will walked into the hall, stopping in his tracks at the sight of the man coming toward him.

His father.

Everyone had always commented how alike the two men were, and there was a time that Will had taken pride in it. His father was as tall as Will, but his dark hair had grayed. Crow's feet etched his face, as did deep frown lines. His father's eyes were cold and distant. It suddenly hit Will that his own eyes had held that same haunted look.

His father was absorbed in a phone conversation, glancing out the side window as he walked. Will froze, torn between what he wanted to do and what he should do—walk away, hopefully without being noticed. But all the destruction his father had caused ignited Will's anger. He clenched his hands at his sides, ready to confront him.

One thing stopped him. Emma. Now that he'd made the decision to find her, he couldn't let his father get in his way. Who knew what his father would do if he knew Warren was after Will? He'd probably turn him in without batting an eyelash. Will couldn't afford to be caught. Stuffing his anger, he took a deep breath and bent down to pretend to tie his shoe.

His father passed by him, his phone to his ear. "...I'll try to be there tonight. Wear that red slinky thing I like so much."

Will recognized the inflection in his father's voice. He'd used it himself more often than he wanted to admit. He suddenly wanted to vomit. His mother was days from death and his father planned to go screw his latest plaything. But Will realized he was just like him. He may have purposely taken a job his father hated, but he tried to emulate him in other ways. Isolating himself from everyone around him. Moving from one woman to the next. At least he never cheated on a wife and kids. At least he had one up on the shithead.

After his father turned the corner, Will stood and took a few deep breaths. He needed to get the hell away from everything that represented his painful past. He needed to find James.

****

Alex had brought her through the main entrance, which she saw as a positive sign, until he ducked into a stairwell and began climbing.

She walked up two steps and stopped. "Where are we going?"

He paused then turned to face her. "Emma, I promise this isn't some kind of trick or trap. If you will keep climbing these stairs,"—he pointed up—"I have a very special surprise for you."

"But—"

He held up his hand. "You will thank me for this. You have no idea how much I'm counting on that fact. But before you discover what I've given you, and before I teach you how to hide your power, you have to promise me something."

She tilted her head with narrowed eyes. "What?"

"One week from tomorrow, I'll be in Albuquerque giving a speech at the Fairmont Hotel for a political luncheon. Your name will be on the guest list. You must promise to meet me there at noon as my guest. It's a public place. You'll be safe." He shrugged with a smirk. "And *I'll* be safe. It's a neutral location. Agree?"

"How am I supposed to get to Albuquerque?"

"You're a bright girl. I'm sure you'll figure it out."

"And what if I don't like your *present?*"

His eyebrow twitched. "Then leave it behind. But you'll already know how to hide from Raphael and that's what you really wanted. My gift is a bonus."

Alex was right. Hiding from Raphael really was her primary objective here. "Okay."

He grinned, then hurried up the staircase. "Come on. We don't have much time."

She raced after him, breathless when he stopped at the door on the third floor.

His hand on the doorknob, he looked down at her. "Find your energy and imagine covering it with a blanket."

Her eyebrows rose. "Just do it. I'm not letting you out of the stairwell until you prove to me that you can do it."

"Fine." Her anger was easy to access, given her irritation. Finding her energy, she imagined shrouding it and instantly felt a change.

Alex twisted his mouth into mock respect. "Congratulations." A scowl of disapproval replaced it. "But you should have figured this out on your own."

"*What?*"

"It's an easy enough task and it's logical. No one's giving you information this week, so you're going to have to use your brain. Let your imagination figure out what you're capable of. If you wonder if something is possible, try it. Also, start working on using external sources of energy. You don't have a shot in hell of winning if you don't, and you only have five weeks to figure it out."

"Anything else?" Sarcasm dripped from her words.

"Yeah." He pulled a wad of bills out of his pocket and handed it to her. "It's not as much as it looks, but if it runs out, you're capable of getting more on your own. Figure it out."

She stuffed the money into her pocket, grateful she didn't have to ask for it, but still pissed at his attitude.

Alex looked through the small window and set her bag down in the corner. "You've got to go. Now."

What in the hell was outside the stairwell?

He swung the door open and shoved her out. "See you in a week."

The door slammed behind her and her heart raced. She nearly tripped, trying to regain her balance. Leaning a hand against the wall, she looked around to get her bearings and figure out Alex's *gift*. She stood in a nearly empty hall. A man talking on his cell phone walked past a man kneeling to tie his shoe, but the ruse was obvious. His head was bent over but tilted slightly to watch the older man pass.

Her blood pounded through her head. Was he with the Vinco Potentia? Had Alex lied and set her up? It wasn't a hard concept to swallow.

The man stood, still watching the older gentleman. Emma prepared to bolt down the opposite end of the hall when his face turned her direction. His eyes widened.

Breath caught in her throat and she forced herself to inhale as her vision blurred. *No, this isn't real.*

He took a hesitant step toward her. "*Emma?*"

She shook her head, biting her lower lip. "You're dead."

He walked several paces and stopped.

"Will?" She choked on a sob and threw herself toward him.

One of his arms wrapped around her back while his other hand held her head to his chest. "You're real."

She laughed through her tears. "And you're not dead."

****

He pulled her into the nearby stairwell then leaned her head back to look at her, overwhelmed by the emotions coursing through him. She was real and she was in his arms. "How are you here?"

"Alex. He said he was giving me a gift. I guess you're it."

"Alex Warren?" Fear trickled down his back. "Is he here now?"

"No, I got the impression this was a dump-and-run mission for him."

Alex. His back stiffened, suddenly unsure. Was she working with Alex and showed up to capture him? That didn't make any sense given the fact that Alex had freed him. "But how... I thought you were with Raphael?"

Her eyes widened. "How did you know that?"

"Jake."

Her face lit up with excitement. "Jake? You've seen Jake? Is he with you?"

"No." The disappointment that spread over her face strangled his heart. "I saw him in a dream, as weird as it seems. He told me that you were dying and wanted me to check on you."

"It was real? You really came to me in my dreams?"

"I've dreamed of you almost every night."

"I dreamed of you too." She pulled his arm loose and looked at his forearm. "But your mark's still gone. How is that possible?"

"I don't know. I don't know how to explain a lot of things."

"But how do you still know me? You lost all your memories of me."

"They're still gone."

Confusion filled her eyes. "Then how do you know me? Why would you dream of me?"

"Because all my memories of you are gone, but none of my feelings. I thought I was crazy at first. I loved an imaginary woman. I knew you were in danger, but I didn't even know who you were. But when Kramer interrogated me, I quickly realized you were real. The only remembrance I have of you was in the woods, after I lost my memory."

Tears filled her eyes as her fingertips touched his cheek. "I thought you were dead. Raphael convinced me you were dead." Her hand dropped and anger spread across her face. "He *convinced* me you were dead. He made me say you were dead while he looked into my eyes, and once I said it, I believed it, like nothing on earth could dispute the truth of it." Her hands clenched into fists. "He used mind control on me. I'm going to kill him. How did you escape?"

"James. And Alex."

Her eyes flew wide. "*James?* Is he here now?"

Her reaction told him to be careful how he answered. "Yes."

A murderous gleam crossed her face as a golden glow enveloped her. "Where is he?

His love for her was overwhelming, growing even more now that she was here with him, but he had to proceed carefully. She admitted that Alex had brought her here, which was a red flag. Just because he loved her didn't mean she was trustworthy, just as his lifelong friendship with James hadn't ensured his loyalty and trust. What he really needed was answers, and one of two sources was in front of him. He just needed to get her with James and maybe the real truth would come out. "Emma, wait. Before you stomp off and do whatever it is you're about to do, let me look at you for a minute."

"James betrayed us."

His throat tightened and he fought to take a breath. "I suspected." He cupped the side of her head, staring into her deep brown eyes. "You've been with Raphael?"

Fear and anger filled her eyes. "Yes."

He noticed the fading bruise on her cheek. "He hurt you." His stomach tightened with a fierce need to protect her, overriding his mistrust. Maybe James was right. Maybe she'd used some kind of manipulative spell on him.

She gave him a tight smile. "It's over now. I'm here with you."

He couldn't get over the fact that her appearance was too convenient. He needed answers fast. He stared into her eyes, looking for signs of duplicity, finding only love. His heart warred with his head. Will lowered his mouth to hers, giving in to the urge he'd felt since the moment he saw her in the hall. Her lips were soft and eager and her arms reached around his neck, pulling him closer.

"Emma," he murmured. The rightness of being with her flooded him. A sense of home and belonging. Was this what it was like before he'd lost his memory?

He pulled her against his chest, needing to feel closer to her, to reassure himself she was really here. This wasn't a dream. But then again, maybe it was. What if it was an illusion she had manufactured?

Will stepped back to clear his head. "Let's go find James."

"Yes." Her face hardened. "We need to find James."

The confrontation was bound to be ugly. "Wait here. I'm going to go get him, then we'll figure out what to do."

She nodded. "Okay."

He opened the stairwell door, surprised by his reluctance to leave her. He turned back. "Promise me that you'll wait for me?"

She bit her lip and her eyes glistened. "I'd wait forever for you, Will."

He walked into the hall, even more confused.

Will entered the waiting room and spotted James in the corner. He looked up, his eyes widening as his hand lowered his cell from his ear. Trying to hide his growing anger, Will gave him a tight smile. "Who are you talking to?"

"A client. He was scheduled for a fishing tour the next couple of days, but I called to cancel." James stood. "How'd it go?"

Will shrugged. "As well as could be expected. Let's get out of here."

"Why don't we go downstairs and get something to eat and talk about it?"

"In a hospital cafeteria? I'll pass."

"We've been traveling for days. Let's just catch our breath and you can tell me what your mom said."

Why was he stalling? If he'd been in contact with Alex and knew Emma was here, he might have told the Vinco Potentia. He felt a new sense of urgency. "I hate hospitals."

"Since when?"

Goddamn him. "Since I passed that prick posing as my father talking to his latest girlfriend on the phone. I'm out of here." He spun around. "If you want to stay here, suit yourself." Will knew he'd follow. James couldn't afford to lose him, although it wasn't for the reasons Will had hoped.

"Wait up," James grumbled as he fell in step. "What's your hurry?"

"I told you. I saw my dad in the hall and I don't want to risk running into him." Will strode down the hall and stopped in front of the stairwell door, preparing himself for the confrontation about to occur. He pushed James in and shut the door behind them.

Emma stood in the corner, glaring at James.

"Emma?" James squeaked, backing into Will. He jerked his head around. "You knew she was here?"

"I just found her."

James seemed to gather courage from Will's brisk tone. "So what do you plan to do with her?"

"Excuse me?" She took a step forward, hands clenched at her sides. "*Do with me?*"

"I plan to get answers from the both of you. And I'll do whatever I have to do to get them." Will pulled out his gun, then picked Emma's bag up and slung it over his shoulder. "Start moving downstairs. We need a private place to talk."

CHAPTER SEVENTEEN

JAMES'S mouth dropped. "What the fuck, Will?"

"Funny, I was getting ready to ask you the same thing. Start moving."

Emma took the lead, fear mingling with her betrayal and disappointment, but could she expect any other reaction? He claimed he still loved her, yet the soldier in him would be wary of the missing memories.

"Emma," James called behind her. "I have to say you're the last person I expected to see lurking in the shadows."

"Given more time to prepare, James, I would have been doing more than lurking."

"Shut up the both of you. You'll have plenty of time to talk."

James grumbled until they reached the basement level.

"Emma, why don't you open the door and lead the way," Will said in a gruff tone.

Her stomach knotted as she moved down the hall, James and Will following. Would Will believe her over James? What would she do if he didn't?

Will stopped in front of a door marked *Storage*. "Let's try this room." The door opened and he gestured inside. "Ladies first."

She entered the darkness, slowing her steps to let her eyes adjust. The fluorescent lights overhead flickered on, their glow dim but enough for Emma to see the room was littered with hospital equipment.

"Head over to those chairs in the back."

What would she do if Will didn't like her answers and decided to kill her? Would he do that?

Emma stopped in front of a row of aged waiting-room chairs.

"Both of you sit down and we'll begin."

Sitting in the chair, she looked into the steely eyed glare of a stranger. She suddenly remembered the day in the woods in Colorado when Will had told her that he'd been trained to extract information from people. How far was he willing to go?

"Over twenty years of friendship and it comes to this," James hissed, his hands gripping the arms of the chair.

Will leaned his hip into a desk, his gun resting on his leg. "You'll get your chance, but we'll start with Emma first." He turned to her, his gaze so sharp it could pin her to the wall. "When did we first meet?"

Her stomach knotted. "In Texas. You were sent to take me to South Dakota. You climbed into my car when Jake and I were escaping from the Vinco Potentia."

"Then what happened?"

"Then we tried to stay a step ahead of them while you took me to South Dakota."

"And you willingly went?"

"Of course not. Do you really think you told me what your purpose was? You told me you had a computer consulting job in South Dakota and you encouraged me to go with you, to put more distance between us and the men after us."

"When did I get my mark?"

"Jake gave it to you in Colorado, although you weren't thrilled about it."

"Is that when I fell in love with you?"

The way he asked the question, so cold and callous, caught her breath in her chest. She forced herself to exhale. "No." Her voice softened. "You always said you fell in love with me the night before, the night we slept in the back of your truck in the cornfield."

He paused, clenching his jaw, then shifted his weight. "So I took you to South Dakota anyway? Even though I loved you? I just handed you over?"

"Yes." She shook her head. "No. You took me there only because I was shot in Colorado and the wound got infected. You said the Cavallo would find me if you took me to the hospital. You figured if the Vinco Potentia was willing to pay you so much to get me there alive, they'd be able to protect me."

"I can't imagine they patched you up and let you go."

"They didn't. You helped me escape."

"So then what did we do?"

"You took care of me the first week and half while trying to track down Jake."

"In Arizona?"

"Yes, the Cavallo had him. Then Alex."

He leaned his head back, stretching out his legs. "Ah, your good friend Alex Warren."

She stuffed her irritation. "Alex Warren is no friend of mine. Alex Warren raped me six years ago and impregnated me with Jake. Then when you took me to the Vinco Potentia, his father decided to take you to Washington, DC and leave me in Alex Warren's *care*. I'm more than a bit terrified to know what that would have entailed."

The certainty in Will's eyes wavered. "But Alex brought you here. What were you doing with him?"

"He was protecting his asset. He was worried Raphael would kill me before he got to benefit from my power."

Will raised an eyebrow.

"Have no doubt that Raphael and Alex put their own self-interests over anyone else's. Mine included. There's more to this than the Vinco Potentia and the Cavallo. This goes back years and years. Millenniums."

"What does that mean?"

"Alex is no mere human."

He swallowed then fingered his gun. "I deduced that from what he did at the compound. What is he?"

"He's the element air."

James laughed. "He's *air*? Let me guess, you make explosions so you're fire?"

She scowled. "No, I'm not fire. I'm the daughter of fire. Aiden Walker is my father."

"So you're not human?" Will asked.

"I guess I'm technically half human."

"And you never told me this before?"

"I didn't know. Not until that night in the woods when you lost your memory. I was supposed to choose Alex or Raphael."

"And Raphael is...?"

"Earth."

"So which one did you choose?"

"Neither. I chose you."

"Because I was your protector?"

"No. Because I loved you."

James leaned forward. "Are you really going to believe this bullshit, Will?"

Will cocked an eyebrow. "Which part?"

"Any of it!"

"Can you contradict any of it?"

"They're elements?"

"Have you got a better explanation?"

"No." James rubbed his chin. "So why am I being interrogated?"

"Because I'm not an idiot. I could see your stories weren't adding up."

His faced paled. "What are you talking about?"

"Let's start with Montana when you were supposedly captured. You said Kramer showed up while you were working on your laptop, but it was in your bag under the cabin. How did it get there?"

"Will..."

"He set it all up." Emma glared. "He sent you to White Horse to look for Jake so he could hand me over to Kramer."

James shifted his weight. "It wasn't personal, Emma."

She shook her head with a snide laugh. "Gee, it felt a little personal when you drugged me. And when Kramer's men carried me out and dumped me in a van. It sure felt

personal when I got the shit beat out of me in the woods."
She clenched her fists. "Don't you dare tell me it wasn't
personal."

Guilt filled his eyes before defiance replaced it. "I
meant it wasn't because I hated you, although I admit I
never cared for you. I did it to save Will."

She swallowed the lump in her throat. "Yeah, well,
look where that got him."

James rubbed his forehead, then returned his gaze to
Will. "Look, Kramer swore he'd leave you alone. His men
came to me a full week before you two showed up. They
convinced me that Emma was using you and that your life
was in danger if I didn't help them capture her."

"You knew the minute I showed up at your door."
Emma's eyes widened as she put the pieces together. "The
lodge. You found out where I was staying after I ran off
from your place, and Kramer's men came to get me."

"Yeah, only somehow you got away."

Her stomach dropped to her feet. "You agreed to
come with us after that so you could keep an eye on me
and figure out when to try to turn me over again." Her
instinct had been right all along.

"Will." James's eyes pleaded with him to understand.
"You were in seriously deep shit. Kramer was pissed that
Emma got away and planned to escalate his plan. He told
me that his deal to not hurt you was null and void unless I
handed Emma over. I knew if I was with you two, I could
try to manipulate things to keep you from getting hurt. I
planned to turn her over at the compound when we broke
in to steal the book, but I realized I'd never get her away

from you. You were so goddamned sure you loved her that I knew you'd do something stupid to save her. The only way to make sure you were safe was to separate the two of you."

Emma clutched her stomach, nauseated. "Which is why you sent Will into White Horse?"

"Kramer warned me about your mind-control trick, and after the forest fire incident neither one of us knew what else you could do, so I drugged you. It seemed easier that way. I also knew from Will that you got your power from your pendant, so I took it off after you fell asleep."

"I hope Kramer paid you enough money to make it worth your time and trouble."

Rubbing his forehead again, James sighed. "That wasn't the point."

The hair on her arms prickled. He presented it all so matter-of-factly, as though he wasn't talking about her. Like he was discussing the weather. "And Kramer told you I was pregnant? That's how you knew?"

"Yeah." He swung his gaze to Will. "Although I didn't understand why you never told me, Will."

She shook her head. Will never told him because he knew James wouldn't understand.

James started to get up, but Will raised his gun higher. "Will, listen to me. We were looking for a way to get Kramer off our backs, and this is it." He pointed to Emma. "If we turn her over, we can buy our freedom."

"You know, James," Will's voice softened. "Everything you've said makes sense."

The hair on Emma's neck stood on end. After everything they'd been through, would Will really give her to the Vinco Potentia? The old Will wouldn't, but the new Will didn't know her at all, and turning her over had been his original purpose.

James's shoulders relaxed. "See, I knew if you heard me out—"

"But there's one more thing." He paused. "Why, James?" Will's voice twisted in pain. "If you knew I loved her, why did you do it?"

James looked up, his eyes pleading. "Because you didn't really love her. She branded you with a mark that compelled you to protect her—and then add your savior complex, and you *thought* you loved her. I could have let it run its course, because we both know you would have figured it out sooner or later, but you didn't have the luxury of time. Powerful people would stop at nothing to get her, Will. And you would have sooner died than let them take her. As your best friend, it was my job to protect you."

"Wasn't that for me to decide?"

"No." James shook his head, his mouth pressed into a thin line. "You were blind to her and the threat she presented. Don't you see? There's no way out of this, Will. There's no way to save her. They will hunt her down until one or both of you is dead."

"After they took her..." Will's voice hardened. "You just let them take me?"

"No! I swear to you, Will. I had no idea that Kramer was going to take you." James leaned back. "I spent two days trying to track you down. Kramer told me they'd leave you alone if I turned Emma over. But you didn't answer your cell phone and I retraced our steps. I decided that Kramer must have taken you after all and went to the compound."

"What? You just showed up and they let you in?"

"Not exactly. I showed up and Kramer said if I could get information about Emma from you that he'd let us both go."

"And you believed that?"

"No," James growled. "I told you, I had insurance."

"Like the book?"

James pursed his lips and bobbed his head. "That was one."

"You have the book?" Emma asked. "With you?"

Lifting an eyebrow, James grinned, refusing to answer.

"The book is in the car." Will's words were clipped. "We'll discuss it later. What else did you have, James?"

James glanced from Will to Emma and back. "I dug up info on all the key members of the group."

"Info. You mean blackmail material?"

"Blackmail's such an ugly word."

Will snorted. "Whatever. So how did we get out of the compound?"

"When you were passed out—"

"Drugged."

"I didn't know they were going to do that. I swear." James wiped a thin sheen of sweat off of his forehead. "Alex showed up and told me to be ready, that he'd help get us out, but he said I'd owe him. He said I had to keep him updated where you were. Getting you out seemed more important at the time. But that's why I wanted to find Jake. I figured if I gave him something he wanted, he'd back off of you. Still, when I agreed, I had no idea what he was capable of."

"You told him we were coming here. To the hospital."

"I had to."

"And what did you think my reaction would be when I found out what you'd done?"

James lifted his chin in defiance. "I never thought you would. I guess Alex had other ideas. The question is, what do you plan to do now that you know?"

Will released a short laugh. "That's an easy choice, James."

Hate hardened James's face. "Really? You're still choosing her over me? You don't even remember her, Will."

"I know she's not shoving her own agenda down my throat."

"Are you sure about that? She's lying to you about what happened before you brought her to me. She made you want to protect her and tricked you into thinking you loved her. I know I've screwed up, but I always had your best interest in mind. How can you be sure she does?" James narrowed his eyes and leaned forward. "How do you know she and Alex didn't set this up together?"

Will ran his shaking hand over his mouth, looking like he wanted to throw up. "I've heard enough. We need to get going."

"*We?*" James asked.

"Yes. All three of us. I have a feeling you haven't told me everything, James. And I definitely want more information from Emma."

"You're bringing *her*?"

Will stood. "She has answers to what the hell happened to me the last month and a half."

James shook his head. "No. No way. How can you trust what she has to say? You choose right here and right now. Emma or me."

"Save your breath, Buckner. Just hand over the keys."

James pulled the key ring from his jeans pocket and tossed it toward Will. "So you're just going to leave me here?"

"Oh hell, no. You're not getting off that easy. You both are a package deal."

"The fuck I am."

Will leaned forward. "Think of it this way. If I find out she's lying, I'll let you have first shot at getting even."

Emma's eyes widened as Will turned his gaze to her.

"You don't have anything to be worried about, do you, Emma?"

This was a set-up for disaster, yet she had little choice in the matter. "No."

"Then let's go."

CHAPTER EIGHTEEN

THEY walked through the hallway in the rehab building. Will no longer needed his gun as a threat. James seemed more sure of himself and Emma hadn't said much.

Grilling her had been harder than he expected. His love for her overshadowed his caution and that scared him. Feelings only made people do stupid things. Will couldn't afford stupid.

Will stopped to the side of the entrance to the parking garage.

Two suspicious men stood on the curb outside the door. They loitered without talking, one smoking a cigarette despite the No Smoking sign behind him. The other guy cast a sideways glance at an elderly woman entering the building, then looked away with a sneer. It was obvious they were looking for someone.

"That's what I was worried about." Will groaned, moving away from the door. "They've been alerted somehow and are now patrolling the entrance."

James glanced outside. "So what do you want to do?"

"They know we're here. I say we go out, guns blazing."

"Are you sure you want to do that?"

Will's mouth lifted into a grin, but his eyes held a wicked gleam. "Why the hell not?" He looked outside again. "We'll wait until there aren't any patients in the garage. James, you take out the guy on the right and I'll take out the guy on the left."

"What about Emma?"

Will held her gaze. "Emma, you stay behind me and keep down."

She nodded, trust in her eyes. "Okay."

Going out there unarmed was a risky move, and in her position he would have asked questions. But she agreed, which implied that she trusted his decisions and trusted him. What had they already been through together?

They waited several minutes until the lot was clear, then Will nodded to James.

His stomach balled in apprehension, his instinct telling him something was wrong. James had already headed outside and Will couldn't leave him uncovered. He glanced at Emma as he ran out the door. "Stay inside!"

Will hated last-minute changes, but something was off and he couldn't have her run out behind him defenseless.

James raised his weapon as the two men turned to him, but gunshots came from behind the men—from two more gunmen hiding behind a sedan. James dived between two compact cars, pointing his weapon over the trunk. Will got in several shots while taking cover behind a trash bin.

The two men on the curb were down and Will spotted only one of the men behind the sedan. This could take all day and Will didn't have all day. Glancing at James, he motioned that he planned to rush the attacker.

James nodded.

As he prepared to run toward it, the car exploded, throwing Will on his ass.

Emma stood in the doorway, surrounded by a golden glow.

Jumping to his feet, Will's mouth dropped. "What did you do?"

Her face was emotionless. "I did what I had to do."

Will ran over to James and found him seated, leaning against the car. Blood drenched the lower right portion of his T-shirt. Will knelt next to him. "Shit."

Emma approached from behind and gasped.

Will's heart nearly stopped, but he moved into action. "We have to get him out of here. He's going to bleed out."

James grabbed Will's arm. "You can't take me into the hospital. They'll find us there."

Running his hand over his mouth, Will sat back on his heels. "Goddamnit!"

Emma took a step forward then hesitated. "I can help."

Will stood and spun to face her. "How?"

She bit her lip, staring at James's shirt. "I can heal him." She looked up, worry and fear flashing in her eyes.

James's eyes widened in horror. "No fucking way! She won't heal me! She'll kill me!"

Will grabbed her arm and searched her face. "Can you really do that?"

She nodded. "But we'll have to hurry."

Screeching tires echoed through the garage. James looked up at Will, his mouth pinched. "Reinforcements are on the way, Will. Get out of here."

"Like hell I'm leaving you here." He grabbed James's gun. "Do it, Emma. Do whatever you need to do and I'll cover you."

She squatted next to James. "I promise I won't kill you, James."

"Why the hell not after what I've done to you?"

She put one hand on his arm and her other hand hovered over his abdomen. "Because if you think I'd kill you out of spite, it shows you don't know the first thing about me. I just killed that man behind the car to save you and Will, and while I did it for a good reason, it still eats me alive. Now shut up and let me fix you."

A golden glow surrounded her and she placed her hand on James's abdomen. "Heal him." An electrical zap jumped from Emma to James. He jerked as she slumped against the car, but Will didn't have time to check on either one of them. An SUV pulled up. The windows lowered and gun tips appeared.

"James! Get behind the back of the car!" Will glanced back. James had gotten to his feet while Emma squatted, leaning against the side.

"I need my gun." James grabbed it out of Will's waistband.

"She really healed you?"

"So it would seem."

"Is she okay?"

"I have no idea."

Will shook his head in disgust. The gunmen in the SUV hadn't taken a shot yet. "Why aren't they shooting?"

"My guess is that they know Emma's here and they don't want to kill her."

Will turned to James with a scowl. "Did you have anything to do with this?"

James snorted. "Don't be a fucking idiot." Determination hardened his face. "But we can use it to our advantage."

Will recoiled. "After she just saved your ass?"

"I never asked her to do that."

"We are *not* handing her over."

"Fine, I'll do it myself."

"The hell you will."

Will dropped to Emma's side and her eyes fluttered open. "Touch me."

"What?"

"Just touch my hand."

Will took her hand, curling his fingers around her palm. The ring on his finger turned icy cold and he sucked in a breath in surprise.

She smiled at him. "Thank you."

Glancing up at James, Will knew he'd fight his best friend to the death before he turned her over. He might not remember her, but it turned out that she was a hell of a better person than James could ever be.

She seemed to regain her energy and sat up straighter. "Are you going to hand me over?"

His chest tightened. "No."

Relief flickered through her eyes. "I can take out the SUV."

"Are you sure? After what you just did for James?"

"Turns out healing someone takes a lot more energy than blowing things up. Do you have another plan?"

"No. But if you blow it up, it will block our only way out of here." Their Toyota was five spaces down and Will had the keys. Will couldn't believe he was making this decision, yet it felt right. "Emma, let's go." He grabbed her wrist and pulled her to the back of the car.

"Where the hell do you think you're going, Will?" James shouted.

Will ignored him, moving behind the compact car next to him.

"Will!"

"Go to hell, Buckner."

****

She followed his lead, scrambling behind the cars until he stopped at an older Toyota.

"You should let me drive," she said. "I'm good and you always had me drive."

"Maybe so, but I think you'll be handier using your power. It will be easier for you to do that if I'm driving. Now get in."

She climbed in the passenger seat while Will ran around to the other side and tossed her bag in the back.

"This is probably going to get ugly."

She tried to swallow the lump of fear in her throat. "Doesn't it always?"

Gunshots echoed in the garage. James was firing on the SUV.

Her chest tightened with fear. "What's he doing?"

Will's face hardened. "He's distracting them and helping us get away."

He swerved the car out of the space and tore down the row, skidding around the corner and past the SUV. "My shotgun's in the bag in the back. Can you get it out?"

"Yeah." She leaned between the seats, her fingers shaking as she unzipped Will's bag. *Calm your ass down, Emma.* Freaking out would only make her ineffective. She searched blindly through the contents, her fingers brushing cold metal. She pulled the weapon out of the bag. "Is it loaded?"

"Yes, but we'll need more ammo. It's in there too."

She found several boxes and pulled them all to the top of the bag. She turned around to the front in time to see the six men pointing guns at them.

"Get down!" Will's hand shoved her head between her legs before bullets pierced the windshield, sending glass raining on her head. The sides and back windows shattered and the car fishtailed. She lifted her gaze to Will. His hands gripped the steering wheel and a gash over his eyebrow dripped blood down the side of his face.

"You're hurt!"

He shook his head. "I'm fine. It's just a cut from the flying glass." Looking in the rearview mirror, his face hardened. "They're coming after us already. I hoped to have more of a head start."

Emma looked out the now open back window. Three cars were in pursuit. "Do you think James set you up?"

He shook his head again. "No. They probably knew my mom was here and waited it out, expecting me to visit her."

"She works here?"

"No. She's a patient." His terse tone told her that now wasn't the time to discuss it.

"Do you have a plan?"

"Other than try to outrun them in this death trap on wheels, which seems highly unlikely? No."

"Then we wing it. We're good at winging it." She wished she felt as confident as she sounded, but she had to believe they'd get out of this. She hadn't just found him for it to end.

Will pulled out of the hospital parking lot onto a four-lane road, the other cars gaining on them. "About a mile ahead, there's an abandoned industrial park full of alleys between the buildings. We might be able to lose them there."

One of the cars pulled up behind them. Emma raised the shotgun and aimed for the windshield, squeezing the trigger. The sedan made a sharp jerk and then righted itself.

"Can you do something to it with your power?" Will asked, swerving between two trucks in front of them.

"I don't know." It wasn't like when they'd escaped in the plane and she had to worry about exploding the gas tanks in the wings. But she hated to take a chance sending her power through the car. "I need to climb into the back."

"No!" He sounded panicked as he grabbed her arm. "If you climb over, they're going to shoot you."

"Then I guess I'm stuck with a gun unless I try something out the side window."

"I can slow down and let them pull up beside us."

Her heart tripped. It was risky but would probably work. "Okay, let's try it."

Will found a gap and moved to the left lane. The car slowed and the sedan pulled behind and rammed the back bumper.

Emma braced herself with her hand on the dashboard and mumbled sarcastically. "I forgot how fun this was," she grumbled.

The sedan edged closer. Will jerked the wheel to try to hide the ruse.

Emma focused on her anger as gunshots hit the side of their Toyota. She aimed for the front of the sedan and released her energy. Smoke poured out of the hood and the car swung to the side of the road, crashing into a speed limit sign.

"One down," she said. But two were left.

The industrial park came into view and Will turned into the first opening in the parking lot, driving at an angle toward the buildings. He drove into a gap between the buildings, turned right, and shot down a narrow alley. Both cars pulled in behind them.

Will pulled into the other side of the lane, barely missing a dumpster as he maneuvered around it. The car pitched as it flew through a pothole.

An opening between two warehouses appeared ahead and Will turned left, skidding around the corner. Pulling out into a parking lot, he sped through the lot, turning onto a narrow road between two more buildings and back into the alley. They were now headed in the opposite direction. One of the cars pulled in behind him. He swerved onto a cut-through to the opposite parking lot again, backtracking to the beginning.

Sirens sounded in the distance and Emma's stomach knotted. "Pull into that road between the buildings and stop the car."

"*What?*"

"Will, the police are on their way. We can't outrun the police. Stop the car."

"Emma, there's no fucking way—"

The cars turned into the alley from opposite ends, both headed their direction. "Listen to me. I can do this. Trust me."

He turned onto the one-lane road and screeched the car to a halt. "What the hell are you planning to do?"

"I'm saving our asses." She opened the door and climbed out of the car.

Will followed with his shotgun.

"Will, you're going to get yourself killed. Get back in the car."

"I'm not leaving you out here."

Emma shook her head in frustration, letting her anger at Will grow so that it overshadowed her fear. "Then get behind the dumpster over there and be my backup."

"But—"

"They can't hurt me, Will, but they can hurt you. Please, go over there."

He relented and aimed his gun toward the closest car. "If you can, don't destroy both cars. We need a replacement."

Emma nodded and moved to the middle of the alley, surrounded by her golden glow.

****

What the hell was she doing and more importantly, what the hell was he doing letting her stand out there?

The glow around her thickened and she raised her hands, her face expressionless.

Will took a shot at the sedan's tire, but it was still too far away to be effective.

Two golden orbs flew from her outstretched palms to the closest approaching sedan, which showed no signs of slowing down. The vehicle exploded, shaking the dumpster next to him and shooting flames into the sky. The car continued toward her, now as a fast-moving fireball. She jumped toward the dumpster as it flew past, nearing the oncoming sedan.

Will ran to a chained sliding door on the warehouse next to them and gave it a jerk. He looked up at Emma. "Can you open it?"

She nodded and stared at the lock, sending a small burst of energy toward it. The padlock flew to the ground.

Will pulled the chain away from the door and shoved the rusted door open enough for them to slide through.

Her eyes flew open and she dragged her feet as he pushed her toward the opening. "You said you had the book. Is it in the car?"

Wrapping his fingers around her arm he pulled her harder. "Forget the book."

"No! Our lives might depend on that book! I have to get it."

His grip tightened as she fought against him.

"Will!"

"I'm not letting you get shot over a fucking book. Now get your ass in there."

A glow surrounded her again as her face contorted from her effort. Her skin singed his fingers and he released his hold. Emma ran into the alley as Will cursed under his breath, raising his gun to shoot anything that looked like a threat.

The burning car had stopped in the middle of the narrow road. The other sedan was nowhere in sight, which meant they were circling around. "Emma! Hurry!"

She opened the back door and leaned inside as the other car pulled in front of the Toyota. The sedan's doors opened before it stopped.

"Emma!"

Her head popped up as the men spilled out with guns. She lowered beneath the seat backs and began tugging a bag out of the car.

Groaning, he ran behind the Toyota before the first shots rang out.

The open back door was her shield as she pulled out two bags and backed up behind the car.

"Emma, just blow up their car!"

"No, we need it. I can blow up our car, but we have to get our stuff out."

Will reached for both bags as two more cars pulled up. "Shit." His heart plummeted. "Now we have two more options. Blow it up!"

Emma looked through the back window, closing her eyes with a heavy sigh as she slid down. She opened them, determination hardening her jaw, and she flashed him a tight smile. "Piece of cake. But Will..." She looked out the window again. "I'm still learning things and I don't have total control yet."

His singed fingers were proof of that.

"I used my power several times and I'm weak. I want you to be aware that I might pass out."

He found the box of shotgun shells on top of the contents of his bag and reloaded his gun. "Then we'll do this the old-fashioned way. With guns."

"But the police—"

"We'll deal with one thing at a time." Balancing on the balls of his feet, he looked through the window again. "You stay behind this car and don't move."

"What are you going to do?"

"Eliminate the threat."

****

Will moved to the passenger side and planted himself behind the open back door.

Well, this is bullshit. Did he really expect her to sit here? Sure, she'd been helpless back in the woods of Colorado, but she'd come a long way since then. Not that he remembered any of it. *Damn it.* But he'd seen what she could do, so that wasn't it. She never should have told him about passing out, yet she wanted to warn him in case it happened.

Nevertheless, she was torn. She trusted Will's judgment. Usually. But he'd been overprotective in the past.

He was going to be pissed.

The car was less than twenty feet away, which was probably too close. She had to make the explosion powerful enough to kill the men around it yet not ignite the Toyota. Yet.

A heaviness filled her bones as she ignited her anger. She was tired. She'd used her power multiple times and hadn't eaten anything. And although she felt stronger, she was sure there were still some residual effects from her contact with Raphael. She needed to be careful. If she passed out, she not only put herself in danger, but imperiled Will as well. Will, who'd move instantly to her side to protect her.

She rose up to peer through the window. Four gunmen hid behind the open doors of the car in front of them. Pushing her energy through the Toyota seemed like a bad idea. She wasn't sure she was strong enough to manage that trick in addition to making a fire. Closing her eyes, she concentrated on the car, imagined it exploding. A peace filled her as she extended her hand, and aimed for the engine. As if firing a gun, she released her energy in a quick burst.

The car erupted, violently shaking the Toyota.

Drained, she sank to the ground, her back to the bumper.

Will's voice boomed in her ear, faint and far away. "Goddamn it, Emma!"

She smiled, but it seemed slow in response. "You're welcome."

He looped his bag over his shoulder and wrapped an arm around her waist, hauling her up. "Come on. We'll move into the warehouse while they're regrouping." Dragging her to the opening, he shielded her body as he held out his gun. They slipped into the darkness of the building moments before shots rang out in the distance.

CHAPTER NINETEEN

SHE was conscious, but something wasn't right. It was as though she'd been drugged. Will was pissed that she'd gone against his orders, yet he knew why she'd done it and he had to admit that it had bought them several precious seconds to hide.

But if anything happened to her...

Pushing the thought away, he concentrated on finding a place to hide as his eyes adjusted to the darkness. Endless rows of shelves filled with sunken cardboard boxes lined the space. It was a perfect place to hide and pick off his pursuers one by one, but his priority at the moment was hiding Emma.

She seemed to regain her strength, putting more weight on her legs while he pulled her down an aisle.

"I thought I told you to sit still," he whispered in her ear.

"And let you have all the fun?"

"Now I'm stuck dragging your ass around."

"And your reward is that you can do other things with it later."

They were about to fight for their lives and she teased him. She'd defended him multiple times, even saved James's ungrateful ass. He didn't think it was possible, but he loved her even more.

A four-foot concrete wall jutted out, parallel to a door in the back corner. He couldn't ask for a more perfect hiding place. He set the bag down in the corner and lowered her to the floor. "Emma, are you okay? Really?"

"Yeah, I just need to eat something. Besides, I feel better already." In spite of her words, she blinked, trying to focus on him. "This is going to sound crazy, but could you do something for me?"

"What?" He would have promised her anything, but after her stunt, he was afraid of what she'd ask for.

"Would you kiss me? I know it sounds desperate and needy at a time like this, but it's an experiment."

He knelt on the floor in front of her, his ears straining for sounds that the warehouse had been breached. Satisfied they were safe for the moment, he leaned forward and caressed her neck, his mouth hovering over hers. "An experiment?"

"I told you it sounded desperate and needy." Her head lifted so her lips lightly touched his.

His hand slid up to cup her head as he kissed her, barely touching her mouth.

She moaned, igniting an unexpected wave of need in his gut. His arm reached around her back, crushing her chest to his as her lips demanded more.

God, now was *not* the time for this, but his body responded to her with an intensity that caught him off guard. He felt electrified and the ring on his finger grew cold on his skin.

What the hell?

The screech of metal echoed throughout the building. They were here.

Emma stiffened as she pulled away. "Will, please be careful. I can't lose you."

The need to protect her was overwhelming. Was this what it had been like before? The thought of something happening to her nearly paralyzed him. "Emma, I thought I was insane. I didn't even know you, yet you were in here." He pressed her hand to his chest. "Most of my life, a huge chunk of me was missing and somehow, I know you fill it. I just found you and I can't lose you, either. I don't want to live like that again." His mouth brushed her cheek and he whispered into her ear. "Stay here. I mean it this time. I don't want to worry about you while I'm out there."

"I'm better. It worked."

He had no idea what she meant and he didn't have time to find out. Instead, he pressed his pistol into her hand. "Shoot anything that comes around that corner. Do not use your power again."

"What are you going to do?"

"Lure them away from you."

****

She shook her head, terrified to let him out of her sight. "No. We stick together. We did this once before. I got shot and you beat yourself up about it for weeks." So she neglected to tell him that he stood next to her when it happened.

His eyes looked haunted in the dim light filtering through the cracks in the roof.

"If you were here alone, what would you do?"

He exhaled twice before he answered, his tone gruff. "I'd climb up on a shelf and pick them off one by one, but that isn't an option."

"Then we stay."

Shaking his head, he took the weapon out of her hand and examined the clip before handing it back. "Use your gun. Not your powers."

They didn't have time for this argument. "I'll save it as a last resort."

Scowling, he held his finger to his lips and pointed out into the warehouse. She nodded.

A rustle came from the middle of the room. Will held up the shotgun, staring down the sight while Emma crouched behind the wall.

He leaned down to her ear. "I know you don't like this, but there's too many of them and they're too spread out. My first shot and they'll rush us. I have to move around."

She choked on fear as it trickled down her throat. Anything could happen to him out there.

"Emma, I trusted you. Now I'm asking you to trust me." His eyes pleaded with her to understand.

The corners of her mouth lifted slightly. "Be careful."

He nodded and reached into his bag, pulling out a knife before he disappeared around the corner.

She scooted back into the corner, her heart slamming against her rib cage. If only she knew how many men he was facing. Not that it mattered. She was stuck behind the wall and wouldn't know the difference anyway.

The room was filled with an eerie silence that lasted several minutes. With each passing second, her tension grew. Other than an occasional rustle or muffled grunt, there was nothing. She knew what Will was doing with the knife, but the thought turned her stomach.

After several minutes she heard the first gunshot, close to her hiding spot. Her finger curled around the trigger. It amazed her that in such a short time, using her power felt more reliable than protecting herself with a gun. But Will was right. She was still too weak. Will's kiss had given her energy, confirming that he hadn't lost that ability, despite the fact that he no longer had his mark.

A man appeared in the opening, a gun pointed at her. She reacted on instinct, sending a small blast of energy at him. The gunman screamed as his shirt caught fire, panic in his eyes. He beat at his shirt, then he jerked, his limbs twisted at odd angles. He fell to the ground, silent and unmoving, while the flames licked his clothing.

She froze. Only a handful of men were capable of doing that to someone. Emma swung the tip of her gun blindly as her heart raced.

Raphael stepped over the body, disappointment contorting his mouth. "You're not going to actually shoot me, are you?"

Her panic ignited. "How did you find me?"

"It wasn't that difficult after you let your guard down. Imagine my surprise when I returned home last night to find you gone. Even more curious was the fact that I couldn't find any traces of your power. So I tracked Alex, thinking he might have convinced you to go with him. You let your guard down about twenty minutes ago and I easily found you. I must say, I saw your handiwork outside. You've been a busy girl."

She stood, thrusting the gun at him. "Leave me alone, Raphael."

"Emma, you know I can't do that. I want you to know that I don't blame you. I haven't been as understanding as I should have been and I'm sure Alex showed up offering you the moon. How could you resist? So we'll just go back home now and forget this ever happened."

She shook her head. "No. I'm not going anywhere with you."

He tilted his head, forcing a patient look that made him look annoyed instead. "Emma, you need to train, and while I didn't find what I was looking for yesterday, I did come up with some ideas to try."

"No, Raphael. I'm not going. I'm done. Now get the fuck out of my way."

"You won't shoot me, Emmanuella."

"The hell I won't."

He took a step toward her, his mouth lifting into a patronizing smile.

She lowered the gun and pointed at his foot, squeezing the trigger.

He jumped and released a growl. "What the hell, Emma?"

She pointed the gun at his chest. "I'll shoot you again if I have to."

He lunged, grabbing her arm. She pulled the trigger, but missed him. The draw to him seeped through her skin and her head fought for control.

"Let her go, Raphael," Will's voice called out.

Raphael laughed, but tensed. "Well, if it isn't Lazarus himself, back from the dead."

Will appeared on the other side of the concrete wall. "Sorry to disappoint."

"Not to worry. Nothing that can't be easily taken care of. Especially since I've confirmed I don't feel anything from you."

Confusion mingled with her fuzziness. Was he talking about Will's mark?

Raphael's hand rose, his palm facing Will. A gunshot echoed and his grip on Emma's arm dropped. He jerked and released an inhuman howl as he lifted his hand to his right shoulder.

Her head still fuzzy, she stumbled several steps away.

Will moved around the end of the wall toward her. "Are you okay?"

She nodded, her senses returning. She picked up Will's bag and walked around Raphael, who leaned against the back wall, cursing in a language she didn't understand.

Raphael dropped his hand from his shoulder, exposing a gaping hole in his blood-soaked shirt.

Will growled. "Lift that hand any higher and I'll shoot it off."

"You know you're not really getting out of here, don't you?" Raphael sneered. "I'll never let you go, Emmanuella."

Will's eyebrows rose. "Funny, last I checked we lived in a country where free choice is everyone's God-given right."

"You're an idiot, Will Davenport, and if Aiden doesn't finish you off, I'll take care of it myself."

"Well, everyone needs something to look forward to, but I suspect there's a long list of people ahead of you waiting for that privilege."

Emma stood next to Will, thankful Raphael hadn't figured out she had the book on her. But why hadn't Raphael retaliated against Will yet? And how could he be standing while he hemorrhaged from the gunshot blast to his chest? "Will, let's go." But that's probably what Raphael wanted and she was playing into his hands. What was the right course of action?

Will backed up, his gun still trained on Raphael.

They moved between a row of shelves as the ground began to shake. The metal racks rattled, swaying from side to side.

Emma ran toward the door, Will behind her. The swaying shelving unit next to them collapsed. Will tackled her as a brilliant white glow surrounded them. When she looked up, the shelves had fallen around them, missing them completely.

How had that happened?

Will was already up, grabbing her arm. The ground continued to shake, and parts of the dilapidated roof fell around them. A giant crack split the ground in front of the door, blocking their exit.

"I have to blast us out." She looked into his eyes to see if he grasped her meaning.

He slipped the bag strap from her shoulder onto his and nodded. "Do what you have to do. I'll take care of you."

A large section of rusted metal fell from the roof and landed several feet away. Emma ducked as a cloud of dust and debris filled the air.

"Emma!" Raphael called. "I'm coming to get you."

Her power was weak, but it was all she had to work with. Finding her anger over Raphael's interference in her life, she tapped into the center of the rage, building her power before she released it into the metal wall. A jagged hole appeared, large enough for them to walk through. Sunlight streamed through the opening.

Lightheaded, Emma remained standing. Will wrapped an arm around her waist and led her to the hole.

"Emma..." Raphael's voice echoed through the building.

Her head whipped around, searching for him. "He's just going to come after us."

"He's playing mind games with you."

"We don't have enough of a head start. I have to do something more. I have to stop him."

Will paused at the opening and looked down at her. "No." He shook his head and started to push her through.

She turned to see Raphael's silhouette between a row of toppled shelves. "Emma, stop this nonsense now before Will gets hurt."

Dread shot through her stomach as she pushed her way back into the building, understanding his threat. "Will, go outside."

"Not without you."

"He's going to hurt you, Will."

"He's going to hurt you too. We're leaving together."

"Then get me out of here when I'm done." She ignited her power, letting it build. A golden glow surrounded her, but it wasn't enough. She needed more. Closing her eyes, she tried to sense an outside power source. She felt the buzz of electricity across the alley. Focusing on the current, she called to it. The energy filled her chest until she felt close to combusting, then she opened her eyes.

Raphael was now about twenty feet away, the front of his shirt covered in blood, the hole in his shoulder partially filled in. A wide grin was plastered on his face. "That is beautiful, Emma. Simply beautiful. I *knew* you could do it. Just think of what we can do *together*."

She released the energy, pushing it with everything in her. The cardboard boxes scattered around the room erupted into flames, and the last thing she saw was Raphael swallowed by the inferno.

CHAPTER TWENTY

HEAT singed Will's face as the room exploded with fire. Emma crumpled and he caught her before she hit the ground. Raphael was lost behind the sea of flames, yet he still called Emma's name. Her explosion wouldn't hold him for long.

Carrying her in a fireman's hold, Will ducked through the hole she'd created and ran for the Vinco Potentia's empty cars, relieved to find the keys in the ignition of the closest one. He placed her in the passenger seat and tossed the bag into the backseat before climbing behind the wheel.

Smoke billowed from the metal building, but there was still no sign of Raphael. No human being could have survived that. But Raphael wasn't a human being.

Casting a glance at Emma, he reached for her wrist, worried that her pulse was faint but grateful she was still alive after what he'd just seen. Electricity had arced across the alley and into her chest. He couldn't believe she had survived an electrocution of that magnitude.

But then, she wasn't human either.

As he pulled onto the highway, the harsh reality of what she was hit him. Even if he didn't fully understand it, he knew that being with her was opening the door to a world he wasn't a part of, not any more, not without his mark. What did he have to offer her?

Yet, when he considered the alternative—leaving her—a knot of panic lodged in his throat. He loved her. Being with her, touching her only made the love he'd felt since he'd woken up on the cargo plane more real. He had no idea how or why he lost his memories, but he didn't want to live without her.

With Emma still unconscious, he drove back toward Kansas City, unsure where their destination should be. Would it take her long to recover? Should he do something to help revive her? He remembered that she'd mentioned needing to eat, which made sense. She'd used energy to create the fires, energy that came from within her, until she summoned electricity.

Thirty minutes out of town, he pulled into a gas station and parked on the side of the building. After he bought a couple of prepackaged deli sandwiches and some water, he opened the passenger door and squatted next to her. "Emma. You need to eat something." When she didn't respond, he rubbed her arms and her cheeks. "Emma, I need you to wake up."

With a groan, she turned her head toward him. "Will?"

Releasing his breath, he took her hand and squeezed it. "I'm here."

"We got away?"

He smiled. "Yeah, completely thanks to you."

"Raphael?"

"He was trapped in the building, although I have no idea how he could survive a gunshot wound like that."

"I think he can heal quickly because of his supernatural powers. I did after I was shot and I'm only half elemental. Raphael is full."

"Well, you're safe now,

Her lips twisted. "No, I'll never be safe."

Unsure how to respond, he kissed her lightly instead.

Her fingers stroked his cheek with a feathery touch as she smiled against his lips.

Leaning back, he put a sandwich in her hand. "You need to eat, Emma."

"This revives me just as much."

He squinted in confusion.

"When I asked you to kiss me in the warehouse, I wasn't lying when I told you it was an experiment. Before you lost your mark, when I overexerted myself, you could revive me with your touch."

He paused. "Like when I touched you in my dream."

"Yes, I thought it was because of your mark, but after I healed James and after I blew up the car and you dragged me to the warehouse, I felt myself growing stronger through your touch."

"So you're saying any living body will do the same?"

"I don't know. I know for a fact Raphael doesn't work. Unless he purposely gives me energy, he sucks the energy from me instead and makes me weaker. Spending the last day and a half away from him has helped me realize that. I was stronger *before* he took me to Tennessee, and that's not saying much."

"You performed some impressive feats today."

"And almost died doing it. I need to practice. The days I spent with Raphael have set me back. Time is running out."

"Running out for what?"

She stared into his eyes for several seconds. "A battle."

Fear tickled the hair on the back of his neck. "What kind of battle? Between who?"

"A battle for control. A battle to survive. *Four will fight, two will remain.* That's what Aiden said."

"And you're one of the four?"

Her head barely nodded. "Yes."

"And who are the other three?"

"Alex and Raphael. And Aiden."

"But wait. Aren't there four elements? You said Alex was air, Raphael was earth, and Aiden was fire. Where's water?"

"I'd like to find out. Raphael has power over me. I have power over Alex. Water has power over Raphael."

"How much time do you have?"

"Five weeks."

Will had seen what Alex was capable of, but he had a feeling that Raphael had been holding back in the warehouse. Probably to protect Emma. "Why does Raphael want you?"

"Several reasons. He loved the Emmanuella that lived before me. So even though I'm not her, I look exactly like her. But most importantly, he wants to join his powers with mine to defeat Aiden and Alex. However, Alex wants the same thing—just not right now, since I have the same effect on Alex that Raphael has on me."

"Why would you join with them?"

"They both think that joined powers are stronger than the two individual powers. They insist it's the only way to beat Aiden and for me to get Jake back."

He sat back on his heels. "So Aiden has Jake? James and I wondered who had him."

Her eyes widened in surprise. "Yes, Aiden has him. Aiden's strong. Stronger than each of us individually."

"Then why don't the three of you combine forces and fight him together?"

"How could we trust one another? Only two survive. One of us would be cast into some shadowy abyss."

"Which one will you pick?

She wrinkled her nose in disgust. "Neither."

"Why?"

"Because joining with one of them means more than joining forces. It comes with a price I'm not willing to pay."

"How are you sure you can dismiss this so easily if it's your only chance at saving Jake and yourself? How do you know the price is too high?"

She leaned forward, furious. "I know it." She put her hand on her chest. "I know it in here. They want to join more than just our energy. What they want is eternal, Will. Eternity is a very long time."

"So if you can't fight Aiden on your own to save your son, what are you going to do?"

Her eyes flooded with tears. "I don't know. I only know that after spending the last month with you, I can hardly face a day with one of those assholes, let alone eternity. Maybe I'll see if Aiden will spare Jake if I forfeit."

"You mean die?"

She looked away and nodded.

"Or we find Water and see if he will team up with you."

"But then there would be five. How would that work? And how do we know he'd be willing or if I even want to join with him? Will, joining is like marriage. Only much more permanent."

"We'll find him first, then take it from there, okay?"

She nodded, blinking back tears.

"And where did I fit into all of this before I lost my mark and my memories?"

Her mouth lifted into a smile, but sadness filled her eyes. "You were my protector, that was the prophecy, anyway. But you were much more than that. Except I was too confused and stupid to see it until it was too late."

"It's not too late. We're together now."

She looked wistful. "Things might have been different. The baby..." Shaking her head, she looked down at the sandwich. "What's done is done. We can't change the past."

He kissed her forehead and shut the door. They were silent until he pulled back onto the highway. "I'm not sure where to go." Used to being decisive and in control, it rubbed against his confidence.

"Neither am I. I need to find someplace remote and relatively fireproof to practice." Glancing out the window, she sighed. "I have to be in New Mexico in a week and it has lots of desert and nothing for miles. I say we head that direction."

"New Mexico?" He had to admit it sounded like a good idea, especially with the fire threat. "What do you have to do in New Mexico?"

"I promised Alex that I'd attend a fundraiser lunch with him." She shook her head. "Wow. That sounds incredibly out of place compared to what just happened."

"Do you think that's a good idea, Emma? Is it safe?"

"It doesn't matter if it's safe or not. I promised, and at this point in my life, the only thing of worth I own is my word. The only way Alex would teach me how to hide my power was to agree. Besides, I'm much more of a threat to him than he is to me."

He had a week to talk her out of it and he planned to use every persuasive technique in his book.

"Which reminds me, I need to hide myself or Raphael will find us again." She closed her eyes for several seconds before she opened them again. "I hope that works."

After a long nap, she spent the rest of the trip telling him how they met and how much she'd detested him in the beginning. At least, until Jake had softened Will's jaded edges, letting her see the man he really was. She told him about her marks, and his, and how he protected her countless times. She confessed that he'd loved her with an intensity that scared her and made her question her own feelings for him until the end. As she told the story, he was amazed at what they'd been through together and saddened that he'd forgotten it all. Emma explained that Will's memory loss was a punishment Emma's father had inflicted on her. She also shared, with few details, what happened after the Vinco Potentia took Will away. How Raphael convinced her that Will was dead. How Raphael descended into madness as she failed to progress. She told him her shock and surprise that the person who'd helped her the most was Alex.

The rest of the time, she scoured the book, becoming frustrated when she discovered most of it was in a language she didn't understand. "This doesn't do us much good."

"We'll figure it out." If Alex and Raphael wanted the book, it obviously contained information vital to her survival. With any luck at all, it would provide information about Water. He'd figure out a way to get it translated.

Will decided to stop outside of Colorado Springs for the night. He pooled his money with the money Alex gave to Emma, coming up with almost two thousand dollars. "Do you think we could spring for a cockroach-free place tonight?" she asked in a hopeful tone.

He winked. "I'll even buy you dinner."

****

After finding a place in Colorado Springs that boasted clean sheets, Will checked in and carried the bag into their room and set it on the dresser. He pulled her into his arms, sweeping her hair from her cheek, his eyes searching hers. He bent down and kissed her, his lips soft and tender.

She hesitated, suddenly nervous. He didn't remember her. This wasn't her Will.

Only he was.

Hope and joy blossomed as she wrapped her arms around his neck, clinging as though he might disappear. His hands grabbed the bottom of her shirt and lifted it over her head. It barely hit the floor before he unfastened her bra and slid it down her arms.

The air hit her bare chest and she shivered.

His gaze traveled down to study her before it returned to her eyes. "You're beautiful."

He kissed her again and she ached with the need to be closer to him, the belief that he could give her the comfort she longed for. The wholeness she had only ever found with him. His hand reached down to her waistband, unfastening the button and the zipper.

Will tugged off her jeans and pulled her down onto the bed. Leaning over her, he studied her with a blank expression.

Her chest tightened. Maybe he decided this was a bad idea. She should stop him before he broke her heart. Just when she was sure he didn't want her, his mouth found hers. She sunk her hands into his hair, pulling him closer.

His lips moved down her neck to her breast. To her frustration, he took his time, exploring her body until she insisted he give her what she really needed, him.

When they finished, he lay next to her and gave her his slow, playful grin. "I can't believe I could forget doing this with you. You're certain we did this before?"

"Many, many times."

"How did we ever get anything else done?"

"You're very efficient." She laughed, rolling to her side.

His thumb stroked her shoulder blade, sending a shiver down her spine. "Are these the marks you told me about? Fire and water?"

She swung her head around. "What are you talking about? It's just fire now."

Will slowly shook his head as his thumb outlined her skin. "No, I'm pretty sure there're two marks. One plainly looks like fire and the one beneath it looks like water."

"But Raphael said the water mark was gone."

Will's eyebrows raised in mock surprise. "Wow. There's no way Raphael would ever lie to you."

She got up and went into the bathroom, looking over her shoulder in the mirror as Will watched her from the bed. Both marks were there. The only one missing was Will's. "I don't understand. What would he gain by lying?"

"You know as well as I do that Raphael wants to mess with your head. I bet this was one more way to manipulate you."

She'd never checked, just taken his word for it. "But he seemed pretty upset when I mentioned that I had water, like he didn't think I should."

Will stood and moved to the bathroom door. "Why are we talking about Raphael?"

"This could be important."

He leaned against the doorframe. "Okay, so what do you think it means?"

"Maybe it means I really am supposed to find Water. Maybe Raphael saw it and it freaked him out and that's why he hid me away in Tennessee."

"So how do we find Water?"

Her mouth twisted in contemplation. "I don't know, but I suspect the answer is in the book."

"We just need to figure out how to translate it."

"Yeah."

He grabbed her wrist and pulled her into his arms, kissing her neck. "I say we worry about it tomorrow."

She smiled as his head moved lower.

"If you need something to take your mind off it, I can take care of that."

Tears sprang to her eyes, grateful she'd found him. Grateful he wasn't dead. She'd been given a second chance with Will and she wasn't going to blow it this time. Nevertheless, he didn't have a mark keeping him with her and he was in real danger if he stayed. Could she live with herself if something happened to him because of her? She pulled his head up and searched his eyes. "Will, you're not stuck with me. You're free to go anytime you choose."

He pulled her to his chest, wrapping an arm around her waist. With his free hand, he brushed the hair off her temple and kissed the top of her head. "I'm not going anywhere."

****

After disappearing all afternoon, Aiden returned in the evening and insisted that Jake join him for a late dinner. Jake's newest nanny brought him into the dining room at nine o'clock. The table was set, and light from a candelabra illuminated the room. Aiden sat at one end, his hands neatly folded on the table. The shadows stood still. Even the shadows were afraid of Aiden.

Aiden's head bobbed with a curt nod. "Thank you, Antonia. That will be all."

The nanny hurried from the room, leaving Jake to fend for himself. Not that she could have helped him.

"Have a seat, Jacob." Aiden waved his hand toward the plate next to him. "It's time for a history lesson. Perhaps if you understand where you have come from you will be able to master your power with more authority."

Jake slid into the chair and placed the napkin on his lap. Kitchen workers usually hung along the wall waiting to serve them, but this time no one else was in the room.

"You're right. We're alone." Aiden scooped food onto Jake's plate. "I wanted privacy."

Jake's stomach rumbled but nerves sent sharp stabs of pain into his belly.

"Years and years ago, four of us ruled the earth. There were lesser creatures, but four of were in control. Fire, air, water, and earth. We didn't manipulate the elements every moment of the day. The world is self-sustaining so there's no need for that. What we have is *command* over the elements. We can generate properties associated with the elements we govern. Your mother and I are fire."

The candle flames lowered until they burned with a blue flame.

"We can create fire and we can manipulate it like the candle flames. But we control it as well. We can create a forest fire and send it one direction, make it stop and send it another. The fire is mine to command. It does not have free will. It must obey my orders, but I must be strong enough to override its true nature.

"As you know, Alex and Raphael are air and earth, but they resigned the majority of their power to me centuries ago. They still possess a small portion of it, but what they possessed in the beginning has weakened over the years.

Plus, it's been so long since they've experienced their full potential that they've forgotten what they are truly capable of. Alex actually has more command over his true talent than Raphael. Raphael's displays are parlor tricks used to impress and intimidate rather than to use with real purpose. Not to mention he's fallen into madness, obsessed for centuries with a woman he continually lost. He forgot his main goal—survival."

Survival. And he and Mommy were a part of it. But Aiden said there were four. "What about Water?"

Aiden tilted his head, a crooked smile lifting his lips. "A very good question. You're a bright boy. Water was part of us, but Water and I didn't see eye to eye on many things. When Alex and Raphael gave their powers to me, Water wanted no part of it and in fact protested the contest. He was concerned about one of us having more power than the others. Water thought it went against the true nature of our existence, that we were all created equal and distributing the equality made the world unbalanced. I thought it was poppycock and banished him. He put up a good fight, but was no match with my increased strength."

"Where is he?"

Aiden studied him for a moment. "Another *very* good question, Jacob. And the answer is simple. I don't know. That's where I was today, searching for him. Usually he comes back every century or so and attempts to kill Alex and Raphael to end things once and for all, but never Emmanuella, not after his first attempt on her life."

Emmanuella? That was Mommy's real name. "Why not?"

Aiden gave him his lopsided smile. "We made an agreement that you needn't concern yourself with. But have no worries. You and your mother are safe from Water. For now."

The shadows behind Aiden grew taller even though the flames on the candles barely lit the area around them. Their tips curled into claws that hung over Aiden's shadow.

The flames shot up several feet into the air and resumed their normal height.

Aiden cut a piece of meat. Stabbing it with his fork, his hand stopped in midair. "Things are not going completely as I planned." He took a bite and watched Jake as he chewed.

Jake fought to keep from squirming under his gaze.

"Water is up to something. We made a bargain a few decades ago that hasn't turned out the way I expected. I love to gamble, but only when I'm sure the odds are in my favor, and in this instance I was sure it was a no-lose situation. If only I knew what he was up to..."

Why was Aiden telling him this?

Aiden laughed. "You need to know that Water is our enemy. He will deceive you. He will not stop until he's seen us cast into the shadow world for eternity. And while he can't personally hurt you, not yet, he can arrange for circumstances to turn against your favor, so never, for a moment, let your guard down."

They ate in silence, Jake forcing himself to swallow several bites. Could Water be scarier than Aiden? He didn't think anything could be scarier than Aiden.

Aiden set his napkin on the table and cleared his throat. "I think that will be all tonight, Jacob. Tomorrow we will resume work on your fire abilities. Good night."

Jake's nanny appeared at the door and he followed her down the hall to his bedroom, trying to ignore the shadows that moved with him down the passageway.

CHAPTER TWENTY-ONE

WILL decided to head to the Farmington, New Mexico area. After using James's laptop to research the area, he found that Farmington was close to high voltage power lines located in the middle of unpopulated desert. It was obvious that Emma needed a lot more practice and fast, and he planned to start that night.

She questioned again why he wanted to help her when he had few memories of her. As odd as it sounded, he did remember her, only with his heart instead of his head. Will convinced her to let him help with her training, which included standing guard to make sure she didn't kill herself or put herself in a vulnerable situation. She'd agreed, not stating what both of them were thinking. He might not have his mark, but he'd resumed the same duties.

While she had more energy than the day before, she still looked tired. She woken in the middle of the night with a nightmare and when he pressed her for the details, she hesitated before telling him it was about a fire. It didn't surprise him. Given his own history with fires, he was amazed he didn't have night terrors of his own.

Will drove while Emma scoured the book, searching for answers. She gnawed on her lower lip as she turned the pages.

Will gave her a quick glance. "I studied the book a little when I was with James. I went over the prophecy, but it just doesn't work. It says the Elevated One and the Supplanter are your children and will battle for control."

She lifted her gaze, shaking her head. "That's the wrong prophecy."

"What?"

"The Vinco Potentia translated the one in the book. In fact, Aiden was probably the one who did the translating. It's different than the one Jake gave you with your mark."

"Do you have Jake's version?"

"Written down? No. Jake burned it into your head. Whenever you thought about it, it just appeared. Let's see if I can remember it." She closed her eyes and recited:

"The land will fall desolate and cold
As it waits for the promised ones
God resides within the queen
While she hides among the people of the exile land
Hunted for that which she must lose
One who is named protector, the Chosen One,
Shall be a shield, counselor, companion
The elevated one will arise from great sorrow
In the full moon after the summer solstice
His powers will be mighty and powerful
He will rise up to rule the land
The supplanter will challenge him
But only one will be overcome
By that which has no price."

"That's completely different."

"It's completely pointless. The prophecy means nothing. Raphael said it was something Aiden came up with to throw humans into the mix and make it more difficult for Alex and Raphael to win."

"So then why did Jake give me a different prophecy from the one the Vinco Potentia has? Why not just give me the same one if it means nothing?"

"I don't know...That's a good point." She gazed out the windshield. "And Alex and Raphael talked about you, the Chosen One. That I, or rather the Emmanuella before me, had never fallen in love with her protector before. That it went against the prophecy."

"So the prophecy does mean something."

"Maybe."

"Jake's version says *promised ones*, plural. Who are they?"

She shrugged. "I don't know. Me and Jake?"

"So then who are the Elevated One and the Supplanter? '*The Elevated One arises in sorrow in the full moon of the summer solstice.*'"

Emma shifted in her seat, tucking her legs underneath her. "The Vinco Potentia said that was the baby. There's no baby now. The prophecy means nothing."

"Let's not dismiss it so quickly. Are you the Elevated One? The Elevated One rises up to rule the land and the Supplanter challenges him. It says you're the queen. Queens rule."

"It says him. It's not me."

"It could be like the Bible. You know, a generic *him*."

"You're grasping at straws, Will."

"You're damn right I'm grasping. We'll sort through every line of this book if we have to. I'm trying to save you, Emma."

She reached over and put her hand on his. "I know you are."

His fingers curled over hers. "We'll figure out how to read it. We'll find Water somehow." Not that he'd ever admit it to her, but part of him balked at the idea of finding Water. Will had to admit he was jealous that she needed someone else to help save her and that he wasn't enough, but he wasn't petty enough that it stopped him from helping her find the bastard.

Raphael and Alex wanted to join with her. What if Emma was right and it meant more than joining powers? From what little Emma had said, Raphael insinuated it was much more intimate. The water mark on her back meant something, but the possibility of *what* it meant was what frightened him. Could Will help her find the man who she might be destined to join with? Could he willingly give her up? Yet he knew the answer, no matter how much it would destroy him.

The fear that Water was just as evil and manipulative as Aiden, Alex, or Raphael gnawed at Will's gut, but there wasn't anything he could do about that. His only hope rested on the fact that Water hated the other three. That alone made Will like him already. Almost.

Emma lay her head on Will's shoulder and sighed. "Thank you."

Kissing the top of her head, he decided if he was forced to give her up, he'd spend every minute he could with her.

****

Emma was exhausted. The stars lit up the desert sky in a blaze she'd never seen before, turning the Milky Way into a creamy band that ran across the horizon. But she didn't have the inclination or energy to enjoy it.

"You have to do it again. Longer this time." Will sat on the hood of the car, thirty feet away.

Nodding, she took a deep breath and held out her hands, one pointed toward the metal towers strung with electrical wires. She twisted her right foot into the sandy ground, trying to get a better foothold. Closing her eyes, she focused on energy and felt it, realizing it felt stronger every time she reached out to it. Her core called to it and, as with every time she'd attempted this tonight, she gasped when raw, powerful energy flooded through her arm into her chest and then out through her opposite fingertips toward a bush. It instantly burst into flames, the desert wind making the fire dance and crackle.

"There's nothing left to practice on," Emma said, slightly winded. She had to be doing something wrong if she felt so tired and breathless. Raphael never appeared this exhausted.

"How are you feeling?"

"Fine. Now what?"

He pushed away from the car. "I don't know. I'm surprised you got it this quickly without passing out."

"But there has to be more. I have to be able to do more than blow things up."

"Which you're quite good at, by the way."

She snorted. "Yeah, whatever."

"You said you could control minds. You could practice that."

A shiver ran down her spine. "No."

"You can practice on me."

"First, we're here for me to practice using outside energy sources. I don't need electricity to control someone's mind. Second, the only other person I see out here is you, and that is not happening."

"Just one little—"

"Which part of no do you not get? For all I know, it could cause you permanent brain damage. No."

"Emma, you need to practice—"

"Yeah, I got plenty of practice on Kramer at the Vinco Potentia compound, and I freaked out that I'd turned him into a zombie." Thinking about Kramer in the compound reminded her of all the people she had killed. If her dreams were any indication, this was only the beginning. "For now, we'll stick with fire."

****

When they returned to the motel in the early morning, Emma collapsed on the bed and fell asleep within minutes. Will had a harder time, his mind a tangled mess as it sorted through the events of the past week. He lay in the dark with his hand behind his head, listening to the slow, steady breathing of the woman next to him.

For the first time, he let his mind go to the topic he had avoided since he left Morgantown.

James.

Never in a thousand lifetimes would Will ever think James capable of betraying him. Not after everything they had been through. Through twenty-five years to hell and back, James had stuck with him through everything. Even after the court-martial and dishonorable discharge. His own family may have disowned him, but James had taken him in and had been the one to kick his ass after he'd spent two solid weeks drinking to forget it all. Not that he could forget what happened.

Ever.

Even now the screams of those kids echoed in his head. But James had shown him tough love, forcing him to get back into the world. Until he realized what Will's new profession involved. He'd been on his ass to quit since the day he'd started three years ago. James wanted Will to come live with him at the lake, but the thought of spending all his time with nothing but peace and quiet made Will want to claw his eyes out. Still, he'd finally caved, telling James that he had a big job coming up that would pay him a shitload of money and then he'd retire. He had no intention of staying with James indefinitely. Just long enough to figure out what he wanted to do with the rest of his life. Turned out he'd found it during the past month with the woman next to him.

Seeing her in person had confirmed she wasn't his usual preference. She was pretty enough but not stunning.

At least until she smiled. When she smiled, the ice around his heart melted, releasing hope.

She whimpered in her sleep and her breathing increased.

He rubbed her arm. "Emma?"

She jerked upright, her eyes open in terror.

Will sat up and pulled her into a hug. "Hey, what happened?"

"I had the dream again."

"The one with the fire?"

"Yes, it's stronger. I think it's getting closer."

He lifted her chin, finding her eyes in the dim light. "No, it's just a dream. Come here." Pulling her down, he placed her head on his chest as he cradled her body against his, amazed at how perfectly she fit. He stroked her hair until her breathing steadied again.

When he woke later that morning, she still slept, rolled over on her stomach. He knew she had to be exhausted from all the work she'd done the night before. He wanted her to sleep as long as possible. His plan was to lay low during the day then go back out at night when it was cooler.

As he studied her face, he found the faint greenish tone of an old bruise on her cheek and near her lip. How had she gotten that? Raphael? His last remembrance of her, her face was bruised, her nightgown covered in blood. Had it been from the baby she lost?

She opened her eyes, looking up with a smile. "Good morning."

"You should go back to sleep. You need more rest."

She pulled him close. "No, I need more you."

He kissed her before looking into her eyes. "Tell me about the baby."

Her eyes widened. "Oh."

"It's...how... I was always very careful about things like that."

Her mouth twisted. "Well, we were out in the middle of nowhere in Colorado and I thought Jake was dead. I pretty much begged you for it and there wasn't anything to use for protection."

He grimaced, surprised how little thought he'd given to taking precautions after years of paranoia. "Kind of like the past two days."

"Yeah, but I just had a miscarriage. We're probably fine."

In the grand scheme of things, this seemed minor. "And how did I feel about the baby?" He already knew, given his grief when he realized she'd miscarried.

She smiled. "You were happy, which made one of us since the baby had a shitload of expectations on its head. I wasn't sure how I felt at first, but then I knew I wanted it. I wanted to have the baby with you."

"And how did you lose it? Aiden?"

Her smile fell away. "No. I don't think so. One of Kramer's men beat me up in the woods after I escaped and he kicked me in the stomach. I started cramping after that, although I refused to consider the possibility of losing it. I was worried you'd be upset with me."

Tucking her hair behind her ear, he kissed her lightly. "How could I be mad at you?"

"You really wanted the baby."

"It wasn't your fault. And when this mess is taken care of, we can make a new one." He tilted his head with a questioning look. "That is, if you want to have another."

Tears filled her eyes as the corners of her lips turned up. "You, me, Jake, and a baby."

A family. The thought nearly took his breath away. Was it really a possibility, or a fantasy?

"I think we should take it easy today, study the book, maybe go buy whatever you need since I left your bag in the car in Missouri. Then after we eat dinner, we'll head back out into the desert and you can work again."

Her eyes flew open in alarm. "Oh, my God. How could I have forgotten?"

"What?"

Terror filled her eyes and she shot out of bed. "I let my guard down to use my power last night and I never put it back up. Raphael can find me."

Will followed her. "He can find you here? Over a thousand miles away?"

"I don't know." She sounded panicked as she pulled clothes out of the duffel bag. "But we can't take that chance. How could I have been so stupid?"

"Hey. It's okay. We'll check out and figure out somewhere else to go. Water's probably not around here anyway. We'd have to go somewhere else to find him."

She nodded. "I'm sorry."

"There's nothing to be sorry for. This is all new to you too. It's going to be okay."

She smiled, but her eyes told him she didn't believe it.

CHAPTER TWENTY-TWO

WILL studied his maps and announced they were going to Arizona.

"But you hate Arizona," she protested.

His eyebrows scrunched in confusion. Then he shrugged. "It doesn't matter. We're going anyway."

Will assured her multiple times that she hadn't done anything wrong, but she knew she'd been careless. She'd been exhausted the night before and hadn't thought through the consequences. Will was right, it was new to her too. But she had a responsibility to protect him and she'd already failed him after only a couple of days.

She read the book as he drove, frustrated that she couldn't make heads or tails of it. Alex said the new rules were in the book but all she saw were the ravings of a lunatic and language she didn't understand.

They would never find Water at this rate.

Will cleared his throat. "We're trying to look for Water, but maybe we should let him look for you."

She lifted her eyebrows, incredulous. "How do you propose that? Don't you think he would have found me by now if he wanted to find me? Besides, Alex is fairly certain that Water will kill me the moment he sees me."

"Why?"

"Let's just say Water isn't a fan of Aiden."

"That's a club with a lot of members."

She laughed. "True, but Alex thinks that as soon as Water realizes I'm the daughter of fire, he'll kill me."

"You keep calling him Water. What's his name? Every one of you has a name that's been handed down since the beginning of time, so what's Water's?"

"I don't know and I'm not sure it's in the book."

"How can you tell? It could be in the part that's untranslated."

"Which I can't read." She rubbed her hand over her eyes in frustration.

"You need to take a break from that."

Shaking her head, she looked up at him. "No, the answers are in here, I just have to figure out how to read it."

"Well, put it down for a little bit and take a nap. I plan to keep you very busy tonight."

She raised her eyebrow with a wicked grin.

"Not what you're thinking." He laughed. "My, my Emma Thompson. You have a dirty mind. I was talking about your training."

She snorted and closed the book. "So that's what you're calling it now. And here I thought you liked when I did that little hip roll."

A grin lit up his eyes. "Keep talking about that and I'll pull over to the side of the road and make you demonstrate it again."

Leaning back into the seat, she reached out her hand to Will's. He grasped it, and her fingertip brushed against his ring. She rolled to her side, watching him as she traced the band on his ring finger. "This is new."

His hand tightened around hers then loosened. "My mom gave it to me."

"When you were at the hospital?"

"Yeah." He kept his eyes on the road.

"You told me you hadn't seen her for years. She was a patient..."

He sighed. "She has cancer. She asked me to come visit her before she died."

Emma sat up. "Oh, Will. I'm so sorry. Why didn't you tell me?"

He shrugged. "I don't know. Other things seemed more important."

She groaned. "Me."

"Emma, don't say it like that. I went to see her because I wanted to know why she sent me away three years ago."

"And did you get your answers?"

"I got answers, but no, it didn't make everything better. I loved her and she..."

"She hurt you, but it's okay to still love her. She loves you."

"How can you say that? She shunned me when I needed her the most."

"I can't pretend to understand why she did what she did, but I can't think of a single thing that would make me stop loving Jake. All mothers are the same, Will. We love our children." Emma liked to think her own mother loved her, somewhere deep inside.

He watched the road, his jaw clenching as he swallowed.

She turned over his hand and examined the blue stone with swirls. "She gave you this ring? Was it a family heirloom?"

"She didn't say. Only that it belonged to someone important to her."

Emma raised her eyebrows. "Her secret lover?"

He shook his head with a laugh. "Or her favorite uncle?"

"So why the big mystery?"

"I don't know, but I can guarantee my mother never had an affair. That was my dad's job."

She stroked the back of his hand. "I'm glad you saw her. I'm glad you got some answers even if you don't think it was what you wanted to hear."

Pinching his mouth, he turned to her, his eyes red with unshed tears. "Thank you."

****

Will leaned against the car, watching electricity shoot into Emma's body and out her hand. No matter how many times he saw it, he wasn't sure he'd ever get used to it.

He looked at the ring on his hand and wondered why his mother wouldn't tell him whom it belonged to. The oval blue stone shimmered in the dark and sent a chill through his body. It made him glad he'd thought to bring a jacket.

Tonight he wanted Emma to work on controlling the amount of energy she took in and released. She'd made good progress the night before, but she needed to make sure she didn't release too much and pass out. He was still amazed she hadn't killed herself after creating the fire in the warehouse. He knew she'd passed out multiple times during the month of his memory loss. The stress had to be hard on her body and he wanted her control to become second nature. In the heat of a battle, she couldn't be concentrating on the amount of energy exchanged. She needed to focus on saving herself.

He got up and handed Emma water. She straightened and arched her back as she took the bottle. Her face was pale, beads of sweat dotting her upper lip.

Maybe he was pushing her too hard. "How are you doing? Really?"

She took a swig and wiped her face with the back of her arm. "I'm great."

He liked that about her too. She loved to complain, but it was mostly an act. She was a hard worker. And in spite of his persistence, he still worried what would happen if she pushed too hard. Could she end up dead?

But he routinely monitored her, whether she realized it or not, ready to scale it back if necessary. She tired out easily though, especially with bigger things, which made her frustrated.

"Emma. Maybe you should take a break."

"No," she spat through gritted teeth, her eyes blazing with fury. A golden glow formed around her. "I have too much to learn."

"You look like an angel when you do that."

"Very funny."

"No, seriously. A badass angel, but an angel nonetheless. All that golden light glowing off of you."

She groaned. "God, I don't have to dress up as an angel to fulfill some fantasy of yours, do I?"

He laughed. "No, darlin', I sure as hell don't want you pretending to be an angel in my bed."

She shook her head and laughed. "Well, I guess I better earn my *reward* tonight. Back to work."

"Hey, that's my line," Will protested.

She reached up and kissed him lightly on the lips. "I'll let you say it next time."

****

Emma sat up in bed in the dark, sweat trickling down her back. Her dream had never been so intense. Fires burned in a valley as she stood on a cliff. Smoke stung her nostrils. Hair tickled her neck as a voice whispered, "You are the destruction of the world."

Forcing her breath to slow down, she turned to check on Will, thankful she hadn't woken him. She'd kept her dreams from him before, worried it would hurt him. But she vowed not to hide anything from him this time. She was sure her dream would happen, but how could she prevent it? She could stop training, but Emma was the only one out of the four who had a fraction of good intentions, even if hers were mostly selfish. She wanted to save her son. That didn't make her selfless. But was selflessness a requirement to saving the world? Wasn't wanting to save it, even if it was a consequence of her selfish motivation, enough?

Will stirred and reached for her. "Did you have your dream again?"

"Yeah." She lay down beside him, curling into his side.

He wiped a tear off her cheek.

She hadn't realized she'd been crying. "I wonder if I'm doing the right thing, learning how to use my power like this." She looked up into his confused eyes. "I think I might destroy the world."

He squinted his eyes and shook his head. "Emma, what are you talking about? That makes no sense."

"When you and I went to Kansas City before you lost your memory, there was an old homeless man outside of your apartment. He had a sign saying the end of the world was near."

"So? There are lots of lunatics like that."

"But this man pointed to me and said I was Jezebel, betrayer of the truth."

He paused, then shrugged. "Okay. So? Lots of crazy old men say weird things."

"Sure, but do the people they accuse have visions?"

Will's eyes narrowed. "What kind of vision?"

"I saw the fire from the night in the woods when my father stole your memory. I heard Aiden telling me that I had to choose. I saw it before it happened, Will." She fought to keep her tears from falling. "Then I was on a hill, looking down into a burning valley and someone said, 'You've caused this. The death of the world is in your hands.'" She swallowed the lump in her throat. "Don't you see? If my power continues to grow stronger, then I might destroy the world."

He took her hand and laced his fingers through hers. "You don't know that."

"But I've been dreaming of it. The valley on fire—what if it's going to happen?"

"Emma, you've been traumatized. Lesser people would crawl into a hole and require massive doses of pharmaceuticals. Of course you're going to dream about it."

"But how can I risk it?"

Will's face hardened. "You risk it because we can't face the alternative, which is you dead, possibly Jake dead, and most likely life as the world knows it over. You really want Alex Warren in charge of the world? Because if he can control minds like you can, just imagine what he's capable of. Or what about your psychotic loverboy? What do you think that monster would do with unfettered power? So you tell me, Emma. Which is better? You learning to use your power to defend yourself and the world, or just giving up and letting them have total control? Which one is easier for you to live with?"

Her anger took hold. "That's not fair, Will."

"Not fair? You know what's not fair? Losing over a month's worth of memories."

Damn him. "But I've killed all those people. What if I kill innocent people? How do I live with that?"

His arm tightened around her waist, pulling her cheek to his chest. "You just do. I'll help you through it and we'll make sure as few people as possible get hurt."

She tried to swallow the lump of fear in her throat. "I don't know if I can live with that. I don't know if I can do it."

He pulled her head back and lifted her chin to stare into her eyes. "Emma, look at the four of you. What are your motivations? Aiden, Alex, and Raphael do this out of ambition, greed, and survival. But you? You do it out of love. You do it to save Jake and me and yourself. And you do it to save the world, which is an act of unconditional love, because you know that none of the other three give a fuck about the rest of the people on this planet. That right there has to count for something."

Tears streamed down her cheeks. "What if you're wrong? That old woman in the woods told me I was a good person, but what if the homeless man was right? What if I *am* the destruction of the world?"

He lifted her chin, looking down into her face. "That's enough. You are not the destruction of the world."

"But my vision—"

"Wasn't proof of anything. Fire. Big deal. You've made fire before. You just made it tonight."

"Not like this."

"Then don't make fire like that. You're not bound to destiny, Emma."

Her eyes widened. "What did you just say?"

"You have the power to change things. You admit that you aren't completely sold on the idea that the prophecy is real. You're not bound to destiny."

"That's what Raphael said."

"That you're not bound to destiny?"

She nodded, wiping her tears.

"Wow. That bastard and I agree on something." He shook his head. "But somehow, I suspect his idea of being bound to destiny and mine are very different. You'll know the line that you can't cross when you come to it."

"Maybe." She settled into his chest, amazed that he was here with her now. What if he or Jake got caught up in this battle and got killed because of her? Could she live with that?

Raphael's threat against Will played over and over in her head. Will had caught Raphael off guard in the warehouse and she was sure it wouldn't happen again. If they ran into Raphael, could she defend Will? Was it fair to keep him with her out of selfish need? Yet he claimed he wanted to be with her and that he loved her. He didn't want to leave her. Surely that had to count for something. While she admitted he'd be safer away from her, she was selfish enough to want him to stay.

If that didn't make her evil, she wasn't sure what did.

****

"Jacob."

Jake woke to a voice he didn't recognize.

He slowly sat up. A man he didn't know sat in his nanny's rocking chair. Jake's heart raced.

"You have nothing to fear from me. I'm your friend."

"I've never seen you before."

He smiled. "I know, but I've been watching you."

Maybe he worked in the gardens or the vineyards. He wore jeans and a button-down shirt, and even in the nightlight glow, Jake could see he had a deep tan. Jake's tummy churned. "Aiden will kill you."

"Aiden doesn't know I'm here."

"Aiden knows everything."

"Not this time."

How could he be so sure? Jake reached out to the man's mind and encountered a wall. Narrowing his eyes, Jake studied him. "Who are you?"

"You can learn to block Aiden. You can block your thoughts so he can't read yours. Or you can filter your thoughts so he only sees superficial things. You can have secrets."

Jake's mouth dropped open at the possibility. Was it true?

"I can teach you."

Jake was more suspicious than ever. "I could call Aiden right now. I should."

"But you won't. The idea of blocking Aiden intrigues you." His mouth lifted into a lopsided grin. "Do you want me to teach you?"

What if Aiden found out? How would he punish Jake? But the chance to have secret thoughts filled him with excitement. He nodded. "Yes."

The man stood and walked slowly toward him.

Jake stiffened.

He held out his hand. "It's okay. I'm not going to hurt you. I'm going to sit on the bed next to you. Is that okay?"

Nodding, Jake twisted the edge of his blanket between his fingers.

The man slowly sank onto the mattress, the down blanket fluffing around him. "Right now, your mind is a pool of thoughts. Some are shallow, like the wading area at the swimming pool your mom probably took you to, but some are deeper, like the diving pool. You have to swim deep to get to them. Does that make sense?"

Jake nodded.

"It takes a lot of effort to dig into really deep thoughts and read them, even for Aiden. But if you're thinking something, it's probably floating around the shallow end of your mind. I only have to peer in and it's right there." The man lowered his head, his eyes probing Jake's. "But if you leave your shallow thoughts there in the wading pool—things like the weather, or you're hungry, or look at that cute kitten—then you can dive into your deep end and think your important thoughts. Like disobeying Aiden. Or talking to your mother."

Jake's eyes widened. How did he know about talking to his mother? "I would never disobey Aiden."

He gave Jake a small smile. "It's okay. I won't tell him."

Excitement coursed through him at the possibility of hiding secrets from Aiden.

"You're in the shallow pool, Jake. Dive down into the deep end and think about it there."

Closing his eyes, Jake focused on the deep recesses of his mind and thought of Aiden. Aiden wanted to hurt Will, but what could Jake do about it?

The man smiled. "Very good. I had to make a real effort to find something I thought Aiden wouldn't approve of. Aiden's so confident, he'll never think to look that deep. But you'll need to practice."

"Why are you teaching me this?"

The smile fell from his lips, replaced by a frown. "Things are changing soon and you'll need to be able to keep secrets." He put his hand over Jake's. "You are a very important player in this game, Jake. More important than anyone else other than Aiden realizes. You'll need to make sure you can hide things."

"Why are you helping me?"

His eyes filled with an icy stare.

Jake swallowed, afraid for the first time since he'd found the man in his room.

"Everyone has their own agenda, Jake. Aiden. Raphael. Alex. Even your mother. I have my own agenda as well. Have you ever played chess?"

Jake shook his head.

"We are all involved in an elaborate game, much like a chess match. Everyone has their own piece in the game. Every move we make affects the others. You are the king in this game, Jacob, whether everyone else realizes it or not. You are the prize." He rose from the bed. "At some point you will be forced to choose sides. Choose wisely."

"But who are you?"

The man moved to the door, his back to Jake. His head turned and he looked over his shoulder with a cocky grin. "I'm surprised you haven't guessed by now. I am Water."

CHAPTER TWENTY-THREE

WILL rubbed his weary eyes. They were both exhausted. Every time Emma used her powers she had to let her guard down, making herself a shining beacon to Raphael. She hadn't figured out a way around it. Instead of practicing at night, Will decided she should practice during the day, then they would move to a new town for the night.

Since Emma still insisted on meeting Alex the next day at his political fundraiser in Albuquerque, Will had returned to Farmington, hours north of Albuquerque, frustrated that he hadn't talked her out of it.

He'd been studying the leather book for over an hour while she slept and showered, and knew nothing he didn't already know when he started. The key had to be the section in the back that wasn't translated, but he couldn't figure out what language it was in, even after searching the internet for hours.

Which left him in the same place he was days ago. With nothing.

The shower turned off in the bathroom and a small grin tugged at the corner of Will's mouth when the door opened and Emma emerged, wrapped in a skimpy white towel, water dripping from the ends of her hair. When she realized he watched her, she gave him a smile. "Find anything?"

He groaned, shoving the book away. "No."

She walked over and sat on the side of the bed. "That's okay. You tried."

"Yeah, but this book holds the key to everything."

She started to say something, then rose and turned back to the bathroom.

"Emma, did you ever stop and think about your name?"

"Emma?"

"No, your full name. Emmanuella."

"No. It was just some awful name my father insisted on naming me." As soon as she finished the sentence, her shoulders stiffened. "Why did I never think if it before? It has to mean something if my father insisted on using it."

Will opened the laptop.

A quick search answered his question. "Emmanuella. Hebrew. God is with us." He turned to look at her.

Her face was a frozen mask.

"Emma, this means something."

His words snapped her out of her thoughts. "It means everything and it means nothing. It would have been helpful information a month ago. Now it tells us nothing we don't already know. My father is like a god, only elemental. I'm his daughter. I'm like a demigod." She gave him a wicked look. "Have you ever thought about the meaning of *your* name?"

He scowled. "Very funny."

She sat on his lap and typed his name in the computer then read the results. "William. English. Strong-willed warrior." Leaning back, she wrapped her arm around his shoulders and kissed him, leaving him breathless and wanting more. "Your name fits you perfectly," she murmured against his lips.

His name fit him perfectly.

He pushed her back. "That's a little too perfect."

"It's a coincidence."

He raised an eyebrow. "Can we really attribute any of this to coincidence?"

"No." She sighed, leaning her forehead against his. "Our names have meaning. The joining words. The untranslated text. Words have power."

"Protector. So my entire life, I was meant to be your protector."

"And my entire life, I was meant to get caught in a supernatural struggle."

"At least you know why you were chosen. Your father is a paranormal creature. Why was I picked?"

Her fingers caressed his cheek and she lowered her voice. "I don't know, Will. I'm sorry."

"I thought I just happened to be in the wrong place at the wrong time, but this was planned before I was even born."

She leaned back and searched his eyes. "Will, I'm sorry. You have no idea how guilty I feel that you're caught up in this. When you had your mark and felt compelled to protect me, the guilt nearly killed me. It wasn't fair to you. You should have had the choice. But you always swore that was what you wanted. That you wanted to be with me. Maybe my father thought he was doing you a favor when he stole your memories, as hard as that is to believe."

He thought about his life before her compared to the past few days and the feelings he had for her. He shook his head. "No, I wouldn't change a thing, Emma. I love you. You have no idea how much you've changed my life."

She snorted. "Yeah, car crashes, gunfights, plane escapes..."

"Love and belonging. I never felt like I belonged anywhere, Emma. Not until I found you. You have no idea how long I searched for that."

"Maybe some of your mark is still in here." She rested her hand on his chest. "Maybe you just think you feel it."

"Now you sound like James."

"God help me." She lifted his chin to look at her. "But maybe it's true."

He shook his head. "Emma, I've been with more women than I care to admit. If I could have manufactured that feeling, I would have done it long before now. This isn't imaginary. This is real."

She started to say something then stopped, and licked her lips before starting again. "Maybe you'd be safer if you weren't with me."

"And maybe I won't get in a car wreck if I never get in a car again."

"The odds of you dying because of me are much higher than dying in a car wreck. And let's say you make it all the way to the end with me, what happens to you if I lose? I don't know if I can take that chance with you, Will. It's selfish to keep you with me."

His back stiffened. "What, I can't make my own decisions? You're deciding what I do or don't do?"

"No...that's not it at all. I just don't want you to feel obligated—"

He untucked her towel, letting the fabric fall open. "There are perks to this job that would be *very* hard to give up."

She gasped as his hand fondled her breast. "I agree."

His mouth lowered to her neck. "Then let's enjoy the perks and not think about the rest."

"I thought we were going back out to practice in the heat."

"The desert isn't going anywhere."

****

The heat was going to kill her before any of the assholes in her life had a chance. Will was right, they needed to change their routine. But...damn.

She stood in a deserted junkyard in the New Mexico desert, the sun beating down and scorching the top of her head. Sweat trickled down the side of her face and she lost all pretense of civility, lifting the hem of her T-shirt to wipe her face.

"Longer this time."

Her brows furrowed as her mouth puckered in protest. "Easy for you to say."

"True, but this is your dog and pony show, princess." He handed her a bottle of water.

She chugged the contents, water seeping from the corners of her mouth and down her neck.

"Don't guzzle it. Sip it. You're going to make yourself sick."

"Who the hell made you the boss?" she snapped as he snatched the bottle away.

He chuckled. "I'm the resident expert on deserts, dehydration, and heat stroke. That makes me the boss."

His reminder of his past tempered her irritation. "How did you stand it, Will?"

His smile fell, but his eyes were warm. "One day at a time, sometimes one second at a time. You can do anything if the alternative is unacceptable." He backed up and sat in the shade of the car. "Which is why you're going to keep practicing. Because the alternative is unacceptable."

"How hot do you think it is?"

Will gulped from the bottle. Wiping his mouth with the back of his arm, he glanced up at her and shrugged. "Hundred? Hundred and five? What does it matter what the temperature is? You're still going to work."

Steeling her back, she pulled power from the electrical lines running overhead and focused on moving a smashed-up VW across the lot. It skittered through the sand and crashed into a pile of cars twenty feet away. Blowing up things only worked when there were objects to blow up. She needed to have more tricks at her disposal.

"That's good," Will said. "But you need to be able to control it."

"If you think you can do better, then you try it." She was improving, but not fast enough to suit her. Her progress had increased exponentially since she'd begun to use electricity as a power source, but she often found trying other things, such as moving heavy objects, was clunky and uncoordinated. And usually left her exhausted.

"I want you to try to pick up a car and hold it over the ground. Don't do anything with it, just let it hover," Will said, twisting the ring on his finger.

"Okay." She took a deep breath, absorbing the electrical energy and focusing on picking up the VW and holding it over the ground. It rose several feet, floating over the ground in a jerky movement.

"You need to make it steady. You need to have better control."

Her temper flared, increasing the pressure in her chest. "If you don't like how I'm doing it, then you do it."

"Maybe I should."

She knew what he was doing, goading her to try harder, but the heat already made her cranky and his words inflamed her anger. Without thinking she directed her temper in his direction and lightning shot from her hands toward him.

He hunched on the ground in a ball as a lightning bolt zapped the car behind him, sending sparks shooting into the air along with a white flash.

Panic swamped her as she shut off her connection to the current and ran toward him. "Will!" The VW landed on the ground with a loud crash.

Emma fell at his side, grabbing his arm. "Will!"

He looked up at her, his eyes wide. "I'm okay. I'm fine."

She burst into tears, throwing her arms around his shoulders. "I could have killed you. I'm sorry."

He took her face in his hands. "It's okay. I'm fine."

"I didn't mean to do it. I didn't know it was going to happen until it did."

"It's okay."

"NO, IT'S NOT!" Hysteria filled her head and she shook with fear. "I lost control and I could have killed you!"

"But you didn't. See? I'm fine."

She glanced around. "But how are you okay? You were right next to the car. Shouldn't you have been electrocuted?"

He shook his head, looking back at the car. "Yeah." He looked up at her, confusion in his eyes. "I felt the electricity and it was like it was blocked somehow. You must have realized what happened and protected me."

Her breath came in hiccupy bursts through her tears. "No. I didn't."

Will pulled her head closer so their eyes were several inches apart. "You didn't mean to hurt me, right? You were angry and it happened."

"I'm so sorry," she choked out.

"It was an involuntary reaction. Maybe saving me was involuntary too."

She bit her trembling lip and nodded.

"Why don't we call it an afternoon? Maybe I've pushed you too hard."

By the time they went back to the motel room Emma had calmed down, but she was more worried about Will's safety than ever. She'd always figured she needed to protect him from the other three. It never occurred to her that she had to protect him from herself.

Emma turned on the water to the shower and walked out of the bathroom to get a change of clothes, when an image on the television stopped her. Alex addressed a large, enthusiastic crowd. A banner flashed across the bottom of the screen announcing his next campaign stop.

Huddled over his laptop, Will glanced at the television and grumbled. "Well, look at Alex playing Mr. Politician on the campaign trail."

Emma sat on the edge of the bed. Alex's face beamed on the screen as he shook hands with adoring potential voters. Her stomach knotted.

Will kept his back to her. "So you're really going to go through with it?"

She knew how upset Will was over her meeting, but there was no way around it. "Of course."

He turned, anger flashing in his eyes. "No, Emma. It is *not* of course. What if this is a trap? What if Alex got you away from Raphael so you could grow stronger for his benefit? What if he led you to me so that you'd be halfway content and focused on training, then set a trap to collect his bounty?"

She couldn't be sure of anything and they both knew it. But it didn't matter. It all boiled down to one fact. "I promised."

He rose from the chair, shoving it into the desk.

Wringing her hands in her lap, she looked up at him. "Maybe it's not a trap. Maybe it's a chance to get more information. Think about it, Will. Alex is the linchpin for all three of our variables. His father is head of the Vinco Potentia, he's part of the Cavallo, and he's one of Aiden's playthings. If I can get him to talk, even just a little, we can learn more than we've learned all week."

Will rubbed his hand through his hair, releasing a heavy breath. "It's dangerous on so many levels, Emma. First, Alex Warren is bound to have a big security detail under his command. They could take you into custody on any trumped-up charge. Second, even though you say you have control over him, what if you're wrong? What if he hurts you? And third, what makes you think he'll even talk to you?"

The muscles in her back cramped, thinking about meeting with Alex, but she had to put her personal discomfort and feelings aside. Jake's and Will's lives depended on her to keep it together. "He won't hurt me because he thinks he needs me, but that's not to say he won't hurt you. He may have put us together, but he did it for his own benefit. He could easily change his mind and decide to kill you." She paused and lifted her chin in resolve. "Which means you can't be with me when I meet him."

Anger flashed in his eyes. "The hell I won't."

She walked over and rested her hand on his arm. "After what happened this afternoon, I want you as far away from all of this power shit as possible. That includes me when I practice."

"Emma—"

"Think about it, Will. He has too much to gain from me. I'm safe, but I can't take the chance with you. I can't lose you again." She cupped his cheek and looked into his eyes. "I'm stronger than I was the last time I saw him. You know this. I have control over him. I can defend myself."

His face hardened. "No."

She hated hurting him this way. Her back stiffened. "I'm sorry, but you don't get a say in this. It's my decision."

Will jerked his arm from her grip and stared into her face, anger blazing in his eyes. "What the fuck, Emma?"

"I love you, Will, and I won't let you get hurt. I know you want to protect me, but your love for me is clouding your judgment. Before you lost your memory, you were the stronger of the two of us. Now, I am."

His jaw tensed.

"It's not a slam against you. In fact, if it weren't for you I wouldn't be this strong at all. Jake is counting on me to win this thing, and your life hinges on this too. Then let's not forget the entire world. I know too little about way too many things and frankly, I'm tired of living in fear. I'm ready to take the offensive and develop a strategy to win this thing. But I need to know what I'm facing, on all fronts, to do this effectively. So like it or not, I'm going to Albuquerque tomorrow and I'm meeting with Alex Warren."

Will's chest expanded as his pupils narrowed. Without a word, he grabbed the keys off the desk and walked out of the motel room, slamming the door behind him.

Emma watched the metal door, stunned not only by Will's actions, but her own. Still, when she replayed her decision in her head, she stood by it. It was the right thing to do.

Hours later the sun began to set and Will hadn't returned. She was hungry and tired but mostly worried about Will. He left the cell phone on the desk when he stormed out, so she couldn't call him to make sure he was okay.

She opened a bag of pretzels, nibbling as she looked up directions to the Fairmont Hotel. Albuquerque was over a three-hour drive, which meant that she'd have to leave early in the morning if she wanted to get there in time.

What if Will hadn't come back by then?

Then again, maybe that was his plan to keep her from going. Could she leave him? It occurred to her that maybe she should.

****

Will drove aimlessly for hours, too mad to go back to the motel room but not mad enough to drive away from the pain-in-the-ass woman he'd left behind.

Will was not a man to take orders. He issued them. Yet, when he let himself cool down enough to think things through, he knew she was right.

And it killed him.

Will's job before his memory loss was to protect Emma, and from what he'd heard, he'd done a piss-poor job of it. He'd failed her before. He didn't want to fail her again. But how could he protect her if she went off alone? Still, Will realized that he was no match for Alex. Emma was better equipped to handle him. It wasn't that his pride couldn't handle that Emma was more skilled than he was for this situation. It was that he wasn't the one to protect her.

And the realization stung.

He loved her. Worried about her. Even defended her. But the desire to protect her came deep from within. It wasn't a want. It was like a physical need. Emma had told him that's what it had been like before, when he bore the mark. His eyes darted down to his arm to see if a mysterious brand had appeared. Nothing.

He knew she'd made the promise to meet Alex before she knew Will was alive, and he knew how important it was for her to keep her promises. But he'd bet his life that Alex wouldn't think twice about breaking a promise. While Alex had set Will free, rescued Emma from Raphael, and ultimately put the two of them together, Will knew without a doubt that Alex only did it to serve a greater good. His.

When the growling in Will's stomach refused to be ignored any longer, he pulled into a truck stop and ordered dinner, watching the rolling banner across the bottom of the news channel. A devastating drought in Africa that was killing thousands every day. A war raging between India and Pakistan that had much of the world looking on with bated breath, both countries a hair-trigger away from nuking each other. Another massive earthquake, in South America this time.

A nagging feeling in the back of his head told him that this wasn't all just one big coincidence. This all came back to Aiden and his twisted scheme. Emma had said that Aiden's power was weakening. Will knew enough about power to know that it didn't weaken, it merely changed directions. It flowed from one pole to another.

Aiden was losing control, and the world was suffering.

He ate, barely stopping to taste the food, his mind whirling as it began to piece things together.

Four shall fight, two will remain.

Emma was stronger than she had been in the beginning. This afternoon was evidence of that. Still, he wasn't sure she was strong enough to win. Perhaps she was right. Maybe taking the offensive, seeing where they stood and trying to get more information from Alex, was the best course of action. Lord knew that in Iraq it had chafed his ass to hole up and do nothing while known terrorists had lurked about. Wasn't this the same? And if his deductions were correct, Emma's survival depended on using anything and everything she could to arm herself.

But when she won, because he refused to accept the alternative, who would rule with her? Would they find Water in time? None of the other three were trustworthy.

When he left the restaurant the sun had set, making him realize how long he'd been gone. He reached into his jeans pocket to pull out his cell phone, then remembered that he'd left it behind at the motel. He felt an urgency to get back to Emma and make sure she was okay. He knew that she was probably worried about him too. He climbed into the car and started the engine, totally unprepared for the voice in his ear.

"Hello, Will. Your time's up."

CHAPTER TWENTY-FOUR

JAKE sat in the gardens, waiting for Aiden. His nanny had brought him outside ten minutes early. She'd made him change clothes twice, brushed his hair three times, and placed him on the bench, moving him inches to either side until she was satisfied with his position.

Now she paced nervously behind him. He was used to it because everyone on the household staff were terrified of Aiden. Until his visit from Water, Jake had been terrified of Aiden too. He'd been practicing, hiding tiny little thoughts from Aiden, deep in his mind. So far it had worked, and it had opened the door to something he'd been missing for weeks. Hope.

Aiden appeared on the path leading to the vineyard, the setting sun basking him in a glow. The nanny stopped, chanting in Spanish, the clinking of her cheap rosary beads giving away her terror.

Aiden smiled as he approached. "Good evening, Jake."

"Good evening, Aiden," Jake said as Antonia had instructed minutes ago. Not that Jake needed reminding.

"Antonia, you may leave us now." Aiden flicked his hand to the side path that led to the house and Jake expected Antonia to fall over dead. He never knew when Aiden would kill one of the staff as punishment for Jake, or just to prove that he could. Jake was surprised when she scurried away, hurrying without a backward glance.

Jake waited for the berating that he knew was coming. Aiden had instructed him to create a thunderstorm the day before. After hours of concentration, he'd managed only a small shower that lasted five minutes.

Aiden bent over a rose bush and inhaled. "There's nothing like the smell of old-fashioned roses. Why do men think they have to tamper with genetics to create what they see as a perfect, yet odorless imposter?" He snapped a bright red bloom off the bush. "Don't they realize that there is more to a rose than its beauty?"

Jake remained still, unsure what answer Aiden was asking for.

With a faraway look, Aiden peered over the hedge and into the rose garden. "Do you miss your mother?"

His eyes widened in surprise. Aiden never showed concern for his feelings. How could he not miss her? She was an enormous hole in his heart.

Twisting the rose between his thumb and index finger, Aiden inhaled. "It occurs to me that you and your mother need to be reminded what's important."

Jake closed his eyes, his back tensing with fear.

"You didn't answer my question, Jacob. Do you miss your mother?"

She was his everything. His world. Without her, he was empty and lonely and scared. Always scared. She was the one who kissed his head when he woke up with bad dreams. She was the one who held his hand and made the bad things go away.

Jake reached out to her in the darkness, surprised to find a crack in the wall that separated him from her. He felt her presence, basked in her goodness. After weeks of living with the stench of evil, she was a breath of soothing air.

Jake opened his tear-blurred eyes and nodded, overwhelmed with her love.

Aiden slowly turned his head to Jake and smiled, crushing the rose in his fist. "And now you remember what you have to lose."

As Aiden's fingers uncurled, the petals caught in the wind and blew onto the path. Aiden ground them into the pea gravel as he walked away.

****

Emma woke with a start, lying sideways on the bed, the TV broadcasting a middle-of-the-night infomercial. She'd stayed up waiting for Will, but exhaustion had finally overcome her. Sitting up, she glanced around the room for any signs of him, on the off chance he'd snuck in without waking her.

Nothing.

Terror stabbed in the pit of her stomach as she bolted off the bed and ran to the cell phone on the desk.

Nothing.

She paced on shaking legs as she tried to reason with herself. There had to be a reason Will hadn't come back, and several came instantly to mind. None of them were good.

Nausea gripped her abdomen and she raced to the toilet, barely making it before her meager dinner made a reappearance. As she rinsed out her mouth, she stared into the mirror, questioning if her nausea was from nerves or her enemy.

"Calm down. Freaking out isn't helping anything."

She took several deep breaths through her mouth, the discomfort in her stomach easing. But was it from her fear or had her warning of approaching enemies come and gone?

Will's bag sat on the floor in front of the closet. Rummaging through the contents produced a shotgun and a handgun, along with enough bullets to get her through a major gunfight. She loaded both and moved to the window, peeking through the cracks.

Vacant cars sat in the dimly lit parking lot, but one in particular caught her eye.

The sedan they'd stolen in Morgantown.

She stood with her back to the wall between the window and the door. She had to think this through, clearly and rationally. Will could have come back and still been so mad he might have decided to sleep inside the car rather than face her. Or someone could have abducted him on his way in. She shook her head, panic bubbling in her brain. No, don't think like that.

Yet she couldn't deny the possibility.

She peered outside again, looking for any signs of trouble, finding none. The car was parked a good twenty feet away, out of the glare of a streetlight. But once her eyes adjusted, enough light illuminated the driver's side of the car to reveal someone sitting inside. The head slumped forward at an awkward angle.

Will.

Heart racing, she forced herself to count to ten before she did anything, only making it to three before she flung the door open and darted behind the front end of a nearby car.

She paused long enough to confirm that no one was shooting at her before she ran to another car closer to the sedan. When she made it without drawing gunfire, she ran across the parking lot, ignoring the rough asphalt on her bare feet. She made it to the car, heart lodged in her throat, then jerked on the door handle. The door refused to budge. Locked.

She bent down to look inside, gasping in horror. His head bent forward at an uncomfortable-looking angle so that she couldn't see his face, but a large red stain saturated the front of Will's T-shirt, the gray one with the rip in the hem.

The one he was wearing when he left.

Not again. Please, God. Not again.

Emma beat on the window with the palm of her hand, hysterical. "Will! Open the door! WILL!"

Her shrieks filled the parking lot, and motel unit doors flung open to investigate, not that she cared. Half of her soul sat bloodied in this car.

"Will!" she sobbed, pounding on the window.

Something deep inside niggled for attention. Use your power to open the door. Her anger had dissipated, leaving only fear and grief. Not enough to even create an ember of power in her chest. Instinctively, she reached out to the streetlight overhead, pulling the energy into herself. "Open!" she cried, pointing to the door. It flung into her hand and she dropped to her knees, in her heart knowing what she would find, but hoping that somehow she was wrong.

"Will!"

She reached for his arm, recoiling when her hand came into contact with unnaturally cold flesh. Sobs erupted as she noticed a note pinned to his shirt. With shaking hands, she pulled it free, her vision too blurry with tears to read the words. A man approached her from the side and she raised her shotgun, trying to steady her shaking hands. "Back the fuck off."

He was an older man, wearing only boxers and a tank T-shirt, and had obviously rushed out without thinking when he'd heard her cries.

She instantly realized he was no threat.

His eyes widened in surprise as he raised his hands in surrender, backing up. "It's okay. I only want to help."

She lowered the gun, sobbing anew, and sucked deep breaths in an attempt to settle down. She had to get out of here before the police arrived.

But she couldn't leave Will.

He's already gone echoed through the dark recesses in her head, but as long as his body was here, he was still here too. "Will," she moaned as she placed her hands on his cheeks and lifted his head.

She gasped, staring into the face of a stranger.

It wasn't Will.

She dropped his head in shock, the man's chin bouncing off his chest, wondering how a man with Will's shirt, build, and hair color came to be sitting in their car. She realized she'd dropped the note in her grief and crawled on hands and knees as a crowd formed around the car. The slip of paper had wedged between the asphalt and the tire of the car next to her.

She held it up into the rays from the streetlight, drawing a shaky breath.

Be at the Santa Maria Hotel in Albuquerque by noon. Go to the front desk and ask for Pedro.

That goddamned fucking Raphael. If she didn't have an incentive to kill him before, she had one now. He'd said he'd hurt Will to get back at her, and this had his name written all over it.

The police would show up any minute, but she couldn't leave their belongings in the motel room. She pushed past the bewildered bystanders, whose numbers had doubled, and went to the room. Closing the door behind her, she jammed belongings into the duffel bag. There wasn't much. She and Will were always prepared for a quick escape, but by the time she was ready to exit the room, the parking lot was lit up with flashing red lights.

The police had arrived.

Taking the car was hopeless. It was parked in the back of the lot, surrounded by at least thirty gawkers from her glimpse out the window. Several people had gathered around the open door, some checking out the body in the front seat. Emma couldn't stop to think about the unfortunate man who shared the same body type and hair color with Will. She couldn't let herself take the blame, either.

Yet.

Instead, she needed to focus on getting away without being noticed by the police. An impossible task, since the front was the only way out.

Emma slung the duffel bag over her shoulder, her knees bending with the weight. Taking a slow, deep breath, she pulled energy from the lights in the room.

Grasping the doorknob with a shaky hand, she opened the door a crack. A bystander by the car was pointing to her door while talking to a police officer.

She threw the door open and lifted her hand, releasing her energy toward a car across the lot, directly in front of her door.

The explosion shook the building. In her nervousness she'd made it bigger than she intended, but it had the desired effect. The crowd scattered, their screams filling the night. She slipped out the door into the chaos of the frantic crowd, refusing to consider that she'd likely killed people in the process, and made her way to the street.

Now she needed to find a car and make it to Albuquerque.

Emma pulled into a public parking lot three blocks from the Santa Maria hotel. No need announcing her arrival any more than necessary. Not that they knew what car she was driving now. She'd gone to a used car lot and stolen one using her power.

Just one more sin to add to the ever-growing list.

Over the past four hours, she'd forced any thoughts of Will to the side, refusing to acknowledge the possibility of what she might find. Instead she sorted through the list of suspects. It seemed too coincidental that whoever took Will knew she was coming to Albuquerque to meet Alex.

The truth was, if the Vinco Potentia had Will, they already knew he was powerless. If it was the Cavallo, she had no idea what to expect. Raphael had the biggest motive, since he blamed Will for keeping Emma from him. But she couldn't dismiss dear old Dad. Aiden. She almost hoped it was Aiden, even if her power wasn't enough to fight him. At least she might get a chance to see Jake. And maybe she could get more answers.

She was early, but only by an hour. She hated to think what would have happened if she'd been detained by the police, or had trouble getting a car. All the more reason to suspect a supernatural being was behind all of this. Humans might consider those things. Supernatural creatures would assume she'd use her power to get out of it.

She planned to use the hour to her advantage.

A coffee shop occupied the corner of the building across the street. Emma ducked inside and ordered a coffee before she sat at the counter looking out onto the street. Pulling the laptop out of a backpack Will had picked up the previous week, she set it on the counter and performed a search for Phillip Warren. The news media reported him being on the East Coast today. But Alex was still scheduled to speak at the luncheon at noon in the Fairmont, three blocks from the Santa Maria. The fact that she was expected to meet Will's kidnapper at the other hotel at the same time Alex was supposed to speak didn't necessarily rule him out, especially since he knew that his lackeys couldn't contain her. Maybe it was a test since she was supposed to meet Alex at the same time. Was he testing her to see which she would choose?

If it was Aiden, she'd never be ready. No matter how she tried to prepare herself for an encounter with him.

She'd spent twenty minutes on the computer. Another forty minutes until noon. What would Will do? Swallowing the rising terror that accompanied thoughts of him, she forced herself to think rationally. Will would probably scope out the exterior of the building. Look for escape routes. That sounded like as good an idea as any.

Walking around the city block, she noted the location of the public and emergency exits, taking note of the restaurant on the northern end. The car was parked in a lot three blocks to the south. If Will was hurt, that might be too far away. She closed her eyes and focused on what needed to be done.

She was ten minutes early, but why not take the offensive and march in like she owned the place? With any luck at all, when she was done, she would.

Entering through the revolving glass door, the conditioned air caught her breath as it cooled the sweat on her skin after walking around in the New Mexico heat. The lobby was decorated like a five-star hotel, with marble floors and columns, and a central atrium that rose through the center of the building.

Emma lifted her chin and strode to the front desk as she hitched the backpack strap higher on her shoulder, leaving her sunglasses perched on her nose. She placed a hand on the counter, fully aware that she looked out of place in her rumpled, slept-in skirt and T-shirt, and her hair pulled back in a ponytail. "I need to speak to Pedro."

If the man behind the counter was surprised by her request, he hid it well. He took a plastic room key out of a drawer, slid it into an envelope, and handed it to her. He stared at her with a vacant expression. "Room 2123."

She paused, trying to determine if he was naturally undemonstrative or if he was under someone's control. She suspected the former.

The elevator was empty and it climbed to the twenty-first floor without stopping. The doors slid open to a hushed hallway with no one in sight. She pulled the handgun out of the front pocket of her backpack and slid back the rack. Her power might be stronger but was still an unknown variable. As she found with Raphael, if she was too scared it might not work. But bullets knew no fear.

Gun raised, she stepped out of the elevator, edging her way down the hall and stopping at the side of 2123, the last door on the right. Taking a deep breath, she ordered her racing heart to slow down. She needed to be calm and in control. Hyperventilating wouldn't help.

After another lungful of air, she hid the gun behind her back, knocked on the door, and waited.

When the door swung open, she wasn't prepared for the face that greeted her.

"Mommy."

CHAPTER TWENTY-FIVE

EMMA fell to her knees, sure she'd lost all touch with reality. "Jake?"

He threw his arms around her neck and buried his face in her hair.

How could he be here? The realization that he couldn't be in a luxury hotel in Albuquerque, New Mexico on his own sunk in. Especially when the last time she'd seen him was two weeks ago in Montana.

She stood and grabbed his hand in hers as she swiveled her head, looking for his captors. "Jake, we have to go."

He locked his knees, remaining in place. "No, Mommy. I can't leave and we don't have much time." He tugged her hand, pulling her inside the room and shutting the door.

They entered the living room of a suite and Jake pulled her to two chairs by the windows overlooking the city. He pushed her down gently and stood in front of her, pressing her cheeks between his palms. The corners of his mouth turned up into a sad smile. "It's you."

"I can't believe you're here." She pulled him tight against her body, hoping to soak in his presence. "I've missed you so much."

"You didn't talk to me," he murmured into her hair.

Squeezing him tight, she choked on the lump in her throat. "I tried, baby. I tried to talk to you. You couldn't hear me, but I was there, dying inside because I couldn't help you."

He buried his face deeper into her shoulder.

If Jake was here, there was only one way for him to be in a hotel in Albuquerque. "Where's Aiden?" she finally squeezed out once her breath recovered. Aiden had to be lurking somewhere and she had to get Jake out before he showed up.

Terror filled his eyes before he masked it. "He has business he has to do."

"Does he know I'm here?"

"Yes. He sent for you."

"Do you know where Will is?"

His eyes widened and he shook his head. "No."

Her heart leapt into her throat. "Do you know where Will is?"

Confusion crossed over his eyes. "No."

"Jake. Someone took Will. Are you sure you don't know where he is? You haven't seen a vision?"

Tears filled his eyes. "No."

She swallowed her rising panic. Maybe Jake didn't know, but Aiden did. "Someone took him." She grabbed his shoulders. "You have to help me, Jake. I have to find him."

He shook his head and looked away. "You don't need him anymore."

"Jake, this is Will we're talking about. Not some random stranger." She let go of him. "Do you know anything about where he is?"

His chin trembled. "I don't know."

Her head dropped, tears burning her eyes. "I have to find him. I have to save him."

He turned back to her, his eyes wide. "No, you have to save yourself."

Her head jerked up. "Who told you that?" But she knew. Aiden. "What did he say, Jake? What did Aiden tell you?"

Squaring his shoulders, resolve filled his eyes. "Will is holding you back. Aiden took away Will's memory for a reason, Mommy. You're done with Will."

Panic flooded her head. With Aiden's attitude, Will might already be dead. "No, I'm not. That's for me to decide. I need to know that Will is okay."

Hurt filled Jake's eyes. "Why are you picking him over me?"

"I'm not! Why are you saying that?"

He remained silent.

"Why can't I have you both?"

"Because Aiden says you can't." His voice broke.

A band of fear constricted her chest. "What will Aiden do if I don't leave Will?" She stood, walking to the windows and looking over downtown.

Jake moved beside her, placing his hand in hers. "Mommy, Will was supposed to help you gain your powers. He was temporary."

Emma spun to face him. "That's not what you told him when you burned that mark on his arm. You told him that the two of you would be enemies."

His mouth puckered before he whispered, "That's why you have to leave him behind. Otherwise, we will be enemies. I've seen it in my head. Who do you think will win, Mommy? Me or him? Who do you want to win?"

She staggered backward, dropping his hand. "No."

"Mommy." He pulled her back to the chair and pushed her down. "You can't fight Aiden." He sucked in a breath. "Please, Mommy. I need you to do this."

"What is Aiden going to do to Will?"

"I don't know."

She leaned back in the chair, gathering her thoughts. Why was Aiden insisting that she get rid of Will? He was the one coming up with new ideas and pushing her harder. She wouldn't be half this far without him.

Jake watched her with an intense gaze.

Her eyes widened as she sucked in a breath. Jake could read her mind.

His face became blurry through her tears. "Jake, please. Listen to me." She took his hand and held it to her chest. "Come with me. I'm stronger now and I can protect you from Aiden. I can teach you how to hide from him."

His face sagged with disappointment. "He said you wouldn't listen. He said that you would pick Will."

"No, Jake. I'm not picking him over you. Please. Listen to me."

Tears filled his eyes.

She pulled him into a hug, crushing him to her chest and breathing in the soft soap smell of his hair. "Has Aiden been nice to you? Are you safe?"

"Yes," he said, his voice muffled.

She pulled him onto her lap, turning him sideways. "Do you miss me? Do you think of me?"

"Yes." His voice broke.

"I miss you so much." Her chest heaved as she struggled to maintain control. "I don't want any of this mess. I never asked for it. I just want you."

"And Will."

She closed her eyes. There was no winning this. "You picked Will for me. You. I can't just stop loving him. Just like I can't stop loving you. I love you both. Why is that not okay? I want you both to be safe."

Jake pulled back and looked into her eyes, his cheeks wet with tears. "No one will be safe until this is over."

She ran her hand over his cheek, smoothing back his hair as she looked deep into his eyes. "Jake, do you know anything about Will? Please, I'm begging you."

His gaze dropped. "I don't know. I'm only supposed to tell you to leave Will."

She raised her eyebrows. "What else does Aiden say?"

"He says that I'm special," he whispered, looking down.

She stroked his head. "Yes, you're very special. We've known that for ages. Which is why I had to protect you."

"Aiden says he can protect me from everyone and everything. Better than you ever could." His voice quivered.

His words pierced her heart. Yet she couldn't deny they were likely true. "I'm his daughter, Jake. Why didn't he protect me from all the bad things in my life? Think about you and me. I did everything I possibly could to keep you safe and I didn't even have powers. He could have saved us both. Why didn't he?"

Jake's shoulders shook with sobs. "He said you wouldn't listen. Mommy, please listen."

Her voice softened as her arms tightened around him. "Jake, I'm going to fix this. I'm going to get you out of this." She set him off her lap and stood, grabbing his hand. "Come on. We're leaving."

Jake pulled against her, frantic. "No! Mommy, please!"

A voice drifted from behind her. "Hello, Emmanuella."

Her back tensed and Jake stilled, his eyes wide in terror. Emma turned around, pushing Jake behind her. "Aiden."

He laughed and walked through a door from an adjoining room. "Going somewhere?"

She lifted her chin. "Yes. I came to get my son and leave."

"I was under the impression you were here for something else."

Her breath caught. "Where's Will?"

He scowled, shaking his head. "I give you your son. He's cowering behind you, yet you still choose that man."

"Give me my son? You took my son, you arrogant asshole."

"Emma, such language in front of Jake. Really." His gaze landed on Jake's face. "Jake, why don't you run into the other room so your mother and I can have a chat."

Jake hesitated, clutching Emma's leg.

"No." Emma's anger grew, filling the room with a golden glow.

Her father sat in a chair and crossed his legs, his face expressionless. "Do you really want to do this, Emmanuella? I think we both know who will win. But if you have any doubt, ask your son." Aiden leaned forward with a tight smile. "Jake, tell your mother who will win this confrontation."

"You," Jake whispered.

Aiden reclined in his chair. "Now there's a smart boy. Tell your mother goodbye and run along."

Jake took a step away from Emma and she grabbed his arm, panic clawing in her head. "No."

With tear-filled eyes, Jake tried to pull loose from her grip. "I can't go with you, Mommy."

She fell to her knees, breaking into sobs as she pulled him into her arms. "I can't leave you here. I can't let you go."

"You have to." His arms tightened around her neck. "I love you, Mommy."

"I love you too." How could she let this monster take her son? Did she really have a choice?

"Mommy, listen," Jake whispered. "You have to listen to Aiden. He does terrible things to people. Please, Mommy. I don't want him to hurt you."

"Antonia," Aiden called out. "I think Jake needs some assistance going to the other room."

A young woman walked up behind Jake and bowed her head with apologetic eyes. "I'll take good care of him. I promise."

Emma clung to Jake tighter. "I'm sorry. I'm so sorry."

He leaned back and cradled her face in his hands. "It's okay, Mommy." He kissed her on the cheek and took Antonia's hand.

Covering her mouth with a shaky hand, Emma watched him leave the room. She couldn't let Aiden get away with this.

"You should listen to your son," Aiden said in a bored tone. "I will stop any attempt you make to kill me."

She rose to her feet, glaring at the demon in front of her.

Aiden chuckled. "You always had a fire in you. I saw it when you were just a little girl and stood up to your mother."

"You saw me?"

He shrugged. "I had to keep tabs on you."

"And you left me with her?"

He leaned forward. "She made you strong, Emmanuella. She made you the fighter you are today. That didn't happen by accident. You should thank me."

Her jaw dropped. He was actually serious.

"You need every ounce of strength to win this. Even though you didn't realize it, you've been preparing since the day you were conceived." He tilted his head. "Emma, sit. I insist." He waved his hand to the chair next to him.

Resisting the urge to run after Jake, she sat across from him.

"You were part of my master plan. I knew I could only hold on for another generation, two at the maximum. The power I acquired from Alex and Raphael had begun to run out. If I continued on like I had, I'd soon be no stronger than those two fools. So I chose to put my remaining excess energy into you."

Cold dread washed through her. "You knew Alex would rape me when you sent him to me."

His face was devoid of emotion. "I needed Jake."

This couldn't be true.

"I told him that you were possibly the queen from the prophecy. But I sent him on several excursions for possible candidates. I may have suggested that there was only one way to know for sure. Most were quite willing."

Had Alex raped other women thinking that they were her? She was going to be sick.

"You're telling me you don't want Jake? You'd rather it never happened and that he'd never been born?"

Her mouth gaped. "Don't you twist this into something it's not, you sick bastard. You practically told the man to rape me."

He shrugged. "The circumstances of Jake's conception are most regrettable and could have been handled much more civilly."

"Much more civilly?"

"Emma, it took care of two things at once. Jake was conceived and Alex proved once and for all that he's a bumbling idiot not worthy of getting his power back. Besides, it worked in your favor too. You got Jake and it made you stronger than ever."

Oh, God. This went deeper than that. "And the Bad Men? The Cavallo? You sent them too?"

The corners of his mouth lifted slightly.

"Do you realize what it did to that little boy? Those men haunted his dreams."

"I did it for you both. Every time they came it made you stronger, ready to fight."

Fight. Icy fear washed through her veins. "What happens to Jake? Please, please tell me that he's not part of this."

He lifted an eyebrow with a smile.

"He's only five years old!"

"And stronger than the two imbeciles who've tried to win your predecessor's favor for centuries."

She leaned back in the chair, trying to take in the information. "So it's you and Jake then. You two are the winners?"

"No," he scoffed. "Four shall fight, two shall remain. It was Raphael's stupid pronouncement, but it fits with my plan. You and Jake can fight Raphael and Alex. The two of you remain."

"Wait." She cocked her head. "I thought it was Raphael, Alex, you, and me."

"I never said *who* would fight. Only that *four* would fight and of those four, only two would remain. The contestant slots are still open."

"What about you?"

"I watch. I don't fight. There are no rules against that."

The air stuck in her throat. They were doomed.

"You have until the very first round to lock in who participates." Aiden winked. "I always think it's fun to keep them guessing. You all have a little over four weeks to fret."

Four weeks. How could she be ready in four weeks?

"So now you see why I need you to focus more on your preparation and less on your love life. That was the whole purpose of wiping Will's memory. That he would disappear. I was sure that Warren and his little playgroup would kill him and I wouldn't have to do it. You would have held that over my head for eternity. How is it that he still chooses to be with you?"

"I don't know." She bit her lip and looked out the window, struggling to hold back her tears. It was hopeless. "So if my training is so important to you, why not take me with you and Jake?"

"And if I took you with us, what incentive would you have? You would already have your son. Would you have willingly agreed to fight?"

No, she would have taken Jake and left.

He waved his hand. "It doesn't matter. I've decided to take matters into my own hands and put a stop to this nonsense."

"Where's Will? Is he alive?"

"Yes, for now. But it's up to you for how long."

She saw no way to stop any of this madness. How could she save Will and Jake from this madman? She couldn't even save herself. "So now what?"

He smiled, his eyes glittering. "I knew if I presented this the right way, you'd see it my way."

"Oh, yeah. Score one for Aiden and his persuasion. What do you want me to do?"

"You go back to training and I'll let you know when and where the battle will be."

"I want to see Will and tell him goodbye."

"I don't think that's a good idea."

"No." She shook her head with a bitter laugh. "If you want me to do this, we're going to do this my way. I want to see him and make sure he's okay, then I'll tell him goodbye."

He studied her, raising an eyebrow. "And then you will leave him?"

"Yes."

He smiled. "Okay, I'll agree to this on one condition. You must promise you will leave him."

Her heart skipped a beat. "What?"

"I'm quite familiar with your honor code. I know how important it is to you, so let's make this perfectly clear. I will allow you to tell Will goodbye and then you will leave him. And if you don't, I will kill him. Is this clear?"

She was losing everything she loved. Again. How many times could she live through this? "Yes." She choked on the word.

Jumping to his feet, Aiden grinned. "Excellent. We've come to an understanding. I'll have my men bring Will to a location tonight."

"I want him released while I'm there to see it."

He cocked an eyebrow. "You don't trust me?"

"Since you seem to have no honor code of your own, no."

He laughed, a rich hearty sound. "You are by far my favorite daughter yet." He walked to a desk and scribbled something on a piece of paper, handing it to her. "They'll meet you in the Sandia Mountains. They'll be at an overlook at nine o'clock tonight."

She nodded, her heart breaking as she took the instructions.

Aiden moved to the door. Pausing with his hand on the doorknob, he turned to her and smiled. "I knew you wouldn't disappointment me."

CHAPTER TWENTY-SIX

EMMA walked into the New Mexico heat with a shredded heart, barely aware of the people she passed on the busy sidewalk. She refused to accept things as they were. So her father raised her to be strong and fight?

Too bad he didn't see that she could also fight him.

There had to be a reason Aiden wanted Will to be gone. It couldn't just be that she was distracted by him. There had to be something more to it.

Alex had expected Emma to arrive by noon at his fundraiser. It was only twelve-thirty. If she hurried, she might not be too late.

As Emma approached the doors to the grand ballroom that held the luncheon, she was suddenly aware of how out of place she would look in her cheap skirt and T-shirt, but quickly dismissed it. She didn't give a rat's ass how she looked. Her sole purpose of showing up was to fulfill her promise. If Alex didn't like it, too bad. He'd never notified her of a dress code.

Two security officers flanked the door and one gave her a suspicious look. "I'm sorry, miss. This event is invitation-only."

"My name's on the list. Emma Thompson."

The man scanned his paper then looked up in surprise. "I'm sorry, Miss Thompson. Mr. Warren is expecting you. His table is in the front."

He opened the door and she walked in, standing in the back of a room filled with more circular tables than she could count. They were covered in white linens with red roses floating in silver bowls. The clink of silverware on fine china filled the air, hundreds of adoring constituents giving their rapt attention to the man in the front of the room.

Alex.

His voice filled the room while the faces of the crowd hung on his every word.

He'd mesmerized them. Literally. No wonder everyone loved him.

"...and I assure you that your concerns are not taken lightly. My father, Phillip Warren, wants to be your advocate."

Emma moved along the outer wall toward the front.

"Alex Warren should be president," a wide-eyed woman said, clutching her hands on the table in front of her.

The man next to her nodded dumbly, his attention totally focused on Alex.

Emma's stomach twisted. Will had been right. If Alex gained control of Aiden's power, he'd be able to do anything.

Twenty feet from the front, she stopped. She could feel him now. Feel the slow roll of energy flowing off of him.

"Do you think Fred Dixon cares? No! While a senior senator, he voted that bill down not once, not twice, but three times, while Phillip Warren worked day and night to push for the right to quality health care. What type of leadership do you want? A man who ignores the will of the people or a man who works tirelessly to heed their needs?"

The crowd cheered and Alex paused, scanning the crowd for dramatic effect. His eyes rested on Emma, and a slow smile lit up his face.

Alex turned back to the crowd. "Send Phillip Warren to the White House! Phillip Warren hears the cries of the people in the land. His heart lies with the poor and the downtrodden. Phillip Warren wants to be your voice!"

The crowd stood and cheered while Alex beamed, raising his arms over his head in a triumphant manner. Emma shook her head in disgust. The crowd was clearly mesmerized. His crappy speech couldn't have elicited this much enthusiasm.

Alex walked off the stage and whispered in the ear of one of his security detail. Holding out his hand, he motioned her toward him. "Don't be shy, Emma. I admit I was worried that you'd stood me up, but better late than never." He tilted his head toward the side door with a grin and a wink. "If you'll follow me."

She froze several feet in front of him. "Where are we going? You said I was supposed to attend the luncheon with you. The luncheon's in here."

He laughed and shook his head. "Paranoid, aren't you. Yes, this is technically the luncheon, but part of the fundraiser is me dining privately with a supportive constituent who's willing to pay for the privilege. Besides, what we're about to discuss needs privacy and discretion."

She scowled. "Won't someone be upset that I took their place?"

"No, since I put your name on the list and donated your fee."

"And how much did you pay for the pleasure of dining with yourself?" she asked as he ushered her through the door.

"More than I'm worth." He laughed again, a self-deprecating tone that caught her by surprise.

The guards escorted them to a smaller room containing a table covered in food, then shut the door, leaving Alex and Emma alone. Alex unbuttoned his jacket as he sat at the table. "You really came."

"I said I would."

"So you did." He waved to the chair next to him. "Please, have a seat."

After her encounter with Aiden, she felt jumpy but sat anyway. "You're lucky you're able to mesmerize the crowd, otherwise you'd need a new speechwriter. That speech sucked."

He raised his eyebrows in mock surprise. "Ouch, Emma. Who knew you had a vicious streak?"

"Oh, I'm just getting started."

He laughed again and lifted the domes off of their plates. The smell of roasted chicken wafted to her nose. Her stomach audibly growled, reminding her that she hadn't eaten since last night.

Alex grinned. "You might as well enjoy it. That dried-up chicken cost me two thousand dollars."

"Two thousand dollars?"

He shrugged. "Small price to pay to gain the ear of the presidential candidate."

"Someone forgot to tell them that you're not running for president. Your father is."

He shrugged again. "Same thing."

"Why are you wasting your time doing this anyway? Shouldn't you be preparing for the epic battle for control of the world?"

Alex cut a small piece of chicken and took a bite, releasing a satisfied sigh. "This is quite delicious."

She raised her eyebrows.

He paused, fork in midair. "There's nothing for me to prepare. I've done all I can do. The only variable at this point is you. I'd be lying if I didn't admit that I'm happy you showed up. I'm quite eager to hear about your progress and I hope that we can come to some kind of agreement." Alex picked up her fork and put it in her hand. "Emma, eat for God's sake."

She held the fork over the chicken, hesitating. What if he'd drugged it?

He reached over with his own fork and tore off a piece and put it in his mouth. "There. Happy now? Eat."

She took a bite and nearly groaned. She couldn't remember the last time she'd had something so good. "Why does Aiden want me to stay away from Will?"

"What makes you think Aiden wants you to stay away from Will?"

"No, don't do that. No talking in riddles. Just answer my question." She took another bite. "Did you know my father sent you to me knowing that you would probably rape me?"

The way the color drained from his face told her he didn't. He took a deep breath, distrust in his eyes. "Why would he do that?"

"He said he needed Jake."

He cocked his head. "You've talked to him since our last meeting?"

"I just left him to come here. He's down at the Santa Maria Hotel."

He turned his attention to his plate. "Ha. Ha. Very funny."

"You think I'm kidding?"

His head slowly rose. "You're serious?"

"Someone kidnapped Will and left a dead man who looked a lot like him in the front seat of my car with a note pinned to his shirt. It told me to go to the Santa Maria Hotel. And guess who was there, ready to chat."

"I'll be damned." Alex put down his fork and pushed his plate away. "Let me guess. You want me to help you rescue your lad in distress again? Really, Emma. Surely, even you are getting tired of his helplessness."

"No," she said, irritation biting the word. "I'm getting him back on my own tonight. What I want to know is why Raphael and Aiden are so dead set that I get rid of Will, when you don't seem to care."

"Why should I care?"

"Then you don't know why they do?"

Alex rolled his eyes as he picked up his crystal water glass. "Raphael is a no-brainer. You may not be the woman he loved, but he can't let her go. You're the next best thing. Plus the whole combining-power thing." He took a sip of water and put the glass down. "Aiden, I'm not so sure about. How do you know that's what he wants?"

"Because he told me to let Will go or he'd kill him."

Alex shrugged with a sigh. "Who can figure out Aiden's mind games?"

"What do you know about the joining words?"

He glanced up, surprised. "What is this? Twenty questions? I don't have time to state the obvious. I'm a busy man."

"Yeah, puppeteering crowds."

He snatched the roll from her plate and tore off a piece. "I'm insulted by your insinuation. I'm a much-sought-after public speaker."

"I bet you are. So what's your plan? Win the battle of the millenniums and then rule the world?"

He pursed his lips with a grin. "It's always good to have a plan. And yes, I'm prepping for my victory. You think I should be preparing my burial plot instead?"

"If Aiden has his way..."

Alex jerked upright. "What did Aiden say?"

"Answer my question first: Do you know the joining words?"

"Of course I do. They're etched into my brain."

"So what are they?"

"You still don't know?"

"Would I be asking if I did?"

"Wow." He ate a piece of the bread. "That's interesting. You should know them by now. But then again, nothing is the same this go-round."

"Could they be in the book we stole from the compound?" Even as the words tumbled out, she realized her mistake.

Alex's eyes widened before he clouded them with nonchalance. "You have the book? Well, well. Look who has a devious streak. For shame, Emma Thompson. You led me to believe otherwise."

"What if I told you that it was destroyed in a fire in Missouri?"

His shoulder lifted in a half shrug. "Oh, well."

"For a politician, you're a terrible liar."

His laughter filled the room. "I wish we'd met under different circumstances. You'd keep me on my toes."

"Yeah...not a chance. Why do you really want it?"

"Why do you?"

"Okay, we can play this back and forth all afternoon and never get anywhere. We wanted to see if the book had answers about who I am. Now your turn."

"I want to see if it specified the new rules." He looked into her eyes. "Did you find any answers?"

"No. But there are pages that aren't translated. Will suspected that they held key information."

"And did they?"

She scowled. "How would I know? I told you it wasn't translated."

He chuckled and shook his head. "For someone so bright, sometimes you are incredibly stupid."

"What the hell is that supposed to mean?"

"It means you're more than capable of reading it if you just apply yourself."

Her eyes lit up with understanding.

He eyed the backpack she'd set on the floor next to her chair. "Do you have it with you?"

She tried to keep her face neutral. "No."

"Where is it?"

"Not here."

"We're talking in circles again."

"Do you think you're going to win?"

His face blanched. "Do you always say whatever pops into your head?"

"I don't have time to dilly-dally around. Do you think you have a chance?"

"I refuse to consider the alternative. Which brings me to my previous proposition."

"Joining with you?"

He stared at her, expressionless.

"Not a chance. But I'm not teaming up with Raphael either. Every man—or woman—for his or herself." She wondered if she should share Aiden's plan but decided to keep that information to herself. "You realize that you are unique in that you have ties to all three of my enemies."

He chuckled. "Do tell."

"Your father's group. The Vinco Potentia."

His lips pursed. "And mine. I belong to them too."

"How can you belong to them and the Cavallo?"

He laughed and leaned back in his chair. "Ah, now there's an interesting story. Take a wild guess at who's behind the Cavallo?"

Her eyes sank closed. "Aiden."

"See? I told you that you were intelligent. Yep, one and the same."

She released a heavy sigh. "Why? What's his purpose for that?"

"What's Aiden's purpose for anything? To confuse? To distract? He formed them about forty years ago, but he was a secret member, playing both sides. They never really did much. The supposed purpose for their split was so that the Cavallo could be more proactive. But the truth is that they never really did anything until five years ago. After I found out about Jake, through Aiden, of course, he suggested I form an allegiance with them. Aiden insisted that it was in everyone's best interest to leave you and Jake alone and bide our time."

"How long ago did you find out about Jake?"

"While you were pregnant."

She chewed on that piece of information. She'd presumed it was later, although she wasn't sure why.

"Three years ago, he approached the Cavallo with information he'd supposedly gleaned from the book. He'd found the whereabouts of the child in the prophecy. He told the group where to find him. They sent several men to bring him back, but of course, you got away."

"And obviously, this kept happening."

"Yeah. Aiden would announce he knew your location, they'd send men out to get Jake, and repeat. Until the end.

When Will showed up at the Vinco Potentia compound and announced that Jake was dead, I was floored. Their goal all along was to capture him and use him, which meant he had to be alive. But I hadn't been in contact with them in weeks so I couldn't be sure until later."

"But you knew he was in Arizona."

"No, I knew the plan was to take him to a safe house in Arizona."

"So when did you figure out who you really were?"

"After you and Will escaped. When I regained consciousness, it was all there in my head. Centuries' worth of memories. I kind of lost it for a day or two, thinking I'd gone crazy. I told Kramer, but he didn't believe me. He thought I'd gone off the deep end. By the time I came to my senses, I realized it was in everyone's best interest to keep my true identity secret."

"So how did you know where to find Jake?"

"Aiden."

She bit her lip, sickened by this entire game. "All roads lead to Aiden."

"In this case, they tend to. Aiden helped me take Jake from the Cavallo and hide him in Montana."

"What happened to the real members of the Cavallo?"

"Aiden used his mind control to get them to let me have Jake and they *forgot* that they wanted him."

"But not me?"

"No, he told them you were in Minnesota. And in the woods in Colorado, when you got shot. But I didn't find out until much later. My goal was to use Jake to lure you to me."

"So you could win?"

"Why does wanting to end centuries' worth of agony make me a bad person?"

"When it involves destroying innocent lives? Yeah, it totally makes you a bad person."

Alex shrugged. "I refuse to apologize."

"For any of it?" she asked, astounded.

He watched her for a moment. "None of it."

"What an ass. You're just as bad as him." Of course he was. These were supernatural creatures that turned the world upside down out of boredom. Over the course of a couple millenniums, how many people had been killed? How many lives destroyed? She was a pawn, perhaps a powerful pawn, but a pawn all the same. "So tell me this: Do I need to worry about the Cavallo?"

"No. I convinced some to forget about you."

"And the rest?"

"Let's just say that you don't need to worry about them. I need you to stay alive and I couldn't trust them."

"And the Vinco Potentia?"

"They've been hit hard twice now, but they're scrambling to recover and recapture you. To them, you and your baby are the key to their success."

"So they don't know there's not a baby anymore?"

Alex grinned. "No."

"And they welcomed you back with open arms after you killed everyone on the compound?"

"They never knew it was me. They suspected it was you when you helped Will escape." He winked.

She shook her head. Of course. She knew he had a selfish motive for freeing Will—now she had confirmation. "It was all part of your plan. You didn't help Will for me. You used it to cover your own break-in." She sighed. "So they're still out there? Rallying the troops?"

"They're scared shitless of you. They want you but they're not sure how to handle you after your mass execution." He laughed as he stabbed a piece of chicken and looked up at her. "Boy, they weren't expecting to see you when they showed up to capture Will in Missouri."

"You sent them? *Why?*"

"You needed real-world practice. I provided it."

"*Really?*" Why was she so surprised? This was the man who'd callously raped her. Squaring her shoulders, she looked into his eyes. "In your opinion, is Aiden my biggest concern?"

"And Raphael, of course."

She lifted an eyebrow. "Of course."

"So, are you ready to join with me now?"

"No."

"Will you show me the book?"

"No, I don't think so."

"I've been extremely forthcoming, Emma."

She studied him. "It appears that you have."

"The book is technically mine. It belonged to the Vinco Potentia and I am their representative."

"Possession is nine-tenths of the law." She stood. "I think it's time for me to be going."

"Where are you meeting your father to collect Will?"

"Why? Wanting to throw Will a welcome home party?"

"Why are you so cynical and distrustful?"

She laughed. "Oh! Now that is hilarious. On that note, I think I'll be off."

Alex stood and rested his hand on the back of his chair. It was a relaxed pose but she saw his fingers clench into a light fist. "Emma, I really need to see that book."

"Your daddy told Will the original is in DC Just look at that one."

"I can't. It's missing."

"Aiden?"

"Probably. Or maybe Raphael."

It occurred to her that she could kill him now and be done with it. She'd killed multiple men, what was one more? Deaths in this game were a certainty. The real question was, how many would die? How many countless lives could she save by finishing him off now? She held a power over him, probably making it easy to accomplish. All it would take was one touch and he would be under her control. Just like Raphael. But didn't that make her just like the demon she had run from? Was she ready to cross that line? "Thanks for lunch."

Alex scowled as Emma walked backward to the exit, keeping her eyes on him.

"I'm going to get that book back, Emma."

She pushed open the doors and looked back over her shoulder as she walked out of the room. "Come and get it."

CHAPTER TWENTY-SEVEN

UNSURE what to do the rest of the day, Emma went back to the car and got the book out of the duffel bag in the trunk. It had been a risk leaving it behind, but now she was glad she had. With Alex's words fresh in her head, she was eager to try to read it now. She shook her head at her idiocy. How did she not think of it sooner?

The truth was that using her power didn't come naturally to her. Sure, blowing things up had become second nature, but the more creative options seemed to be a last resort. And she couldn't ignore the fact that every time she used her power, it came with a price. With each use, she sacrificed her humanity bit by bit, making her more like the fiends she feared. Still, the hard reality was that she had little choice in the matter. She had to sacrifice her soul to save the people she loved.

Ducking into another coffee shop, she ordered a drink and hid back in the corner. She laid the book on the table, trailing her finger over the embossed letters on the cover. She silently offered up prayers to whatever deity would hear her plea. Anyone but her father.

She took a deep breath, her stomach crunching into a ball. She'd never know unless she tried, but she'd have to uncover her power to do it. Unmasking her power would make her a target, but her options were limited. One, she could try to read it now and hope she found answers to help save Will tonight. Or two, she could wait until she was far from Albuquerque. The latter was unacceptable. She'd take her chances. Opening the cover, she carefully flipped the pages until she came to the questionable text. It scrawled across the page in thick ink, clearly illegible, a mixture of lines and swirls. How did she use her power to read it? Maybe it wasn't as difficult as she made it out to be.

"Show me the words."

Magically, the lines on the page rearranged themselves, forming a flowing cursive script.

First, the prophecy appeared. The one that Jake recited to Will, and not the Vinco Potentia version in the back of the book.

After that, the title "Joining Words" appeared. Emma felt the walls creep in closer and she looked up, swamped with paranoia. Yet she couldn't deny thick shadows had formed on the walls, edging toward her.

She slammed the book shut, drawing the attention of a harried mother with an obnoxious toddler at the table next to her. Emma offered a small smile of apology as she gripped the tome protectively.

Could the shadows hurt her? They felt ominous. That night in the forest, Aiden had said that part of his, Alex, and Raphael's purpose was to rule the creatures that had been banished to live in the shadows. What were the shadows capable of that they needed governing?

She was in a public place. What could happen? Emma couldn't hold back her laugh at the irony.

The mother cast Emma a questioning glance then picked up her coffee and pastry, rolling her stroller several tables away.

Smoke singed her nose and her vision faded as the voice from her vision and dreams filled her head. "You are death. You destroy those you love and those who don't even know you. You are the destruction of the world." The blackness just as quickly fell away, leaving Emma shaken and scared. Who the hell was that?

The shadows inched closer and coldness seeped into her bones, beckoning her. She shivered, shaking it off. She was imagining things.

Or was she?

There was no question that the shadows had thickened around her. Did they whisper in her head?

She needed to read those words.

Cracking the book open, she turned it away from the wall at an angle, sure that she looked even more like an escaped mental patient.

The words had gone back to their original language so she repeated her earlier phrase and watched the prophecy form the title "Joining Words." She held her breath as the letters slowly appeared.

With echoes from the beginning of time
To the last ray of light from the stars at the end
I join my heart with yours
onto an endless path that winds through infinity
and sears our souls and power into an unbreakable bond

Through life and death, and all that lies between
I vow to be yours, forever

As she silently read the words, she felt them etch into her brain, forever available if the need should arise.

One thing was for certain. She'd been correct to presume that the words didn't represent just a joining of power. It was literally a vow to merge souls—and at least with wedding vows it was till-death-do-us-part. Or divorce. This joined the two together for eternity. Death be damned.

So if one were to vanish into the shadows, would the other go with them?

She read before and after the vows, looking for instructions but finding none. Not that it mattered. She had no plans to use them. Ever. She'd rather be cast into nothingness than be joined for eternity with either of those assholes.

The fake prophecy that Aiden had written was printed in the back pages. There was no doubt it had served its purpose to coerce the Vinco Potentia to look for her and think one of them would be the Chosen One. Emma couldn't help but wonder how many others Aiden had duped over the years. Groups, families, kingdoms. With Aiden, there were no boundaries.

She found a page that told the story Alex and Raphael had shared. Ancient creatures, bored and drunk, gambled away their power for what they thought to be a relatively short time. Until Aiden tricked them, sending them on a perpetual loop through history, destined to search and attempt to win the key to their victory. Aiden's daughter. All elemental, fire, air, earth. Water.

Where the hell was Water? After a week of no information, if the book didn't give her clues to find Water then she was at a dead end. Unless she could use her powers and say she wanted to find him. She suspected, and hoped, that wouldn't work. Otherwise, Raphael would have found her six days ago.

The text looked old and smudged but underneath was a newer section with a freshly inked prophecy, which was odd, given that the text read as chaos to the normal eye. *This* was why everyone wanted the book.

> The battle shall end the fight
> When all four unite
> Four will fight, two will remain.
> And the—

A wave of energy hit her and she looked up, knowing it was Raphael before he opened the door. He grinned when he saw her, his pleasure filling the waves that lapped at her. She could feel his emotions now.

She pulled the backpack off the floor and stuffed the book inside as he sat in the chair across from her.

"Well, if it isn't old-home week," she mocked. "The gang's all here."

"You saw Alex, I take it?"

"And you know this...how?"

He crossed his legs and leaned an arm along the back of his chair. "I know things."

"Then you know I met with Aiden as well?"

His momentary pause before he grinned gave him away. "But of course."

"Liar."

"What did Daddy Dearest want?"

"Who said he called me? Maybe I was the one to go to him."

"No one just drops in on Aiden. He always sets up the meetings."

She scowled. In this case, it was true. "He told me that I had to get rid of Will."

He studied her with an intense gaze before he swung his head around. "I don't see Lazarus around anywhere. Did you cut him loose?"

"You lied to me. You made me believe Will was dead."

With a heavy sigh, he leaned forward, lowering his head. "I did it for your own good. He's human and he's going to hold you back. You can't join with him, which makes him worthless to you."

"Wasn't that for me to decide?"

"No, because you could have gotten yourself killed trying to rescue him. I was thinking about your survival, Emmanuella."

"I think you're jealous."

His lips puckered as he tilted his head with a half shrug. "Perhaps. But the fact remains that he is human."

She turned her glance out the window. "I can't help but think that you and Aiden know something you're not sharing."

Which raised the question, what did they know? The newer prophecy said that the four would join together. Four shall fight, two will remain. Everyone seemed to have their own interpretation of what it meant. But what if it meant the four elements were together again. The four shall unite again. What if it wasn't referring to Aiden, Alex, Raphael, and Emma? What if it included Water?

Raphael leaned his elbow on the table, his head moving closer to hers. "You know, if we joined together, there would be no secrets. We would know everything there was to know about one another. No secrets, no way to lie."

"Everything? Why would anyone want that?"

"I'm sure it has its advantages."

"Maybe, but I guess you'll never know. With me, anyway."

Raphael frowned. "Why are you being so difficult? Surely you see the advantages of joining together to fight your father." His mouth pinched in disdain. "Unless you've decided to join with Alex."

While she understood his persistence, she was weary of the debate. "What if I sided with Water?"

Raphael's face paled as his eyes widened. "What did you say?"

She cocked an eyebrow. "Air, earth, fire. Water? There are four elements. Where's Water?"

Relief crept into his eyes and he released a breath. "He was one of us many years ago." He looked down his nose, skeptical. "Why the sudden interest?"

"If this is my world now, I should know more about it. Don't you think?"

Raphael shifted in his seat. "There was never any love lost between any of us, and while he would enjoy nothing more than to defeat Aiden, he'd never side with either of us to do it. Water will not show up."

The gears in her head kicked into overdrive. From the new prophecy, it sounded like Water *was* coming back. Which made sense. If he wanted his realm back, he'd definitely turn up for the showdown of the millenniums. What happened to him if he *didn't* show up? It sounded like Raphael didn't want Water to show up. And Aiden probably didn't want him around either. Her breath stuck in her throat.

Could Will be Water?

She made herself calm down. "What is Water's name?"

Narrowing his eyes, Raphael's voice had a sharp edge. "Why?"

Emma shrugged and tried to look nonchalant. "Why the big secret? What are you afraid of?"

"Why would I be afraid of anything? This is ridiculous, Emmanuella."

She stared into his face, waiting. "So then why not tell me?"

"Marcus. His name is Marcus. Happy now?"

No, she wasn't happy. But then again, she couldn't trust that he was telling the truth, either.

"What else did you find in the book?"

It was Emma's turn to feign confusion. "What book?"

Raphael grabbed her arm on the table, leaning closer. "Don't play stupid, Emma. You know exactly what I'm talking about."

She jerked her arm out of his grasp. "What does it matter anyway?"

He sneered, clenching his jaw. "With the added information in the book and joining our power, we could not only defeat Aiden but use our unlimited power to achieve *anything*."

Her mouth gaped.

He snorted, seeing the horror on her face. "Don't get all self-righteous on me. What good is power if you can't use it?"

She rolled her eyes in disgust. "Maybe you and Aiden should hook up after all. You both have the same belief system."

"Really, Emma. What do you plan to do with it?"

"Honestly, Raphael, I hadn't given it much thought. I'm trying to get past the saving-my-ass part, thank you very much." She leaned closer and lowered her voice. "Now, are you going to tell me the real reason you want to get rid of Will or not?"

He leaned forward so that their foreheads almost touched, and grinned. "There's nothing to tell."

She sat back. "You bastard."

He chuckled. "Technically, I think that title goes to you, love."

Grabbing the backpack, she stood. "I'm done here. Stay the fuck away from me, Raphael. Don't stalk me.

Don't come near me. If I see you before hell freezes over, it will be too soon."

"I'll be around anyway. To keep track of Will and make sure he's not impeding your progress."

"No worries, Daddy dearest has taken care of that one as well. When Aiden's men hand him over tonight, if I don't tell him goodbye Aiden will kill him."

"Well, there's one way to take care of the threat."

She paused then sat back down, leaning toward him. "Wait. Threat. What threat?"

His eyes widened in mock surprise. "I didn't say anything about a threat."

"Oh, yes you did. I heard it plain as day. Why does Aiden think Will's a threat?"

"I never said he thought that. Enough nonsense, Emmanuella." The tremor in his left hand belied his self-assured attitude.

"You think he is too or you wouldn't be so nervous."

"Who the hell says I'm nervous?"

"Please. Sweat is oozing from your pores. What has you so worried?"

He grinned, but it didn't reach his eyes. "Enough questions, Emma. I'm done with questions. Join me or not. I'm done persuading you, but be warned. I'm not doing this on my own so if need be, I will team up with Alex. The two of us together are still stronger than just you."

Too bad he didn't seem entirely convinced of that.

She stood and started to walk past him when he grabbed her arm. She jerked away.

"And one more thing." He looked up into her eyes. "I'm going to need that book."

Curling up her upper lip in disgust, she glared. "Get your own."

"I tried. It's gone."

"Wait, you don't have the original?"

"No, which is why I need to look at the one in your bag."

"As I told Alex, possession is nine-tenths of the law. It's mine." She walked to the front door.

"I'm sorry, Emma, but I really need that book."

The floor pitched violently and she fell to her knees as ceramic cups rattled off of shaking tables. Customers squealed and dove for cover.

"Earthquake!" a man yelled.

But Emma knew better.

She spun around, ducking out of the way of a toppling chair.

Raphael stood in the middle of the room, unaffected by the commotion.

"Have you lost your mind?" she shouted.

Judging by the crazy look in his eyes, he had.

She ran out the door before he could do any more damage inside. Instead, she led him straight into downtown Albuquerque.

CHAPTER TWENTY-EIGHT

WILL had a headache that threatened to crack open his skull. It pissed him off that he didn't see the guy hiding in the back of his car before he smashed a flashlight on his head. While he didn't know who had tried to smash in his head, he had a pretty good idea why.

Emma. God knew where she was or if she'd gone to see Alex. She might have thought Will left her and she'd moved on. Or she might be sitting at the motel waiting for him now.

From the looks of the room he was in, he was in a place similar to what he and Emma stayed in. Dark and seedy. A man sat in the chair by the door, his beefy arms crossed over his chest as he watched a game show on the TV chained to the dresser. The other guy was in the bathroom and had been in there too long, from the irritated looks the first guy kept shooting at the closed door.

So far during the few hours he'd been conscious, they hadn't given him any indication why they'd taken him, although after he woke up they tossed him a crumpled bag with a cold hamburger and soggy fries. Food meant they didn't plan to kill. Yet.

There was a knock at the door and the man in the chair jerked upright. The bathroom door opened within seconds and the second guard emerged, drying his wet hands on his jeans.

Will presumed it was a shift change. He'd only been aware of his surroundings for a few hours, but they'd already changed guards twice. One new guy in and one old guy out. However, the attitude of his current guards suggested otherwise.

The man by the door looked through the peephole and jerked back, scrambling to open the door.

Will swung his legs over the side of the bed, sitting upright, his head swimming with pain and dizziness in the process.

A man dressed in a dark suit walked through the door, casting a look of distain on the furnishings. He glanced at Will and smiled. "Hello, Will. Good to see you again."

Will squinted. "I'm not sure I can say the same. For multiple reasons."

The man lifted an eyebrow in amusement. Whoever he was, he reeked of money with his expensive suit and perfect hair. "No, I'm sure you can't, but I daresay you've been an interesting find."

"What the fuck does that mean?"

"Of course you wouldn't remember me." He tilted his head to the side with a smirk. "I'm Aiden."

Unable to contain his surprise, Will's eyes widened. "Aiden? As in Emma's father?"

"One and the same."

Raphael and Alex he could understand kidnapping him, but Aiden? "Why did you take my memory away?"

He laughed. "No wonder Emma likes you. The two of you are so much alike. Direct and to the point. I did it to protect you both. You really don't know what you're dealing with and I plan to keep it that way. There's much too much at stake." He squinted and inched closer. "There is a resemblance. I wasn't close enough before to see it."

Aiden's words meant nothing other than he saw a connection between Will and Emma that he saw as a threat. Will couldn't ignore that Raphael saw it too.

Will grinned. "I've got one of those faces."

Aiden smiled, but his eyes were cold. "He's a flippant, arrogant ass as well."

"Sounds like he's a lot more fun than you are, whoever he is. Mind telling me what this is all about?"

"You're a threat to my daughter's safety. You are a distraction at best and will get her killed at worst. She refuses to listen to reason and send you away so I've had to force the issue."

Fear squeezed Will's chest. "What did you do to her?"

Aiden snorted. "Do to her? Nothing, other than shake her up a bit and make her see reason. I've convinced her that she no longer needs you. However..." A shadow fell across his face. "She has refused to cut her ties with you until she sees that you are safe and can tell you goodbye."

Will looked around the room, shaking his head and sending a fresh wave of pain rippling through his brain. "I don't get it. Why go to all this trouble? Why not kill me last night or the night you took my memory away?"

Aiden's eye twitched. "Are you suggesting I kill you and be done with it, William? That does surprise me. I never took you for suicidal."

"Thanks for the offer, but no thanks." How much manpower had it taken to kidnap him and bring him here?

And the round-the-clock guards? All of that took time and money. Sure, Aiden was notorious for his mind games and he was obviously loaded with cash, but this seemed like too much effort, even for Aiden. "Why go to all this trouble?"

"Because I hope to rule eternally with Emma, and she'd hold a grudge against me forever if I killed you."

"Won't she hold a grudge for forcing her to make this choice? Emma doesn't like to be forced into anything, especially something she would never choose for herself."

Irritation swept across Aiden's face and Will knew that his questions were getting too close to the truth.

"You can't kill me, can you?"

"That's the most preposterous thing I've ever heard. Of course I can kill you."

Will knew he was playing a dangerous game, but he needed answers. "I don't think you can or you would have done it already. A half a dozen times. The question is why."

"I refuse to waste my time on this discussion, William. I am here to tell you that you will be seeing Emma tonight. If you care anything about her, make it as easy as possible when she tells you goodbye."

"And why would she do that?" But he knew even as he asked.

"Because I've threatened to kill you if she doesn't."

This made no sense. There was something here Will was missing, but he couldn't place his finger on it. "And if I don't?"

Aiden shook his head. "You're only making it harder on Emma."

Will glared, refusing to promise anything. There was no way in hell that Aiden cared anything about Emma or her feelings. "Cut the bullshit, Aiden. Why are you really here?"

Aiden studied him with cold eyes that would have made a lesser man shrink in fear. "You know, Will, I think under different circumstances we could have been allies."

"Again, that doesn't answer my question."

"You're hardly in a position to demand answers, but lucky for you, I'm feeling generous." He grinned. "Let's just say curiosity. After all of this time, I had to see you for myself."

There was a knock on the door and a guard poked his head in the crack. "Sir, we've become aware of a situation in downtown Albuquerque."

Will's gaze jerked to the man. Alex was in downtown Albuquerque and Emma had planned to go see him.

Aiden shot the guard an impatient look. "Go on."

"Sir, they're reporting multiple earthquakes and explosions."

"Anything else?" Aiden asked with a bored tone.

"Well, no...but..."

"Thank you. That will be all."

The man shut the door.

Aiden sighed. "They're trying to accelerate the timetable. I'm going to have to go put a stop to this."

"Who?"

Aiden's brow furrowed. "Raphael and Emma, of course." He turned toward the door.

Raphael and Emma? "Wait!"

Aiden stopped and glanced over his shoulder with a curious expression.

"The last time she met with Raphael, she barely got away and it nearly killed her. She's stronger now, but I'm not sure she's strong enough."

Aiden stared with a blank expression. "Not to worry. Raphael has more to fear at this moment than Emma. He wants to use her so it's in his best interest to keep her alive, while she has no use or interest in him. See? No real concern."

Will expected Aiden to leave, but he studied Will for several seconds. "It's very curious how much you really care about her. I took away all your memories of her yet you're still with her. It's as if you really do love her. But that's impossible."

"Is it?"

"It would seem that it's not." Aiden walked out while three guards entered.

Two grabbed Will's arms and pulled him off the bed. "Time to go."

****

Emma ran out onto the sidewalk and across the street, ducking around the corner of a building. A crack split the street, creeping toward her as the ground shook in a continuous roll.

"I want that book, Emmanuella!" Raphael shouted over the screams of the pedestrians running for cover. There was nowhere for them to run. People poured out of the buildings, onto the street and into danger.

Emma plastered her back against the brick building. "Raphael, enough of this!" she called out.

"This is your last warning, Emma. After this, I'm going to start making promises. Promises you won't want me to keep."

An elderly man emerged from a doorway beside her, confused and disoriented. A cut above his eyes dripped blood down his face, and he gripped his awkwardly bent left arm. He staggered toward Raphael's direction.

Emma tugged his good arm and pulled him back. She spun him around to face the opposite way. "Go that way. Run!"

People swarmed past her as she stepped onto the corner. "Raphael, stop this! Innocent people are getting hurt!"

Raphael held his hands out from his sides. "Whose fault is that, Emma? Just hand over the book and be done with it."

She clutched the strap that she'd slung over her shoulder. She'd love nothing more than to hand it over, but she also knew that if he was willing to go to this much trouble and risk this much exposure, there had to be a reason.

Giving Raphael the book would be a disaster.

But would it be any worse than the disaster unfolding before her now?

"What do you expect to find, Raphael? What do you think is in here?"

He took several steps toward her. "I already told you, Emma. I hope to see if there's anything about the change of rules. You have an unfair advantage if you have the information. Now be a good girl and share."

Her instinct screamed no.

Raphael waited for several seconds before he pointed across the street. "Okay, time to start paying, Emma. I'm giving you three seconds to hand over the book before I destroy the building on that corner."

She turned her gaze to the six-story office structure. People spilled out the doors. How many were left inside? Surely, he wouldn't really do this. Yet she had no doubt that he would.

Uncertainty mingled with her panic. Hundreds of lives depended on her decision. But if she gave him the book, it might not just be hundreds. It might be thousands. Or millions. She gulped deep breaths, her mind nearly paralyzed with indecision.

Maybe it wasn't an either/or situation. She could try to stop him.

"One."

The screams of the people around her filled her ears as she pulled energy from the building next to her.

"Two."

It would take a lot to stop him. She let it build until it was nearly intolerable.

"Thr—"

She released it, pushing the mass toward Raphael. His eyes widened in disbelief as he threw his body out of the way a second before it would have hit him. The energy hit a car parked parallel on the street, exploding it in a fiery ball. The car behind it blew up, and each car behind blew up in rapid succession. Emma suspected it had more to do with the intensity of the force she used than pure combustion.

Raphael scrambled to his feet, a murderous gleam in his eye, and raised his hand. The building he'd threatened shook violently and collapsed, filling the street with dust and horrified screams.

Emma hid around the corner holding a hand over her mouth to smother her scream, trying not to think about how many people had just died. Choking on concrete dust, she swallowed the bile that rose in her throat. She had to get away from here. If she could lead Raphael away from all of these people, they'd be safe.

Scanning the horizon, she looked for the least populated place to run, devastated to see that there was none. It was all buildings and people for miles.

She had to get to her car.

Emma took off running, the plume of dust hiding Raphael, but she felt him behind her. His energy and his anger. The ground shook and she looked over her shoulder as he emerged from the white cloud. He raised his hand and a crack in the asphalt shot toward her, sucking cars abandoned on the road down into the crevice.

Struggling to maintain her balance, Emma pushed a ball of energy toward him, knowing it wasn't enough to do him serious injury but would hopefully slow him down. It landed at his feet, throwing him off balance, granting her enough time to gain some distance.

The parking lot was two blocks away.

"I'll destroy this city, building by building, block by block, until you give me the book," he called after her. He stood between two cars, one with the driver's door standing wide open. The back tire of the other hung over the edge of the crevice.

Absorbing electricity from the sources around her, she focused on igniting the gas tanks of the two cars. The explosions rocked the ground, sending plumes of dark smoke into the air and engulfing Raphael. She held her breath in hope that she might have defeated him.

Until he walked out of the haze toward her.

He raised his hands toward the buildings on her left and the ground pitched and bucked, the buildings collapsing like brittle gingerbread houses. An explosion quickly followed.

Emma lost her balance on the quaking ground and fell to her knees as the structures crumbled. She scrambled to her feet and took off running toward her car until another building collapsed beside her, blocking her path.

She spun around to face him. "Raphael, stop. I'm begging you. You're killing innocent people."

"No, Emma, you are killing innocent people."

She wondered how right he was. She should just give him the book and stop his madness. She slipped the strap off her shoulder, holding the bag to her side.

Raphael moved closer, a smile spreading across his face. "There's my girl."

Her hand fumbled with the zipper as fear shot down her spine. Was this really the right decision?

"Emma, don't give up."

She stopped, sure she had an auditory hallucination. "Will?"

His relief filled her. How was this possible? "Emma, I don't know how but I can feel that you're scared. Just don't give up."

"Raphael wants the book."

"He's destroying Albuquerque for the book?"

"Yes."

"Then do anything and everything you can do to keep it from him."

Raphael stood about ten feet away.

"Stop right there," she shouted. "That's close enough." Will was right. She couldn't give it to him. If he wanted it this badly, God only knew what he'd do with whatever was inside it. But how was she going to keep it from him without getting more people killed? "Back up, Raphael. You're making me nervous."

"That's too damn bad, Emma. Now hand it over."

Emma pulled in power and held the backpack out at arm's length with her right hand. She held her left palm toward it. "Back up now, Raphael, or I'm going to burn it up."

Panic filled his eyes. "You wouldn't do that."

"I've already read it all," she lied. "I've got nothing to lose."

Raphael backed up two steps, his arms out to his sides. "Emma, don't do anything hasty. You don't know that you've found out everything you need." He reached a hand toward her, palm up. "Just let me look at it and I'll hand it back when I'm done. I promise."

"I've learned better than to trust one of your or anyone else's promises. Your promises mean nothing to me."

He nodded his head, hand extended. "Fair enough. I deserve that. Just don't destroy it. You still need it."

"Why? What's in it?"

"Let's look at it together and I'll show you."

He was bluffing. "First tell me how you know something is in here. Surely, you've read this or a copy at some time if it's so important. The chain-link fence at the Vinco Potentia compound wouldn't be enough to keep you out."

Sirens wailed in the distance, adding to Emma's anxiety. This had to be over before the police showed up or more people would get hurt. Raphael would probably kill them all.

"You're right. I have seen it before. But after the rules changed, I went to the compound the day I left you back in Tennessee, and found that it was gone." He took a step forward. "Emma, you don't understand. The book holds the rules. The sovereign rules. If the game changes, the rules will appear in the book. I don't trust Aiden to tell them all to me. In fact, I think he purposely has withheld key information. I need to know what's in there."

Emma watched his face, fairly certain he was telling the truth.

"Emma, can't you see that my survival depends on the information in that book?"

"Which is why Alex wanted it too."

A wild look filled Raphael's eyes. "Yes! Exactly! The one with all the rules has a better chance and knows all the loopholes. All I'm asking for is a fair chance."

He was right. It wasn't fair to fight a game that you didn't know all the rules to. Her arm lowered and relief covered his face.

"That's it, my love. Just hand it over."

She remembered his words in the coffee shop. *What good is power if you can't use it?* Raphael deserved a chance at survival, but did he deserve a chance at controlling the world?

"Well, isn't this cute, you two, playing in the street together," Alex called from down the block. He was an odd sight, picking his way through debris in his expensive loafers and pristine dress pants, shirt, and tie.

"Alex." Raphael held his hands out to the side, grinning as he turned to face him. "What a pleasant surprise. Or should I call you President Alex now?"

"Ha! Just Alex for now. Perhaps His Royal Majesty later. I haven't figured out what my title will be." He looked over at Emma. "I take it we're both after the same thing."

For once, Emma knew it wasn't her they were talking about.

She lifted her chin. "How'd you know where to find us?"

Alex laughed. "Really? You sent a calling card through the whole city. My biggest problem was getting away."

Emma took several slow steps backward.

Raphael lifted his hand and the ground cracked behind her, the street separating several feet. "Not so fast, Emma."

She wobbled but kept her balance. "You know, Raphael, I might be more willing to cooperate if you weren't so hostile."

"So did you figure out how to read it?" Alex asked.

"She claims she's read it all and now she's threatening to destroy it."

"What?" Panic laced Alex's words. "Emma, I know we've had our differences, but be reasonable."

The sirens grew louder. They'd be here any minute. She had to get out of here. "I don't want to fight you two. I don't want to fight anyone. This isn't my fight. I just want my son and to be left alone. Can't you understand that?"

"It's not us you have to convince of that, Emma," Raphael said. "It's your father."

Which was hopeless.

Alex moved closer to Raphael. If she could push the cargo van beside the two men into them and make the gas tank explode…

She held the backpack out again, her palm facing it as she let the energy fill her. Tears burned her eyes. This could all go so terribly wrong. "I'm sorry," she whispered.

Fear covered Raphael's face as he lunged forward. "Emma! Don't do it!"

His approach scared her and her power released in Alex's direction before she had a chance to aim it at the van.

Alex hit the ground as Raphael pressed forward.

"Go back!" she shouted, her energy pushing him away.

The sky filled with dark clouds and thunder boomed overhead.

The first police cars screeched to a halt a half-block away.

She aimed for the van, her energy crashing into the gas tank. The explosion rocked the ground as she pushed it toward them then turned to run.

"Emma!"

She'd forgotten about the crack in the ground but had enough momentum to leap over, falling to her knees as she landed.

As she took off running, she ignited cars behind her to slow Raphael and Alex down. Police cars blocked the end of the street, the officers filling the road.

Damn it.

She ran down the sidewalk, tearing around the corner of a building to the parking lot, just before the building crumpled to the ground. An explosion followed, shooting debris higher into the air. She fumbled with the car door and climbed inside as pieces of concrete fell around her, then took off toward the street on the opposite side of the lot.

Raphael stood in the middle of the exit, his eyes wild with rage, his body encased in a dense green glow. Alex was nowhere to be seen. The police were behind her, entering the parking lot, drawn by Raphael's gleam.

Raphael seemed like her biggest concern at this point. The parking lot was ringed with a metal chain slung through posts, with only two exits. One blocked by police and the other by Raphael. He took a step toward her. "What are you going to do? Run me over?"

She would if she had to.

She floored the gas pedal and Raphael created a crack in the ground. A light pole fell on the hood of the car, smashing in the engine.

Goddamnit.

Gunshots rang out behind her but didn't seem to affect Raphael. The bullets bounced off his glow.

If she got out of the car, she was likely to get shot. If she stayed inside, Raphael would get the book.

The back window shattered from gunfire. She turned and held up her palm, thrusting energy toward the parked cars behind her. The entire back of the lot erupted with flames and she hoped it would buy her a minute or so from the police.

Raphael appeared at the driver's door, pulling on the locked handle as panic clawed at her sanity.

Alex rounded the corner, brushing dust off of his pants. Two against one.

She closed her eyes to gather her strength. She couldn't let them get the book.

The door clicked as it unlocked.

She looped the backpack over her shoulder and pushed the door open as Raphael pulled. "Move." The door flung open with unnatural strength, ripping off the hinges and carrying Raphael with it at least ten feet. Raphael landed on his back, the door on top of him.

Emma burst from the car and leaped over the metal chain onto the street, running the opposite direction from the police and Alex.

Thunder rumbled overhead and a torrential rain fell from the sky.

"Emma! Stop!" Alex shouted. "Just listen to me!"

She flung energy to more parked cars, blocking her path with explosions. More law enforcement vehicles filled the street ahead. She had to get out of here, but if she got away from Raphael and Alex, how could she outrun all these police?

The ground shook, glass shattering in the buildings around her. If she hid her power, then she could get away once she was out of Alex's and Raphael's sight. First she had to get out of view from the police, then she could try to hide her energy. Halfway down the street, she spotted an alley. If she went inside and blocked the entrance, then she could escape from everyone at the opposite end.

She neared the passageway, Alex behind her and emitting a dense blue glow, clearly visible to the police officers. As she made it into the entrance, she looked back. The policemen slumped on the ground and over car doors. Alex had killed them all.

Swallowing her horror, her nausea intensified when she realized that the second part of her plan wouldn't work. There was nothing to ignite. Unless she burned the wooden buildings encasing the alley.

"Please be empty," she begged as she lifted her hands and shot energy into the structures. Fire ripped through the sides, spreading burning debris in the alley. When she reached the opposite end, she turned to see the alley behind her engulfed in flames. With no sign of Alex, she covered her power.

Rain, wind, and sirens filled the air, but she was nearly oblivious to it all. She only wanted to get a car and find Will.

Everything else would sort itself out.

CHAPTER TWENTY-NINE

WILL stood, chained to a picnic table, looking down onto the city below. Fires dotted the landscape in the setting sun. Emma had been part of that mess. Worry for her safety gnawed in his belly, but somehow he knew she was all right, as though he could feel her deep within. She had mentioned they had a similar connection before he'd lost his memory, back when he had the mark. Even though the idea should have freaked him out, he found it comforting. He felt like he possessed some part of his past with her.

But if Aiden had his way, he'd lose her soon. She'd drive up and tell him goodbye. Will had little doubt that she would. With the threat of his death hanging over her head, she would see no other alternative. Somehow he had to convince her not to go through with this.

A car turned into the overlook parking five minutes before nine. The men with him shifted nervously. He didn't know their allegiance to Aiden—Vinco Potentia? Cavallo? Will waited, anxiety jolting through him until he realized it was Emma in a vehicle he didn't recognize.

Opening the car door, she stepped out wearing her sunglasses, her mouth pursed. It shocked him that he could read her so well. She was prepared for the worst as she scanned the area, her hand gripping the strap of the backpack slung over her shoulder, the book presumably inside. After what she'd just gone through, he would have been surprised if she'd left it in the car.

Even wearing her glasses she looked alert yet leery, not that the men with him noticed. They tensed the moment she pulled up, having been told what she was capable of. She stopped six feet away and scanned the group, not acknowledging Will. "I'm here. Now what?" She was sharp and direct.

The leader of the group moved to Will's side. "We've been told that you're to tell him goodbye and then we release him."

Her jaw tensed. "Then your job is done. Go."

The men stayed in place.

Emma took a step forward. "Let me make this clear, you fucking assholes. I just blew up half of Albuquerque. I can blow you halfwits up in my sleep. Now move."

The men looked at their boss, then moved across the street and climbed into their cars. The man in charge glared at Emma before he backed up toward the road, his hand on a gun holstered at his side. He got into a van and the vehicles took off down the mountain.

Emma watched them, her body so rigid Will wondered how she hadn't shattered with tension. When she was satisfied they'd left, she turned her attention to Will.

Her jaw trembled. Her first sign of weakness since she'd arrived.

His heart broke. Without thinking, he moved his hand to reach for her, jerking the chain that tied his hands to the table behind him.

Still, she said nothing, her glasses covering her eyes. Her gaze turned to the valley below and her face paled. "It's my vision," she whispered.

"Emma, no. No, it's not." Goddamnit he wished he could touch her.

Her gaze stayed on the scene as she walked closer to the edge. "It's just like I saw." Her voice choked on tears. "I saw a valley dotted with fires and a voice saying 'You are the destruction of the world.'"

"There's no one here saying that, Emma. You didn't cause this. Raphael did."

"I should have just given him the book."

"No, you did the right thing. We need to look at it again and see if we can find something new. I'll figure out a way to translate the text."

She turned back to him, tears streaming down her cheeks from beneath the glasses. "I read it. This afternoon before Raphael showed up."

"How?"

She gave a half laugh. "I told the book to show me the words."

He closed his eyes and shook his head. They'd had the answers all along yet it never occurred to him to try that. "Emma, take off your glasses."

She hesitated before sliding them off and looking at him with red, puffy eyes.

"I know why you're here. I know what you're supposed to do."

She bit her trembling lip.

"You don't have to do this, Emma. Aiden came to see me this afternoon."

Her eyes widened in surprise.

"He told me what he threatened."

She turned back to the devastation below.

Will tugged on the chain again, his frustration mounting. "Don't look down there."

"I told you it would come true. I'm the destruction of the world."

"Emma, look at me," he ordered.

She swung her head, tears filling her eyes.

"You don't have to do this. Unchain me and let's go. You can tell me what the book says and we'll figure out where to go from there."

She shook her head, holding back sobs. "I can't. He's going to kill you. I can't save you from him."

"Emma, no. You don't have to leave me here. Listen to me."

Her sobs broke loose when she finally touched him, placing a hand on his chest and the other on his cheek. "I don't think I'm strong enough to leave you." She buried her face in his shirt.

"You listen to me," he said, his voice firm. "You're strong enough to do anything you have to do, but I'm telling you that you don't have to do this."

She lifted her head. "I do. Even if I save you now, he'll kill you later. I have to protect you, Will, and this is the only way I know how. Besides, I promised."

His heart dropped. "Emma, I know what it means to you to promise something, but this was coerced."

She cried into his shirt, clinging into him.

"Listen to me! You made a promise to the devil himself. Do you think he'd keep a promise to you?"

She stepped away and ran a hand through her hair. "I don't know. I don't know."

"No, he wouldn't. You don't have to do this."

"I couldn't protect Jake." Her voice broke and she took a deep breath. "I saw Jake this afternoon. He was terrified of Aiden, but I couldn't save him. What does he think of me? Does he think I abandoned him?"

"He loves you. He knows you had no choice. We'll get him back."

She shook her head. "Aiden's plan is for Jake to fight. Not Aiden, Jake."

"What? He's a child! How could that work?"

"I don't know. But the book mentions Water. We were right. Water is somehow involved in all of this. I think he'll be at the battle."

She seemed calmer now, but he wondered if that was good or bad.

"The joining words are there."

"That's good. See? That's something to work on. Together. Unchain me, Emma."

She looked into his eyes and slowly shook her head.

Panic rose. She might go through with this. "Emma, listen to me. Aiden can't kill me. If he could, why wouldn't he have done it before? Why not just kill me last night when his men found me? Or the night he took back the mark?"

"He said he didn't kill you because he worried I'd be angry with him for eternity."

"Since when did Aiden care about anyone's feelings?"

She paused.

"Emma, he doesn't give a fuck what you think, otherwise he wouldn't be doing this now. Why would he take Jake? Why would he orchestrate all of this if he worried what you thought?"

Her shoulders heaved as she turned back to the valley. "I don't know."

"They're threatened by me. Aiden and Raphael. They know something we don't and they see me as a threat."

She held her knuckles to her mouth. "I know. I've been thinking about that all day as well. And for a bit I thought you were Water."

"Me?" Will's brain scrambled to use this to his advantage. "See? Maybe I am. If I am, you need me."

"No." She shook her head. "If you were him, you'd know who you were by now. Like Alex and Raphael. You would have developed powers."

He didn't believe it was possible, but if Emma did and she'd set him free, he'd push the idea. "Maybe they're dormant."

"No, you would know if you were. And surely I would have felt *something*."

"You do feel something, Emma."

She looked into his eyes. "It's not the same."

"But you can't deny that Aiden and Raphael want me gone for a reason that has nothing to do with your feelings. They see me as a threat."

"I know."

This was good. She was listening. "I called Aiden on it. I accused him of not being able to kill me. He didn't deny it."

She was quiet for several seconds. "But he didn't confirm it, either," she whispered.

"No, but—"

Her tears broke loose. "I can't take that chance, Will."

****

Her heart was breaking. The pain threatened to split her chest open and consume her. She sucked in a breath as she held back her sobs.

"Emma," he pleaded. She heard the panic in his voice, which broke her even more.

What remained of downtown Albuquerque lay below in smoldering ruins. She had hoped beyond hope that the vision was wrong, but here it was, spread below her, nearly identical to what she'd seen.

And it was only the beginning.

"Emma."

Will's broken voice brought her back to the present. She'd been selfish to keep him close. Every moment with her was a risk. She could never live with herself if something happened to him. She'd nearly shattered into pieces this morning when she thought the dead man in their car was him. This was the right thing to do, but she still wasn't sure how to do it. Leaving Will was like cutting out part of herself. She inhaled, willing herself to be strong for the both of them.

"I love you, Will. I love you too much to let you get yourself killed."

"Emma, just listen." His voice cracked. He was begging.

Her tears burst. "Please don't make this harder than it already is." She pressed his cheeks with her trembling palms, her chest shaking against his. "I've never loved anyone like I love you. I was so stupid not to realize it sooner."

Will's eyes bore into hers. "Emma, please…" His shoulders jerked as he tried to pull free. The chain holding him clanged against the metal table.

Her fingers trailed down his cheek. This was the last time she would touch him and she wanted to remember the feel and the smell of him. His face was blurry through her tears as fresh waves of pain surged. "Even though you don't remember most of our time together, what you've done for me these last few weeks is more than anyone has ever done for me. Ever." She took a breath. "And what we had before…" She broke down, leaning her head against his chest, trying to recover enough to say what she'd rehearsed the last hour. "You own half my soul, Will Davenport."

"Emma, stop this right now." He pulled on the chains. "Goddamnit!" He took a breath. "Emma, look at me. Please."

She pulled back, her hands on his chest, and stared into his eyes. The eyes that had watched her live through hell and heaven and everything in between.

"Unchain me. I have to touch you. You can't leave me without letting me touch you one more time."

She hesitated.

"I have to be unchained to be set free. Just do it now."

"I can't."

He leaned his head back and took a deep breath, then leveled his eyes to face her. "We both know you're stronger than me, Emma. What's the real reason you've left me chained? Because you don't trust me or you don't trust yourself?"

They both knew the answer.

"Just one hand, okay? I have to touch you."

She nodded. But freeing him meant she had to reignite her power. Which meant she had to leave before they found her. Or Will.

She closed her eyes and let her anger burn, igniting the flame in her chest. When her eyelids opened, she was surrounded by a golden glow. "Release his right hand."

The chain links fell to the table with a clatter and Will's arm wrapped around her waist, pulling her to his chest.

His mouth found hers as she cried her frustration and sorrow into him. The irony that their beginning and their end came drenched in sorrow wasn't lost on her.

"I love you, Emma."

She kissed him with a desperation that matched his. In spite of her heartbreak, she knew what she had to do. Raphael's words from ages ago echoed in her head. You have the power to release him. Perhaps that's why Will couldn't let her go. Maybe part of his mark was buried deep in his heart, binding him to her. It had been up to her all along.

Reaching down, she grabbed his arm and pulled his hand into hers as she stepped back.

Will's eyes widened in panic. "Emma, no. Don't do this."

Emma sucked in a breath to steady her voice and found her power to make this work. "Will Davenport, I release you. May you have the life you were destined to live."

They glowed in a golden light as Will's mouth dropped open in surprise. He fell to his knees gasping, and she worried that she'd injured him, but the light faded and his head jerked up.

****

She walked backward, shaking her head. Fresh tears slid down her cheeks. He felt her grief, her guilt, her anger. They rippled off her in waves.

Scenes flipped through his head as memories rushed in, overwhelming his senses. Emma and Jake in the car. Emma in the cornfield, on the night he started falling in love. Jake branding his arm. The explosion. Emma in his arms in bed. Escaping from the compound. Emma nearly dying from the infection in her leg. The fire in the forest from her explosion. Flying the plane. Standing in the forest and holding Emma as she lost the baby. Stopping with the last image of her in his erased memories: the horror on her face as her father stole his memories of her.

She backed up toward the car, sobbing so hard she stumbled and righted herself.

"Emma, wait! I remember."

"No. You're just saying that to make me change my mind." She turned her back to him, leaning against the car. Her shoulders shook before she opened the door.

"Emma! I remember!"

She paused, watching him before she got into the car and leaned her forehead against the wheel.

"Don't you dare leave me. Not after everything we've been through."

Her head jerked up, her eyes wide as she stared at him.

"The cornfield. I remember the cornfield. The night I fell in love with you."

She shook her head.

The chain on his left hand fell away as her car backed up onto the highway. She'd freed him.

He ran after the car, the taillights disappearing around the curve down the hill.

Then he felt it. An oppressive stench swamped his head and without knowing how, he knew that Raphael was close.

If Raphael was coming, it was for the book. And Emma.

"Emma!" he shouted in his head, encountering a black hole of nothingness. He panicked, wondering if Raphael had killed her.

No. Raphael needed her alive. Will turned in frustration. He had to get to her, but he was alone on a mountain road.

The ring on his hand turned icy, burning his hand. What the hell?

He jerked his gaze down to the glowing blue stone, gasping as he realized the marks in the gem were swirling. Emma's pendant had heated and glowed when she needed to use its power.

A chill washed through him. Could it be true?

Tires squealed down the road and Will ran to the edge of the overlook to see if he could determine the source. He caught a glimpse of Emma's car round a corner, dangerously close to the edge. A dark sedan was in pursuit. Anger and fear intertwined. He had to get to her.

"It looks like you need a ride."

Will spun to the voice behind him, his chest tightening. He'd been so worried about Emma he hadn't heard a car approach.

A middle-aged man dressed in jeans and T-shirt stood at the edge of the road next to an idling sedan. He placed a foot on the curb and leaned forward, his mouth lifting into a familiar grin. "You need to go save her."

Will took a few steps closer. "Who?" How much did this man know?

The man's grin spread wider, wrinkles crinkling his eyes. "We're wasting time. He's going to kill her this time, and we can't have that now, can we? Get in."

Will didn't trust him, but he saw no other option. He'd do anything to get to Emma. But then again, this stranger might know it and use it to his advantage. After a half-second of hesitation, he ran to the man's car and climbed in, barely shutting the door before the man took off down the winding road.

"Who the hell are you?" Will asked, bracing his hand on the dashboard.

The man shot him an amused look. "Actually, Will, I think the more appropriate question is who on earth are you?"

CHAPTER THIRTY

EMMA hit the brakes, the car skidding around the corner before she punched the gas, trying to outrun the vehicle behind her. She was at a disadvantage. The car she'd stolen was an older sedan. The car in pursuit was a BMW.

She was screwed.

Who was behind her? Vinco Potentia? Cavallo? Raphael? Not that it mattered. She needed to focus on getting away.

The car behind her tapped her rear bumper, pushing her close to the edge of the road.

She swallowed her fear and swerved away from the narrow shoulder. As she rounded the next curve she saw an overlook below. If she could slow down, she might be able to turn around and head back up the mountain. And perhaps the car chasing her would fall off the edge.

"Emma." Raphael's voice called out.

Slamming on the brakes, she jerked her head around the empty car.

He laughed and she realized his voice was coming through the radio.

"Nice job of hiding yourself. Lucky for me you showed yourself just long enough for me to find you."

She'd turned her power off after she released Will and gotten in the car, but she lit it again. Her nightmare was realized. Raphael had found her and she wasn't sure how to escape this time. She needed every bit of help she could get.

Thank God, Will was safe up the hill.

The car rammed into the back of her again, harder this time, and she fought to regain control.

"That was just a warning, my love. Pull over. We have things to discuss."

A straight stretch of road lay ahead and she floored the gas pedal, but Raphael's car swerved around to the driver's side and pushed her off the road. The car pitched wildly as it drove over the rough terrain until slamming into a tree.

Momentarily stunned, she came to her senses and looked in the rearview mirror. Raphael had parked on the shoulder and he walked toward her car with purposeful steps.

The glass had shattered in the driver's window. She grabbed the door handle and tried to open the door, meeting resistance. Looking through the open window, she saw that the crash had caved in the engine and crumpled the driver's door.

"I want the book, Emmanuella!"

Using her power, she focused on the door. "Open." The metal groaned in protest.

Emma looked up to see Raphael bathed in a green glow, his light pressed against the car door.

"I'm making the rules now, Emma. You have three choices. One, you bring me the book and we join together. Two, you simply give me the book. Three, we do this the hard way."

Obviously, one and two were out. "I've never been one to do things the easy way."

A sadistic grin lit up his eyes with a red glow. "Somehow I knew you were going to say that."

The car jerked as the ground shook, the vehicle sliding sideways away from Raphael. Emma sat up to look out the passenger window, her breath freezing when she realized what was on the other side: a V-shaped crevice at the edge of a cliff.

"Raphael!"

"The book."

At least if she went over the edge, the book went with her. But not without a fight.

She shot a ball of energy toward him. He was prepared, blocking the glow and sending it into the trees, which exploded with a force that shook the car.

Raphael glared. "I really wish you hadn't done that."

The car slid to the edge as Emma searched her brain for a way to counter him.

"Raphael!"

Screeching tires filled the air, followed by shouts. Shit. She'd deal with whatever was outside later. She needed to focus on getting out of the car.

Her vehicle stopped, teetering on the edge. Emma held her breath and spun to face him. Raphael's smile was the last thing she saw before the car toppled over the edge.

****

Will jumped out of the car before it stopped. He saw Raphael's BMW but Emma's car was nowhere in sight. Instead he saw a streak disappearing at the edge of the cliff.

His heart jumped when he saw the fresh tire marks leading to the area.

"Emma!"

Raphael stood at the edge, peering over. When he heard Will's voice, he turned and put his hands on his hips. "Ah, Will. I thought you were history."

"Funny thing about history, it has a way of repeating itself." Will walked closer, forcing his breath to come in even bursts and not give away his terror.

Raphael glanced over the edge then looked at Will with a cocky grin. "I never pictured you as a philosopher, Will."

Will gave a half shrug. "History major."

Raphael laughed, the sound echoing off the hills and cliffs surrounding them. "History won't help any of us this time."

"Where's Emma?" But he already knew.

"You could say that Emma decided to take a more scenic route."

Will eased closer, his heart pounding. "I think I'll have a look myself."

Raphael curled his lip and shrugged a shoulder, moving away from the edge. "Suit yourself. Maybe you can help me figure out this dilemma."

The tire marks showed that a car had run off the road and hit a tree. Then the marks moved sideways, ending at the V-shaped precipice. He held his breath as he found the courage to look down. Emma's car rested on its side six feet down, wedged between two boulders.

Oh, God. "Emma?" Will shouted.

Raphael smirked. "It seems she took a little spill."

"Will?" Emma's voice called out from below.

He couldn't repress his intake of breath at his relief. Will turned his attention to Raphael, who seemed unconcerned for Emma's safety. A murderous rage filled Will's chest, the ring on his finger burning a circular band into his flesh. "You did this."

Raphael looked up in exasperation. "I have spent all day trying to make this woman see reason. It's obvious that she needs to be shown the extreme."

"Raphael, stop this madness!" she shouted through the broken window.

He chuckled. "You brought this on yourself. You've been incredibly hardheaded. It was time to get your full and undivided attention."

"Because destroying half of Albuquerque wasn't enough."

"Obviously not."

"How'd you know I wouldn't plunge to my death?"

He paused. "I didn't."

Will's heart skipped a beat. The rules had changed. "You son of a bitch."

Raphael turned to him and glared. "Don't push me, Will. You are inconsequential and irritating at best, and I can kill you with the snap of my fingers."

"Will! Stop!" Emma sounded terrified, but Will knew she was scared more for him than herself.

"I'm done with the games, Emma. I've given you every opportunity to join with me and you still refuse. If you won't join with me, then I'll make sure you don't join with Alex."

Will had to stop him. "That's not what Aiden thinks. He's sure you won't kill her."

Raphael's eyebrows rose in indignation. "Are you calling my bluff, Will? How could you possibly know what Aiden thinks?"

Slick, foul-smelling waves of anxiety and anger lapped at Will's chest, leaving him stunned. It was coming from Raphael.

Will forced his breath to even. "We had a nice chat this afternoon. You were one of many topics."

"So Aiden feels threatened by me, does he?" Now pride added to the mix of emotions. Along with distrust.

"No, I think he sees you as more of an annoyance."

"Just like I see you."

Will gave him a smug grin. "Exactly. But you both have something in common."

"What's that?"

"You agree that I'm a threat to you if I'm with Emma."

Raphael paused, cocking his head as he narrowed his eyes. Wariness rolled off of him, along with a hint of fear.

What was Raphael afraid of?

"Now that is an interesting theory, Will, if not somewhat delusional. Why would I be threatened by you?"

"We both know that I'm not holding Emma back. In fact, I've pushed her harder than she would have pushed herself."

Raphael stayed frozen, eyeing Will with distrust. "That hardly explains why you think we're threatened by you."

"Why can't Aiden kill me?"

Raphael shook his head as though he tried to clear it. "What the hell are you talking about?" But dread oozed from his pores. "Did Aiden say he couldn't kill you?"

Will stared into his dark eyes. "Yes, which is why Emma didn't follow his orders. His threat is empty. Just like yours."

Raphael snorted, turning his head slightly but keeping his gaze on Will. "I assure you that my threat isn't empty."

Will could sense he told the truth, but his fear had increased. Raphael was afraid of him.

"So, how long has it been since you've seen Marcus?"

Raphael's eyes widened before he caught himself. "What do you know about Marcus?"

"More than you think."

A slow, wicked grin lifted the corners of Raphael's mouth. "You don't know anything. You're bluffing."

"Are you willing to take that chance?"

The sound of fatigued metal echoed from the crevice.

"Emma!" Will rushed to the side, but Raphael held up his hand.

"Not so fast. Try to save her."

"What the fuck do you think I'm trying to do, you moron?"

Raphael laughed with a smirk. "You're lying. You don't know anything. You can't save her. But I can." He moved closer. "What's her life worth to you, Will?"

He'd finally gotten his memories back. He loved her with every fiber of his being, but there was no way he'd trust this asshole. "Quit playing games, Raphael. The fucking games are endless. What the hell do you want?"

"What I've always wanted. With an added bonus. The book."

"What you want isn't mine to give. But you've known that all along. Emma is free to make her own choices."

Raphael raised his hand to the car. "Then I'll have to do things my way."

"Wait!" Will took a step toward him. "Let me try to save them both. The book and Emma."

"Why would I do that?"

"Why not? What have you got to lose? We'll both be down there, nowhere to go. And I'll get the book."

Raphael eyed him with suspicion before he scowled. "Okay, you have five minutes."

"Emma, hang on. I'm coming." Will didn't waste time lowering himself over the edge and climbing onto a tree growing out of the side of the cliff.

****

How was Will here? She'd left him several miles up the mountain. There was no way he could have run here that fast. And what was her father going to do to Will when he found out Will was with her?

"Will, you have go." Her voice cracked with fear and she cleared her throat. "You have to leave."

"Sorry, princess, you're stuck with me." The car creaked as his head peeked three feet over the passenger window. "Are you all right?"

She nodded. "Yeah."

"This thing's not very stable and I have no idea how far down this crevice goes. No sudden movements. Okay?"

"Yeah." She had no desire to plummet to the bottom.

Will twisted his head to look behind him. "The back end is resting on a ledge, but it's not very wide. Can you stand up and climb out the passenger window?"

She bit her lip. "Every time I move, the car drops."

"Then we'll take this slow, okay?"

"Okay," she said, her voice shaky.

"Reach up and grab the top of the passenger seat."

Taking a deep breath, she grabbed hold. "Okay."

"Now gently pull yourself up, tucking your feet underneath you."

"The side window's gone."

"Then when you tuck your legs, brace yourself on the window frame."

She nodded, pulling her body with her hands and sliding her legs underneath her. The car slid forward several inches, her feet slipping on the metal. She released an involuntary shriek before finding a foothold.

Wood cracked over her head and her gaze rose to Will, who had scooted farther down the tree. The branch bowed with his weight.

"Will, stop! You're going to get yourself killed. Go back up."

He looked down at her, his eyes so full of love and longing that it took her breath away. "I just got back every memory I ever had of you. I'm not going anywhere. Got it?"

Tears burned her eyes. Was it true? She thought he'd been lying about getting back his memories, but he had no reason to lie now. She nodded.

He grinned. "If we weren't hanging over a bottomless crevice, I'd show you how much I love you, but now doesn't seem like the right time for makeup sex."

She laughed through her tears. "No, I guess not."

Grim determination set his jaw. "We've been in rougher spots than this. It's a walk in the park, princess."

She and Will belonged together, her father be damned. "Yeah, piece of cake."

"The car's wedged but obviously not very securely. My plan is for you to climb out the window and I'll grab you when you're in reach and help you crawl across the side of the car."

"Is there any other way out?"

"No." Will looked up. "Any chance you could toss down a rope, Raph?"

Raphael's laughter filtered down. "No."

Anger filled Will's eyes before his face softened. "Don't move until I tell you to. If we shake things around too much this thing might go crashing down."

"I've got to tell you—I'm not a fan of crashing down."

"Are your feet underneath you now?"

"Yeah."

"I want you to slowly stand. *Slowly* is the key word."

She'd maneuvered her feet into a squat with her last effort. Centering her weight on the balls of her feet, she straightened her legs. The car dropped, her stomach plummeting as her feet slipped off the frame. She dangled out the open window, her sweat-slickened hands slipping on the vinyl passenger headrest. "Will!"

"Don't move, Emma. Just don't move." She heard him grunt in frustration as she struggled to get her feet back in the car. "Can you use your power to get out of there?"

"No, I have no idea what to do. If I lift this car or myself out of here, I might fling one or the both of us down the cliff."

"Just keep thinking of something, okay?" Terror filled his voice.

Shit. "What is it, Will? Just tell me."

"The ledge that's holding this car up is crumbling."

"Time's up," Raphael called down.

"Son of a bitch fucking psycho," Will growled. "I need more time!"

"Emma's time is up. Literally."

****

Will had never wanted to kill someone so badly in his entire life. But losing his temper now wouldn't help Emma. He needed to focus.

He looked up at Raphael, glowing in his ghastly green light.

Oh, fuck no. "You're going to lose the book too."

"I'll get it at the bottom." Raphael raised his hand and Will felt energy flowing from the ground into Raphael's body and out through his hand.

Will instinctively lifted his arm and blocked Raphael's power.

Raphael's mouth dropped and formed an O that opened and closed in shock. He dropped his hand and the power flow stopped. "What the hell? How did you…"

"You know exactly how, don't you Raphael?"

"I suspected but didn't see how it could be true. Yet Emma said she had a water sign on her back and it was gone after Kramer took you away. It was like the one she got with Jake, the fire symbol. If she was telling the truth, there could be only one reason for her to have the sign of water."

"So you didn't want me around her."

"When I saw you at the warehouse, I didn't feel any power rolling off of you so I didn't see how it could be true, but better to play it safe and get rid of you. I hoped to do it the easy way."

"You mean me just walk away?"

"Yes."

"You know I'm not going anywhere now, right?"

Raphael waved down to Will's position on the tree branch. "You've made this painfully obvious. Now I need that book more than ever."

The car groaned again, the metal screeching on the side of the earthen wall.

"Fuck the book." Emma's head appeared at the top of the window, the backpack slung over her shoulder.

Will froze. "Emma, stop right there! What are you doing?"

"I'm getting myself out of this death trap, that's what I'm doing." She inched across the door toward Will when the car dropped another foot, jerking to a halt. Emma bounced with the car, sliding halfway off the hood. The vehicle slid down, pinning her against the wall. She cried out in pain.

"I need that backpack, Emma." Raphael called down.

She pushed against the metal, her face straining with the effort. "You need me!"

Raphael glanced at Will with a grin. "No, not anymore." Raphael sent a blast of energy toward Will, catching him off guard and knocking him off the tree.

Will slid down the earthen side, rocks digging into his back until he landed on top of the sideways car.

"I promise you that I'll save Jake," Raphael said. "If you just toss up the backpack."

"I can't," she said through her gasps. "It's stuck."

"Then I have no choice but to free it." Raphael raised his hands.

Will looked down at Emma's panicked face. It glowed in the fading sunlight. "I know what you plan to do, Raphael. You want to join with me instead of Emma."

"I always knew you were bright."

Will slid across the car and grabbed hold of another scrub tree, straddling the sideways trunk. "How is that possible? Isn't it like a wedding ceremony?"

"There's another bond, a seal of brotherhood. It's not as strong, but it will do."

"No!" Emma shouted, grunting as she leaned her weight into dislodging the car. "Will, for God's sake, don't do it."

Will's chest tightened. "What about Emma? I want her safe." He looked up to see Raphael's answer.

He shook his head.

Without knowing how, Will absorbed power, creating a white glow that surrounded him.

"Emma, do you trust me?"

She paused for less than a second and lifted her chin. Love filled her eyes, replacing her shock. "I trust you with my life."

"Do you love me enough to spend eternity with me?"

She snorted. "Now isn't exactly the right time for a marriage proposal, Will."

The fact that she could joke in a situation like this made him love her even more. "No sense wasting any more time, princess."

Tears fell down her cheeks. "Yes, I love you more than enough to spend eternity with you."

He reached his arm across the earthen wall toward her.

Her chin trembled. "I'm stuck, Will. I'm wedged in here and I can't get out."

"I know. Just hold my hand. Please."

She reached her hand toward him, their fingertips barely touching.

"Get away from her!" Raphael called out.

Will leaned farther off the tree branch and laced his fingers around her outstretched hand.

"Do you remember when you told me that words held power?"

"Yes."

"You were right. But do you know what makes the words more powerful?"

She shook her head.

"Love."

****

She didn't know how he was doing this, or how he knew what to do, but she felt his intention simply through their connection.

Staring into his eyes, filled with love and devotion, loyalty and trust, the words leapt into her head. They recited them in unison.

"With echoes from the beginning of time
To the last ray of light from the stars at the end."

Bursting stars erupted overhead, their light sweeping from the sky, the tendrils swirling around Will and Emma.

"What are you doing?" Raphael screamed.

"I join my heart with yours
onto an endless path that winds through infinity
and sears our souls and power into an unbreakable bond."

The streams of light wound around their hands, swirling down their arms and around their bodies.

"Through life and death, and all that lies between
I vow to be yours, forever."

A bright-burning light pierced her heart. White and golden lights burst from their bodies in rays, lighting the sky in an unearthly glow.

"What have you done?" Raphael shouted overhead.

Will's grip slipped down her hand to her wrist. "Hold on and don't let go."

"Never."

The wall behind her shook, and she searched his face for reassurance. She had no idea how he knew the joining words. Or had powers. How could this happen? But she knew. It happened because she released him. May you have the life you were destined to live. Emma had given him this gift, whatever it was.

The earth behind her shook until something cold and wet seeped into her shirt. She squirmed in panic, but Will's grip on her wrist tightened.

The entire side of the rock was now covered in water, a stream of it trickling over the cliff above them, down to the crevice, sweeping down around the car. Emma spit out a mouthful as it drenched her head.

The car moved, now pinching into her abdomen. She cried out in pain.

Will's fingers bit into her wrist, his face hardening as he concentrated.

The water gushed now, washing over her. She gasped for breath as it poured over her head.

The car dropped several inches, pulling her down with it. Her hold on Will loosened.

"Don't let go!" he screamed in her head.

She swallowed her panic. They were bound together now. Her power could help him. She filled herself with it and pushed it through her connection to him. If nothing else, maybe she could give it to him to keep if she fell with the car and died.

The torrential water engulfed her, pulling her down, but Will's hand held tight. Fuzziness filled her head from her lack of oxygen. Her fingers loosened their hold but Will's grew tighter. She felt the car give, heard metal crunching from the stress. Pulling her with it.

But Will held on and the car finally slipped away, freeing her. She dangled over the cliff with nothing but Will's grip saving her. The rushing water stopped and she coughed, fighting for breath as he pulled her up onto the tree branch. She laid her head against his chest and gasped for air.

"Are you okay?"

She nodded, holding back her tears of happiness and relief.

"What, no sarcastic retort?" he asked, running his hands over her as he searched for injuries.

She threw her arms around his neck, burying her face into his shoulder. He wrapped an arm around her waist as he scooted back against the cliff.

"I realize being tied to me for eternity is like a death sentence, but no need for hysterics."

She hit his chest with her fist. "Shut up, Will."

He tilted her head back, staring into her eyes. "Thank you."

She had released him to his destiny, yet she didn't know how he did the things he did. "What about Raphael?"

Will grinned. "He left. Once he realized he was out numbered, he hightailed it out of here."

"Once he realized who you were."

His eyes hardened. "Yes."

"So you are Water."

Will straightened. "No."

"But…how?" she looked up at him in confusion.

He cupped her cheek, his eyes filled with love and devotion. "I told you that we could change destiny."

She shook her head in confusion.

"I'm the son of Water." His mouth found hers as he finished the seal to their vow.

A slow, methodical clap echoed overhead. Emma's head jerked up, terrified that Will was wrong and Raphael had returned. Instead, a man she didn't recognize stood at the edge. "Emma, I hear you've been looking for me," he called over the edge.

Emma's eyes widened as she glanced from Will back to the man.

"Who are you?"

"I'm Marcus." A lazy grin spread across his face. "And I'm your worst nightmare."

ABOUT THE MARKS

THREE intertwined symbols are on The Chosen Series covers: a trident, fire and water. All three appeared on Emma's shoulder blade at various times.

The trident was the symbol that Jake branded on Will's forearm as proof that Will was The Chosen One, the protector of his mother Emma. That mark was highlighted in *Chosen*.

In *Hunted*, the symbol for fire is highlighted on the cover and embedded on the title and chapter heading pages. Fire is the symbol that appeared after Jake was conceived and the symbol on the pendant Emma's father gave to her mother.

Water was highlighted in *Sacrifice* because Emma realizes Water has control over Raphael and sets out to find him. Also, Will discovers his birthfather is Marcus, the element water.

The fourth yet untitled book will have a new symbol.

ACKNOWLEDGMENTS

THANK YOU to my children for tolerating Mom's crazy work schedule and spontaneous, yet embarrassing, dance numbers. At least I don't do it in public. Yet.

Thank you to my critique partner and friend, Trisha Leigh for keeping me sane and talking me off a ledge when my new developmental editor sent me an email that began with "Sometimes it's good to start these editorial letters with a big glass of wine."

Thank you to my new developmental editor, Alison Dasho. I loved her instantly when she encouraged more wine consumption. (Ironically, I did not drink before reading her lengthy editorial letter.) She not only jumped into Will and Emma's world feet first and running, but was excited to be part of it. Her enthusiasm, encouragement, and fantastic ideas, made Sacrifice a much better book.

Thank you to Bill Cameron, mystery writer extraordinaire, who I'm lucky to call a friend. Not only has he offered encouragement and advice in a whole variety of subjects, but also introduced me to the wonderful Ms. Dasho. For that alone, I will be eternally grateful.

Thank you to Jim Thomsen and Jill Mueller for line edits, copy editing and proofing.

Thanks to Laura Morrigan for creating another awesome cover!

And finally, thank you to my readers. There are a million books to chose from and you chose to read mine. I'm honored, flattered, and humbled. I cherish every email or comment I get. I do not take you for granted. Ever.

ABOUT THE AUTHOR

DENISE GROVER SWANK lives in Lee's Summit, Missouri. She has six children, three dogs, and an overactive imagination. She can be found dancing in her kitchen with her children, reading or writing her next book. You will rarely find her cleaning.

You can find out more about Denise and her other books at www.denisegroverswank.com or email her at denisegroverswank@gmail.com

Made in the USA
Middletown, DE
16 June 2015